MW00716758

MY NAME
IS
TOM DORIN

Theresa C. Crawford

My Name Is Tom Dorin

ISBN 10:0991080114
ISBN-13: 13:978-0-9910801-1-3

Dedicated to
my great-great-grandfather
Richard L. Crawford,
who served in the Confederate army
and survived to help reunite the nation.

CONTENTS

ACKNOWLEDGMENTS

First of all, I want to thank my son, Caleb. You endured far more discussion about this book through the years than any one human being should have to suffer in a lifetime. You've always been my best critic, a wonderful sounding board and my most enthusiastic supporter. Thanks for never being afraid to give me a swift kick in my sagging self-confidence when I needed that, too. I thank you for the cover image concept, too.

Mom and Dad, if it wasn't for your support down through the years, this book wouldn't exist. Mom, thank you for reading it even though it's a physical struggle for you. Thank you too for your suggestions and your ideas. Every typo that isn't here anymore, is thanks to you! Dad, I know fiction of any sort isn't your reading preference, so hearing that you enjoyed this book is high praise I'll treasure forever. Thank you too for your suggestions on editing that improved this story with every stroke.

There is a special friend who walked with me through the early mutations this tale endured, Michel Huber.

Chel, I wish there was a stronger way to say 'thank you' than those two poor, overworked words. Without your friendship, your brainstorming, your opinions and your encouragement, this book would still be nothing more than an archived, unfinished file on my hard drive.

Of far more importance than this novel, though, I will always be enormously grateful to you for your suggestion of a possible diagnosis for my son. You proved precisely correct, and that diagnosis led to better treatment for his condition and the resolution of some major issues for our family.

So again, thank you with all my heart!

On a less personal note, I'm also indebted to all those far-sighted individuals who preserved original letters from soldiers on both sides of the conflict, and all the fine historians who have presented their views of the history and sociology of those tumultuous times. I found the work of James M. McPherson especially helpful, in particular his books *For Cause and Comrades: Why Men Fought in the Civil War,* and *What They Fought For: 1861-1865.*

I would like to thank all those who maintain websites on all aspects of the Civil War and the 19th century in general. I've been helped by far too many to individually list here, but that doesn't diminish my gratitude for your work and your generosity in sharing it with the world.

Although I used artistic license to put fictional characters and events into the history of the 19th Tennessee Volunteer Infantry, C.S.A., I tried to keep everything else as historically accurate as possible. Any omissions or mistakes are not the fault of my sources, but are entirely my own.

An unusual website that I found particularly invaluable is Douglas Harper's Online Etymology Dictionary, (www. etymonline. com.) I had it up in my browser through every writing session. It's incredibly exhaustive and it's also a lot of fun to randomly explore.

Steffen Thorsen's website Timeanddate.com also proved itself a huge help. The ability to generate calendars for years past and future is a godsend.

Thank you all!

PART ONE

CHAPTER ONE

July 31, Present Day
Nevada

Jon was almost ready to leave this shabby little roadside museum. King Gila, the Two-Headed Lord of the Lizards, proved to be deceased, preserved in a pose of pathetic fierceness long before Jon was born. The rest of the exhibits were even less lively.

Time to head back to the car, Dee, and the long road to Vegas.

Then, recognition struck like a sharp blow to the head. Jon's grip tightened on the tarnished brass railing skirting the old-fashioned case. He stared down at the tintype photograph inside.

"Outlaw," the crude lettering on the yellowed label declared. 'Hanged March 13, 1874 in Cooper's Creek, Arizona Territory.'

Its subject glared up into Jon's eyes with a dangerous intensity undiminished by the passage of time.

Jon's reflection glimmered on the glass of the case. He shifted, bringing his image parallel with the face in the photograph. The man's features were sharp, his skin pulled close over his bones. His mouth was set in a harsh line and the camera had captured his contempt for whoever was behind the lens.

1

None of those differences blurred the resemblance. This long dead criminal was his double. Jon pressed closer to the case, blind to everything but that disturbing portrait.

"He was a mean-looking sonuvagun, wasn't he?"

Jon flinched, startled by the reedy voice behind him. He turned to the antiquated man, who looked even more worn and tattered than his collection. "What do you know about him?"

"Not much," the old man admitted, but the elbow he propped on the showcase warned Jon that this might be a lengthy lecture. "Found out a little while back that his name was Tom Dorin...."

18 May, 1861
Polk County, Tennessee

"Them Federals has spit all over the Constitution and they's gonna march down here and try to steal our land!" Tom squared off in front of his brother. "You join up with them, and you're sayin' you're willin' to give away this farm and the whole blessed South to a bunch of lyin' thieves and lawbreakers. Besides, you can't go, you're the eldest!"

Josh gave him a hard shove. "That's why I'm the one that oughta go. You're the runt, you stay here and help plow. Them filthy Rebels you like so much ain't gonna be hurt none by not havin' you taggin' along. Besides, nobody round here cares whether all them darkies is slave or free, so why are you so lathered up and blowin' about shootin' a bunch of white folks just to keep a heap of darkies from runnin' all around the countryside like stray cattle?"

Tom spat his contempt, and it would have landed on Josh's foot if his brother hadn't snatched it back quick enough. "I ain't in it to keep them people slaves, you ig'nert heathern. It ain't right in no way to own folks like livestock, but that ain't why I'm Sesech. This war is about our right to govern ourselfs as we see fit without no Federal say-so, but you ain't got enough brains to tell states' rights from a rooster's arse."

"Don't much matter what it's about when folks start shootin', and I got enough brains to know this war ain't gonna last three months no way. You won't be missin' much while I'm off seein' the fight," Josh said.

"I ain't gonna miss nothin'! All you're gonna be seein' in the back end of the mule!"

"Purtier than your face!" Josh shot back.

The sneer on his brother's face was unbearable, but they'd both get their hides caned off if they came to supper again with blackened eyes and fat lips. It took all Tom had in him to speak instead of walloping Josh a good one. "How do you want to settle this?"

His brother stuck a hand into his pocket. "We flip for it. Winner goes, loser sticks up for me with Pa."

Tom looked down in shocked awe at the shiny coin in his brother's dirty palm. "Where'd you get that?"

"Ain't none of your nevermind." The dime rang as Josh flipped it into the air. "Call it."

"Tails." Tom grabbed for his brother's wrist before Josh could slap the coin onto the back of his hand and cheat the toss.

"Blame you, Tom! Now it's lost in the grass!"

"Ain't neither. I seen where it dropped." Tom squatted and parted the long, coarse blades. "I ain't touching it. You look for yourself."

The coin lay tails-up. Josh couldn't put his frustrated rage with words, falling to sputtering and stamping on his own hat instead.

Tom laughed till his sides were sore. "Tonight, after supper, we're gonna talk to Pa."

◑

Tom slipped out of the house and down to the old puncheon bench under the oak, a sullen Josh trailing along behind. His father's pipe glowed, a red firefly in the dusky-dark beneath.

Tom stepped up, squared his shoulders, drew a good breath and dove in. "Pa, I want to go join up to fight against the Federals. Me and Josh agreed he'll stay and help work the farm. I jist need you to come with me and sign for—"

"No."

That one word was as implacable as what Moses heard on Mount Sinai and held nearly as much authority in Tom's mind. Even so, the desperate ambition eating at him prompted a protest.

"But, Pa, I'm sixteen now and a crack shot and I-"

3

"I said no." Abram Dorin laid aside his pipe and rose to his feet.

Tom had all he could do not to quail back. He'd have stepped all over Josh at any rate.

"Pa, I did tell Tom I'd do his part and mine of the work," Josh put in staunchly as he'd promised. "He ain't lyin', he can shoot a keen bead. I ain't sayin' I cotton to him joinin' up with the Sesech but—"

"Enough!" Abram's voice was as sharp and curt as the crack of a whip. "This war is an abomination to the Lord and this family ain't takin' no part in it."

He pointed back up to the house. "Get inside and if I hear one more word out of either of you'uns about this I'm gonna take the razor-strop to your backs. You hear me, boys?"

"Yes sir," both brothers answered almost as one, though only Tom's voice betrayed begrudged obedience.

"You got somethin' else to say for yourself, Thomas?"

Tom glared hot defiance into his father's narrowed eyes, his heart pounding fit to burst his eardrums.

"Well, boy, do you?" Abram stepped closer, his gnarled hands closing into ropy fists.

Tom dropped his eyes to the ground between their feet. "No, sir."

"Then get!"

Tom turned to find Josh already clean out of sight. He salved his smarting pride with the fact that he strode back to the house like a man instead of tearing off like a scolded child.

July 31
Present Day
Las Vegas, Nevada
~ Early Evening ~

"Baby, wake up," Dee called, extending the pattern of a downshift to draw its twin on Jon's thigh. "Welcome to Sin City. "

Jon blinked, his eyes trying to bring the haze of bewildering light into focus. He smiled an apology for his grogginess to Dee in the rear view mirror.

He looked out the window. "Oh for cripe's sake! I don't believe this! Look!" Jon pointed to a billboard further up the block.

A buxom Native American maiden with amazingly Anglo features looked up worshipfully from the booted feet of a bare-chested man brandishing two revolvers.

'VENGEANCE!' the billboard shrieked in flamboyant scarlet font. 'The Newest Marshal Maxx Starr Adventure! Book signing with author Chris Hansen, July 31, 4-6 pm. Only at Bordens Books, 6521 Las Vegas Blvd!'

Dee slowed down and gave Jon a saucy grin. "There's still time to make it to the signing." She put her blinker on.

"Don't you dare," Jon growled. "Or I'll sic King Gila on you!"

"Gah! Anything but that!" She flicked the turn signal off and drove on to their hotel.

CB

Dee settled in at a slot machine, and Jon took the opportunity to wander away through the casino. The vast room was disorienting, fiendishly seductive, all random dancing neon over a constant drone of chimes, electronic fanfares and the clatter of a few hundred human conversations. There were no shadows allowed in the brilliant lighting, but there were also no windows, no clocks, no natural light of any kind to trigger thoughts of sleep or even common sense.

For a man with no money in his pocket, and a long drive in his recent past, the scene lost its charm quickly. Jon shot Dee a quick text: *Tired. Going 2 room.*

He made his way to one of the elevators against the side walls.

In contrast to the casino, the hallway leading to their room was normally lit and rather bland, offering nothing to entice a guest to linger there. When he went into their room, he didn't bother turning on the lights. The multicolored flickering from the strip below was enough to cast a glow through the room. The shadows felt restful after a day driving through desert glare.

Jon caught his own reflection in the dresser mirror, a trick of the dim light exaggerating the tired smudges under his eyes into shadowy hollows. He switched on the bureau lamp, then reached into his shirt pocket and drew out a small envelope. He slid the antique photograph out and glanced between Dorin's face and his own.

Because of the tintype's silvery gray-scale, it was impossible to know what color Dorin's hair was, but Jon could see it was neither blond nor black. It could have been a medium brown, much like his own. Dorin's eyes were light-colored, probably blue, staring out in sharp contrast to what was either a dark complexion or a deep tan.

Dorin's eyes and cheeks were sunken beneath the high arches of their bones, as if he was emaciated at the time of his hanging. Even so, give or take twenty pounds between them, and they could be brothers. Maybe even twins.

"I've heard everybody has a doppelganger, but I thought it was superstitious crap," he informed the unsettling image.

Dorin glared back, his truculent expression frozen, eternal.

An outlaw, so that meant armed robbery, probably murder too, since he was hanged. Pretty much the same as any of them: Jesse James, the Youngers, Billy the Kid. People are still writing about them, historians as often as paperback hacks like his brother. Why wasn't Tom Dorin famous?

Slow, avid excitement flooded his veins.

"I can make you famous."

21 May, 1861
Polk County, Tennessee

Tom lay in the moon-faded darkness of the back porch, arms behind his head, sleepless in the heat. He was certain the three everlasting days since his talk with his Pa had flown by, up where he most wanted to be. He sat up and eased off the bed, careful not to jostle his brother. The last thing he needed was Josh waking up and flapping his lips.

Tom slipped inside the house and crept upstairs to their stuffy room, careful of the boards that squeaked. He took his extra shirt and pants off the hook and stuck his spare socks in his other pocket.

He made it back downstairs without mishap. Silent as shadow, he tarried long enough to grab a sweet tater and scoop up the half-pan of cornpone left from supper. These he wrapped in one of his Ma's dishrags and tucked into the pillowcase with the rest of his plunder.

"Thomas."

"Yes'm?" His heart sank as he turned towards the back of the room.

His mother came through the doorway, her shawl wrapped close around her nightgown. "You'll need more than that with you. It's a long ride."

"You're lettin' me go?"

His mother moved to the cupboard and drew out a wrapped bundle. "I know how it is between you and your father. Joshua is the one that would stay here, war or no. I always knowed we wouldn't be keepin' you with us. This war's jist hurried it all along."

She laid the bundle aside and wrapped her arms tight around him. "Make us proud, son," she whispered near his ear. "But more than that, you come back to me, you hear?"

"I will, Ma. I promise," he said and patted her back. He hadn't realized until then just how small she was.

She kissed his cheek and then stepped back. "Go on now, it'll be daylight soon." She followed him to the doorway and stood at the threshold.

Tom sat down on the stone back porch step to pull on his boots. Josh watched, silent. He waved once when Tom stepped off into the yard then lay back down with his face towards the house.

When he entered the barn, his filly lifted her head and Tom hurried to lay his hand across the bay's nostrils to head off her greeting nicker. "Hush now, Flit," he murmured. "You got to be quiet or we're gonna get skinned."

A few moments later, he tied his bundle and a small sack of oats for Flit to the cantle of his saddle and mounted up. Flit's hooves were almost silent on the packed dirt of the barnyard as Tom rode out at a walk.

His mother waved from the doorway as he passed the house. When they reached the road, he touched the filly's sides with his heels and urged her into an easy lope.

They headed north, towards Knoxville and the gathering Army of Tennessee.

August 1
Present Day
Las Vegas, Nevada
~ The next morning ~

Dee frowned as the waiter carried away Jon's credit card. "I thought we agreed we were going cash-only on this trip."

Jon drained the dregs of his orange juice. "That assumed I would have cash at this point."

She groaned and rubbed her forehead. "You've lost it all already? We haven't been here twenty-four hours!"

"I didn't lose it, I invested it."

"Okay.... Explain?"

Jon leaned forward, propped his elbows on the table. He felt the hair rise on his nape in a rush of excitement. "I found it, Dee. Already! I found my thesis, back at that lizard museum, of all places!"

"And it cost you a thousand? Uh, you do know that buying a Master's thesis is frowned upon, right?" Dee's irritated expression gave the lie to her playful tone of voice.

Jon ignored her conversational feint. "It's source material, Dee. Unpublished, undocumented source material. A piece of history nobody else has seen before."

"Okay, on what?"

"A Civil War veteran who turned outlaw."

"Still gonna have to sell me on it." Dee leaned back in her chair, her expression softening a little.

"His name was Thomas Dorin. He was born somewhere in Tennessee. He served in the Confederate Army." That was pretty much everything the old museum owner knew, so Jon added in his sketchy plans for his Master's thesis.

"I'm thrilled that you've found your inspiration, and I accept you're a history junkie, but I still don't see a grand's worth there," she said.

"You will." Jon grinned at her and reached into his shirt pocket. He drew out the tintype photo and presented it with a flourish.

Dee took it with much less enthusiasm, but she stared at it a long moment. Her eyes wide, she looked up at him and back down at the photograph. "Okay granted, this is truly weird. Still, I wouldn't have given some old fart my last dime for this."

She handed the picture back to him with a sigh. "But since you did, I better hit a big jackpot and you better write one hell of a thesis, honey."

24 May, 1861
Camp Cummings
Knoxville, Tennessee

The doctor looked bored and almighty hot in his uniform. By the time Tom's turn came, he figured he pretty much knew why the man looked bored.

"You got a cough?"

"No sir."

"Lame limbs or stiff joints?"

"No sir."

"Pains anywhere?"

"No sir."

"Bowels move regular?"

Tom felt himself redden a little. "Yes sir."

"Can you see and hear good?"

"Yes sir."

"Open your mouth."

Tom complied, feeling like a horse at market.

"Sound teeth. You pass."

The boy following the doctor around marked a piece of paper and the Doctor scrawled his name on it and handed it to Tom. "Go on over there, get sworn in."

Tom took the sheet of paper and went where he was bid. He took his place in another line of men and boys. Once again, he had plenty of time to learn the expected process. He was especially glad he'd taken the advice of another fellow about his same age that he'd met up with outside the camp. Tom felt the coin slide around in his boot with every step.

"State your name."

"Thomas Anderson Dorin."

"Where you from?"

"Northeast of Benton, in Polk County, sir." Tom held his breath. One of the enlisters asked the next question one way, the other put it different and they seemed to swap off at irregular periods, probably just for a change.

"You over eighteen, boy?"

"Yes sir." Tom's relief overshadowed a niggle of guilt at shaving the truth paper-thin. He was, indeed, over eighteen. The coin in his boot was stamped 1858, and he was standing over it so solid it was about to give him a stone-bruise. If he'd been asked how old he was, he would have had to tell an outright lie.

"Can you read and write?"

"Yes sir."

The man showed a flicker of relief. His voice was hoarse, probably from reading the oath so many times to those who couldn't. "Read this and sign your name here."

Tom wrote his name where indicated. It was done. He'd vowed his life to the service of Army of the State of Tennessee until the end of the war or an unlikely three years. That didn't mean he had any more idea what he was supposed to do now than when he'd started the process a couple of hours earlier.

The camp traffic seemed pure confusion at first, but by the end of the afternoon Tom was in a rather ill-fitting new uniform, carrying a new rifle that fit him fine and searching out the tent where he was to bed down. He was better fitted out than some of the new recruits, for all that his britches were cinched up in folds around his waist and his jacket pulled tight across his shoulders.

The 19th Tennessee was infantry, so he enlisted Flit into the Army too. She drew more of an enlistment bounty than he had. Tom had helped birth the clean-limbed bay filly, and it was a hard thing to watch Flit be led away to be put into the cavalry's service, but he needed a good rifle and such more than a mount.

CB

As Tom approached the tent that was to be his quarters, he saw a slight, tow-headed young man squared off with a taller, older one. He couldn't hear the words exchanged between them for all the ruckus around, but it was clear to sight alone that whatever was between them wasn't much friendly. The tow-headed fellow ducked inside and the lanky dark one set himself down onto a camp stool by the tent flap and began to load up a pipe.

"Afternoon," Tom greeted him. "I's told this was where I'm to draw quarters."

"Make yourself at home," the man told him, with a quirk of his head towards the open tent flap. "The congregation's still gatherin'."

Tom shuffled his plunder around to free his right hand and stuck it out to the fellow. "Tom Dorin."

The other man clenched his pipe between his teeth and gave his hand a hard squeeze and pump. "Taylor Malloy. Where you from, Tom?"

"Up in Polk County, near to Benton."

"Local boy, nearly," Taylor surmised.

"How 'bout you?"

"Barren County in Kentucky claims me, when they ain't got no other choice about it." Taylor punctuated his sentence with a puff of sweet-smelling smoke.

"You're a long way from home."

Taylor grinned around his pipe stem. "That's the general idea."

He was hailed by someone a few tents down, and it was clear Taylor lost all interest in Tom then. "Go on in and claim yourself a wallow," he tossed over his shoulder as he sauntered away, hands in his pockets, trailing smoke like a locomotive.

Tom stepped inside the tent. It smelled of fresh straw and new canvas and the sunlight filtered through in a soft glow. The 'wallows' were heaps of straw piled up for pallets, with only enough room down the middle for a man to walk if he took a care. The tow-headed young man was smoothing a blanket over one that looked more like a feather bed it was tucked up so square and neat.

"Afternoon," Tom greeted him.

"Afternoon." The man smiled. "Feel free to settle in anywhere." He pointed towards the other two pallets that had been claimed. "That one's Malloy's, and that one over there is Bird's."

Tom noticed that this man's pallet was as far from the one Taylor had claimed as it was possible to be. For himself, he didn't much have a care one way or the other, so he unloaded onto the pile nearest this fellow's.

"I'm Carl Lynd," the fellow offered along with his hand as soon as Tom had his free.

"Tom Dorin," he smiled back, more at ease with Carl's sort of friendliness. He glanced over at one of the other claimed pallets. "Is that feller's name really Bird?"

Carl chuckled. "It's his true surname. How are you finding soldiering so far?"

"Confusin'," Tom confessed with a grin.

"Don't fret over it. A couple of days from now you'll be considered one of the Old Guard, like us." A drum rattled outside somewhere and Carl grabbed his rifle. "Time to fall in for afternoon drill."

Tom followed him out, leaving the rest of his plunder to square away sometime later. As they made their way to the parade ground, a couple of fellows hurried to get in step beside them. Both were black-haired and dark complected, but that was about the end of their resemblance. One was tall and spare, and his hair was glossy and straight as string. But it was his eyes that were all a body noticed first off. They were over-large for his narrow face and so pale a blue they looked spooky, set into the dark brown of his tan.

His companion was built low, round and fleshy, and it was a wonder how his cap found purchase to stay on, crammed down on top of an unruly mass of curls. His black eyes were near hid in folds from his grinning, and he was breathing hard from the work his bandy legs had to do to keep up with his companion.

"Hey, ya'll," the taller one drawled as they drew alongside and fell into line beside Carl and Tom.

"Tom Dorin, this is Shine Bird," Carl told him, nodding to the tall fellow.

"Hey, Tom. This here's Will Flynn." Shine nodded, his voice friendly even though his expression stayed solemn. "He's in our mess now too."

"Pleased to meet'cha," Will greeted Carl and Tom with a wholesale grin.

"Hey, Will, Shine," Tom answered back with a smile and nod.

The Drill Sergeant bellowed an order. Further introductions would have to be made later, when they were allowed to converse again.

August 1
Present Day
Las Vegas, Nevada
~ Later that day ~

"It's nice of your brother to come pick us up, but we could have taken a cab," Dee said.

"I'm betting he sends a limo," Jon answered from the bathroom. He tilted his chin, sweeping the last swathe of shaving cream away with his razor.

"Come on, he wouldn't do something like that, would he?" she asked.

Jon wiped his face. "With Chris, we'll go by camels if he thinks it'll make a big splash."

"Then I'm glad I'm wearing shorts!" Dee moved to the foot of the bed to pull on her sandals.

Jon chuckled and finished up his own preparations. It was good to hear Dee relaxed, upbeat and happy. She'd kept herself so wound up while she was going for her paramedic certification, so determined to get the highest score possible on every single detail. This trip had been a good idea, a celebration of her achievement and a last hurrah before they really had to start tightening their belts when he went back to school full time.

As it was, they'd be paying off this jaunt for months. When he looked at Dee standing there, a soft smile on her face as she slipped her earrings into her ears, Jon considered it worth every cent. He put his arms around her waist from behind and she leaned back against him, her hands warm over his. She looked up at him and he bent his head, turning her into his kiss.

The trill of his cell phone evaporated the moment.

Dee stepped back, shaking her head with a little rueful smile. "Uh... make a note to get back to this later?"

"You bet." Jon grinned. "Let's not linger over the ribs."

Dee giggled and hurried to grab her purse. Jon admired the view. Legs for days, and the outfit she wore only made her longer and sleeker. Chris wasn't the only Hansen brother with a stunner on his arm these days. Jon flipped open his cell.

"Ready to go?" his brother asked.

Oh yeah, on so many levels. Jon resigned himself to barbecue instead, however.

"We're heading downstairs now," he answered Chris and followed Dee out the door.

α

It wasn't a limo or a camel caravan awaiting them, but a sleek Jaguar sedan. Chris opened the back door for them with playful panache. "Good to see you both." He smiled at Dee. "Even though I've never had the great good fortune to see you before."

"Dee, this is Chris, my rogue of a brother," Jon said. "Chris, this is Dee Collins."

Dee held out her hand for Chris to shake but Jon wasn't terribly surprised when his brother kissed her knuckles.

"Enchanté," Chris said with a grin as he released her hand.

"Don't even start, Chris," Jon said in playful warning and punched his brother's arm.

"Start what?" Chris asked with wide-eyed innocence.

"I think he means using your Hansen charms on me," Dee interjected. "But I'm already completely under the spell of this Hansen."

"Alas, my heart will never recover from this shocking lack of opportunity," Chris said, holding his hand to his heart. "But, speaking of wounds, want to get in before we get mugged?"

Jon rolled his eyes and handed Dee in first.

Chris turned towards them from the driver's seat. "Before I forget," he handed Jon a package the size of a fat cigar box. "Your birthday present!"

"My birthday was on Tuesday." Jon chuckled. "You're late. Again."

"So what? You think I'm going to give up the family tradition? Go ahead and open it."

Jon tore off the wrapping paper, revealing a wooden box. He slipped the old-fashioned catch and raised the lid, then caught his breath at the handgun nestled inside.

Dee leaned forward to see Jon's gift and gasped. "Is that real?"

"Yep. A genyoowine Colt 1860 Army. Still fires, too." Chris said. "But be careful if you load it. The man who sold it said it's got a very light trigger-pull."

Jon chuckled. "That's ok, I go off half-cocked myself sometimes." He looked down at the beautiful old pistol again. "This is practically a museum piece. Thank you, this is... amazing."

Chris beamed. "Happy birthday, little brother."

"Chris, I'm almost speechless. I don't know what else to say, except thank you!"

"You're welcome." Chris grinned. "Consider it my nod to your desire for authenticity."

"At least you're nodding at it now. That's progress." Jon settled the box beside him and gestured towards the front passenger seat. "So where's Angela? Is she going to be joining us later?"

"Nope," Chris replied. "The current Mrs. Hansen is in Italy, trying to wear out my credit cards."

"I told you she was a gold-digger." Jon turned to Dee. "For some reason, Chris can't seem to stop getting married. How many exes are you supporting now?"

"I think Angie will be five. You'd have to ask my accountant." Chris said with a shrug. He pulled out into traffic. "So, what do you do, Dee? Jon hasn't told me much about you."

"I'm a paramedic. I've been an EMT for four years, but I got my paramedic certification last month."

"Ohh. So you get to drive around in an ambulance with all the flashing lights and shock people like on TV?"

"Well, yeah. But trust me, it's nowhere near as glamorous as it looks on TV. I wouldn't want to spoil your dinner by telling you what it's really like," Dee said.

"Point taken." Chris raised a hand from the wheel in surrender. "I'll change the subject. Are you from Arizona?"

"Born and raised. My grandfather settled the family down here when he came back from World War Two."

"Settled the family?" he repeated. "You make it sound like some kind of clan migration."

"Actually, that's pretty accurate. Granddad brought Nana, her mother and brother, two of his sisters and all of their spouses and kids down from Illinois."

"Wow. Sounds like a big family."

"You have no idea. We practically have to rent out the convention center for family reunions."

"I have a hard time imagining what that would be like. It's pretty much only me and Jon now."

"It's a lot like living in a small town, I think. Everybody knows everyone else's business, and there are always well-meaning busybodies telling you how you could run your life better, and despite all of the petty, picky, absolute crap you have to put up with, the sense of belonging, the... love, I guess... makes it worth it. Most of the time, anyway." Dee interrupted herself with a self-deprecating chuckle. "And that is way more than I usually tell people the first time I meet them."

"It's one of Chris' talents. He usually has most of the significant portions of a woman's history by the end of the first course."

"Then I'm in big trouble because we've not even gotten to the restaurant yet," Dee said with a smile.

"It's not my fault you're too polite to shut down a shameless snoop." Chris flashed a smile at her in the rearview as he pulled into the restaurant lot.

Jon watched Chris and Dee, as they left the car with a valet and went into the restaurant. He wondered what she thought of them. There was a family resemblance, but Chris was brawnier, blonder. He knew he was handsome in an average way, but Chris looked like the hero on the cover of one of his own damned books. Regardless of what Dee may or may not think, Jon was certain that Chris was more comfortable in the current environment, in almost any environment, for that matter.

Chris took up their earlier conversation again as soon as they were seated. "So, Jon, I don't think you told me how you two met."

"You know, sometimes I wonder if you ever notice anything that doesn't have to do with you," Jon said. "Do you at least remember the last time you were in Tucson? Your last book-signing tour?"

"Mmm, yes. Lindsay. Strawberry blonde. She wanted me to sign her cleavage."

"And she had her hands under the table, until I left because I felt like a voyeur," Jon retorted. "So I guess I'm not terribly surprised that you don't remember me telling you about the stunning brown-eyed woman in uniform who agreed that your novels were dreck?"

Chris bit his lip in concentration. "Come to think of it, I do remember the Van Morrison song going through my head that night. I take it this is the woman with eyes that made you 'see home, and peace'?"

"You said that?" Dee asked Jon.

Jon felt himself go red, opened his mouth, but Chris beat him to the punch.

"He did." Chris grinned. "I'm gonna use it somewhere in my next book. It's a nice turn of phrase."

Jon raised his water glass. "To my very own brown-eyed girl."

"Hear, hear," Chris agreed, raising his own glass toward Dee.

Jon noticed that Dee breathed a sigh of apparent relief as the waitress' arrival with the menus saved her from further Hansen dramatics.

"So what have you doing with yourself lately?" he asked Jon after they placed their orders and got their drinks.

"General construction and home repair, mostly. Building decks, putting in ceiling fans, laying carpets, fixing plumbing, a little bit of everything."

"Oh? I thought you had been accepted into the graduate program?"

"I was. I'm heading back to school when we get home. But I've been helping Dee out over the summer until she got her paramedic certification."

"I guess he really does like you," Chris told Dee. "When he finally started college, Jon took to it with all the enthusiasm of a fresh-hatched bookworm in a library. I didn't think anything would tear him away before he got a PhD."

"Nothing but a very special woman," Jon said, placing his hand over Dee's.

Dee turned red to the roots of her hair. "Okay, stop it, you two. My head's gonna swell up so much that I won't be able to get back into the car!"

"If his can fit into it, yours certainly can." Jon shrugged.

Dee shot him a sharp look. Chris chuckled and the subject changed again.

A few moments later, Dee excused herself. Chris turned in his chair to watch her make her way through the restaurant.

"She's not bad, little bro," Chris mused. "Shortchanged on the tits, but I can see why you fell for the eyes. And I sure wouldn't mind having those legs wrapped around my—"

"Damn you, Chris! Don't you have enough bimbos dancing in your lap that you have to drool all over my girlfriend? For the first time in my life, I've got a woman who's interested in me, for me, not because I'm Chris Fucking Hansen's little brother. I'll be damned if I'm gonna let you waltz in with your smarmy snake-oil charm and your black AmEx card and your Hollywood veneer job and sell her a Hansen upgrade. You go through women like rubbers and you've got as much use for either when you're done with them. You're not going to do that to me again."

Chris looked like his eyes were about to bug right out of his head. "Whoa there, Jon. I was joking. Where the hell is all this coming from?"

"Laura Pettinger, for starters. I'm sure you don't remember her. Imagine my surprise when I went to pick her up for prom and her family tells me she's gone with you. To a Beta Sig kegger. Did you ever wonder why I quit Beta Sigma? I didn't have much choice when one of my 'brothers' let me know that the only reason I'd been rushed was because of my illustrious brother."

Chris took a long swallow of his beer. "This does throw a whole new light on why you suddenly transferred out here from OSU."

"At least here, I'm not constantly asked 'any relation?'"

"Well excuse the friggin' hell outta me for making something out of my life!"

Hostile silence fell until Dee returned from the restroom and their waitress hurried up with a staggering amount of barbequed ribs.

Just another festive evening for what was left of the Hansen family.

He and Chris talked to Dee through the rest of the meal, instead of to each other. Jon could tell that Dee had no idea why she was the center of attention, but after a few confused glances his way, she relaxed and drank up the dual attention.

»

At the end of their dinner, Chris tossed his wet-wipe and napkin onto the table and leaned back in his chair as if it were a recliner. He excreted a long sigh, a stifled belch and a doleful expression.

Here it comes. Jon simply sipped his beer. If he was going to be subjected to a rambling account of the tribulations of the rich and famous, Chris was going to have to work for it.

Another gusty sigh, though, was all it took for Dee to bite. "Is something wrong?"

Chris' expression altered to one that wouldn't be out of place on an icon of some martyred saint. "Angie served me with divorce papers today."

"What a shock." Jon drained his beer. The toe of Dee's sandal tapped his shin.

"I'm so sorry, Chris." Her voice as well as her face displayed mild sympathy, but Jon wasn't sure if it was genuine or her work-face.

"You had to have seen it coming," Jon added, with no effort at sympathy at all. "Like, from the day you said 'I do.'"

"Yes, I suppose," Chris admitted. "But I wasn't expecting it so soon. According to our pre-nup, she gets to keep full rights to the house. That's only fair, it was hers when we married, but the agreement states that if she files, I have to move out within the week. It's the worst possible time. I've got a deadline looming and my editor's really breathing down my neck. There's this movie deal in the works and we have to get this next novel out in time—"

"Rent a suite," Jon interrupted as he poured himself another beer.

"I need a quiet, peaceful, homey environment to work in," Chris informed him with the same tone most use to admit to a life-threatening allergy. "A hotel suite doesn't cut it for me, I've tried while I've been out here."

He shook his head, his voice pitiful. "I'm already stressed with work, and now I've got to deal with this divorce. They're always ugly, no matter how good the pre-nup. This movie deal is contingent on me being free to write the screenplay. If I don't get this novel finished by the deadline, I'm screwed. Double-screwed, with all the hassle and stress of moving out and finding another place to live. Even if I do lease a place, there's a real estate agent to deal with, viewings, movers..."

Another long sigh, minus the belch this time.

"You'll handle it." Jon shrugged. He gave his brother a smirk instead of a smile. "You always land on your feet."

"But I've never been completely homeless before." Chris managed to look more like a spanked puppy than a spanked puppy.

Jon laughed. "You talk like you're going to be sleeping on a park bench!"

"You can stay with us."

That unexpected statement had Jon's head whipping around to Dee. She looked as startled as he felt, as if she wondered who'd blurted that out.

"I can? That's great Dee!" Chris' mournful demeanor flashed over into one closer to his normal manic glee.

Jon's jaw clenched. If the damned conniving bastard had demurred for the least fraction of a second— but no. He felt for Dee's sandaled toes and gave one quick, firm press.

Dee flinched, and seemed to shrink in her chair a little. "For a little while, until you can get settled somewhere else. We've got a spare bedroom, and we're outside of town, so it's pretty quiet."

"I really appreciate this, Dee." Chris leaned forward, crossed his arms on the table. "I give you my solemn word I won't be a pain in the ass. I'll do my own laundry and I'll fend for myself in the kitchen. I can pay rent or the utilities or something. I don't want to be a mooch."

"You're family, not a boarder." She smiled. "You take care of your own necessities and we'll call it even."

Her eyes slid over for a furtive glance at Jon, the look in them making her smile a lie.

Jon could feel a muscle beginning to twitch in his left eyelid. He applied himself to keeping his face blank and his beer glass emptied.

"That okay with you, Jon?" Chris asked, far too late of course.

"It's her house." Jon shrugged.

Dee cast him a pleading look. He pretended to find great interest in the décor beyond her.

Dee blinked, and looked back at Chris. The two of them became absorbed in working out the cohabitation details. By the time the waitress set another pitcher of beer down on the table, Chris even had Dee laughing and looking as happy as she had when they first met at the car.

CHAPTER TWO

11 June, 1861
Camp Cummings,
Knoxville, Tennessee

"Well boys, I didn't expect to still be bunkin' with y'uns after today," Taylor said as he plunked his gear down, claiming a spot by the tent flap.

"You ain't the only one 'round here that can shoot sharp," Willy answered, "And today proved it."

"Maybe so, but I'm the best there is, in this here Army or any other." Taylor lit his pipe and made himself comfortable.

Tom paid heed to that with only a snort through his nose. He was more amazed that all five of them were still together, in the same company and even the same mess, than that all of them qualified as marksmen. He'd expected them to be scattered through their new regiment to the four points and some in between, regardless of their skills.

Carl seemed the only one of them not inclined to crow about their success and good luck, not even a little.

Tom moved to squat beside Carl's pallet. "What's wrong?" he nodded towards the letter that Carl had been studying for way too long. "Is it bad news from home?"

"Yes." Carl didn't look up, only turned a page.

"Aw, Carl, I'm sorry. What's happened?" Tom laid a hand on his friend's shoulder. Going by Carl's face, that letter had to be news that the Lynd's house had burnt down, or maybe his father's warehouses. It wasn't a death, for a mercy, for the pages weren't edged with black.

"My mother has taken into her head to throw a cotillion ball in my honor. Worse yet, my father used his influence to have a half-day's furlough granted for that purpose," Carl said.

Tom couldn't help it, the woeful expression on Carl's face as he spoke was too much, and he laughed. He bit it off right quick and tried for sympathy instead. "How's that bad news? You look like your best hound's died."

"I'd rather he had, than this. A ball and a leave are bad news, as you would know if you'd ever made the acquaintance of my dear mother. She's... rather a force of nature, as if a whirlwind donned crinolines and set its mind to raising its social standing through sheer implacable will alone."

Carl sighed and folded the letter, tapping it against his thigh. "I am her only surviving child, the sole male scion of the Lynd family, and all her extraordinarily ambitious hopes rest upon me. It is, at times, quite a throttling yoke to bear."

Tom gave a soft whistle through his teeth. "If that's so, how'd you ever persuade her to let you join the Army?"

"I didn't ask her permission to do so." Carl straightened, his nervous hands going still. "It is my one and only act of rebellion against her domination, and I do not regret it."

The paper resumed its rustling tap-tap against his thigh. "Although, it is clear she has found a way to make me pay."

Tom chuffed. "It's just a dance, Carl. A few hours for one night."

"Oh yes, a fleeting, festive affair that may end with me chained for life to some brainless lump of biscuit dough in petticoats, if Mother feels such a marital alliance will gain her entrance into the upmost strata of society."

It took a second or two to work all that out, but Tom grimaced when he got the sense of it. "Anything I can do to help?"

Answering took Carl a second or two, but a slow sly smile curved his lips. "Yes, there is. Go with me, protect my flank from maternal espionage and lobbed debutantes."

"Carl, I ain't never been to anything fancier than a barn dance!"

"All the better!" Carl's wicked glee tempered itself with sympathy. "Don't worry, I'll help you, so you won't feel out of place."

"How many weeks you got for that task?" Tom muttered with a roll of his eyes.

Carl laughed. "Trust me, four days is plenty of time. All you need is polished boots, a few tucks and gussets tailored into your uniform, and a pair of white gloves. You'll catch onto the bowing and scraping required in less than an hour of drill."

"There always seems to be drill no matter what," Tom said with a sigh. "But for you, I'll do it."

Carl gripped his shoulder. "You're a good friend, Tom," he said, his voice low and his expression serious. "For more reasons than this alone."

"You're the same to me," Tom answered.

Carl grinned and clapped the shoulder he'd squeezed, then turned to the others. "Hey, fellows— any of you want to go to a fancy ball?"

15 June, 1861
Near Knoxville, Tennessee
~ Four days later ~

The evening was warm, that late June evening. Under the shimmering candelabras in the ballroom, it was downright stifling from candlelight and the effect of his nerves. Tom felt as out of place as a hog in church.

He stood on the sidelines, out of the way of swishing silks and stamping boots, nursing a cup of punch and feeling like a fool. He considered the social implications of stripping off his new white gloves, for he'd probably sweated clean through the silly things by this point anyhow. At least the music was first-rate.

Taylor sailed by with a laughing, lovely little ornament on his arm and gave Tom a broad wink. Tom lifted his punch cup in salute and wondered if he'd mortally offend Carl if he slipped off and went back to camp.

He never got the chance to follow through on that urge to desert, as Mrs. Lynd approached like a ship in full sail.

"Private Dorin," She smiled as he bowed to her politely. "I am so glad I found you. There is someone I would like you to meet."

"Yes ma'am, thank you," he murmured obediently and meekly offered his bent arm as she lifted her gloved hand with studied elegance.

She led him to the other side of the bedecked pavilion, to where a gaggle of young women perched on the edges of spindly gilt chairs, giggled behind gloves and fans, and waited to be asked to dance.

They all politely rose at the approach of their hostess and her escort. Mrs. Lynd smiled and nodded at them all, but barely gave Tom time to nod his own courtesies before she planted him in front of the duck among the swans.

"Miss Sarah-Elizabeth Beattie," Mrs. Lynd announced, "Allow me to introduce Private Thomas Dorin, lately from Polk County."

The girl inclined her head, and Tom made his own nodded bow. "I'm pleased to meet you, Miss Beattie."

"The pleasure is mine, Private Dorin." Her voice was surprisingly low-pitched, and musical as a mountain rill gurgling over stones.

"I'll leave you to become acquainted. Pardon me." Mrs. Lynd smiled, content with her success in getting the most obvious wall-flowers paired up. She stepped away to waylay Carl as he passed with a young woman lightly touching his arm. Tom sent him an apologetic look. Carl returned a slight shrug and a smile. They'd known there'd be casualties, going into the fray.

Tom smiled then at Miss Sarah-Elizabeth Beattie. She was an amazing-looking little creature that was for certain. So short the top of her head wouldn't reach his chin, with hair of an astounding red— it was orange, to be truthful- and so curly that tiny ringlets sprang free all over her head, giving her a slightly disheveled appearance. Her skin was as pale as milk and her nose and cheeks as freckled as a wren's egg. Her face was round with a little snub nose and her figure curved with a lushness that even her corset couldn't fully conceal. Her eyes were powerful pretty, green as a cat's and set tilted, and there was a merry light in them that brightened when she smiled back at him.

"May I have the honor of this dance, Miss Beattie?" He held out his hand, as Carl had instructed.

"I'd be delighted, Private Dorin." She laid her small, kid-gloved fingers in his palm and he led her towards the twirling couples. Tom paused at the edge of the dance floor, and cleared his throat.

"Miss Beattie," he leaned down to make himself heard over the music and chatter, but hopefully, not overheard. "I have to confess, I might step on your toes. I'm not over familiar with these dances tonight."

She blushed and cut her pretty green eyes sideways at him from under her lashes, gave him a smile that edged on wicked, and rose onto her tiptoes, balancing herself with a fleeting touch to his shoulder.

"Don't worry," she breathed near his ear. "We women are quite adroit at leading our men, all unawares!"

He chuckled, charmed and startled by her transformation from plain to lovely in that informal instant.

"Lead on then, fair lady!"

She laughed and they took their places in the forming figure of the next dance. True to her word, she managed to keep her slippers away from his boots and vice versa, and put him so at ease he forgot to be nervous or to feel out of place.

When the dance ended, he bowed to her and she curtsied, her ivy-colored skirts crumpling elegantly around her.

"May I fetch you some refreshments, Miss Beattie?" he offered, the formal courtesies making him feel awkward once more.

"Actually, Private Dorin," she demurred, "I would prefer a stroll. It is so warm here." She flicked her fan open and gave him that sidelong, impish glance again. "And truly, I would prefer to be addressed as Beth, if you don't mind."

"I don't mind one bit," he smiled back, and led her towards the garden just beyond the ballroom's tall French doors. "And I'd be real pleased if you'd call me Tom. 'Private Dorin' always makes me feel like the Master-Sergeant's lurkin' jist behind somewheres, anyhow."

She rewarded him with that warm, throaty laugh of hers and they joined the couples promenading along the graveled garden paths, away from the more brilliant illumination of the dance floor.

The rest of the evening they spent in each other's company, other than for the brief separations demanded by the movements of the dances. Tom enjoyed her every word, treasured every time he was rewarded with her quick, coy glance and chuckle. The night fled away and left them under a bower, the moon-vines covered with fragrant blooms.

"I'm sorry, Beth," he told her, holding her hands in his. "I have to go."

"Can't you linger a little longer?"

He shook his head. "Much as I'd like to, there's a curfew for us. I don't want to start off by makin' a name for myself as one who flaunts the rules."

"Then forgive me for tempting you," she smiled, and rose. "I don't want to besmirch the record of a man who will surely be soon proven a hero."

He followed to his feet as well, their hands still linked, and he felt the heat of a flush surge up from under his collar. "I doubt I'll be a hero."

"I have no doubt on that count at all," she murmured, and to his surprise, lifted one of his hands to her face, laying her cheek against his knuckles for a fleeting instant like an affectionate kitten. "May I ask a favor of you?"

"Anything at all," he breathed, his heart thudding in his throat.

"May I write to you?"

"I'd like nothing better," he assured her. "A letter from you will be the bright spot in my day."

She gave a playful giggle. "Then prepare to be deluged. I warn you now, sir, I'm a voluminous correspondent!"

"Well, we'll see how you feel about it after you strain your eyes tryin' to make out my hen-scratchin' in return," he grinned.

"For you, I'll risk eyestrain to the point of putting myself into spectacles," she declared merrily. "Would you still wish to keep the acquaintance of a girl with spectacles perched on her nose?"

"Of course," he said. "For once all them other gals see how charmin' you are in 'em, it'll be all the fashion for miles around."

Beth laughed. A soft cough nearby behind them caught their attention. They turned and Carl closed the distance, a faint smile around his mouth.

"I'm sorry, Tom. We have to go."

Tom nodded, and gave Beth a bow as fine as any at the Ball. "Good night, Miss Beattie."

She curtsied pretty as a queen. "Good night, Tom. God speed." She favored Carl with a shallower dip. "Good night, Private Lynd."

Carl paid his courtesies in due kind and they headed away into the dark, back towards Camp Cummings. As soon as they were out of earshot, Carl spoke with a sly smile in his voice.

"So you're Tom and I've known her all our lives and I'm Private Lynd all of a sudden?"

"Yeah." Tom couldn't wipe the fool grin off his face all the way back to camp.

August 10
Present Day
Tucson, Arizona
~ Ten days later ~

Jon lay tangled together with Dee in the hammock. They swayed gently as the night breeze began tempering the heat from the patio's paving. The last skeins of a brilliant sunset faded on the horizon.

"I talked to Mom today," she murmured.

"How did that go?"

"Better than usual, only three digs in a thirty minute conversation."

"That's a first. What had her distracted?" Jon traced lazy meanders down her arm.

"She was calling to let us know that the reunion is on Sunday and everybody's meeting at Danny and Marta's this year."

"Good lord."

"I know, but it's their turn." Dee tilted her head back to look at him. "Will you go this time?"

Jon groaned. "Honey, they've already seen me and passed judgment."

"Once, and you haven't been around since so they can change their minds. Please? It's just one day."

The silence stretched out between them. The twilight deepened to dusk.

"Okay," he said.

ɔ꙯

21 June, 1861

Deer Beth,

I was most pleesed to git yor leter to day an if i draown in thim i wil go undr the see of ink with a big grin on my face.

I hope you hav a good eye doktor in mind becaus you wil shorly need one after readin my skrawl. My hand is turrible i no an my spellin is worst an it is no fawlt of my Ma for she tryd her verre best to teach me but it were a task akin to makin silk purrsis frum sows ears.

Carl Lynd sends his regards—he dont call hisself Carol here an for that i can not blaym him. He ketchs enuff guff as it is an bars all th teezin with a pashunt disposishun. I rekon he has had lots of practis at it if his Mother is as you say.

I am verry graytfull to yor Mother for her kind invatashun an i would be pleesd to hav suppr with yall when an if i kin. I wil find out abowt it an let you no direktly.

As for my famly i do not no as i hav not reseevd a leter from eny of them thoh i did rit to my brother Josh. My Pa is a man who xpekts to be obayd and who is quik to anger and slow to giv it up when he is crossd so in all truth Beth i do not no if i wil ever be welcum at his suppr tabel agin. I jist no i dun the rit thang evn if mebe i went abowt it the rong way an i jist hope that Pa wil com to se it that way two sooner er latr.

But as you sayd yor self, on to happeer subjeks. Yor Ball is one my happeest memrees to and i am glad u fownd thet moonflowr catchd up in yor skirts as somthin to remembr it by. As long as i liv, when i smel moon flowrs i wil think of you an our first meetin.

I am in Carls debt for invitin me and in his Mothers debt for interdusin us. I felt so out of place amungst that fine Crowd but you put me at my eez at oncst and for the rest the evnin, thar was no one else be sides you who was thar as far as it kinsernd me.

You mayd a clod of a man from Jump Off Nowhar fel lik a Gennelman for a chang and for that if for none else i wil always remembur you fondly.

Now Beth you askd to here of my days and it is the trooth of it to say that yors ar shorly mor innerstin then mine. Me and i rekon ever othr feller in this Grat Army sind up to fiyt the Yankes but what we do is Dril frum befor day liyt till 6 o'clok in the evening wich is Suppr, and sum free time wich i am njoyin in rihtin this dul leter to you, por Deer Girl.

I am in a tent with my mess mayts. A mess of men is lik a mess of soop beans— jist as much as the pot wil hold. In this canvas pot that numbr is five. Thar is Carl, and Taylor Malloy, and William Flynn who you have not met i do not think, and Shine Bird— that boy you sed had purtyer eyes then any man had the riht to have— and yours trulee.

With all of us undr the canvass its a rit close skweez but we mannij it awl riht. Our beds is heaps of straw with blankits ovr and whil that felt lik sleepin on a plank at first the Sarjants has tawt us well that if you tar a man out enuf he kin sleep on enythang or probly even standin strayt up.

Shine jist askt what i was rihtin an when i told him he askt me to ask you if mebe that littl yaller haird girl in the pink dres sprigd with roses mite be so kind as to rit to him. Now Shine caint read nor riht more then his own name so i dont no how he'll mannij the trik if she agrees but i am jist the faythful mesenjer here.

I had best finnish up kwik here for soon thar wil be the tatto which is a rol on the drums that tels us to fall out for anuthr Rol Call befor a bugul sounds an we are all to sak out for the nite. But at leest thar aint no more Dril for the day.

So far, eny how.

In hopes i aint ruint your eyes nor bord you to weepin.

Your good frend,
Tom

August 25
Present Day
Tucson, Arizona
~ Fifteen days later ~

Dee was on a forty-eight hour shift, so the two of them were left to fend for themselves. When Jon came home, he and Chris decided it was easier to order pizza than to decide which one of them would cook. They managed to say nothing much to each other after the usual toppings debate.

ଔ

Jon shoved the empty pizza box to one side, and took the last swallow of his first beer.

Chris twisted the cap off his second round and lit a cigar.

"Dee—" Jon frowned.

"Is not here," Chris interrupted. "By the time she gets home, she won't notice a thing."

Jon shook his head. "You never learn, do you?"

"Oh, I learn," Chris grinned, "But the lessons are so much fun, I can't help but repeat them."

"Then you'll never graduate to real life."

Chris flicked ash into his empty bottle. "As opposed to you, the perennial student, who intends to make a career out of hiding out in some museum basement?"

"There will be a graduation in between the two," Jon said around a bite of pizza.

"But not to a real life," Chris countered, his demeanor going serious. "Especially if you wind up driving Dee away. She's the best thing that'll ever happen to you, Jon-boy. You need to start acting like you're glad she's around. Hell, you should marry her, quick, and count your damn blessings every day."

"You say that like you're some sterling example of marital bliss."

"Don't make this about me." Chris's eyes narrowed. "You and Dee have a good thing going. Whether you admit it or not, she makes you happier than I've seen you since Mom died, or at least it seemed like that in Vegas. I don't know what's going on with you two, but it's been nothing but downhill since you started back to school."

"Don't make that all about me. We were fine till you horned in and you don't know jack-shit about what she's really like." Jon drained his beer and set the bottle back onto the table with a sharp clack. "Put out that damn cigar. You're stinking up the house."

He turned and headed for his study. Once Chris got wound up, leaving the scene was the only way to end the conversation.

"Asshole" accompanied him on his way.

24 September, 1861
~ Nine Days after the Ball ~

As Tom read Beth's second letter, he frowned. After going back to the rough patch half a dozen times with no more idea of the sense than he had the first go-round, he looked over at Carl.

"Hey, Carl. Can you help me with this here?"

"Of course." Carl laid his journal and pen aside and went to sit beside Tom on his pallet. "What's the trouble?"

"I ain't got the least idea what these words is." Tom pointed to the indecipherable portion.

"Débutante soirée. That's French. It's a high-toned way of saying 'coming-out party.'"

Tom sighed with a little shake of his head. "I know I can't write for beans, but 'til I started gettin' her letters, I was mistaken I could at least read purty good. It's for certain sure she's thinkin' she's befriended the village idjit after readin' what I wrote her back afore this 'un."

Carl didn't laugh, which was a bit of a surprise. Instead, he tilted his head like a blue jay eyeing a robin's egg. "I have an idea."

He reached over to his pallet and retrieved his journal, pen and ink. He handed Tom the pen and book, and held the bottle of ink at a convenient angle. "Write down what you just said to me."

It took far longer to write it than it had to say it, but eventually Tom was able to hand the journal back.

Carl quickly scanned the unfettered spelling and bold, sprawling scrawl that starkly contrasted with his neat, tight script on the facing page. "I believe I see your problem. You're not stupid Tom, you're only ignorant."

Tom felt his ire rise some. "Never figured there were any difference between the two."

At that, Carl did chuckle. "Ignorance is easily cured with regular and diligent applications of education. Stupidity is a life-long intractable affliction." His fingers tapped a silent rhythm on his thigh.

"You spell the way you speak, the way you hear the words. That will help you improve, I believe, once you have the keys to it all. You see, English has certain rules, and once you learn them, you'll be able to speak and spell properly and read much more easily."

Tom frowned, considering this entirely novel information. "How does a feller learn them rules?"

"He studies a grammar textbook," Carl said. "That's the usual way."

"Then I'm whipped already, for I ain't got one nor money to buy any."

"Don't count yourself out so quickly." Carl nodded towards the sheets of fine, pale rose paper in Tom's lap. "There's an excellent grammar and spelling primer for you, and believe me, it's a far more appealing one than I ever had to endure. Memorize how she spells her words, and how she forms her sentences, and you'll cure that ignorance condition of yours in jig-time."

Tom smiled, feeling entirely better about the situation. "Thank you kindly."

"My pleasure," Carl smiled, then gathered his writing materials and went back to his bed.

Tom unfolded Beth's first letter, and spread it out beside the new one. He took up his own paper and pencil and began to write, searching her letters for each word he wanted to use, one by one.

ɔʒ

At the call to muster, Carl ripped a few pages from his journal and handed them to Tom as they fell into formation. "This might help a little," he smiled.

Tom glanced at the first line. It was a rule, about vowels. Carl had written out a whole passel of them. He grinned at his friend as he folded the sheets and tucked them into his shirt pocket. "This'll help a heap more'n a little."

August 28
Present Day
Tucson, Arizona
~ Three days later ~

When he came of out the bathroom, Deidre was sitting on the end of the bed, still in her robe.

"Honey, we need to talk," she said.

Dee had a lot of shining qualities, but her timing sucked rocks. "Now's not a good time."

"There never seems to be a good time anymore," she said.

He dropped his towel and pulled a pair of briefs out of the dresser. Saying anything to that would start an argument he didn't have time for.

"Would you please stop and listen to me?" she demanded.

He avoided her accusing gaze, reflected in the mirror. "For heaven's sake, I can listen to you while I get dressed. I'm already running late."

He went to the closet, pulled out his shirt and jeans.

"Your collar's frayed," she said, her voice soft.

He picked up his comb and started pulling it through his hair, smoothing the longer strands back behind his ears. "So what?"

"It looks shabby, honey."

He shrugged and bent to tie his shoes. "I'm not teaching today."

"Still, I would think you'd care abou—"

"Funny how you say we never find time to talk, but you always find time to nag. You gonna start in again on how I need a haircut too?" He locked gazes with her in the mirror.

Dee dropped her eyes, her fingers fidgeting with the tie of her robe. "I'm sorry."

Jon tossed his comb onto the dresser and turned to face her. "So what's important enough to make me miss my first class?"

She shook her head, still watching herself fold that belt end into tight pleats. "Nothing."

They just got better and better with the communication thing. "You think clamming up like a pouting kid's going to help? What do you want to tell me?"

She sighed and looked up at him. "Never mind. You're right, it's not a good time."

"Jeez, Dee!" He scooped up keys, phone and wallet, not willing to coddle and sweet-talk her complaint out of her this morning. "When it is the right time, send me a damn memo or something."

When she didn't say anything, he headed out the door. Now he was running really late.

03

The front door banged against its frame. Deidre's shoulders twitched. She shrank into her robe, her hand clenching over the stubby plastic wand in the pocket.

Deidre crouched and picked up the towel lying in a crumpled heap in front of the dresser. She headed for the bathroom, but stopped in the doorway.

The debris of Jon's morning routine littered every surface. Damp terrycloth slithered through her fingers.

"I'm not," she whispered. "I'm not cleaning it up this time. I'm not."

Deidre bolted towards the toilet, dropped to her knees, barely making it in time. She heaved until the relentless nausea subsided. Wrung out and aching, she reached up to flush and then rose on shaky legs to wipe her tear-streaked face and swish her mouth with water. Spitting into the sink threatened to set off a second surge of morning sickness.

Deidre clung to the cold porcelain rim of the sink, swallowing hard against the rising bile. She straightened, blew out a breath and looked around the bathroom again from one thoughtless mess to the next.

She walked out and slammed the door.

29 June, 1861
Camp Cummings
Knoxville, Tennessee

"What's it gonna be this evenin'?" Taylor looked down at him with the taunting grin that seemed to be his sole variety. "You gonna go down the line with me for a touch of oh-be-joyful and some horizontal refreshment, or are you gonna go wanderin' off with the holy rollers again?"

Tom looked up from cleaning his rifle, more suspicious of Tay than he'd ever been of Josh. "Why are you so all-fired innersted in gettin' me drunk and screwed?"

"Since you ain't never experienced either of them conditions seems to me you orta grab on while you got the opportunity. Be a sorry shame for a young feller like you to maybe catch a ball between the eyes and go out of this world without never knowin' what it's like to be a full growed man."

Tom felt a chill along his spine as if a crow lit on his grave. He sighted down the barrel of his rifle at the lantern's flame. The grooved surface inside flashed back at him, bright and smooth with no dark flecks of corruption marring the shine. "Seems to me, if a feller like me was to catch a bullet, it'd be to his favor to go out of this world without that particular knowledge."

Taylor rocked on his heels, sending out a few puffs from his pipe while he considered that. "Maybe so, but what if this War don't send you straight on to Glory? It won't be to your favor to go into a marriage with that virtue of yours intact. Chastity's for the gals. A man's supposed to know what the hell he's about. All respectable women expect it to be so. You want go fumblin' around on your weddin' night like a blind man tryin' to get his key in a new lock and set your woman to wonderin' if she's done made a terrible mistake?"

As Tom reassembled his rifle, he had to admit that Tay hit a tender spot there. "I reckon I'll figure it out quick enough. I ain't an idjit."

"Never said you was, ol' hoss," Tay amended. "Jist sorely innocent. 'Sides, it ain't hardly healthy to deny your male nature when the sap's runnin' the highest."

That there smelt of pure fresh manure, but arguing about it had his thoughts deserting over to Tay's side of the fight and in alarming numbers. His rifle and kit squared away, Tom set them aside and rose to stand near nose to nose with Taylor.

"All right then, tell you what." He looked Tay straight in the eye and gave him a cocky smirk right back. "You tell me what's in this for you and maybe I'll take you up on it."

Taylor looked as if he was mortally offended. "They ain't nothin' in it but havin' some good times with a mess-mate."

Tom laughed in his face. "You need to plow that furrow straighter."

Tay knocked the ashes out of his pipe. He grinned at Tom. "All right, here 'tis. All this hurry up and wait we's doin' lately is gettin' right tedious. I need some diversion and I expect I'll laugh my arse off at the look on your righteous pie-eatin' face after you're liquored up tighter than a drumhead and one of them gals has showed you what's it's for."

"See there? The truth does serve you better," Tom answered. Despite the sure promise of future ridicule, tonight Tay wasn't the only one of them who was getting powerful bored and restless and ready to kick up some sand. "Let's go."

ᘓ

A little less than a mile outside the Army's camp, another motley sort of camp had been established. Like any human habitation, it had stratified itself. Camp followers attached to the officers dwelled in one orderly section, the enlisted men's wives, the sutlers, bakers and washerwomen comprised another neighborhood and farther off from both of these a far more raucous little settlement flourished.

Unlike the others, its organization was more freeform than otherwise. Men and women, civilians and soldiers alike wandered between the wall-tents, plank shanties, Sibleys, shebangs, lean-tos and brush arbors that made up its architecture. Loud conversations and exclamations of every possible tenor and snatches of a dozen different tunes forced out of nearly as many instruments blended together into a general din that ebbed and surged.

Intermittent illumination was provided by campfires and pine knot torches, while inside some of the shelters, an interior light occasionally provided a shadow play that startled Tom but seemed to be largely disregarded by the other passers-by. Taylor shepherded him through, obviously familiar with the place. They made their first stop at a wall-tent set up as a makeshift saloon. Tay slapped a coin on the packing crate bar and got a bottle and a pair of tin cups in return. After pouring a generous shot into each, Tay handed one to Tom. He held his own at the ready and the dare in his gleeful expression was unmistakable.

Tom took that dare. He nonchalantly knocked back the liquor as if he'd been drinking all his life. The fumes came surging up through the back of his nose to singe off all the hair in there as the fiery liquid itself lit him up from the back of his throat straight down to his belly.

Tay sipped at his own cup and snickered while Tom turned bright red, wheezed and hacked like the nearly drowned. "Have another," he chuckled as the paroxysm passed.

This time, Tom put prudence before pride, so the whiskey went down a lot smoother. By the time they abandoned their empty cups on the bar, Tom was enjoying a buoyant sense of wellbeing. He did, however, find the ground a good bit more uneven than it had been on the way in. Taylor led him down a side path lined with smaller tents and thick with milling men and bawdy women in every state of dress conceivable, and a few inconceivable, for Tom at least.

"See one you favor?" Tay inquired as they made their way into the crowded alleyway.

Tom squinted to bring the scene into clearer focus. "That 'un." He pointed to a bosomy girl about halfway down with sorrel hair hanging loose down her back, wearing nothing but a gaudy colored corset and a lace petticoat.

Tay pressed three coins into his palm. "Go get her then. Give her this when you're inside and be damned sure she keeps her hands out of your pockets."

Floating on liquid confidence, Tom swaggered off on a slightly zig-zag trajectory. He wasn't quite sure what to say to the girl when he stopped in front of her tent, but he was pretty certain formal introductions wouldn't be required. "Hey."

"Hey there handsome," she smiled at him, swaying her veiled hips in a figure-eight. "Care to keep me company tonight?"

He blinked, near as enthralled by that motion as a rabbit by a rattler. "Yes'm."

She laughed, slid a red rag up to the top of the guy-rope, then took his hand and tugged him into the tent. "What's your name, handsome?" she asked as she flicked the flaps together.

"Tom." His tongue felt thick and he was definitely losing his higher faculties, probably from the blood rushing away from his brains.

"I'm Essie," she informed him. "Put your three on the table there."

ᘓ

39

Tom left Essie's tent wobbly in the knees and on a definite cant, but he grinned from ear to ear and felt like he could whip the entire Army of the Potomac single-handed. "TAY!" he bellowed. "TAYLOR! Where are ye?"

He bumbled happily through a good bit of the camp before Tay caught up to him and offered him the bottle. Tom's mouth was practically numb by this point, so this long swallow of whiskey went down like water.

Tipping his head back to drink would have sent him on over into the dirt, save for Taylor's snatch at his collar to jerk him back upright.

"You havin' yourself a good time, ol' hoss?" Taylor grinned as he retrieved the bottle from Tom's uncertain grasp.

"Yesh I am," Tom stated with an ebullient laugh.

Tay towed him into the circle of light thrown by a nearby torch. He grinned into his face and Tom grinned back, swaying like a sapling in a windstorm. Taylor laughed and Tom laughed right along with him, mainly because he couldn't make himself not.

"Worth ever' damn dime, pie-eater," Taylor chortled.

"Oh hell yeah!" Tom agreed. Taylor handed him the bottle again.

 C3

The blast of reveille was surely a foretaste of eternal damnation, but even with a pounding head and a mouth that tasted like it had been swabbed with horse manure and dirty socks, Tom felt no real regrets. The whiskey he could take or leave, but Essie— no doubt in his mind he'd be paying her another visit at his earliest opportunity.

C3

He'd come back with Taylor on his sixth time, so he was ranging on ahead, for Tay liked to take a few swallows before he got down to his own business and Tom let him have most of those swallows alone. His first experience with the wages of alcohol overindulgence had learned him but good. He never again drank more than two shots despite Tay's ragging.

The flag was up on Essie's tent, so Tom settled himself on the stump set beside the flap to wait.

Taylor walked up and took exception to that for some reason. "She ain't the only whore here, ol' hoss."

"I know."

"She ain't sweet on you, no matter what she squeals when you're pokin' her. It's strict business to these gals."

"I know that too. I ain't as dumb as you think I look."

"Then why the thunder are you wastin' your time sittin' there?"

Tom kept a straight face as he looked up at Tay. "'Cause she's got this swirl she does with her hips while she's ripplin' inside her belly somehow at the same time." He described a lazy figure-eight in the air with a forefinger, and then he did grin. Could hardly help it, with that move in mind.

Taylor barked a laugh. "Aw hell, hoss! You done took to this like a drake to water!" He eyed the closed tent with speculation. "If she's as good as you say, I might have to give her a go."

Tom shrugged. "Suit yourself but wait your turn. 'Course, she'll likely be all tuckered out after I been at her."

Shaking his head in mock dismay, Taylor clucked his tongue. "You sure turned into one debauched sonuvabitch awful quick, Thomas."

"Yeah, and whose fault is that?" Tom called after him as Taylor strolled on up the way.

☙

Essie made the wait worth his while. They were well into the proceedings when all of a sudden there was an animal roar right behind and somebody yanked him onto the ground and lit in on him with a vengeance. Tom took a few good licks, stunned by the sheer horror of what was assaulting him, but then he started swinging to keep from getting beaten to death right there.

"Don't hurt him! Don't hurt him!" Essie kept yelling, but Tom didn't have the luxury of figuring out which one of them she meant. His assailant slung spit and fists and spewed random profanities, bellowing declarations that made no sense from one word to the next.

Tom's strategy was craven retreat by that point, but he got in one good gut-punch that rolled the grotesque lunatic up and gave Tom space to regain his feet. Essie flung her arms around the madman's arms from behind and he turned into her like she was his mother, rolling his good eye at Tom, the white showing all the way around like a frightened colt's.

Breathing hard and shaking, Tom wanted to bolt like a skittish colt himself, but they were blocking the door and her tent was sided with planks. He kept a wary eye on the pair as he gathered up his scattered clothes and pulled them on.

"Paul, sugar, shh now," she crooned, rocking the monstrosity. "He weren't hurtin' me. You know better'n that. How come you're out here, huh? You know you ain't supposed to go nowhere without Danny. Leonard's gonna whip us both if you keep makin' such a fuss...."

Paul toyed with her corset-strings and muttered something that didn't even sound like English. Half his face was destroyed by thick, raw lumpy growths and most of the rest was cratered with oozing sores. One eye was white-blind, almost swallowed up by the ruination.

"What the holy hell happened to him?"

"He's eat up with the French pox," she snapped, helping the poor wretch to his feet.

"Why ain't he locked up in a madhouse? He's rabid crazy!" Tom stamped his feet into his boots.

Essie looked over at him with the first true emotion he ever saw on her face. It was bitterness. "He's my brother."

She led the sniveling wreck out the tent flap. Tom waited just long enough to give them a head start then made a beeline back to Camp.

☙

"Thet's one glory of a blinker there, Tom. What happened?" Shine asked.

"I got in the way of a runaway fist."

"What'd the other feller look like?" Willie chimed in.

The thought of that made the hairs rise on his arms. "Worse," Tom said.

He fingered his split lip. It was swelling out like he'd been hornet-stung, and his abused eye was down to a slit.

"You've taken up brawling now along with drinking and whoring?" Carl asked, almost under his breath.

Tom shot him half a sharp warning look. "I didn't start this."

"Yes you did, when you first went out there," Carl answered and got up. "I'll go draw our rations for tomorrow."

"Was Tay in on it?" Shine asked as Carl walked away.

"Nah, jist me and the other feller," Tom said, his mind more on what Carl had said. How anybody could flay him right down to the bone with fewer than a score of soft-spoken words, he couldn't figure but Carl sure had the knack.

"Why'd y'all get into it?"

"He took exception to me pokin' his sister, near as I kin figger. He lit in on me when she and me was right in the middle of the operation."

Willie gave a long, low-pitched whistle. "If I come up on you ridin' my sister, I'd beat the stuffin' outta you too!"

Tom started to laugh but gave that up as a bad idea as soon as his lip stretched. "I doubt your sister will ever sully herself by offerin' her favors to any an' all passersby, so you don't have to trouble yourself there."

&#x2og;

"Can't sleep?"

Tom rolled back over to face Carl's pallet. "Sorry," he answered in a similar whisper, more breath than sound. He'd been so restless, he'd squirmed himself through the straw onto the hard-packed earth beneath.

"It's all right. Something troubling you?"

Somehow, it was easier to confess his fear in the moonless dark, with Taylor out walking sentry and Shine and Willie snoring on the other side of the tent. "How long d' you figger it takes for a feller to know if he's catched the French pox?"

Carl propped his head up on his hand, the straw rustling beneath him. His face was a paler oval in the darkness. "Why? Are you feeling ill?"

"Naw, jist wonderin'."

Carl blew a little breath through his nose. Tom figured his friend took that excuse for the feeble thing it was.

"I have no idea, really," Carl whispered, "but I would imagine that if your privates don't start dripping or breaking out in sores or buboes within two or three weeks, you're probably safe. If you don't go back and risk it again before then, of course."

"I've had m' fill of that."

Again that scornful little exhalation.

"I have," he protested.

"Sure you have." Carl rolled back over, away from him. "Good night, Tom."

"Good night," he whispered back. "Hey Carl?"

"Hmm?"

"Thank you."

"Glad to help," Carl breathed back, then yawned and burrowed deeper into his bedding.

Tom scraped enough straw back under him to cut the chill seeping up out of the ground. He lay on his back then, an arm bent under his head. Two or three weeks—that seemed a very long time to wait to find out if you were going to end your life raving mad and looking like an abomination.

He couldn't close his eyes without seeing Paul's ruined face or hearing his maddened yells. At least Paul had Essie to look after him and take up for him. There wouldn't be anybody like that for him. He'd rot away chained up in some bedlam somewhere.

Tom spoke again, this time his words too soft even for Carl to hear. "Lord? I know I ain't been actin' proper here lately. I ain't got no good reason for it but givin' in to the lusts of the flesh, so I ain't gonna make things worse by makin' somethin' up You an' me both know ain't true."

He sighed. "I ask fergiveness and I do sincerely repent. Jist— if Y'd be so merciful as to spare me the pox? I swear to you on m' honor if you spare me that I won't never again lay with a woman who ain't m' proper wife. Amen."

Nothing left to do then but wait on the divine decision; Tom rolled over and drifted into a dream-troubled sleep.

31 July, 1861

Well, He was right well known for sending plagues of locusts as a sign of His almighty wrath. Wouldn't be such a stretch nor a blasphemy to figure He could muster up a company of smaller bugs to express a milder state of holy vexation. Especially ones so small that can make a man itch so powerful bad in such an inconvenient area.

"I told You true I weren't gonna go sport with them gals no more," Tom muttered real low under his breath. "But I reckon too I'd a whole lot rather scratch like a mangy hound then rot away crazy with the pox. So I'm real grateful to You for sparin' me that. Amen."

His somewhat grudging but deeply sincere thanks given for a somewhat hedged but powerfully merciful answer to prayer, Tom indulged in a good thorough scratch then buttoned his fly and left the reeking latrine ditch.

It wasn't as if he were the only one in the camp who had taken on boarders of one stripe or another. Wasn't an uncommon sight already to see some fellow skirmishing through the seams of his spare clothes of the evening or another raking a nit-comb through hair generously dressed with lamp oil.

Much as the idea of taking that particular cure in a more southern location unsettled him, the itch was reaching a maddening degree and he could scarcely chance reeking like a kerosene keg when he was ranging. Regardless of lamp oil's lack of explosive qualities, Tom was going to be bedrock sure there was no chance of a stray spark anywhere about when he applied the remedy.

August 30
Present Day
Tucson, Arizona
~ Two days later ~

"Afternoon, sleepyhead." The light pressure of Dee's lips against his was enough to catapult him out of the dream he was having. He'd been talking to Tom Dorin, but couldn't hear him over the sound of their horses' hoof beats. He groaned in frustration and sat up, rubbing his eyes. "What time is it?"

"Almost one. I didn't want to wake you up when I got in this morning, since I know you haven't been sleeping well. But I—"

"One?! Dammit!" Jon jumped off the couch and hastily finger-combed his hair. "Shit! I was supposed to meet Joe Finnegan at the library half an hour ago! His great-great grandparents lived in Cooper's Creek. Shit!"

He picked up the phone and dialed the library.

"Eric? Hey, it's Jon. I was supposed to meet Joe Finnegan there about half an hour ago." He paused, listening. "He's already left? Dammit! Sorry, no, not you. Thanks for letting me know. Yeah. Bye."

The receiver slammed back into its cradle and Jon slammed his fists against the desk. "Great. This is just friggin' fantastic. I'm gonna have to drive up to Carson City to talk to this guy now. He was only in town for the day. Dammit, Dee, why didn't you wake me up?"

"Jon! Jeez, I'm sorry you missed the guy, but you didn't say anything about meeting anyone, so how was I supposed to know you needed to be up at any particular time? I love you, but I can't read your mind!"

He stared at her for a moment, anger and frustration and resentment pounding through him. Then he clenched his jaw and took in a deep breath through his nose. Still clenching his teeth, he gritted out "I'm sorry. You're right. You couldn't have known."

Sitting down in the desk chair, he booted up the computer. "I need to do some damage control. I'll leave you a note next time."

Bringing up his email, Jon looked for his last correspondence with Joe, and started trying to compose an apology with another interview request. He realized halfway through the email she was still standing there staring at him. "What?"

"Nothing." she said, and turned away. "I'm going into town for a few hours."

"See ya later." Jon turned his attention back to the computer. She'd be over it by the time she got home.

ርጽ

19 January 1862
Dear Beth,
Well as you have probly already heard our Brigade has 'seen the Elephant' and to be truthful to you if to no one else I was more than a little spooked by the roarin Beast. I hardly know how to start tellin you of the battle for it is like nothing else you—or I—knowd.

It is a very quair feeling to start out marchin and look to your comrades on either side and know that some of you wont be there come the next muster.

We was set off marchin near midnight and the mud was halfway to my knees and thick as bread doh and I aint stretchin the truth a word. We hoped to surpriz the Enemy but we met up with Yankee pickets round daybreak and we chased them boys for a good quarter mile. The fight took up right and proper then and we charged them Yankees plum into the woods but between the poorin rain and fog and powder smoke and all it tangeld up the ranks right bad.

We lost General Zollicoffer, God rest his soul.

Colonel Cummings took comand of the brigade and he done as good as any could do, but we hadnt enough artilary and that cursd rain was playin hob with most of our boys rifles for it drownded the powder and fowld the actions.

Come late morning the Yanks fixed baynets and chargd and I am shamed to tell you that was the end of it for us.

The things I seen in that fight aint fit to speak of to a woman. I feel like they aint something nobody should have to see or think on but I know that there is a time for War as for all things and truly the South was pushed past all indurins by Northern insult and abuse and there is nothing left to do but go and fight.

We lost some fine men in this battle. Not so very many the officers say but enough I cant bear now to think on it to say a numbr but God spared all in my mess. None of us was so much as skint up though it was a near thing for Taylor. A ball came so close to his head that it left a black mark on his hat. A mark I have to say he is insuffrable proud of as if he had some hand in saving his own life but you know that is jist the way Tay is.

I will tell on Shine and I dont reckon he would mind as he told it on hisself to our mess when we was back to Camp. When the bullets first started whizing around us like a swarm of bees I seen Shine runnin back from where he had been sent out to skermish like he was being chased by the Devil hisself.

As he come up to where me and Carl was shootin from cover I hollered out Why is you runnin?

And he yelled back Cause I caint FLY!

Carl jerked Shine down beside us and give him a right strong talkin to. Told him he knew Shine werent no coward and he werent about to let him act like one now. Shine drawed up his mouth like a little tike that had jist got a switchin and shouldered up his rifle and fought then like a cornered bear. I dont want you thinkin that he is a cowerd for the truth of it is that we all wanted to bolt but I was too afraid of gitting shot in the back to jump up and tear out and Carl said he was so blame froz inside he didnt even think of runnin and as the battle ended up the whole army fell back to the Cumberland at the end of it so we was all brave or all cowerds together dependin on your disposishun I reckon. Still and all I reckon Shine will be teased for his atempt at flyt for the rest of this War and maybe his life!

As I write I make a picture of you in my mind and purtend we are sitting in your parlor or on the porch swing and talking. Your letters is more preshush than I can say but it is you I miss despite our short aquaintance face to face. I feel like we know each other very well now through our letters and I promise you that I am jist as I show myself here for good or ill. You are a better friend than any other I can claim and I hope to prove so to you. When my time in this War is up I hope I may meet you again under some flowerin bowr and tell you persnal jist how much your kindness means to me.

I am a ignert man of low birth and likely always will be a poor one too specially compared to your folks but even though I am not truly a fit companion it is my most fond hope that you will not be ashaymd to call me Friend even after this War is through.

I must close now for it is about too dark to see to write more and we is not to burn lights here for fear of drawing sharpshooter fire even at night so I will close with the wish this finds you well and safe. You are in my every prayer Sarah-Beth and always in my thoughts.

Your affectionate friend,
Tom

September 1
Present Day
Tucson, Arizona
~ The next day ~

He'd forgotten the damned Collins-Hughes family reunion. Dee threw a fit last night when he suggested meeting up with some of their friends at the Rendezvous. It had gotten ugly before he apologized. Which led to the long aggravating drive up to Flagstaff today, with no noise in the car but the radio. Nobody could give the cold-shoulder silent treatment like Dee; must have learned it from her mother.

CS

"Will you at least pretend you're happy to be here?" she said as she found a place to park among the rows of vehicles that turned her cousin's property into a temporary used car lot.

"Yes." Jon felt a resigned sense of dread. Her Collins grandparents alone had seven children, who married young and multiplied with great dedication, except for Dee's mother. Each of those grandchildren married young and spawned at least four kids each, again, except for Dee.

The oldest of the great-grandchildren were already practicing pairing off in preparation for another round of impetuous fertility. Walking into a Collins-Hughes family reunion was like walking into a small village. A raucous, matriarchal, slightly hostile village.

He had never met his own grandparents. The closest he'd come was the funeral of the last one, his father's mother, when he was twelve.

CS

By the time the extended official feast was over, Jon's frayed nerves were being sedated by the oncoming inertia of a food coma. Not that feeling gorged and sleepy on top of dull and disliked was much of an improvement. The noise level alone was stupefying. There were almost as many conversations going on at once as there were relatives. A shrieking flock of little kids was in constant motion at top speed, bursting inside, thundering back out, weaving around the adults with the deftness of starlings. Above it all, the TV blasted a game that was either ignored and talked over, or enthusiastically cheered.

Jon escaped out the back door in a swirl of pre-schoolers, broke away from the herd at the gate of the swimming pool, and sought refuge under the pergola. Being alone wasn't a possibility, not in this tribe, but at least there was a chance of less chaos out there under the mister, now that everyone was stuffed full of barbecue and other delights.

He dropped into a vacant chair with a heavy sigh of sincere relief. He stayed where he was for the rest of the long day. The heat was the lesser of discomforts, compared to being grilled as to his relationship timetable with Dee, his career plans and current and projected earning potential. He'd even dozed off a few times before Dee came looking for him.

She wasn't any more pleased with him leaving than she had been arriving, but at least on the return home he had driving to distract him from the icy silence radiating from her side of the car.

ભ

6 May, 1862
Dear Beth,
You ask me me to tell you partikulars of my own duties in battle and so I will for if you can not uphold my part as right then you need to know it soonr than latr. I am a sharpshooter. It is my part to slip from place to place alone or with one of the others in my Mess way out ahead of our Boys as we advans or to gard them from behind when we must retreet.

I do this to remove oficers and artilry men from the field and to halt Enemy pickits and skirmishers and yes Yankee Sharpshooters too as much as I am able to do so. Some call me and such as me Murdurers and Scowndruls and Sneek Cowards because we shoot from conseelmunt and pick off our targits one by one. Some even say this who are amungst our own Army. Maybe you will think me so as well which will greeve me sore but we both have promised truth to one another and this is the truth I live in this War.

I stand before you Beth and before God and say that I take no pleasure in the killing of men but I do take comfort in Duty. For it is sure that the death of an oficer causes confuzshun and saps the will to fight out of his men and as I see it by the death of that one oficer many more enlisted men are parhaps saved amung the Gray and even amungst the Blue. It is with out dowt that every enemy artilry man put down and out of the fight saves scores of our own good soldiers.

I will not say more in this letter for fear I may have lost your good regard but will wait to write again until I know your mind about my sort of service to our struglin Nation. While the loss of your sweet company would pain me sore it would not compair to the pain of seein our best men fall if I do not dis charge both my sworn duty and my good Whitworth rifle.

Your most affectionate Friend and in hope I remain your own,
Tom

ભ

29 May, 1862
My dearest Tom,
You may note the date of this letter betrays that I did not pen this reply with my usual impetuous haste. That is because I had to reflect long and

somberly on what you told me. I must confess that I feel most terribly disturbed by your revelation of the duty you must perform. It is not because I think what you do is immoral or cowardly, please do not take my words in that mistaken way!

It is more, I think, because I know <u>who</u> you are. I feel I am coming to know your heart, Tom, as well as a woman can know a man's. I know we are all sinners before God, but I also know almost as certainly that there is no real evil within you. It is to think of you, the fine young man I know, having to sight down the barrel of a rifle and end a stranger's life— I confess, it is almost more than I can imagine.

I will never know, of course, but I would think that in the swirl and smoke and confusion of battle that perhaps most soldiers never know for certain if it was their shot or another's ball that brings down the enemies who fall dead in the charge, and the lack of that certainty would be a help and a comfort to those of a gentle and kind nature such as yours.

But you… oh my poor Thomas! But you, when you pull the trigger, you know that you have destroyed a life. Lives that we know, for all we rightly despise their perverted "Union," are as precious to Our Heavenly Father as yours and mine. To think of that burden upon you makes me weep bitterly, not because of what you do <u>but because you have to do it.</u>

When I tell you this next, please, please do not think of me as disrespectful or flippant about your most solemn duty, for it was purely an attempt to… well, to put myself in your place, as imperfectly as I am able to do so. To see through your eyes, perhaps? The first day after I read your letter I was too upset to think clearly, but early on the next morning I made my way up to the attic and took down my grandfather's old flintlock musket from the wall. (Do not worry, its "teeth had been pulled" when my father and uncles were little boys.) I sat there, far back in the shadows where none below could see, and sighted out the window with that heavy old firearm held steady to my cheek and I watched the folk move along the boulevard and thought—BANG! You are dead, sir. Hurry on Madame, you may live yet another day. That teamster is surely hauling materiel that will aide our Enemy. BANG! Now his mules will run wild without anyone at the reins. A minor officer—a real one, albeit one of our Own—wandered through my sights. BANG!

I could not carry on this little mental exercise for another "shot." My nerve broke and I dropped the old gun and ran downstairs as if my skirts were afire. I could not explain to my mother and sister why I was in wild tears, and I am not sure I can do better at that task with you, my dear friend. Know this, that I am as convinced of your mettle and of your courage and devotion to our Nation as I am of sunlight and rain.

Although I do not dare claim their equal in my own character, I do know the depth of my devotion to you.

I will no longer chide you for withholding "particulars" as you say, when you wish to do so, but please also know that our former agreement still stands for as far as it lies within me. I want to help you bear your burdens, now more than I ever did before. When something weighs on your soul, yes, I am sure you pray. But sometimes, dear Tom, we all "need to talk to someone with skin on" as my little sister once cried. I want to be that someone for you. Tell me what you can, and what you wish, and what you can no longer bear to hold to yourself in silence.

I give you my most solemn word, by all that we hold Holy, that I will not judge or ridicule or reveal what you say to anyone else, but will only comfort and cheer you as best as I am able to do from this vast distance.

Please forgive the spatters, for I found I could not pen this letter without another torrent of tears, foolish weak girl that I am!

I am now, more than ever before, your most loving own,
Beth

CHAPTER THREE

September 9
Present Day
Tucson, Arizona
~ Eight days later ~

Dee came into the kitchen, fresh-scrubbed and in her good robe.

"Mornin', babe!" He kissed her, just a light peck, his hands full with an apple and his travel mug. "Mmm… you smell good…"

"Morning, sweetie. I didn't know you had to rush off today." She sounded as disappointed as he felt. When she wore that robe and put on perfume….

"Yeah, got a meeting with my advisor. I'll call you later, okay?" He inwardly cursed their mutual bad timing.

"Sure." She didn't keep her disappointment out of her voice.

Another hurried kiss and he was out the door. Jon sighed as he got into the car. Maybe tonight they would both be in the same place at the same time.

ধ

3 June, 1862
Dearest Beth,

Picturing you sittin up in that cold attic with that old musket rifle sighted on folks passin by made me want to jump up and yell NO BETH! STOP! STOP! Not because I thought you would be in real danger though you could well have been if you had been seen especially in takin a beed on that officer! But more because I do not want you touched by the uglynes of what fighting this War does to all of us who has to do it. It is right and honorable and it is shorly necesarry, but there aint nothin about it that is pure or lovely and very little of good report or virtue and only bloody sacrifice to praise for us fighting it to think on.

But you sweet Beth are true and honest and just and pure and lovely and of good report and of highest virtue and shorly worthy of praise so it is no wonder that I much purfur to think on you instead.

Your last letter and the one before made me so proud of you I feel fit to bust. Aint no dowt in my mind that if you was born to britches instead of pettycoats that you would be a By Word and Boogerman to ever Yankee between here and the jump off of Main and I would count it a honor to bear arms by your side. I know that no truer nor braver heart than yours has ever beat in any brest whether of man or woman.

Insted of having you at my side as a comrade in arms in this War my darling I will content myself with holding you in my arms the rest of my life, if your willing to tie your fate to mine. When this War is past I want no other honor than to be your husband if you would stoop to have me.

I feel so full of love and pride for you that I could cover all the paper in the world with it but all the paper I have in the world is this little scrap and they jist called us to muster out so I must go. Stand or fall, at least now you will know my true mind towards you sweet Beth—

With all my love,
Tom

ᘓ

17 June, 1862
My Dearest Tom,

Yes! Yes! YES!!
A hundred thousand times over YES....

ᘓ

    Tom's whoop of joy lifted him to his feet and brought the camp traffic to a halt around the fire in front of his tent.

"Well that there don't sound like bad news," Shine said with a grin.

"It's not!" Tom waved the letter. "She's gonna marry me!"

"So good news for you, but for her, mebbe the worst," Tay teased.

Tom ignored Tay as Willie and Shine thumped him on the back and said their heartier congratulations.

"Beg pardon, fellers," Tom grinned then. "I gotta find Carl!"

He took off through the camp, hunting for his best friend to ask him to be his best man.

September 12
Present Day
Tucson, Arizona
~ Three days later ~

He wasn't drowsing at his desk on that quiet afternoon, but the rap on his office doorframe was as startling as an alarm clock. Jon lifted his head up from his book to see Dee standing there in her uniform, her expression strained and pale.

Jon stood up so fast, his desk chair crashed into the shelves behind. "Baby, what's wrong? What happened?"

Dee took two running steps towards him. "I can't do this anymore!" she burst out, and threw her arms around him so tightly he could hardly breathe.

Jon did his best to completely enfold her in his own body. "What happened sweetheart?"

Dee was silent for a very long time, trembling in his arms, her face buried against his shoulder, but not crying as far as he could tell. Jon shuffled them both over to the battered couch and shoved stacks of files and books to the floor. He pulled Dee into his lap.

She tucked her long legs up onto the cushions, and even though her lips were almost against his ear, he still had to strain to hear her first few words.

"We'd been called for a little kid choking on a piece of candy. It hadn't completely obstructed her airway, luckily, and when we got there, we were able to remove it and she was laughing with me by the time we got to the hospital. She asked me to help her name one of those teddybears we give away. A good call."

"George and I were almost back to the station after leaving the ER. We were stopped at a light. Right as it turned green, three little kids darted off the sidewalk out in front of us. They couldn't see the other lane because of the rig—Oh God, Jon, they ran right out in front of a car! It had to have been making at least thirty-five! It hit two of the boys— I can't stop seeing them, flying through the air. Like broken dolls… twenty feet down the street…."

Jon felt his stomach heave and he had to swallow burning bile back down. "Sweet Jesus! Dee, I am so sorry!"

Dee began to sob, but her words kept spilling out as if she heard neither his words nor her own weeping. "The driver hadn't seen them in time either, because of the rig. She was hysterical. Her babies in their car-seats were screaming. The boy who hadn't been hit was in shock….He kept staring straight ahead and asking over and over 'What happened? What happened?' Me and George… after we got them to the ER, it was like our legs gave out from under us both at the same time… "

Her voice drowned in wrenching sobs. Jon rocked her, crooning soothing nonsense, feeling more helpless than he ever had in his life. How do you comfort someone through something like this?

"It all happened so fast. Barely two seconds. I saw what was going to happen, but I couldn't stop it!" she wailed.

"I know, baby," he assured her. "Nobody could have. It was a pure accident. A horrible, horrible accident. It's not your fault or George's or that poor woman's. It could have happened to anybody."

Finally, Dee's weeping started to wind down a little. He shrugged out of the shirt he'd wore open over a tee that day, then offered it to Dee. "Here, honey—blow."

When Dee cried, it was as if every drop of water inside her tried to come out her eyes and nose. The process of blowing and wiping took quite a while, especially since she kept jerking with residual sobs.

Dee moved off his lap, and he watched the slow-motion process of her shattered composure being drawn back together. He could all but see her stuffing the experience tightly down into whatever dark psychological hole held all the awful crap she experienced on a day to day basis.

Dee shook her head then let it fall backwards onto the back of the couch. She closed her eyes. "I can't do this any more."

"Hey, I know you feel that way now, but—"

Dee jerked upright, glared at him through red, swollen eyes. "I mean it. I can't do this any more."

Jon drew a deep breath, let it out. "Dee, sweetheart—you've been through a horrible experience. 'Traumatized' doesn't cover it here. But I can't believe that you really want to throw your whole career in the crapper because of one terrible day."

She gave him a look that he didn't try to interpret and heaved herself up off the couch. "I'm going to go take a shower."

"Okay, babe," he murmured and let her go.

He was sure she only came back out when she ran out of hot water, but it gave him time to meet her with a big mug that was more sweet cream and whiskey than hot chocolate.

She murmured thanks, but that's all she said as she dropped down onto the bed he'd already turned down. Jon sat beside her, his arm around her shoulders, until she set the mug aside on the bedside table and lay back.

Jon held her, spooned up as closely as possible, wrapped in both his arms and legs.

"I mean it," she mumbled. "I don't want to do this anymore."

"I know, baby. But let's talk about it later, okay? Try to rest now."

She went quiet again after a deep sigh. Jon wasn't sure if she slept, but eventually, he did.

Dee woke him a couple of hours later, having a nightmare, but he was able to coax her out of it without completely rousing her. He turned onto his back and laced his hands behind his head, thinking about their situation now.

If Dee quit, they'd be flat broke within two months. He'd have to drop out of his graduate program, go back to work as a sweating grunt.

He wouldn't let her quit. It would be stupid for her to throw away everything she'd been working towards for over two years because a couple of kids didn't know how to safely cross a street.

Moving slowly so as not to wake her, Jon got out of bed and went back to his office. She wouldn't quit, he decided. This wasn't the first time she'd been shaken up enough to consider it, but it was the worst. Still, this is what she loved. He couldn't imagine her doing anything else, and he doubted she could either.

CȢ

Chris woke her, coming in well after midnight from wherever he went, but Chris respected the quiet darkness of the house and didn't make any more noise than necessary. Dee turned to see if Chris had wakened Jon too, but she was alone in the bed.

She rolled over and reached for her cell phone on the nightstand. She had the number for U of A's trauma unit on speed-dial. Part of the life of a first responder.

"Hello, this is Deidre Collins, paramedic with Tucson Fire. We brought in two minor male victims of an MVA at two-fifteen pm. I'm calling to check on their status…."

Dee listened, murmured a thank-you and a goodbye. She dropped her phone back on the nightstand and then dropped her arm over her eyes. She lay very still, but she didn't sleep again until daylight began seeping around the edges of the blinds.

CȢ

28 December, 1862
My dearest sweet Darling,
I am so very sorry to start off my reply to you this way but I am shorly in terrible need of some one who loves me tonight. What I need to tell you is so ugly that I almost have scratched out even this part three times but ever time I put my pen down to do it more words come out instead so I reckon I'll go on ahead and say it all since you told me in no uncertan terms I am to do so when heavy laden.

I am sitting by the fire in my un mentionabls hoping my clothes will dry by morning. I had to scrub them despite the weather because they was spattered with meat and bone and muddy blood from where a shell burst near enough to throw dirt and bits of men from the next rifle pit over on to us like Hells rain and I could no longer bear the thought of it nor the stink of it. Four men I called friends Beth and nothing left of a one of them bigger than a post stamp.

58

Feelin them bits spatter hot and wet against me about made me lose my courage then and there. I seen men die by shell often enough but never so close I had to carry them in rags and tatters with me through the rest of the Fight. Being blowed to pieces by a burstin shell is a kind way to die compaired to most in this War I reckon but it is a sickning thing to witnes.

So there it is Beth. After day on day of seens like that, one on another and being half deaf from the noyze and half blind from the smoke it is a respit and a refuge to git to sit by a fire and write to you my dearest girl and think of some one sweet and alive and good and know that you and all like you are worth going out and fighting for to protect when the drums roll again to call us to battle. When it gits too much to bear again I will speak to you of it I promise but for now you have let me warsh my heart and mind cleaner than my cloths.

I come through just with my ears ringing like church bells but Shine got cut up some by shrapnul from the shell acrost his right arm and cheek. The wounds is not dreadful and he is otherwise holdin up well and is back in with us and takin a good rest as I write. He looks right pityfull with the bandages bound about his head and arm and I got no doubt both parts pounds like a drum tonight and though Shine is silent as a sufferin sheep you maybe might put a word in the ear of Pink Dress Alice to send him a cheerful word or two soonest.

That is all the bad news so I will go on and tell you some things to make us both smile again instead of weep.

You asked me a few letters back how Shine is being treated after his bolt at Fishing Creek and I kept forgiting to say till now. No one thinks him a Coward for he has proved himself as brave as any time and again since that day. But that dont mean nobody lets him forget it oh no!

Any dead bird that is found is sure to give up its wings and they show up tucked in his bedroll or stuck in his knapsack or even in his boots and hat band if the genrous person is early and quiet enough. When ever poltry comes to the pot the Wings are his porshun and it is a good thing he favors them any how because he would not git a bite of any other.

Shine has had the last laugh about it and the way he done it makes me wonder if he is as simpul as ever one thinks. He somehow brought down a huge barn owl and took them big white wings and spread them out in the hot sun so they dried up instead of rotting. Then he fasend them to the straps of his knapsack so that when we marching down the road he looks like a way ward Angel fallen in amungst us. I jist hope him wearin them dont make him a Angel for truth. He orta know better, but when

59

Shine gits his mind set on somthing you might as well argue with a boar hog for all the good itll do you.

Speakin of Shine reminds me of something else to tell you I am no longer lowly Tom A. Dorin but high and mity Lord Byron so you must bow and kurtsee low the next we meet and let me kiss your hand like a Frenchy.

I got dubd that for writing to you all the time and of coarse they call them Love Letters (rekon they are now but were not when we started!) and Carl is fancyer still and dubs them Billay Dooz which means the same thing he tells me.

Shine you would think was nick named enough by his own folks by being called Shine but now he is comonlee referd to as Dohdoh because he is a Large Flytless Bird and surely the only one of his Kind.

Willie has been Fat Willie from the start because he was right fleshy at Camp Cummings but he has been meltin away like a candel so now he is lean as a black snake as we all are but he could be skinny as string and he will still be Fat Willie.

Taylor is Breez because he never shuts his mouth and Beth I do not lie by one word when I tell you that he sometimes even talks in his sleep.

Poor Carl gets the worse of it as usual for all ours was dubd in fun but his nick name has some meanness in it so I do not use it but I will tell you so you will know how it goes for him. They call him Lady Mac Beth because he is always warshing or ringing his hands with that nervus habit of his or they call him worse yet Darling Angel Precious for that stinkin mean Mr No Acount (You know who I mean) yankd one of his Mammas letters away from Carls grip and read it out loud in a squeeky voice thinking he was bein as funny as a minstrul. I will fix ol No Acounts wagon but good when I git the chance to do it and not git caught by the officers. He is nothing but White Trash and if he gits blowed to pieces there will be no water wasted in tears here.

I will tell you that I think less now of Tay for taking up No Acounts meanness and chayfin Carl when the whole hurt full situashun would of died away purty quick if he had kept his big mouth Shut. He has had it in for Carl from the first and I caint figur out why because Carl aint been nothing but good to all of us, Tay as well. Tay has already taken to teasin Shine a little about how the Yankees clipped his wing today. He left off quick when me and Carl lit in on him but the way Shine rolled his eyes at Tay I figure Tay had best let it drop or he might regret his fun when Shine gets the full use of both arms back!

I will stop barkin like a bull dog now and end this by telling you again how much I miss you and at the same time how much company your letters are to me. Ever one is like a little visit because I picture sitting beside you and I can even hear your voice saying the words.

You said in your last that you are not pretty and that is a lie from your own lips and I will not hear it again, so you mind me as your betrowthed and the one who loves you best. No you do not look like them drawings of women in Godeys Book but you look around and point out the lady who does and I will show you one very pecular looking lady!

I will tell you this Beth not to be forword or corse but so you will know how it is for me when I think on you. I dreemd night before last of us when we is married and in our own house. You was before the fire in your gown and robe and brushin out your hair for bed. I took the brush and began workin out the snarls as I used to do for my sisters and the fire light seemed to be coming from your hair as if it were alight on its own and it crackeld and wrapped itself around my hands as Hannah Graces would do in Winter. I told you in the dreem what I would tell her. Your hair is huging me I said and you turned and huged me your self. I would not trade that dream for any other but it was a sorrow full thing to wake up and find myself rolled up in wet blankets in the drizzle instead of warm in our bed with you.

I love you Beth and I long for the day when I am free from Service and we can start our new life together in our New Country.

With all my love,
Tom.

CHAPTER FOUR

September 17, Present Day
Tucson, Arizona
~ Six days later ~

Earth to Hansen. Come in Hansen. Do you read me Major Jon?

Jon read the text message then glanced up at the clock in the department carrel. It read two hours and forty-five minutes past the last time he'd checked. Almost ninety minutes past the time he'd intended to leave. The time he'd promised to pick Dee up at the auto-repair shop.

Jon's face screwed up into a tight grimace and he lightly bashed the phone against his forehead then began cramming laptop, books and papers into his bag. As soon as he was out in the hallway, he called her. "Aw crap! Honey, I am so sorry!"

"It's okay," she sighed, amusement and mild irritation mingled in her voice. "I've been keeping myself amused by flipping through the channels. I never realized that daytime TV is such unadulterated crap."

"I'm on my way, baby. Really. Like, keys in my hand and running for the car on my way."

℈

Dee met him at the doorway of the shop's waiting room. "I'm sorry, sweetie. The shop's too busy to spare someone to take me home, and we can't afford a taxi this week."

Jon blinked at her. She looked and sounded genuinely contrite. "Dee, I was the one who screwed up here. I can't believe I lost track of time that badly."

"I can," she said as they got into the car, so softly he wasn't sure she intended him to hear it.

"I guess this is what we both signed up for, huh?" she continued at a conversational volume. "I didn't realize how all-consuming this process would be, though."

"Honestly, I didn't either," Jon confessed as he pulled onto the street. "I knew it intellectually of course, but the actual experience? I feel as if I've got to consume and process this warehouse full of information that's coming towards me on a conveyor belt, and the faster I stuff it into my skull, the faster the belt runs."

Dee reached over and squeezed his thigh, her expression sympathetic. "I don't want to have to dig your crushed and mangled carcass out from under a pile of books at the end of that belt one day. Every conveyor belt has an emergency stop button."

"Stopping's not an option," he countered. "This is what I want, Dee. All I want. I'm not shooting for tenure— I'd have better odds playing the lottery, frankly. But history is what I love and to become an archivist or a curator, I have to have at least a Master's to my name."

She laid her head back against the rest with a sigh and looked over at him out of the corner of her eyes, a small odd smile playing around here lips. "It's a relief to hear you say that."

"What do you mean?"

"I've… I've been afraid you're going off the deep end about that guy in the picture. From what I've seen, that seems to be where you're focusing the most."

He covered her hand with his own. "I admit, he fascinates me. Come on, if you found a photograph, more than a hundred years old, that looks nearly identical to you, wouldn't you be intrigued? Yeah, I'm probably spending more time on him than I should, but besides the curiosity factor, he does make a pretty good poster boy for the disaffected, damaged, unpardoned human train-wrecks that a lot of Confederate veterans became."

"That makes sense," she nodded. "And even I can see at least a half-dozen ways you could go with that to tie it into our society's current problems."

"Exactly. Wish I could find out what his deal was, though."

Dee blinked. "Huh?"

"As far as I can determine, he's not a relative from either side of my family. So why the close resemblance?"

"Who knows? Science hasn't really proven that no two snowflakes are alike, right? So who's to say DNA can't spit out a replica every once in a while?"

"Nothing's impossible, I guess," he agreed, "And that makes sense. The combinations can't be truly infinite. I'd sure love to be able to put myself in his head for a while, though."

"That's where I figured it was today." Dee pulled her hand away, turned on the radio. "I can fix you some lunch when we get home. There's some of that roast left, and I can make a salad."

Jon's stomach growled. "Nah, thanks baby, but I've got to teach a class in a few. I'll barely have time to make it back as it is."

He'd grab something later, or eat when he got home. Hunger always passed when ignored long enough. Besides, most of his day was spent sitting and reading. He didn't need much fuel for that.

☙

12 February, 1863
Darling Beth,
Are you well? Are you gettin enough to eat darling? I wish your Papa would send you and your sisters and Mama on out to Arkansas or somewhere on the Western border where the fighting aint so thick. I fear that things will get worse for yall in Richmond before it gits beter. I am grown akustomd to danger hard ship and hunger for that is the lot of a soldier in the field but it near madens me to think of you and yours suferin any thing near the same privashuns. Its near driven me to

distrakshun not knowing how your faring and that is not a scold because I know you write so faithful but the Post is not up to leepin the herduls throwd up by this War.

I got your letter yester day marked three weeks ago so there is a likely a whole passul of them wandering around somewheres. I have not got the package you spoke of neither but maybe it will still come as will the letters. Being as how our rations aint caught up with us neither its no surprise about the other.

I hope you can read this as either the rain or jist the paper is making the ink spread something awful and pencil wont mark dark enough on it before it cuts clean thro. It will make a gay envulop though.

Tay jist read over my sholder and told me to stop belly aching for once I start I aint goin to have enough paper nor ink to whine about it all and I reckon he is right.

I will tell you about the little fellow who I stole this wall paper from instead. Now before you start to fuss I did not spoil some poor womans best parlor. The house was ruint and this paper was hanging in loose strips mostly. When I pulled one off there was this little bat humpd up under neath fast asleep. Ive seen bats flying around all my life but never seen one eye to eye so to speak. He werent a lowthsome looking creechur as you might expect. Glossy brown as if he had been freshly curryed and his black wings neat folded as a ladys parasawl. He had his head tucked down against his breast till I poked him with a finger and woke him up. He blinked at me with little eyes like jet beads. He had a head like a fat field mouse and he yawned right in my face with a pink tung and tiny white teeth like a kittens and then crawled up the wall a bit using these clever hook feengers on the elbows of his wings. I was rude enough to give him another poke and he took flight going off woblin through the air like a drunk sparrow. I hope he finds another good warm spot to sleep.

Oh Beth, if I could fly to you I would whether I was on big soft owl wings or them black leather bat wings! It feels like this War has lasted an age and a half and there will never be anything but War and rainy cold gray days like these. I will close now before I afflikt you with the mullee grubs too and roll up in my blankets and hope to dream of you and warm nights and the smell of moon flowers.

You are always first in my heart and in my prayers without ceasing.

With all my love my darling,
Tom

September 25, Present Day
Tucson, Arizona
~ Seven days later ~

"May I join you?" someone asked in a husky feminine murmur.

Jon looked up. The coffee shop was crowded, and the chair opposite him was one of the few available. "Uh, sure."

He discreetly looked her over as she took her seat and settled her coffee, pastry and laptop. She was cute. Short and curvy, with a bright smile, smooth skin the color of well-creamed coffee and crazy auburn curls, the complete antithesis of her voice.

She took a bite of her scone, studying him far more overtly. "You look so familiar to me. But I'd remember you if we'd met." She gave him a smile that seemed more than conversational, though that was probably only because of her voice.

"I can say the same," he smiled back, and offered his hand. "Jon Hansen."

"Callie Darger." Her handshake was firm, but soft. "Oh! Hey, I bet I know where I've seen you. You're a student, right?" She indicated his computer and notebooks with a slight wave of her coffee cup.

"History," he nodded, "working on my Master's."

"Ooh, a grad student," she purred, lids and long lashes dropping down over her eyes, then she chuckled and dropped the sex kitten demeanor. "I'm only a lowly undergrad. Organic chemistry."

"I'm impressed," Jon smiled. "I barely got out of high school chemistry alive."

"Ah, but in high school chemistry, if you never have anything spontaneously burst into flames or get the building cleared because of noxious fumes, then where's the fun?"

Jon chuckled. "So, we've established that we're both U of A students, and we're both closet anarchists, but where do you think we've crossed paths?"

"The bookstore," she declared with absolute certainty. "I work there part-time."

"You have my deepest sympathies," Jon said. "I served my sentence under Mac the Knife my sophomore year."

"It's good to see you survived. I went in my first day thinking, hey, a bookstore, how hard can this be?" Callie chuckled.

"Then, he has one of his infamous quiet but deadly melt-downs and you're ground zero," Jon commiserated.

"Exactly," Callie grimaced, "which explains why I'm here drowning my sorrows in about a bazillion calories of pastry and a four buck mochalattefrappeventipooftigrande with extra whipped cream. And sprinkles."

Jon chuckled, then shook his head. "Never, ever let him smell fear. If Mac thinks he can intimidate you, you're doomed."

"I'm going to let you in on a little secret, Jon Hansen," Callie murmured, her voice an earthy caress as she leaned closer across the table. "I don't allow myself to be dominated."

That one statement, in that voice, with that look in her eyes, made him momentarily lose the thread of their conversation. "I don't think Mac... Uh... yeah."

She was used to having that affect, apparently, because she laughed off his moronic non sequitur and they chatted on as if she hadn't caught him with his libido hanging out.

Over an hour passed before she excused herself and left. Jon looked down at her name and number, written on a scrap of notepaper in looping script. He tucked it into the depths of his wallet. The last thing he need was for Dee to find that in his pocket and get the wrong idea.

25 February, 1863

"Dorin!"

Tom stepped forward, his heart thudding and a broad grin stretching his face. Finally!

Stewart's face was set in doleful lines as he handed over a long-anticipated letter. "I'm sorry, Tom."

The envelope was marked with a broad black border. Tom's hands started shaking. By the time he stepped back from the crowd and broke the seal, they were quivering so badly that he could barely pull the letter free.

He scanned the lines, then crumbled letter and envelope together into a wad and flung it viciously into the mud. Blind, he all but ran through the encampment, with no end in mind but away and alone. He paid no heed to those he jostled in his flight, whether officer or enlisted man.

Behind him, Carl picked the sodden paper up from the mire and smoothed it out.

"What does it say?" Shine urged. "Who died?"

"Beth." Carl looked over his shoulder towards the wake his friend was cutting through the traffic of the camp. "Beth's dead of typhoid."

"Oh lord," Shine groaned. "I'm gonna go—"

Carl caught his shoulder. "No. Leave him be for a bit."

"I never seen no man set more store on a woman," Shine commented softly. "This is gonna put him in the ground too."

"It might indeed," Carl agreed, his voice thickened. He folded the note almost reverently, and tucked it into his shirt pocket.

October 1, Present Day
Tucson, Arizona
~ Six days later ~

"Happy birthday, Dee."

Dee looked up from her fruit and coffee, her startled expression blooming into one of happy pleasure. "Thanks, Chris. I hadn't even thought about it."

"You shouldn't have to, that's our job." Chris flicked a glance towards Jon, then handed Dee a small, beautifully wrapped package.

Whatever message Chris was trying to convey didn't make it through the urge to spring across the kitchen table and throttle his brother. Leave it to Chris to upstage him. Make him look like he'd forgotten.

Sure, the date had slipped his mind in the early morning brain-fog, but he hadn't really forgotten. He made plans a week ago, plans which didn't include her picking up this extra shift without telling him. So much for spontaneity.

Dee picked at the tape and unwrapped the little package with a precise deliberation that set Jon's teeth on edge. Whatever was in that damn thing, he wanted her to hurry the hell up and get his humiliation over with.

Her gasp of surprise when she opened the jewelry case didn't help. "Oh! Chris, it's gorgeous!"

On the dark blue velvet lay a golden Star of Life pendant polished to a mirror sheen, its caduceus serpent and staff fashioned from green and rose gold. A bright diamond winked in the snake's eye.

Jon felt his breakfast curdle.

Dee closed the case and slid it across the table towards Chris, all joy gone from her expression. "It's so beautiful, and it's incredibly sweet of you, but I'm sorry—I can't accept this. It's too much."

"Bullshit," Chris retorted. "I said it was *our* job to remember your birthday. This is as much from Jon as from me."

Jon could tell Dee didn't buy that one any more than he did. She obviously found it more endearing, since she didn't look as if she wanted to cut Chris' heart out with her grapefruit spoon.

"Still…" She glanced from Chris to him.

Jon shrugged.

Chris wasn't finished laying it on. He was never finished laying it on.

"What you do is important. Special. There's no way in hell I could do what you do, even if I wanted to. Neither could Jon. We figured you wade through enough blood, puke and chaos on a daily basis that somebody should hang a medal on you."

Chris scooped up the case and tossed it back so fast that Dee caught it by reflex. "So, happy birthday, Deidre Collins, and thank you for taking care of this county's sick, injured, stoned and crazed, even when some of the idiots should be euthanized for the common good."

Dee gave a little laugh, her cheeks flushing bright rose. "Well, since you put it in such flowery language… I accept. Thank you." She looked at Jon. "Both of you, very much!"

Dee lifted the pendant out and rose to kneel by Jon's chair. She offered him the necklace. "Would you fasten it for me, please?"

Jon clipped the chain around her neck, and Dee settled the pendant beneath her uniform. She turned and kissed Jon. "Thank you, really," she whispered by his ear and hugged him hard.

"It's nothing," he shrugged, making minimal effort towards a smile.

Dee gave him an odd look, then sprang to her feet. "As much as I hate to grab the gold and run—I don't want to be late!"

Jon didn't walk her to the door. He didn't want to give Chris a chance to slither out the back. As soon as the front door closed behind Dee, he was on his feet and around the table. Chris backed away fast.

"What the HELL is the matter with you?" Jon yelled, his hands fisting.

"What the hell is the matter with you?" Chris fired back. "All I did was give Dee something nice for her birthday— and tried to cover for your sorry forgetful ass. You're welcome."

"I hadn't forgotten her birthday, you bastard— you didn't give me a chance to say anything before you rushed in and she knows as well as I do what you pulled in there."

Chris listened to that with his arms folded loose across his chest, leaning back against the counter, that superior smirk on his face. The disrespect of his casual, 'I've got nothing to fear from you' posture made Jon want to punch him.

"First, if I kept waiting for you to get your act together this morning, she wouldn't have heard happy birthday at all," Chris said. "When she gets home, it won't be her birthday any more. Second, why don't you tell me what I pulled, so we're both on the same page here?"

"Why do you always have to upstage me, make me look bad?" Jon gritted. His knuckles ached, his fists were so tight. "What do you get out of it? Is your ego so fragile and your dick so damn small that you're driven to make me look like a failure and a fool at every possible opportunity?"

Chris came up out of his slouch then, and faced Jon with all his snide nonchalance gone. "You want to know what I get out of it? Nothing. Not one friggin' thing. I don't try to make you look bad."

"Like hell! You do it every time we're in the same room with someone else."

Chris shook his head. "It's all in your head. You're jealous. You're jealous and you blame me for everything that's gone wrong in your life, so you don't have to take responsibility for any of it. Mom petted you rotten and you've spent your whole life looking for a replacement!"

"Don't you drag Mom into this. For shit's sake, if anybody's got a clinical mother fetish, it's you. You're the one who keeps marrying even though you can't keep a wife around for more than a year and a half!"

"Ah, but I don't ask them to feed me, clothe me, shelter me and wipe my pathetic ass. You're damn near thirty years old. Start acting like it instead of like a whiny emo teenager. Yes, I got Dee a nice gift. I can afford it."

"God, how could I not know you can afford it? Every time you show up, the first thing you do is start waving money around like it impresses people. Now you're trying to buy off Dee and you're not getting away with it this time!"

"If the way I choose to spend my cash bothers you, you can kiss my ass! Dee's earned that damn necklace and a hell of a lot more for putting up with your immature shit for years. Her only problem is she's too soft-hearted to give you the swift kick in the can you've needed since you were ten!"

Blind furious, Jon threw a punch. The next thing he knew, he was on the floor with Chris standing over him like Bruce friggin' Lee.

"Are we done, or would you like to try again?" Chris smirked.

Rage made him agile. Jon sprang off the floor. Chris moved back, still in a fighting stance, still with that smirk on his face.

"Get out."

"This isn't your house," Chris shrugged, his smirk wider than ever before.

"It sure as hell isn't yours. Get out!"

"Jon—"

"GET OUT! Get out before I kill you!"

Chris tensed. "I know you don't mean that."

"Don't push, Chris. Get the hell out. Now."

Chris moved around him, still cautious, and left the kitchen.

~ The next day ~

"Welcome home, Dee!" Chris sang out as she wandered into the kitchen just before noon, with her hair hanging wet over her tee shirt. "Want a burger? I made extra."

"No, thanks. I ate before I left the station." She yawned and headed for the coffee.

"Okay. By the way, Jon's probably going to be pissed when he gets home today."

"Lovely." She plunked down into a chair. "Dare I ask why?"

"He kicked me out yesterday."

"And yet," she waved her mug like a magic wand, "you're still here."

"Well, yeah. You didn't kick me out, so I spent the night at a motel and came back once he left for school this morning." Chris put a fully loaded burger and a handful of chips on his plate then settled in across from her. "You aren't gonna kick me out, are you?"

She snorted at his plaintive, little-boy-lost tone. "Depends. Why did Jon toss you out on your ear?"

"The usual," Chris said around a bite. "I'm showing off, making him look bad. Basically the same things we've been fighting about since we settled it by banging each other over the head with toy trucks."

Dee's fingers touched the pendant that glittered against her ratty tee. "Ugh. I was afraid this hadn't gone over well."

"Look," Chris pointed at it with a potato chip. "Don't start feeling guilty about that necklace. I gave it to you because nobody else should own it. Hell, Jon would have given it to you himself if he'd seen it first."

"He couldn't afford it."

"Since when has he started worrying about spending money he doesn't have?"

"Chris—"

"Just sayin'," he shrugged and shoved in another bite of hamburger. Thankfully, this time he swallowed before he spoke again. "Anyway, the point is, he's gonna be ticked off when he gets home and finds out I came back. But since it's okay with you, he'll get over it. Be prepared for it to take till Thursday, maybe."

"You sound pretty sure of the timing."

"Not like we haven't had this same fight before." Chris swigged his iced tea. "Fact is, about the only thing I can think of that would make him truly hate me for life is if you and I started messing around."

Dee stared at him, coffee cup halfway to her lips. She burst out laughing.

CHAPTER FIVE

13 March, 1863

Tom eyed Taylor with dull curiosity. Ever since Tay had come in from the front, he'd been moping around solemn as an undertaker with hardly a word to say to anyone.

As Tom passed him to get some more wood for their fire, he thumped Tay's boot sole with a light tap from his own. "What's the matter? I ain't heard three words outta you since you come in."

Tay started as if Tom had shouted him from a sound sleep. "Huh? Oh, nothin', ol' hoss. Jist tired I reckon."

Satisfied with that— Lord knows, he was weary to the bone— Tom went on. When he got back with the wood and began to lay it on the fire, he saw that Tay was still looking glum, sitting right where he had been, shaving a stick of cedar down into tinder almost as fine as hair.

Affected by the dampening fog of battle-fatigue and Taylor's uncharacteristic gloom, the rest were unusually quiet as well. Every one of them found something to do that didn't require any conversation.

Willie laid his much-read novel aside. "You sure you ain't gettin' sick or something, Breeze?"

"No, not sick," Taylor muttered, then scratched at his beard and looked from Fat Willie to the rest of his messmates. "Well, I'll tell you, boys. I killed one today that's working on me. On the line this mornin' some jasper picked me out and began shootin' from up in a tree. I watched for his smoke to line up a shot, and took it. He bounced down through the branches like a dead coon. He was a boy. No more than thirteen, fourteen years old and I'd shot him clean through the head."

Tay shook his head and sheathed his knife. "I tell you, fellers, I signed up for this war to kill men, not children!"

"When did you grow scruples, you blowhard arsehole?" Tom muttered under his breath.

Taylor lurched to his feet, his hands balling into fists. "You got something to say to me, Dorin?"

Tom sprang up, glaring at Taylor with fury. "I do. That filthy little bluebelly son-of-a-bitch was tryin' to kill you in case you didn't take note of it jist then! He sure as hell wouldn't have wasted no regrets over your carcass."

"You're saying you could shoot a beardless boy and not turn a hair then," Taylor retorted scornfully.

"Damn right I am." Tom's voice came out as a near-snarl, his lips drawn up away from his teeth in rage. "You may not have the guts to do what needs doin' but I ain't sufferin' under the same affliction. I intend to blow the worthless brains out of ever mule-fuckin' Yankee soldier I can set my sights on and I don't give a shit if they's a man, boy or yeller dog!"

Taylor said nothing to that, glaring into Tom's eyes, hands still clenched tight.

Tom wasn't about to blink first.

It was Willie who broke the rising tension with a long, shrill whistle. "Don't hold back none, Dorin. Tell us what you really think about it!"

"You done, pup, or am I gonna have to bust your mouth?" Taylor rumbled, their gazes still locked.

"I've said what I have to say." Tom left the tent, slamming his shoulder against Taylor's as he passed with enough force to bruise them both.

Taylor turned to watch him stalk away. "Whooeeee, look out, boys!" he taunted. "There goes a thoroughly dangerous man!"

Shine and Will gave short, nervous laughs but Carl was silent, his hands beginning to wring against each other until he shoved them into his pockets and ducked by Taylor to leave the tent. He headed in the direction Dorin had taken.

18 March, 1863

Tom shuddered as another runnel of icy rain slid down the back of his neck and traced the groove of his spine like the fingertip of a corpse. The afternoon was dark as midnight under the heavy-branched pines. The narrow road was nothing more than a darker smear in a world of dull gray. Every thread he wore, every inch of his body beneath, was soaked through. The brim of his hat was so sodden that it almost blocked his vision. He no longer shoved it up, too tired to do anything but stay upright and moving. Sleep kept ambushing him from the fuzzy edges of his mind. His thoughts drifted, straying away into dreams even as he walked.

Tom's boots stuck and slid in the greasy red mud, but the lurching kept him startled awake. He stumbled into a thicket of young pines, growing so close he could hardly push his way through.

If I slithered under thet brush, I could jist lay there an' let this whole damn war march on by.

Tom shook his head to clear it and stumbled on. Even if he managed to avoid both armies, his own conscience would torment him enough for both. The Dorin name had never been worn by a coward and he wouldn't be the first to sully it. Men's lives depended on his guts and his aim. He had to find high ground, a vantage point to watch this road, to protect his comrades and harass the enemy following behind.

Eventually the rain lessened and the trees thinned. A whiff of wood smoke lazily drifted by his face. Tom turned into the fitful breeze, feeling his muscles tighten as the scent grew stronger. False vigor smoothed his movements as he approached a break in the thick underbrush. The acrid tang of old ashes mingled with fresh smoke now. Tom crept to the edge of a clearing, just beyond the tangle of fallen trees, muscadine vines and poison ivy that concealed him.

A large house, once fine, sat in the center. Fire had eaten the porch and left a huge hole in the front. With its windows broken and black, its white paint singed to sickly yellow-gray, the place looked like an unburied skull. It also looked like dry shelter and a good place to take a long shot from the attic dormers. Only hitch in that was that someone else had found the place first.

Tom checked his pistol. The powder, despite his precautions, was as wet as everything else on him. Mouthing a curse, he pulled his knife instead and began working his way closer to the house. Whoever was inside was in the upper story or the attic, as the smoke was dropping in the heavy air.

Once he gained the cover of the building, Tom paused to let his eyes adjust to the darkness. Slowly as a stalking cat, he picked his way around broken crockery and scattered furniture. The blaze had damaged the stairs, destroying some of their support. Tom began to climb, wary of a squeak or the crack of breaking wood. He kept his shoulder pressed against the wall, easing his weight onto each stair, pausing for long seconds between to listen.

He held his breath as he peeked just past the attic door frame. A man in faded Union blue sat huddled close to a tiny fire built in a rusty wash pot.

The man cut loose with a long, rasping snore.

Tom's heart almost jumped clean out of his mouth.

The man's blood felt scalding, gushing over Tom's chilled skin. He kept the man's chin in his hand, the back of the man's head held hard against his chest as the Federal sharp-shooter sprayed blood from his gashed throat, kicking and bucking as he clawed at Tom's hands.

That Yank settled down pretty quick. A man can't struggle too long with his throat cut right down to the backbone. Tom dragged the twitching corpse down the stairs and across the rutted, muddy rear yard. He dropped the dead man just inside the brush and wiped his hands on the wet leaves.

Back in the attic, Tom surveyed the spoils of his victory. A dry spot with a long sight-line, a stash of firewood, a haversack and, he noted with a grin, a battered tin pot holding an inch or two of coffee. Real coffee, not chicory root nor ground acorns nor any of the other nasty truck a man would use when forced to do without.

"Much obliged, Billy," he mumbled. "This'll go down real easy." Settling onto his haunches beside the tiny fire, Tom helped himself to a trail-worn hunk of hoecake and a long yearned for cup of coffee.

When he bit into the bread, he realized that blood tainted it, speckling the crust like pepper. He could taste it, sharp and bright, like copper. Tom closed his eyes, forced himself to swallow. The next bite went down easier.

October 2, Present Day
Tucson, Arizona
~ One day later ~

Dee sat at the table with her chin resting on her hand. She tapped a pen against the papers in a nervous rhythm. No matter how she ran the numbers, the sum always came up on the calculator with a minus sign in front.

Chris sauntered in, grabbed a soda out of the fridge and swung one of the chairs around to sit straddled. He leaned on the back and took a sip, then gestured at her work. "Too much month left over?"

"Bordering on too much year." She sighed. "Thanks to certain people writing checks and hitting the ATM without checking the balance first, it looks like I can pay the mortgage or the utilities this month. Got a preference?"

"Yes. Rent income." Chris held up a hand to head off her knee-jerk protest. "Look, I know you're letting me live here out of the goodness of your heart, and maybe to wind up Jon, I dunno— that business is between you and him— but it's crazy that he's not letting me help you two out."

"You know as well as I do, that accepting financial help, especially from you, is practically a capital offense."

"And my darlin' little brother can be a putz. You know that as well as I do. Come on, Dee, let's be honest about this, just between us. This is an ideal situation for me right now. I have the house to myself most of the time, none of my usual bad influences and major distractions know where

I am, and it's giving me the opportunity to meet my deadline and start that screenplay without having the added pressure of finding a place right away hanging over my head. That's worth more than a few bags of groceries and take-out per month. Let me make the mortgage payments while I'm here."

"I appreciate the offer, but the mortgage is—"

Chris took advantage of her demurral to slide the mortgage statement out from under her elbow. He scanned it and gave a decisive nod. "Less than I'd be paying for rent. Certainly less than a suite would cost me per month."

Dee chewed her lip.

Chris leaned closer, waved the mortgage statement in front of her eyes like a hypnotist's watch. "Come onnnn," he coaxed. "You know you want to do it. It's the right thing. It's the best thing. It'll feel soooo gooood…"

Dee couldn't help a little laugh. "Yeah, it'll feel good till Jon finds out. Then it'll feel like falling into molten lava."

"Who says he has to find out?" Chris folded the statement and tapped the checkbook lying in front of her. "How often does he balance that thing?"

"Uh… well…"

Chris pressed on. "When does he pay the bills?"

"When I ask… and remind him."

"Does he even know how much you owe on this place?"

Dee shook her head. "I don't think so, or at least, we haven't talked about it in so long I'd say he's forgotten."

"If you didn't have the student loans from his undergrad studies on top of the household bills, could you make ends meet on your salary?"

Dee considered that for a long moment. "Yes, we could. We still wouldn't have much surplus, but we'd be solvent again."

"There ya go." Chris tucked the statement into his shirt pocket. "Look, Dee. I love my brother but I care about you too. You're good for him. He leans on you more than he realizes. Probably more than he ought to. There's no reason you should lose your house because you're carrying the weight of my brother's dreams. This doesn't have to be anything he ever has to know. It's simply a business agreement between you and me. Consider it a loan if you have to, but don't be in any hurry to pay me back."

Chris grinned. "Just promise to take me in between wives if I show up on your doorstep again."

"We can put that in writing," she said with an uneasy chuckle.

"Oh, between us, a handshake will do."

Dee decided on a hug, instead.

19 April, 1863

Tom rarely spoke now beyond the sparest syllables necessary. There was no more joking, no more amiable smiles and of course, no more letters. Carl respected his friend's self-imposed solitude, but even so he kept as close a watch over Tom as he was able.

The rest tended to give him wide berth. Tom would flare furious at the slightest provocation now and even he and Shine would catch the heat of it if they crossed his temper's capricious dead line. For days, he was the only one of their mess who chose to bed down near Dorin.

"You need to eat," Carl said.

Tom didn't look up. The steady, slow movement of the file against his rifle stock didn't falter.

That soft, inexorable rasping was setting his teeth on edge. Carl rose and dropped his hand over Tom's to still the movement.

Dorin stiffened, looked up into his face. His features were sharp now, his skin pulled close over his bones. His mouth was set in a harsh line and his eyes glowed blue-hot, sunk deep in their sockets. "What?" he snapped.

"How many will it take?" Carl asked softly, keeping his hand over Tom's.

"What the hell are you sayin'?" Tom jerked his hand away from Carl's touch.

Carl ran a fingertip along the long row of homicidal notches. "How many will it take to avenge her?"

"How many of 'em is they?" Tom started up with the file again, but this time his movements were sharp and savage.

"Tom, this won't bring her back."

"You think I don't damn well know that?" His expression was murderous, the file clenched in his fist like a dagger.

Carl laid his hand over that fist again. "What would she say if she could see you this way? Could know this is what her love has done to you?"

"Fuck you, you pious little prick! You ain't no better'n me." Tom flung the file down and sprang up to head out into the darkness again. But this time, he left his rifle leaning against the log he had been sitting on.

October 12, Present Day
Tucson, Arizona
~ Ten days later ~

"Are you okay in there?" Chris' voice was muffled by the door, but his concern came through as loud and clear as the noise of her puking must have.

Kneeling in front of the toilet, Dee rested her head on her arms, folded on the rim of the toilet bowl. "Yeah, give me a second."

When the gagging didn't start up again, she slowly rose, flushed, and rinsed her mouth. Chris was waiting, practically against the door, when she opened it.

"You sure you're okay?" he asked.

"I'm fine, Chris. Honest." She stepped around him to go down the hall.

He blocked her path. "This is what you call fine? Dee, you've been sick for more than a week, and you still look pretty green."

She turned to look at him and decided, what the hell. It wasn't as if Jon gave a damn about anything outside his obsession anymore. "Morning sickness is normal."

Chris blinked and she could swear his jaw went slack for a second or two. Then, his whole face lit up with a huge smile. "You're pregnant? Dee, that's great!"

His smile faltered then, probably because of the look on her face. "Isn't it?"

"I'm not sure." Her lip started trembling on the last word. She bit it hard. Damned hormones.

"Hey… Dee…" Chris reached out and put a hand on her shoulder. "Come on, kiddo. Let me fix you some tea and toast or something while you tell me what's going on, okay?"

She nodded, not trusting her voice. As she headed for the kitchen, Chris walked beside her, his hand sliding over till his arm was around her shoulders instead.

"Does Jon know about this?" he asked.

She shook her head again.

"How come?"

She dropped into a chair at the table and Chris moved to drop bread into the toaster. "That apple juice is okay," she said. "You don't have to make tea."

"Alright." Chris poured a glass for her then sat down across the table. "So… why am I hearing the good news before Jon?"

Dee took a cautious sip of her juice. "I've tried to tell him, but he keeps brushing me off," she sighed. "Or biting my head off. There never seems to be a good time."

"He has to have noticed you puking your guts out every morning."

Dee lifted a skeptical eyebrow. "As hard as he sleeps? Unless I puke on his chest, he's not going to notice. Besides, usually one of us is up and gone before the other wakes up."

"Well, that's one way to make sure he takes the time to listen to you." Chris snorted. "But I'd hold that as a last-ditch move. Look— I know my brother can be a real jerk, especially when he gets fixated on something. This thesis thing, this obsession he's got with that antique lowlife, it's the worst he's been in a long time."

Dee took another sip of juice, since the first was obediently staying put. "I'm worried about him. I've never seen him like this. He's barely eating and sleeping, much less taking time out for me. I feel like I'm nothing but an irritation to him now, like a mosquito in the room."

"He's gone way overboard this time, that's for sure," Chris grumbled. "I can usually jolt him out of his craziness, but Dee, this huge announcement has to come from you."

83

"I've tried to tell him," she said. "But he won't—"

"But nothin'!" Chris interjected. "Kiddo, you have to stop being afraid to rattle Jon's cage. Sure, he explodes, but he gets over it. His temper's like a passing thunderstorm. There's a lot of noise and the house shakes, but there's nothing you can do about it so you sit back and wait for it to blow over."

"He scares me when he gets that way," Dee confessed, feeling herself shrink back in her chair from the memories alone.

Chris stiffened and he reached out to touch her hand, clenched around her juice glass. "Dee… does he hit you?"

His voice was harsh and when Dee looked up, the fire in Chris' eyes was more frightening than the worst of Jon's outbursts.

"No! Never!"

The relief that passed over Chris' face was obvious. Dee turned her hand to squeeze his. "It's not that he's threatening me when he goes off. I'm… I'm a wimp, I guess. I'm not used to grown people, who're supposed to be in love, yelling at each other, calling each other names, slamming doors, breaking things. I never had to deal with that with anyone before."

Chris' grip on her hand tightened. "Why do you put up with it, then?"

Dee blinked. "I love him."

"Trust me, kiddo— love can't overcome much of anything."

"It overcomes Jon's temper." Dee pulled her hand away. "Or it did, before this thesis got its hooks into him. He was good to me, before. Sure, we'd have a fight, he'd blow up and I'd get the cold shoulder for the rest of the day, then it would be like we hadn't argued at all. But now?"

She shook her head. "Everything changed after he found that tintype. It's like that damn thing's possessed him or something."

"Come on, Dee." Chris leaned back in his chair. "That's crazy talk and you know it." His mobile expression shifted into a sudden, sick dread. "Does Jon believe that?"

"No, of course not." She forced a chuckle. "Neither do I. It's that he's so wound up in writing the best thesis in the history of ever, he's losing his perspective."

"Sounds like he needs some serious help if this is taking over both your lives."

The toast popped and they both jumped. Chris rose and laid it on a saucer. "Want butter and jelly?"

"Ugh, no."

Chris set the saucer in front of her.

"Thanks." She took a fragrant slice and nibbled a corner. "I don't think he's that crazy. It's hard to get past his focus now. I don't know how to break this to him subtly."

"Dee, you're going to have to get in his face and say straight out, 'I'm pregnant.' Subtle doesn't work when Jon's got tunnel vision."

She shivered and laid her toast back down. "That's not going to be fun."

"Well, kiddo, your other option is to say nothing and wait for him to notice. Of course, by then you'll probably look like you've swallowed a beach ball."

"Hey, I kind of like that plan." She gave him a smile and picked up her toast again. "Do you think he'll notice before or after I go into labor?"

"Great— he's oblivious and you're a procrastinator. You're made for each other." Chris rose to drop more bread into the toaster.

When he poured himself a cup of coffee and pulled the eggs out of the fridge, Dee grabbed her second piece of toast and evacuated the kitchen.

CHAPTER SIX

10 July, 1863
Near Chattanooga, Tennessee

The sun was high and glaring just past noon when Tom spied a flicker of bright, fresh green through a copse of trees ahead of him. He edged forward for a better look.

It was a small stand of corn, healthy and tall. The tassels on the ears were drying. Tom's mouth watered, so much he had to swallow. There wasn't a blessed thing to eat in this world he favored more than sweet corn. Of course, whoever had hidden this patch away didn't plant it for his benefit.

Tom eased closer with all the stealth of a panther on the stalk, alert for any sign of movement. He reached up and pulled an ear of the new corn. The tender kernels burst between his teeth, so sweet his mouth ached at the taste. He gnawed down to the cob then moved a few steps, breaking and stripping another ear.

A brief glimpse of blue and a gunmetal line arcing too quickly toward horizontal were all it took for Tom's war-trained instincts to take over.

A high-pitched scream told him his shot had found its mark.

The man fell, his rifle sailing into the corn.

Tom moved quickly away from his firing position, so any of Billy Yank's friends would have a difficult time in drawing a bead on him.

When he heard no answering reports, Tom concluded that the Yank had been alone – a forager like him or maybe a picket. He crept toward the terrible screams at an angle, alert for any signs that the soldier was still capable of an attack.

He wasn't.

Tom shoved his arm through his rifle's sling and settled it back against his spine, eyes never leaving the kicking figure.

The little coot rolled his head towards Tom, wide wild eyes set in a youth-smooth face.

"You done aimed at your last Confederate, boy."

"Help me!" The high-pitched whimper was pathetic, choked with pain and terror. "Please, mister… help me!"

The boy's hat fell off as he writhed. A long, copper-brown braid slithered from underneath onto the hoed dirt. A calico bow bound the end of the plait.

Horror knocked Tom to his knees as hard as any shot. He reached out to the woman, his hand brushing over hers as they clenched and unclenched over the gushing wound that was quickly turning her sweat-stained work-shirt from indigo to the most brilliant scarlet.

"Help… me…" She fixed on his face, her eyes already going glassy and distant.

"I can't," he moaned. There was no hope when a gut wound bled like this one. Still, he ripped off his own shirt-tail, wadding the cloth into a ball. He wrenched her grip away from the wound to press his make-shift bandage against the hole. He felt throbbing spurts of blood spreading hot and wet against his palm as the dry cloth sucked it greedily.

The woman's face was going pale beneath her sunburn, ominous gray-blue tinting her lips. Death-dew coated her forehead. She kept her eyes on his face, gasping for breath.

"Why'd y'have to draw a bead on me?" he asked, dull anger mingling with sharp regret. "I wouldn't have hurt you if you hadn't been fixin' to fire. I ain't never hurt no woman before."

"I…" she whispered, moving one hand to close it around his wrist, there at her ruined belly. "I didn't… even see… you."

"Then why'd you bear down on me with your rifle, you lyin' bitch?" He pulled his hands away and reached for her weapon.

His hand closed around a hoe instead, its broken handle wedged into a piece of iron pipe worn smooth and bright from hard work.

Her breath rattled in her throat. She still stared at him, but whatever she saw now, it wasn't his face. A long, soft sigh escaped her, and her spasmodic struggles ceased. Her body relaxed into the bloody mud.

The sun-warm metal dropped from his hand; his fingers gone numb.

A fly lit on her eye. It strolled across the still, glassy surface and paused to sip at her last tear.

Tom lurched to his feet. He crashed back through the corn, all caution gone.

October 15, Present Day
Tucson, Arizona
~ Three days later ~

After his third conversation with Callie, Jon gave up his feeble ruse that he happened to have frequent business at the bookstore. They started meeting at the Student Center or having lunch together somewhere off campus. Jon ignored his uneasiness when she'd touch him as they talked or brush against him as they walked. That's just the way she was, an indiscriminate flirt. He and Callie were nothing more than friends. Comrades in arms who'd hit it off on first meeting.

They were in the middle of a rather philosophical discussion that late afternoon as he walked back with her to her apartment.

"I think the 'tell the Universe what you want' belief system is magical thinking and really pathetic," she offered, "But I'm all for asking for what you want from an actual human being."

Jon hesitated as she moved from beside him to in front of him.

"Like right now," she continued. "What I want is…" Callie closed the distance between them, her body warm and soft along the front of his. She put her hands on his shoulders and whispered beside his ear. "You, naked, with my legs hooked over your shoulders."

Jon heard himself make a startled wheeze. For a crucial few seconds, he couldn't think of a damn thing to say to that.

Callie laughed and her hands traveled from his shoulders to his behind. "Though I'd settle for them wrapped around your waist. So long as we keep the naked clause in there."

For one, brief, reckless moment, he was willing to give her what she wanted, and more. He could feel her skin against his, could almost hear her throaty voice crying out, hoarse with passion.

"No." Jon stepped back, and Callie let him slip out of her embrace. "I... I can't. I'm living with someone."

Callie lifted an eyebrow. "Wow. Wasn't expecting that. Not at this stage, anyhow."

"I'm sorry," he offered. "I'm in love with her."

Her chuckle startled him. He expected anger, accusations, not amusement.

"I'm sorry too— for her." Callie's smile was sardonic. "Considering that this is the first time you've mentioned her, seems as though love's the wrong label."

"Her name is Deidre, and yes, we're in love."

Callie moved in again, kissed him quick and hard, then stepped back. "I suggest somber reflection on your definition of the term, Jon Hansen. What you have with Deidre sounds more like friends with benefits."

"It's not like that at all…"

Callie walked away as he spoke but turned back to smile over her shoulder, the expression wickedly sensual. "Too bad, you can have more than one friend. You call me when you stop deluding yourself."

CHAPTER SEVEN

25 November, 1863
Missionary Ridge, Tennessee

In the scant space between one running stride and the next, Tom skidded, face down, mouth and eyes suddenly filled with cold mud, his rifle flying from his hold, discharging when it too hit the ground. His right leg dead after that first almighty slam and jolt.

He was hit! Oh God, he was hit bad!

Tom managed to squirm around onto his back without sitting up. Wouldn't matter if his leg was gone if he took a bullet to the head.

His hands shook as he reached down, craning his neck to see, his breath short and high in his throat. It was still all there, his leg. His fingers found a ragged hole the size of his thumb, high on the front of his thigh. A scalding stream of blood ran over his fingers, but it didn't spurt. He'd live through this, maybe, long enough to suffer for certain.

He lolled his head, straining to see how far he'd fallen from the cover he had been trying to reach. Shot whirred over and around him, from foe and friend alike. He had to slow the bleeding, he decided, or getting to cover would make no difference.

Tom slid one of his galluses off his shoulder, cut it free with his knife. He wound the strap around his thigh, around and above his wound, and tied it as tight as he could manage with clumsy, blood-slick hands.

He squirmed himself up onto his unwounded side, and as he began to hitch himself along with his arms and good leg, agony rose up and swallowed him. Every breath drew in with a shudder and went out with a shriek and there wasn't a mortal thing he could do to stop the racket. Not that it mattered. His screams were no more than a few thin, shrill notes in the hellish racket all around.

Tom set his focus on the upturned root-ball of a small, storm-killed pine; nothing else mattered but getting himself behind that natural earthwork. The screams and shouts, the constant rolling thunder of shot and shell faded to nothing as he struggled to reach that promise of refuge.

When he rolled into the leaf-filled depression left by the uprooted tree, he lay panting, shivering, exhausted. The freezing rain beat down on his face. Every heartbeat slammed through his body, jerking his chest from side to side. He was cold to the bone but his blood turned white-hot at the hip, scalding his veins as it surged.

He curled himself around his shattered leg. He vomited up bile then kept on heaving, helpless to stop, straining hard over nothing at all. As soon as he could draw a breath without gagging, the torn flesh of his thigh would draw up in another wrenching spasm and set the heaving off again.

Soon thirst took the reins of his torment. The icy water in his canteen was quenching as dust. He drank it in sips, puked most of it right back up, and wondered if it was worth the pain to stay alive.

By the time the cold rain began to slacken, Tom lay with his empty canteen still in a slack hand, the pain now a familiar thing like the biting cold, a continual torment to be borne without struggle.

"Tom! Hey Tom! Still here?" The voice was loud, almost against his ear, then it disappeared and the sharp crack of a rifle fired at close range replaced it.

Dragging his eyelids open took an appalling amount of effort. "Tay?"

"The very same, ol' hoss." The rifle cracked again then Taylor's face and warmth leaned over him. Tay's back was against the root ball, his rifle between his knees as he reloaded. "How you holdin' out?"

"Don't let the surgeons get me," Tom rasped. "Spare me one of them rounds."

Taylor frowned, and swung around onto his knees to fire again. "Cain't do that." He dropped back to reload, with nary a pause in his speech. "Against my religion since you're wearin' what's left of the gray. Buck up, Tom. This way, at least the majority of you'll be goin' home."

The whistle of an incoming shell interrupted what shooting at his enemies could not. Taylor threw himself over Tom, and the pain from that protective impact sent Tom into a faint, his scream lost in the explosion.

⚃

It was the groaning that roused him. A resigned, weary groaning from pain so long endured it wore down the will for any sharper protest. At first, he thought the droning noise came from his own throat, but when he roused a little more, Tom realized that it was the man lying beside him who moaned.

He managed to raise himself up on an elbow, shocked by his own weakness. The blast of answering pain in his right hip and thigh knocked him flat again. Something fluttered against his cheek and he half-heartedly slapped at it. It was a paper tag, on a string around his neck. "AMP RGT L" was scrawled on the scrap.

When the meaning of that sank in, horror drowned the pain and revived some of his strength. His wound was so high, he'd have no leg left. He would die of the surgery, surely. A death far more horrible and lingering than his end if he'd been left out in that stump-hole to bleed to death.

Tay and his religious scruples could go to hell. Tom would rather have perished out there than face the fate set for him on that tag. He drew a deep breath, raised himself up onto his elbows, then pulled himself backwards along the ground, moving himself with his hands and the heel of his uninjured leg.

A few inches gained.

Where he was going to go, he didn't think. Distance was all. The agony from his leg sent tears rolling down his face. He ignored them, clenched his teeth till they were near to shattering, and gained another few precious inches away from the group of men awaiting the surgeons' saws.

Nobody noticed his struggles. How could they take note of one writhing man among the moaning, crying, dying masses? The only notice anyone took was notice enough to not step on him when he paused to breathe and try to blink away the gray fog that kept seeping in from the sides of his vision.

A hand closed around his shoulder. Tom cried out in frustrated rage and swung a fist upward, awkward, unbalanced enough that he would have collapsed save for that restraining hold.

"Tom! Tom, it's Carl!"

He dropped his head back, to look up into his friend's anguished face. "Don't let 'em, Carl. They're gonna take my leg— don't let 'em!"

Carl crouched, and pulled Tom back against him, supporting him with an arm around his friend's chest. "Tom, they must! If they don't, you'll die of blood-poisoning."

Tom gave a furious snarl that broke on a sob, tugging at his friend's arm that felt more a restraint than an embrace. "Get the hell away from me then! I'd rather go quick of blood-pizen than rot slow with gangrene!"

Carl didn't release his hold. "I don't want to watch you die."

Tom craned his head back against Carl's shoulder, the move a mockery of affection. "So you're gonna hand me over to the butchers to die out of your sight."

"What the hell do you want me to do, then?"

"Git me away from this buzzard-nest," Tom gritted. "Wrap up my leg and let it take care of its own self."

Tom tugged frantically at the tag around his neck, succeeding only in tearing the bit of card off the string. "Well? You gonna help me or not? I don't wanna keep sittin' here on my arse till the surgeon's boys shows up!"

Carl chewed on the edge of his wispy mustache. "I'll help." The concession was soft, the command came stronger. "You'll have to stand, and walk as best you can. I can't carry you outright."

It took some grunting, many curses, some outright screams, and a near brush with a full swoon, but Carl soon had Tom upright, Tom's arm held tight around his shoulders.

Tom leaned so heavily upon the slighter man that Carl staggered under the weight. "If you faint, I can't do anything but break your fall," he warned.

Mortal fear is a powerful motivator. Tom shook his head like a wet dog. "I ain't gonna faint," he swore through a clenched jaw.

It was a near thing, more than once, but somehow Carl managed to half-carry, half-drag Tom to the outskirts of the field hospital, near the less gravely wounded. He laid his friend down close to the warmth and glow of one of the fires.

Tom sagged, limp, onto the ground as Carl eased him down. His eyes rolled back and closed. Carl held his own breath until he saw his friend's chest rise and fall.

"Now what do I do?" he muttered to himself, squatting by Tom's bloody leg. He sprang up to accost a passing orderly, commandeering the basket of lint the boy carried.

His nose wrinkled at the grayed cloth strips and wads of cotton lint inside, flecked by bits of foreign matter. "This is foul."

Still, it was all they had. All he was likely to get. Carl postponed that decision, his internal discomfort driving him to rinse and wring his hands with water from his canteen. The nervous habit got him mocked, called Lady MacBeth and worse, but he couldn't break it.

He corked his canteen, set it aside and tore Tom's britches leg away from the wound. Gingerly, he plucked a few shreds of cloth and loose bone from the mouth of the gaping hole. Fresh blood welled up.

Carl shuddered, and uncorked his canteen again. This time, he poured some over Tom's wound, till only a slower seep of bright, clean blood was left within it.

The thought of touching the filthy stuff in the basket, much less layering it over that raw, vulnerable hole in his friend's flesh, was repulsive enough to make Carl grimace.

If only the dirty cloth didn't have to touch the flesh… Carl looked down at his shirt. Every stitch he had on was as grimy as the bandages in the basket. Only the variety of dirt differed. Tom's clothing was no better.

Carl leaned close to Tom's ear, his hand on his friend's clammy forehead. His voice was a hoarse whisper as he spoke. "And when I passed by thee Thomas Dorin, and saw thee Thomas Dorin polluted in thine own blood, I said unto thee Thomas Dorin when thou wast in thy blood, Live; yea, I said unto thee Thomas Dorin when thou wast in thy blood, Live."

As Carl dropped his hand, he felt his Testament shift in his breast pocket. All those soft, thin pages, soiled only on the edges. A quick thought to ask forgiveness for any offense given, then Carl began ripping away the leaves from the little leather-bound book.

Psalm Forty-one, he made certain to put against Tom's skin. Blood seeped into the paper, obscuring the Psalmist's certainty. Once the blood flow was staunched by a thick layering of God's word, Carl tied the sanctified packing in place with the suspender strap Tom had tied around his leg. It was saturated with drying blood, but at least the blood was Tom's own. Carl surveyed his handiwork with a critical frown, then moved away to scrounge up the makings of a splint.

Once Tom's leg was bound up from hip to foot with green-cut limbs and bandage linen and he lay under a purloined blanket, Carl refilled his canteen and left it under his friend's hand. It was the last he could do, his official duties impossible to be set aside any longer.

ᑐ

"Are we all that's left?" Shine asked, his voice almost a whisper in the darkness of their battle-camp.

"No," Carl assured him. He moved to sit beside his friend. "Tom's wounded though, badly."

"Lord, lord," Shine groaned, and the words sounded more like a prayer than an idle exclamation. "What happened?"

"He took a ball to the top of his right leg. He asked... he asked me to get him away from the surgeons."

"Did you?" Shine's pale eyes caught the gleam of a passing lantern.

"Yes." Carl wrung his hands before stuffing them into his jacket pockets. "I fear I may have signed his death warrant, doing so."

"Then you done him a right fine favor, for he was beggin' me to shoot him in the head out on the field." Taylor dropped down beside their banked fire.

"You think he's gonna die, then?" Shine asked in between them both.

Carl's hands fisted in his pockets. His jaw clenched. "I don't know. I pray not."

"Wouldn't make any plans with him for after this fight, if I's you," Tay shrugged. "Any of you'un's seen Willie?"

"Not since we mustered out," Shine answered.

Carl closed his eyes, that ominous news almost too much to bear after Tom's ordeal.

"Willie missin' in action, Tom's as good as dead; this War's whittlin' us down with a will, boys. We should make the best of it, start us a big wager on which'll be the last 'un standin' when the big frogs call it quits." Tay stuck his pipestem in his mouth and sucked on the cold, empty bowl.

Carl lurched to his feet. "Why waste a wager? You're sure to survive, for the Devil takes care of his own." He left their smoldering fire, the damp cold more comforting.

Taylor's voice raised to follow him on his way. "I'm gonna hammer that tetchy little milksop into the ground like a tent peg one of these days."

Carl flipped his jacket collar up around his ears and didn't break stride.

∞

Case XLII—Private Thomas Anderson Dorin, Com. A, 19th Tennessee Volunteer Infantry, C.S.A., age eighteen years, was wounded in the battle of Missionary Ridge, November 25th, 1863, by a conoidal musket ball, which entered at the outer aspect of the upper of the right thigh, and transversed the entire thickness of the limb, moderately comminuting the shaft of the femur in its progress. He lay upon the field for about five hours, and lost a good deal of blood, although none of the larger vessels appear to have been damaged. He was then conveyed to a temporary field hospital, and his wounds were dressed and the injured limb was put into a crude splint.

On November 29th, 1863 he was admitted to the Newsom Hospital in Chattanooga, Tennessee. On the evening of reception the original improvised dressing on his wound was removed. On removal the wound was remarked to be free of suppuration and almost entirely free of necrotic tissue. Numerous detached bony splinters, about half a handful, were extracted. On the patient's violent insistence that the wound not be further treated, the wound was re-dressed. For six weeks, extension and counter-extension were maintained, but so much suffering arose from this treatment that it was discontinued and the limb simply supported in a comfortable position. The patient was confined to bed for six months. Ever since the reception of his injury the patient has been in severe pain and taken morphia very freely. On May 10, 1864, it was found that the fracture was quite firmly consolidated, with some enlargement of the thigh and shortening of the limb by approximately one and three-quarters of an inch. The patient began to sit up in a chair and soon began to ambulate upon crutches about the ward. His appetite was fair and his general constitution was excellent throughout his convalescence. The patient weighed one hundred forty-seven pounds upon entrance to the hospital, and one hundred thirty pounds at release. On June 20, 1864, by order of the Medical Director at Newsom Hospital, he was honorably discharged from the military service of the Confederate States of America due to permanent and irreparable lameness resulting from gunshot fracture of the right femur which renders him unfit for further duty.

CHAPTER EIGHT

October 17
Present Day
University of Arizona, Tucson
~ Two days later ~

Jon paused in the open office door. "Good morning, Dr. Rosner."

"Come in, Jon." She got right to the point as soon as he'd closed the door and taken a seat. "I'm afraid I'm the bearer of bad news."

Jon swallowed hard. "I wasn't aware there was a problem this semester."

"I've been keeping an eye on your progress. Unfortunately, your coursework doesn't seem promising so far, and we discussed my issues with your thesis earlier. The draft you turned in to me this week didn't fully address those concerns."

"Dr. Rosner, this semester had been especially difficult for me, due to situations in my family. I know I can improve now that I know that those stresses are affecting my work here."

Dr. Rosner's expression was kind, but her voice was still somewhat cool and formal as she replied. "Jon, we all have stressors. Situations are always going to arise in life that distract and worry us. Graduate school in itself is a major source of stress. It is also, as you are well aware, highly competitive, especially in this specialty. Our candidates have to give their

99

best, despite those pressures. Those who can't? Well, it serves the best interests of both the student and this University for them to move on to other endeavors. Are the family situations you spoke of on a catastrophic order, such as a death or major illness?"

"No ma'am," Jon answered. What else could he say? I'm sliding towards bankruptcy and my relationship with my domestic partner is on the skids? Yeah, him and about three-quarters of the rest of the student body.

"Then I'm afraid this meeting must serve as notice of probation. You have the remainder of the semester to demonstrate improvement and bring your average up. You'll be mailed a copy of the official notice for your records."

Jon slumped, his heart pounding in his ears. This meeting was stress of a catastrophic order, all on its own. "Yes ma'am."

"Jon," Dr. Rosner's formal demeanor softened, and she leaned forward. "I'm sorry. I dreaded doing this, but I have no choice. You know your GRE scores were marginal, but I urged your admittance to the program because I saw potential and an admirable drive to not only preserve and document history but to make it relevant to current concerns. This semester, that drive has seemed to turn inward on itself and become distorted. I don't want to see it consume you. I think you may need help in coping with whatever is causing you to lose focus. Please, take advantage of it."

She slid a card across the desk. 'Counseling and Psychological Services' was emblazoned beneath an emblem of a rising, or perhaps setting, sun.

Jon's fingers left a fleeting shadow of moisture on the glass desktop as he picked it up. "Thank you."

ଓ

His first impulse after he left the office was to call Dee, but he squashed it almost as soon as it entered his head. This was a warning, that's all. He had till mid-December to bring his grades up. He would do it. He didn't have any other choice.

Why worry Dee about something that didn't pertain to her at all? The last thing he needed was for her to do more of her helpful nagging anyway.

Jon dropped the Psych Services card into a trashcan as he passed.

17 July, 1864
Near Benton
Polk County, Tennessee

Hours bled into days, days into weeks under a weary tread. Dragging his feet up the long incline, a storm wind at his back, Tom could almost convince himself that he'd fallen into some sort of fitful delirium after his wounding, and only came to himself now, as he climbed the ridge that overlooked home.

Tom paused in the underbrush, as instinctively conscious of concealment as a buck deer, and leaned against a pine. He tucked his crutches tighter under his arms and looked down into the peaceful valley. Smoke rose from the chimney of the house. Someone was awake then, stoking the fire in the stove for Ma before going out to milk.

Milking, and coaxing the banked coals back to life in the cook-stove, had been among his chores before he joined up. How often since then, had he dreamed of being home, being in this valley with never another soul to see for days but those who shared his own blood?

Tom's muscles tensed, ready to hurry down the ridge he'd climbed so many times. Ready to go home.

Finally, home.

He heard his mother call out the back door, though the strong, wet wind to his back didn't allow him to catch the sense of her words. His father moved just outside the barn door and called back. He was leaning on a cane. Tom felt a clenching in his chest, and took three quick lame strides downhill, his make-shift crutches slipping and tangling in the grass, then stopped short.

How could he go home now?

He was a useless cripple and worse than a cripple. A coward and a murderer, stained with innocent blood. He was an insult to his family name and to the very ground beneath his rag-wrapped feet.

Tom sank back into the concealing underbrush like the filthy beast he'd become. The word of God, sharp as a saber, rose up in his mind, clear as the day Reverend Collier preached on it.

Tom's lips trembled as he whispered the ancient words of divine damnation for his sins. "Cursed be he that smiteth his neighbor secretly. Cursed be he that taketh reward to slay an innocent person. Cursed shalt thou be in the city, and cursed shall thou be in the field. Cursed shall be thy basket and thy store. Cursed shall be the fruit of thy body, and the fruit of thy land, the increase of thine kine, and the flocks of thy sheep. Cursed shalt thou be when thou comest in, and cursed shall thou be when thou goest out."

His breath caught in his throat. How could he visit that wrath upon his family, the souls he held most dear in this world? His name might still be Dorin, but his true identity was signified by the indelible mark of Cain burning within.

Tom turned his back on what his heart yearned for most desperately, and trudged along the fence line at the top of the ridge. A thin whinny rose through the rattling of raindrops. He stopped and after a long still moment, worked his way down the side of the rise. A pasture nestled in the valley, out of easy sight of the house in the oncoming storm.

"Hey, ol' lady," he called to a sway-backed, sag-bellied mare.

She ambled away from the other brood mares to greet him and frisk his ragged coat for apple slices.

Disappointed, the mare swung her head away, but Tom caught her mane. He ran his hand down her side. "Didn't catch this last time, huh?" he murmured.

She was Flit's dam. She'd been the dam of a whole line of fine colts and fillies, almost as long as he could remember. She carried no foal now.

Tom scratched along her neck and she dropped her head to crop the wet grass again. The old mare was about played out. Not long before she was entirely worthless.

Tom pulled a length of string out of his pack and knotted a loop around the mare's lower jaw. She shook her head and snorted, but stood willing while he laboriously pulled himself up onto her bony back,

102

gathered the make-shift neck rein in one hand and his crutches in the other, held tight across his lap.

"Let's go, Annabelle," he murmured and squeezed her ribs with a grimace against the protest from his ruined thigh. "You stay here and they'll be feedin' you to the hogs and the hounds 'fore next spring."

The mare obediently ambled away towards the far fence gap, undisturbed by a rumble of thunder overhead.

He was a murderer, a coward, and had outlived his usefulness as surely as the mare had outlived hers. In light of that, what difference did the extra sin of horse-thievery make to his certain damnation?

CHAPTER NINE

10 April, 1865
Somewhere on the Western border

The church bells clanged all day and through the night when the news came over the wire.

It was over.

Honor, glory, bravery, sacrifice, suffering, rights, dreams, lives, blood, all wasted.

The Bonny Blue Banner and the Cause, shot to hell and gone, for nothing.

The Confederacy and all it stood for, signed away at the Appomattox County courthouse on a Sunday evening. Thousands and thousands of soldiers turned traitors, pledging their allegiance to the enemy nation they tried to destroy for all the four years before, on even the very day before....

Two objects lay on the table in front of him, a bottle and a pistol. The bottle of whiskey had been emptied and overturned hours before.

The pistol, he hadn't touched since he checked the load and laid it there when the first peals began to ring out.

... forgive me for tempting you. I don't want to besmirch the record of a man who will surely be soon proven a hero....

"I weren't never no hero, Beth." He picked up the pistol.

…Know this, that I am as convinced of your mettle and of your courage and devotion to our Nation as I am of sunlight and rain. Although I do not dare claim their equal in my own character, I do know the depth of my devotion to you….

"I'm a coward. Worthless. I failed us all." He pulled the hammer back.

A callused hand gently covered his fist. "What would she say if she could see you this way? Could know this is what her love has done to you?"

"It don't matter. It never did. She's dead…." He pressed the muzzle against his temple.

His finger began to tighten on the trigger.

My dearest Tom… I give you my most solemn word, by all that we hold Holy, that I will not judge or ridicule or reveal what you say to anyone else, but will only comfort and cheer you as best as I am able to do from this vast distance….

A broken, bitten back sob choked him. He lowered the gun, eased the hammer down, shoved it into the holster at his hip. Tom grabbed up his saddlebags and left the stark, shadowy room.

He rode out of town at a gallop, heading west. Heading nowhere, anywhere, beyond the noise of bells tolling dirge.

CHAPTER TEN

~ Seven years later ~
3 November, 1872
Cooper's Creek, Arizona Territory

"Whoa, gal."

The small bay mare planted her hoofs almost in midstride. She was not much bigger than a large pony, but she was the most willing mount he'd ever encountered. Tom combed his fingers through her mane, patted the satiny hide beneath.

Sukie curved her neck, side-danced like a spoiled little girl, and he let her. She was so willing, so soft-mouthed, that he often let the reins lay slack, guiding her with voice and knees. Such an obedient temperament bought her a good many indulgences.

Tom continued to pet her idly as he gazed down into the prosperous town spread below. It had been well-planned from the get-go, with a main street wide enough for two wagons to pass while others were pulled in to the hitching posts along the sides.

Broad turn-arounds were laid out at each end. The town's public well-house marked the center of one. In the other, an ancient palo verde tree, a good forty feet tall, spread welcome shade.

Both sides of the main street were built up and some of the adobe buildings flaunted wooden fronts. A few even had a second floor, and one imposing edifice was of brick.

Even now, some of the businesses spilled light out their front windows onto the board sidewalks. It was getting near to sunset, the cool night wind already beginning to whisper against his cheeks. If luck was with them, they wouldn't be spending another night out in it.

"Now Sukie, tell me true. Does a night knee-deep in straw with a full trough in front of you strike your fancy?"

She bobbed her head, though he knew it was to hear her slack curb-chain jingle rather than any recognition of what he said. He kneed her into motion once more. Her small hooves clopped smartly against the caliche, belying how many miles she'd borne him that day.

"I ain't flush often, little girl," he warned the horse, "So you best enjoy it while it lasts."

Sukie flicked an ear back to catch his voice and swished her tail.

He'd had a good run of luck at a faro table in Pantano Station, proving himself the only man willing to walk away while he was ahead. The trait wasn't considered a virtue amongst that particular bunch, so he'd lit a shuck out of there. Didn't matter where he was now, or what this town was called, it was two-day's ride northwest and that's all that mattered.

Tom let Sukie amble down the street at her own pace, nodding and touching his hat brim to the folks still on the streets at supper-time. He dismounted in front of the livery and led her inside.

"Evenin'," he called out to the stableman, who was filling a hay rack for an over-eager gray. "Got an empty box tonight?"

"Evenin'." The man turned and then jerked his arm away from the gray's yellow teeth. "Leave off, you filthy dog! Try that again and Doc's gonna be makin' his rounds on foot!"

He grinned at Tom, showing a friendly demeanor and a lack of teeth of his own. "Last on the right's free, but that little lady could lay herself out crossways in a stanchion."

"Maybe so, but I reckon she could out-last that leggy gray there that near took a piece outta you. She's earned herself a box tonight."

Tom led Sukie back to the box stall, jawing with the stableman as he tended to her needs.

108

Felt real good not to have to slink into town like a hungry cur, nosing around, hoping for a kind word and a few scraps. "Say, is there somewhere a feller can rent a room and get a hot meal around here?"

"Yes sir," the stableman replied, leaning on his pitchfork now, clearly preferring conversation to cleanliness. "We got a hotel, but between you and me, ol' Rodgers charges a liver and light for a night there. Then there's the saloon, couple of rooms over that 'un for cheap."

He flashed gums in a lascivious grin, "If ya don't mind sharin' your bed and eatin' coosh and beans three times a day. Or if you jist want a decent room and board and you're plannin' on stayin' a spell, there's Miz Perkins' boardin' house."

"I done et enough coosh to last me till doom's-day," Tom said, "So I reckon I'll go by and see if Miz Perkins will take me in."

"Probably will, she's got a soft spot for strays." The man gave him a wink and pointed in the direction of the eastern side of town. "Down the street, across from the bank."

"Much obliged." Tom paid up Sukie for the night and went off to find his own place to bed down out of the wind. He rolled his shoulders and flexed his neck. Felt as if he'd been beaten with a hoe-handle. Everything ached from his boot heels up. Sleeping off the ground and under a roof would feel like a piece of heaven tonight.

He strolled down the street, leaning heavily on his cane, looking over the busy town with interest. He nodded and spoke greeting to those he passed and got polite replies in return. Friendly enough place, too.

Some towns, you rode in and folks eyed you like they expected you to steal the hitching posts. There was a bath house just up from the stable, and the promise of the soothing effect of good hot water was too much of a temptation to pass up. Tom stepped inside.

An hour later, he moved much more freely on up the street. Even so, by the time he got to the boarding house, Tom was glad the town was no larger than it was. He opened the gate, crossed the neatly swept yard with its cosseted brittle-brush shrub, and scraped his boots on the jack beside the porch steps. He stepped up into the pool of light cast from the window and rapped on the door, shifting his saddlebags and bedroll higher on his shoulder, his hat in his hand.

After a few moments, a dark-eyed woman with a lovely, long neck opened the door. "Good evening, sir. May I help you?"

"Yes ma'am. Forgive me if I've come at an inconvenient time, but I was told down at the livery you might have a room to let?"

"I do," she nodded, "But I must inform you that I let my rooms by the week only."

Tom shifted a little to ease his leg as he considered that. "That'll be fine, ma'am."

One place was as good as any other, among strangers. If he couldn't find work, he'd stay till his stake ran low and then move on.

"Please, come in." She stepped aside and he entered the foyer. It was spare, but pleasant with lamplight and the scent of supper. His stomach growled impatiently, though he hoped not audibly to her.

"May I ask your name, sir?" She drew a little notebook out of her skirt pocket and the stub of a pencil.

"Tom Dorin," he replied, and she recorded him in her book.

He paid her a month's rent, for the rate she named was reasonable enough for room and board.

She tucked the money into her other pocket, and smiled up at him as she offered her hand. "I am Mrs. Perkins. Welcome to my home, Mr. Dorin. I'll show you to your room. Harold will be up shortly with water for you. Supper will be served in half an hour."

"Thank you," he answered, and took her hand for a fleeting moment. It felt fragile as a bird, refined and delicate, but callused from hard work. He didn't think her less of a lady for that.

25 November, 1872
~ Three weeks later ~

"Mr. Dorin? Might you spare me a moment of your time?" Mrs. Perkins asked him after breakfast, as he was heading out.

"Yes'm." Tom turned and followed her into the kitchen. He nodded to Ophelia, who nodded back, a queen to a commoner, before returning to scrubbing the pans.

"Please, sit down." Mrs. Perkins sat down at the table and Tom followed. "Have you had any success in finding employment, Mr. Dorin?"

He shook his head. "Not enough, ma'am. Lem Hokes took me on to break the new stock, but there ain't enough need at the stable to keep me workin' steady. I ain't fit for work out at the mine, of course. I can pay you for next month, then I reckon I'll have to be moving on."

She traced a square of the gingham tablecloth. "I suppose you've heard I had to let my previous hired man go, shortly before you arrived."

Hoo howdy, had he ever. But more than two-thirds of that wasn't fit to repeat back to her, and he reckoned a good portion of the whole was gossip anyhow. "Yes'm, I know you had to ask him to leave."

"Despite his... regrettable lack of initiative, his absence has caused Ophelia and me hardship even in this short time. Frankly, Mr. Dorin, I am finding it to be quite difficult to carry on the work required of this business if I do not have a reliable hired man to assist. Would you be willing to step into that position? I'm afraid I can't afford to pay a fully commensurate wage, but I would give you room, board and laundry to make up the deficit."

"So long as I got enough coin to keep Sukie in high clover," he nodded, "whatever you pay, with room and board, will be enough. I don't require much for myself."

Mrs. Perkins closed her eyes, then looked back up at him with a soft smile. "You have greatly relieved my mind today, Mr. Dorin."

She rose and he did as well. She offered her hand across the table. "Thank you. I'm sure we'll work well together."

"You're welcome, ma'am. I got no doubt we will." He gave her hand a gentle shake. "I've begun to feel right settled in here. I was dreadin' havin' to move on down the road the first of the year."

"So, now you won't have to," she smiled. "Which simply proves the old saws about ill winds and silver linings, I suppose. I'll have a list of your duties drawn up in the morning for you to look over. Of course, your obligation to Mr. Hokes comes first, for as long as he requires your services."

"He's got a couple of saddle horses I'm to lady-break to harness for him, but I won't be more than two weeks doin' that. Afterward, he won't need me til he gets another string in, this spring."

"Excellent. I don't want to keep you from your work, but there is one other matter." Her eyes went to his cane, propped against the edge of the table. A splash of high color lit her cheeks. "I must beg your pardon for my thoughtlessness, for I haven't considered the inconvenience of our rooms for you, before today."

"There's no need to apologize, ma'am. I made peace with the world not smoothin' itself flat for me a long time back."

She gave him a slight smile. "Regardless, I shall make the downstairs room yours the moment Mr. Merrit vacates."

"Much obliged," he said, with a polite nod.

Hattie rose. "Well, I shan't keep you from your work any longer, Mr. Dorin. Thank you again, and good day."

"You're more than welcome. Good day, Miz Perkins." Tom glanced back to where Ophelia was still rattling around. "Good day, Miz Lefler."

"Mr. Dorin," she acknowledged without turning around.

Tom let the slight snub roll off. Mrs. Perkins had set him straight in a hot hurry the first time he'd thoughtlessly addressed her hired woman by her first name. It appeared Mrs. Perkins had forgiven him for his breach of enlightened household etiquette, but Ophelia— Mrs. Lefler— surely hadn't.

26 November, 1872
~ The next day ~

"Mornin', Mr. Dorin!"

"Mornin' Harold." Tom glanced around to where Harold peeked over the side of the stanchion.

"I'm sure glad you're milkin' now. That ol' cow is mean."

"She does have her bad habits." Tom deftly rescued the full bucket from the threat of yet another kick. He handed the milking stool to Harold then reached around cautiously to untie the string that held the cow's club of a tail captive against her hock.

Harold gave a little chuckle. "I never thought of doin' that!"

"I got tired real quick of gettin' smacked upside the head by that nasty switch of hers."

"I tried to pull the burrs out of her tail once and she butted me clean out into the hall," Harold told him as he handed Tom his canes.

"Well, maybe this calf she's carryin' will be a heifer so we can sell off ol' Queenie."

"Or we could have her for Sunday dinner," Harold suggested, grabbing up his schoolbooks as they left the barn. "Bet she'd be tough as a boot, though, just for spite."

"I expect you're right," Tom nodded.

"Is it true you're gonna stay on and work here now, with Mamma and Miz Hattie?"

"It is."

"Good! I didn't like ol' man Lair. He was meaner than the cow."

The school bell started ringing.

"Gotta go!" Harold took off like he was fired from a pistol.

Tom paused to watch the little boy dart up the street before he went on up to the summer-kitchen with the milk. Mrs. Lefler still didn't approve of him in the least, but he and her son hit it off from first meeting. He expected he'd have a small chattering shadow a lot of the day now and he found he looked forward to it.

"I hope I don't find hair in the milk again this morning," Ophelia sniffed as she took the bucket from him at the stoop.

"I did my best, ma'am, but it'll take a few more days to get Queenie used to bein' curried and havin' her bag washed before milkin's. She don't tend to cooperate with the notions long."

The fact was, it would be a wonder if there weren't at least a few cow-hairs in the milk. The scurrilous and skedaddled Mr. Lair ought to have been taken out and whipped for a good many misdeeds, his shameful neglect of that cow among them.

"I would expect you could control a cow, Mr. Dorin."

"It's been a long while since I've had to deal with one regular, Miz Lefler, but me and Queenie will come to an understandin' purty soon."

"See that you do. I have enough work without having to strain the milk repeatedly."

She closed the kitchen door between them with a sharp whap.

Tom shook his head and went on to his other chores.

CHAPTER ELEVEN

October 17
Present Day
~ Later that day ~

The house was deserted when he went inside. Jon went to the study and pulled his daypack out of the closet. Chris had called him nuts all his life and Dee was beginning to act like she thought he was losing his marbles. Even Dr. Rosner hinted he needed psychiatric help.

He had to keep his head down, not let them get to him. Make it through and present his thesis. It was the only way to shut them all up, get them all out of his damn way for once.

He checked the contents of his pack then headed for the front door. As he scooped up wallet and keys, it occurred to him that while checking out Cooper's Creek for the sake of research wasn't crazy, to do it alone without letting anyone know where he was going was insanity.

Jon left his daypack by the door and went back into his office. He scrawled a note and laid it on the keyboard of his open laptop. If he wasn't back by morning, Chris would know where to start looking.

03

Jon paused on the narrow spine of the ridge, breathing heavily, to look down into the valley below. The sight of the remains of Cooper's Creek sent a burst of renewed energy through his system. Logically, he knew there would be nothing in the ruins that would answer any of his questions. Only to himself, he admitted that logic had very little to do with the fascination that prompted him to make the trek.

Ramshackle ruins lined both sides of a wide street, now narrowed by encroaching cacti and brush. Both ends terminated in once-generous turnarounds. In the center of one was a heap of collapsed wood and tin. The town's well, its death-blow when the spring feeding it failed. The other round was marked by the weathered trunk of an ancient palo verde, as dead as the town. Massive branches littered the ground around the tree's standing corpse.

The early afternoon sun was beginning to lengthen the shadows as Jon made his way through the abandoned town. The farther he walked, the more aware he became of a discomfort in his chest. He hesitated, rubbed his sternum with a frown. It wasn't pain exactly. More an ache. He turned back towards the ridge, and the sensation eased.

Relieved, he turned back towards the center of town. The sensation intensified. He turned and the sensation ebbed then surged, as if he were the needle of some odd compass. Jon closed his eyes, focusing inward, trying to grasp the ache that tugged in his chest. He stopped at the strongest point and took three blind steps forward. The odd sensation increased to a steady pull.

Jon opened his eyes, found himself blinking at a wooden building sagging behind a surviving stretch of warped boardwalk. Half of the double door hung on by the tenacity of a lone rusty hinge. Only faint traces remained of the gaudy lettering and buxom bird that once sprawled across the false front of the building.

"The Speckled Dove," he read aloud, and chuckled. "Someone had a sense of humor."

Jon cried out then and stumbled forward, the pull on his chest increasing, as if to force him where he already wanted to go. The weather-beaten walk creaked and whined beneath his weight as he stepped up to the doorway of the old saloon.

What he saw inside knocked the breath out of him.

Sunlight trickled in streaks through a failing roof, spotlighting fragments of a debris-littered floor, the cracked dusty mirror, overturned chairs, broken tables, a lizard sunning on a fallen beam.

Sunlight poured in the doorway and through windows, casting shadows of opaque lettering across a varnished bar with polished brass. Bright beams played off of the bottles behind the bar, danced in dust motes, tapped the hunched shoulders of the few men who lounged inside.

Past and present, overlaid like some moving double-exposure. The drawing inside his chest was nearing agony, as if something was hooked into to his sternum and trying to yank it straight out through the skin.

The bartender poured another round for a broad-shouldered man in a faded frock coat.

A ghostly woman in a low cut dress and striped stockings stepped into the doorway. Oblivious that she was nose to nose with him, she peered down the street, her hand shielding her eyes.

He might be losing his mind, but this was all so clear. Crazy or sane, the camera would see only what was really here.

He stepped back to the edge of the sidewalk and lifted the camera. The image on the screen was a miniature of the impossible double image before his eyes. He pushed the button.

The camera whirred as it recorded. The lizard scurried down the beam and across the ruined floor into the dusty shadows.

That dark-haired barmaid glanced his way. She smiled at someone who wasn't beside him.

"Hey! Can you see me?" he called to her, lunging towards the doorway.

His sternum felt as if it were being ripped out of his chest. With a yell of pain, Jon fell through the doorway of the saloon. His right knee banged into the floor as he tried to break his fall. His camera bounced across the floor, shedding pieces through the cracks.

He was alone. Nothing stirred but dust.

Jon grabbed his camera, lurched back onto his feet and ran. He didn't slow down till he was halfway up the ridge.

CB

"I saw something weird!" Jon's eyes went huge in his sunburned, dusty face. "A man in a frock coat and a bar-maid and a whole room full of people. Right there in front of me, like I could walk right in and join them!"

Chris was tempted to slap Jon hard across the face. That was supposed to shock someone out of hysteria, wasn't it? He wiped his hand over his own face instead. "Jon, I'm sorry. There's no such thing as ghosts, singular or plural."

"Listen, I wouldn't believe me either if I was you, but I know what I saw." Jon brandished his battered camera in Chris' face. "Better, what this saw!"

Only then did his crazed brother seem to realize the abused condition of the device. "If it's not busted."

"If it's not, I'm gonna buy stock in the damned things because they're indestructible," Chris said.

Jon moved to drop into his desk chair and focused on pulling the memory card out of the camera.

Chris followed him around the desk. He drew a deep breath and breathed it out through his nose. "I know you think I'm being a jerk denying your reality, but Jon, you've slipped your chain here. The stress or something has gotten to you. When did you last get more than a couple hours of sleep?"

"Dunno," Jon inserted the card into his laptop, eyes intent on the screen. "Tuesday before last maybe?"

"That's not funny. I'm worried about you. You dive off the deep end on stuff all the time, all your life, but this time it's edging into certifiable obsession."

"I'm not insane," Jon looked up at him with manic rage glittering in his eyes. "And I'm not obsessed and I'm not seeing things that aren't there, so you can take your touching worry and shove it up your ass."

"Fine. You're completely rational and I'm way out of line. Sure." Chris threw his hands up and backed away. "I'm out of here."

"About friggin' time." Jon turned back to his computer screen.

ᙣ

Chris wasn't far down the hall when the study door slammed behind him. The lock clicked.

He stopped, pulled his cell phone out of his pocket and pulled up Dee's number. His thumb hovered over the Send button.

Chris shook his head and shoved his phone back into his pocket. She was in the first twenty-four of a forty-eight hour shift. There was nothing she could do for Jon that he hadn't already tried. Maybe this flare-up of madness would burn itself out before she got home.

଀

Jon closed the image file and leaned back in his desk chair. He'd done everything he knew how to do to the picture, and it was still ambiguous. Still nothing more than a milky blur of roughly human size and shape.

His memory was in far better focus. She had dark hair, and her dress was deep blue. Her stockings were striped with broad vertical bands of black and white. He couldn't have imagined those, they were too ridiculous.

The memory haunted him. He winced at that internal pun. But there was hardly a better word. She did haunt him, just like Dorin. Neither of them would leave him alone, their mysteries too intriguing to ignore.

Dorin, however, was tangible. Real. Recorded by objective history. This saloon girl was a phantom, but a phantom as real as the scowling man in the tintype.

The sound of the front door opening interrupted his thoughts. Jon closed the image files. A few seconds later, Dee came down the hall and leaned against the doorframe. She looked exhausted, dark circles under her eyes.

"You're up early," she said.

"You're up early," he corrected her, punctuated with a yawn. "I'm up late."

"Come on Jon, not again."

Jon left the desk to put his arms around her. "I'm okay."

"Sure, because sleep deprivation is the cornerstone of perfect health," she rested her head on his shoulder. "And you're limping. What happened to your leg?"

"It's nothing, I'm fine."

119

She lifted her head and frowned at him. "Let me look at it."

"Baby, I'm fine. I bruised my knee, that's all. You've got to be worn out, though. How about we both go to bed and work on our respective sleep debts?" He gave her a smile and a kiss.

Dee nodded with a yawn. "Works for me. So, what did you find out there so exciting it kept you awake all night?"

Jon led her down the hallway, his arm around her waist. He decided not to say anything about the ambiguous photo. She was way too pragmatic to take a ghost sighting seriously.

"Sadly, it was my coursework that kept me up, not some exciting unexpected discovery." He opened their bedroom door.

"That's too bad," Dee said, sounding more tired than interested.

"Yeah, just another day in post-grad paradise. How was your shift?"

"Long. Very long." Dee gave his waist a squeeze then shuffled off to the bathroom and closed the door.

Jon got into bed. When he closed his eyes, he could still see the shadowy image he'd captured with his camera. That photograph could be of anything or nothing to someone who hadn't been there. If he went spouting off about it, Dee and Chris would have justifiable reason to have him committed.

Chris. There was no reason for him to keep hanging around. He and Chris were going to have a come-to-Jesus meeting tomorrow about Chris getting his lazy, meddling ass out of this house.

His thoughts faded into dreams before Dee came to bed.

CHAPTER TWELVE

17 October, 1873
~ Eleven months later ~

As he made his way down the boardwalk, Tom became aware of a growing uneasy sensation in his chest. It wasn't pain, nor even an ache exactly, but more a drawing sensation, an odd tugging. By the time he was halfway down the street, he figured that maybe he was a touch sun-struck.

Tom paused near the open doorway of the saloon. The sight knocked the breath out of him.

Harsh afternoon sunlight poured in the doorway and through the windows, casting shadows across the bar from the opaque lettering on the glass, and setting the mirror behind the bar gleaming and the bottles in front sparkling. Doctor Hackler and few other fellows loafed at their leisure, finishing up their lunches.

The sunlight trickled in streaks through a failing roof to pick out fragments of a debris-littered warped floor, a splintered bar, glittering shards of the broken mirror behind it, leaning tables, overturned chairs.

Reality and ruination, laid one over the other.

Fred passed Doc a beer.

A lizard scurried down a fallen beam.

The drawing inside his chest was nearing pain, as if something was hooked into to his breastbone, trying to yank it straight out through the skin, trying to yank him into the Dove.

Tom staggered one involuntary step towards the threshold, the drawing overpowering.

The bar-whore glanced his way with idle curiosity, unaware she was now a vapor, almost as clear as water.

The newly solid lizard darted across the newly-ruined floor.

Tom all but threw himself backwards, and tread on Lem who'd stepped up just behind.

"Whoa there!" Lem caught his shoulders. "Law, Tom, you look like you seen a ghost. You okay?"

"Yeah, I'm all right," Tom hastily assured him. "Jist took a turn for a second. Reckon it's the sun."

"It's blame near boiled my brains today, and I ain't been out in it much," Lem agreed with a nod. "Let's go on in and get us a cool 'un."

Tom threw a glance over his shoulder at the Dove. Everything inside was just as it always was. His chest felt fine, the unearthly drawing vanished.

He shook his head. "Nah. Thanks all the same, but I reckon I better get on back to work. It'll be shaded in the barn."

"Suit yourself," Lem clapped him on the shoulder and went on in.

Not love, money nor wild horses could have dragged Tom over that threshold. He hurried up the street fast enough to draw a few curious glances.

CHAPTER THIRTEEN

October 20, Present Day
~ Three days later ~

Maybe she had gone about it the wrong way. Maybe starting off with 'Honey, we need to talk' really did make a man's gonads crawl up into his abdominal cavity. Maybe she'd picked a terrible time to broach the subject before. She hadn't exactly been thinking at her most rational capacity that morning.

Dee gave up pushing the remainder of her lunch around on her plate and looked across the table at Jon. Today had been such a good day, nothing special, just the two of them loafing around the house and running errands together, nothing stressful. She hated to shatter their peaceful interlude. But if she didn't talk to him about it soon, he'd figure it out for himself and that would be worse. He was getting that far-away, 'I need to be studying' look in his eyes, too. Tick tock, tick tock. "Honey?"

"Yeah?" he answered.

"Something's come up that you need to know about, and I've been putting off talking to you about it because I'm not sure when would be a good time."

"How about now?" He smiled at her, but it was an uneasy little quirk of his lips. "Nothing too serious, I hope?"

"Pretty serious, yes." She sighed. Might as well blurt it out, like diving into a cold pool. "I'm pregnant."

Jon stared at her, silent. Motionless. For so long that she began to feel sick.

"What the hell, Dee? I thought I didn't have to worry about that."

"No, Jon. *We* knew this could happen." Her fear and nausea gave away to anger. "Once again, you're ignoring a decision we *both* made, and shoving all the responsibility off on me when it goes wrong! We discussed the odds of pregnancy way back when we first got serious, before you even moved in. I told you I couldn't use hormonal birth control and that a diaphragm isn't a sure thing. You're the one who decided you didn't want to use condoms as insurance!"

"If I wanted to wear a rubber every time I screw, I wouldn't be in a committed relationship!"

"Is that all I am to you? A clean fuck?" For a horrible instant, she thought he was going to say yes.

"Of course not. Don't be such a damn drama queen."

"Drama queen? You think I'm being a *drama queen* after what you just said?"

Jon lunged up. Dee expected him to keep going right out the door, but instead he paced back and forth a couple of times before dropping back into his chair. When he spoke, his voice was tight.

"Okay, look, I'm sorry. That crack was out of line. Yes, obviously I should have worn a rubber each and every time. Mea culpa. Can we move past that now?"

All she trusted herself to do by that point was nod.

"You know I don't want a bunch of kids," he went on. "That's something else we talked about when we first got together."

"But I didn't think that meant you never wanted any at all."

"I figured we'd have one or two, someday, maybe. I sure didn't intend to start now. Dee, we can't do this. We're barely scraping by as it is. We can't make it on that pathetic handful of pocket change they throw me at the University, and you won't be able to keep working for long."

"You'll have to drop out of school, at least until I can go back to work."

"No! Damn it, Dee, we're talking graduate school, not community college! I'm almost thirty— I've already taken the risk of waiting two years for you to get your shit together. If I drop out now, I'll never get back in. I'm not going to give up my goals because you can't take a friggin' pill!"

"This baby isn't going to go away, Jon."

"Yes, it can."

"What are you saying?"

He glared at her, white around his lips and nose. "Get an abortion."

Dee felt the blood drain out of her face. Her lips went numb. Her mind went numb.

Jon stared at her with terrible, cold fury on his face, then rose and strode towards the kitchen door.

"Jon?"

He stopped, but didn't speak, didn't turn around.

"Wherever you're going? Don't come back."

He left the room then as if she hadn't spoken at all.

She didn't flinch this time when the front door slammed. She flung his glass against the wall instead. "Drop dead, you cold son of a bitch!"

CF

It was nausea that finally drove her from table. She felt hollow after the purge, distant, as if her mind was operating somewhere a few feet above her body and there was no sensation flowing between. She took a box of garbage bags from under the sink and went to Jon's office.

Moving at random, she raked books off shelves, papers off the couch. When she filled that bag to bursting, she dragged it out to the porch and started on another one. She worked her way around the room, cleansing it of any trace of Jon and his obsession.

She didn't realize she'd been avoiding his desk until there was nothing else to eject. Suddenly exhausted, she dropped into the desk chair. She found herself looking straight into Dorin's disapproving scowl.

She grabbed the tintype in its worn wooden case. "You evil bastard. This is all your fault!"

Dorin went sailing across the room to whack the wall above the couch. The old case broke in half, both pieces falling down behind the sofa. She didn't bother to rout him out. Let him stay buried there with the dust and the dead spiders. The desk chair slammed against the empty bookcases behind as she stood back up. Dee cleared the desk with a sweep of her arm, laptop and all. The contents of the drawers rained in wholesale after.

After that bag was deposited out the front door, Dee started on Jon's half of the bureau in their bedroom. She ignored the doorbell the first time it rang, but decided that she had a bagful and whoever was out there wasn't going to go away by the third ring. Dragging the bag along with her, she opened the door.

A courier stood there, a cardboard box at his feet. "Good afternoon, ma'am. I've got a package for Jonathan Hansen."

"I'm Dee Collins," she told him. "Jon lives here." Putting that in the past tense would only confuse the issue and maybe set her off crying. She didn't want to do that until she could do nothing else for a very long time.

The courier checked his delivery sheet. "Looks like you're authorized. Sign here, please?"

After he left, Dee sat down on the threshold and studied the package. It was from a town in Tennessee she'd never heard of. It was addressed to Jon in a woman's handwriting.

Dee drew her knife out of her pocket and slit the tape. Inside, there was a letter in the same feminine handwriting. She read it, dropped it, and lifted out one of the small books inside. It opened at random, its deteriorated binding falling apart in her hands. She read a few pages before she threw it back in with no regard for its fragility and tossed the letter in on top. She lifted the box, carried it out to her car and put it into the trunk.

☙

By this point, Chris ignored the occasional slammed door. It was the constant slamming today that got on his nerves. He abandoned Marshal Starr to an unintentional cliffhanger and left his room to investigate. He met Dee in the hallway, dragging a bulging trash bag. "Have we generated that much garbage already?"

Dee ignored his reach for the bag. "No."

The look on her face, and the flat, dead tone in her voice sobered him past any joking. "What's going on?"

Her flat aspect ignited into towering rage. "What does it look like? I'm throwing your worthless brother out!"

Chris did grab the bag then, to make sure that she was speaking figuratively. It was heavy, but he could tell it contained clothes, not body parts. "I know you two are having some problems, but I didn't know it's gotten this bad. What happened?"

"It doesn't concern you." Dee snatched the bag back and headed for the living room.

"Yes, it does," he countered. "I know he can be a real dumbass. Come on, Dee, talk to me. At least tell me if I need to go knock some sense back into him."

Dee rounded on him again. "I told him I was pregnant. You know what he said?"

Chris shook his head.

"Get an abortion!"

She made it to the front door, that information shocked him so much. Dee flung the bag out onto the porch to land with a considerable pile. Chris reached out to put his hands on her shoulders when she slammed the door.

"Dee, I can't believe he would say something like that—"

"Are you calling me a liar?" Dee whirled around, fist clenched.

Chris stepped back, not sure she wouldn't throw a punch. "No! God no! What I meant was I'm stunned he'd blurt out something so heartless, but I can't believe he meant it."

Dee's shoulders slumped and any fight she had in her bled right out. "He meant it."

"Dee, sweetheart," he groaned and reached out to her again. This time, she didn't shake off his touch. "Jon's always spouted off extreme bullshit when he's mad. He told me on your birthday he was going to kill me if I didn't leave."

He drew her closer in a tentative hug. "I doubt he was any more serious about what he said to you than what he said to me."

"Does it matter?" Dee put her arms around his waist and laid her head on his shoulder. "It can't be unsaid."

Chris had the feeling she was holding onto him to keep anchored and upright. He stroked her back. "It can be apologized for. Made up for. Forgiven and forgotten. They were only words, sweetheart."

"Words scar, Chris," she whispered. "And it had to be in his heart for it to come out his mouth."

"Come here, sweetheart. Sit down." Chris walked them over to the couch and kept his arm around Dee's shoulders as she dropped down beside him. "Look, there's another person we have to consider here."

"Yeah? Who?" Dee frowned. "You?"

"The baby. If there's any possible way you and Jon can get past this, don't you think you owe it to your kid to try and give him two parents who can stand to be in the same room together?"

Dee's hands curved protectively over her belly. Her face crumpled. "It hurt so bad, Chris. You can't know how bad it hurt!"

"I'm so sorry, sweetheart," he crooned as she began to cry. There was nothing else to do then but hold her while she sobbed. His brother had always envied his life, but Jon threw away something today, with three thoughtless words, that Chris had long before given up hope of ever having.

As Dee soaked the shoulder of his shirt, Chris was sorely tempted to let his fool brother bumble on his pathetic, deluded way. Maybe Dee and this baby both would be better off if for once he really did engineer a Hansen upgrade

CHAPTER FOURTEEN

20 October, 1873
~ Three days later ~

"Come on, gal. Time for your constitutional."

Sukie squealed and rushed the rope that formed the stall-gate, tossing her head.

"Oh, yeah, you're fierce," Tom murmured as the mare proved her hurry was that of eagerness rather than viciousness. She pressed her forehead against his chest, her breath hot and grass-sweet, blowing right through his shirt.

Tom scratched the hollow between her jaws and smoothed his hand over her neck, laying stray strands of mane back onto her near side. "I ain't been payin' enough attention to you lately, huh?" he crooned.

Lem chuckled from across the stable aisle. "You pay more attention to that horse than I do to my wife."

"I reckon that says more of your faults than mine," Tom said.

"Maybe so," Lem agreed with good humor, then leaned on his manure fork and watched as Sukie stepped out of the stall, free, moving along at Tom's side like a well-trained dog at heel. "How do you get her to bow? I tried askin' every way in the world and she just snorts and turns her tail towards me."

"That's 'cause she only curtsies to gentlemen," Tom informed him seriously.

A horse apple bounced off his shoulder. Thoughtfully, a drier one.

"Sukie, mind your manners and say howdy to Lem."

The mare bent a foreleg, crouching down, her neck tightly curved alongside her straight front leg, for all the world as close to a curtsy or a bow as a horse could manage.

"You two orta be in Barnum's Museum," Lem grinned. "I still couldn't see how you signaled her."

"That's 'cause critters watch us a whole lot closer than we watch them," Tom answered. "Come on, Sukie, we're burnin' daylight."

He lifted her hackamore off the peg as he passed the tack-stall. He could ride her now with sewing thread for reins, or none at all, but it made other folks nervous. He slipped the headstall over her ears, carefully lifting her forelock from under the strap then smoothed the hair on her muzzle under the bosal.

He leaned his cane against the stable wall and swung himself up onto her bare back. "Let's go, baby-girl," he murmured for her ears alone.

They ambled out of town, past the houses, the loop of her mecate rein hanging in a loose arc.

It hadn't taken long after their first acquaintance for Tom to discern that she liked the noise of a curb chain, though she needed no bit at all. To please her, he'd attached jingle-bobs to the mecate's tassel and popper.

Vain as a young maid with a fancy new dress, Sukie shook her head to make them ring and arched her neck, prancing down the street as if she were on parade.

When the road began to fade back to wilderness, he tightened his thighs.

"Take off," he commanded, and the little mare squealed again, giving one twisting crow-hop out of sheer joy and beans, before she straightened out in a full gallop.

Tom let out a whoop and bent down, his cheek nearly against her neck, urging her on. She wasn't as fast as most— she couldn't be, small as she was— but she purely loved to run and being atop her when she cut loose felt as close to flying as he would ever come.

When she started to slow, her shoulders breaking out in foamy sweat, he pressed a knee against her barrel. Obediently, she began a wide turn, still at a gallop.

The sudden whir of the snake's rattles undid them both. Sukie screamed, trying to shy away and rear all at the same time. She went over backwards, crushing Tom beneath as she fell.

The thud was sickening as they hit the sand. Tom saw stars, felt an awful pressure for an instant, as Sukie rolled off him onto her side and then onto her belly. She struggled to stand, her legs tangling with themselves.

Wheezing, his breath and his senses nearly knocked clean gone, Tom gasped, "Whoa! Sukie, WHOA!" but the frightened little mare disobeyed him for once.

She thrashed, made it upright, stepped in a hole and fell again. This time there was an ominous snap, like the sound of a green branch breaking.

Sukie squealed and limped a single stride forward, holding one foreleg off the ground, horribly distorted at the cannon.

"Oh baby," Tom groaned. "Stand now. Whoa." His own limp intensified by their fall, he came towards her slowly, his hands out to her.

She stood, breathing hard, hide shuddering all down her back, making low, groaning little pain-noises as she breathed. Noises that sounded very human.

She stretched out her head towards him and he kissed her between the eyes, then ran his hands down her neck, to her shoulder and on down the injured leg to the knee. Sukie let out a sharp whinny that sounded for all the world like a woman's scream of agony, but she neither struck out nor snapped at him.

Instead, she dropped her nose into his hair, breathing against his scalp as he stared down at the twisted leg in horror. There was no doubt. No hope. A bloody-white point of bone pierced her glossy black foreleg.

"Sukie..." he groaned, easing her shattered leg back down. He straightened and she pressed against him again, burying her head under one arm. With every breath, she groaned.

"I'm sorry, baby-girl. I'm so sorry," he whispered, and drew his pistol. The two steps back he took from her felt like miles.

She stretched her neck towards him again, made to move but drew up short. She whinnied again, a low, pitiful, pleading sound.

Tom gritted his teeth, narrowed his eyes. Pulled back the hammer. He stepped forward, flung an arm around her muzzle in one last desperate, violent embrace, jammed the end of the barrel right up against her forehead between her eyes and pulled the trigger.

The report deafened him. Blowback spattered his face and hands with a hot mist. Sukie dropped in her tracks, flinging blood and brains in thick ropes across the sand as she writhed in her death-throes.

Tom watched, gun hanging forgotten at his side. When she stilled, turned and staggered back towards town. His mouth was set in a tight line, a muscle jerking in his cheek. His eyes were dry.

"Tom— what happened to Sukie?" Lem rushed out of the stable as Tom grabbed his cane from where he'd left it behind.

"Stepped in a gopher hole."

Lem shook his head, giving a sympathetic click of his tongue. "Now that's a damned cryin' shame. I'm sorry, Tom. I know how much store you set by that little mare."

Tom didn't answer, didn't seem to hear as he passed Lem. He got a coin out of his pocket, lifted his saddle off the rack, balancing it against his good side. He laid the coin on the cross-piece, and left the stable, heading for the boarding house.

"A damned dirty shame," Lem muttered to himself as he retrieved the coin. He'd be on the lookout for a new mount for Dorin, next time the drover came through. It was little enough to do, but all there was.

"Evenin' Mr. Dorin!" Harold called from his perch on the boardinghouse gate. "You missed supper!"

Tom passed through the gate and by the boy as if neither existed.

Harold's eyes widened as he took in Tom's burden and the dried blood on his face and clothes, and he darted inside the boarding house ahead of Tom. "Mr. Dorin's cartin' his saddle and got blood on 'im!"

The boy's excited announcement was almost lost in the ringing in Tom's ears. Almost.

"Mr. Dorin, have you had an accident?" Hattie rushed to meet him in the front hall. It was only when she reached out and gave his sleeve a little tug that he came back to himself and realized she was by his side.

"Yes'm," he managed, his tongue wooden in a mouth as dry as the dust on his boots.

"Are you hurt?"

He swallowed. "Jist banged up some, ma'am."

Hattie frowned slightly as she took in his battered demeanor. "I'll bring you up a bite of supper."

There was an unusual lag between hearing her words and getting the sense out of them, between his thoughts and speech.

"I thank you," he said, "But don't trouble yourself with the food. It's most kind, but I ain't hungry. Beggin' your pardon, Miz Perkins."

He turned and started up the stairs. He knew it was inexcusably rude to walk off before she dismissed him, but he couldn't bring himself to care. That hateful staircase seemed a mile long, and every step a yard high.

Tom's bad leg was buckling on every step by the time he reached his room. The saddle he flung into the corner. He hobbled towards the washstand, yanking his shirt off as he went, sending buttons skipping across the floor.

He poured water into the bowl and scrubbed his face and hands. When he lifted his head, he met his own eyes in the mirror.

Hollowed. Empty.

The gaze of a corpse.

Tom lifted the mirror off the wall, folded it almost at the expense of the glass, and shoved it into the drawer.

ᘓ

The sun's last rays had long since disappeared below the horizon when a heavy tread sounded in the hall.

"Tom?" a man called, tapping on his door.

He looked over at the door, scarcely moving his head. He didn't stir from the bed, his throbbing leg stretched out straight, cradled on his rolled up quilt. "Come in."

His door opened, and the light from the hallway lamp revealed the silhouette of a very tall, broad-shouldered man.

"Evenin', Doc. What brings you by this time of night?"

"Good evenin', Tom," he said as he stepped inside. "Mrs. Perkins told me you were thrown from your horse, and asked me to make certain you weren't seriously injured."

Tom noticed that the doctor stepped out of the lamplight spilling in from outside, so that it fell across him but left the doctor still in shadow.

"I'm all right," he answered. "Jist banged up some."

"I'd like to confirm that," the doctor replied. "If only to set Mrs. Perkin's mind at ease." He gestured towards the unlit lamp on the table beside Tom's bed. "May I?"

"Suit yerself."

Hackler took the matches lying beside the lamp and struck one. He lit and adjusted the wick, then replaced the lamp chimney. Tom squinted against the light.

"Is it uncomfortable for your eyes?"

"Nah, jist laid in the dark too long, I reckon."

"Where are you hurting?"

Tom gave a soft chuff. "It'd be quicker to tell you where I ain't."

"What happened?"

"Sukie shied from a rattler and reared over backwards. I wound up underneath her for a few seconds."

Doctor Hackler grimaced, a formidable expression considering his beetling eyebrows and walrus mustache.

"Mrs. Perkins was prudent to send for me. You should have, you stubborn mule. Will you undress so I can examine you?"

"Sure, Doc." Tom sat up, biting back a groan. Felt like every muscle he owned from the neck down had settled in stiff while he was lying there. When he got his undershirt off, with discreet assistance from Hackler, he realized he was bruised almost black from the chest down.

Hackler checked him out as thoroughly as a new plow horse, right down to running his hands along each leg to test for soundness. Which was a virtue he only half-had, on the best of days. It was no surprise that

Hackler spent more time probing around the scar and misshapen lump of his right thigh.

"Minie ball?" Hackler murmured, his expression blank but intent with concentration, as if sight had been transferred to his fingertips.

Tom's answer was superseded by a soft grunt as the doctor's fingers explored an especially tender point where the mended bone kinked over towards the outside.

"Yeah. And if it hadn't healed with that bow to the outside, I'd never been able to sit a horse again. Reckon I'm so damn lucky I orta set up a standin' poker game down at the saloon."

"The fact that you still have both your legs, and your life, is proof enough that you're an exceedingly lucky man." Hackler straightened. "The fact that you also had a horse fall on you without receiving a grave injury— well, my friend, you might want to give serious consideration to that gambling career."

Tom got dressed again, this time with more overt assistance from the doctor.

"Have you taken a piss since the fall?" Hackler asked.

"Yeah. Why?"

"Any blood in it?"

"Not that I could see."

"Good." Hackler settled the sheet back over Tom, then stood at his ease, hands shoved into his coat pockets.

"Tom, as far as I can determine, you've got no broken bones or internal injuries. My professional opinion, however, is that you're likely sorer than a ripe boil from one end to the other."

"And you had to go to doctorin' school to learn that?"

"The first lesson," Hackler solemnly informed him, though the corners of his mustache quirked up. "Do you have something you take regularly for pain?"

Tom nodded. "Laudanum."

"How much?"

Tom gave a supine shrug. "Ten or fifteen drops in the mornin' to loosen ever'thing up. Sometimes six or ten round dinner, depending. Thirty, thirty-five or so in the evenin', right before I go to bed."

"You've been following that routine since you were wounded?"

"Yep, pretty much. Took more back then, but I've slacked off some over the years."

"Have you taken your usual evening dose?"

"Nah," Tom shook his head. "Once I laid down, I didn't want to get back up. It's over there on the wash-stand."

The doctor moved away to pick up the small bottle, and filled Tom's cup with water from the pitcher. He measured out a dose, stronger than Tom's usual.

Tom knocked it back like a shot of whiskey. Even after all this time, the acrid, musty flavor tightened his lips against his teeth.

Hackler refilled his cup with fresh water and set it close to hand on the lamp table.

"Rest well, Tom. I'll be by tomorrow around noon to check on you."

"No need," Tom said. "I'll be fine, what with that outstandin' good luck of mine and all."

Doctor Hackler gave a short, low little chuckle, blew out the lamp and left the room.

Tom dropped his arm over his eyes. He felt anything but lucky and about a hundred years old, and not only because of his badly bruised body. At least, Doc's whopping slug of laudanum did its job. Tom slid under the surface of a deep, drugged sleep before the parlor clock struck another hour.

CHAPTER FIFTEEN

October 20, Present Day
~ Several hours later ~

He had nowhere to go. He had nowhere to come back to, either. When Dee's soft, cold statement of finality shoved him out the door, Jon got in his car and drove. He must have traveled every street in Tucson and surrounding. No reason, no destination, just circling. Lost.

As the sun set, Jon was far out into the desert, alone on a stretch of empty highway. Without the distraction of Tucson traffic, he had no choice but to deal with his thoughts. Jon stared out the windshield at nothing as the sky darkened to night. He had no future. No home. No lover. No child.

The last thought froze him. What if she did what he'd told her to? What if it was already too late? He made a squealing U-turn. He called Dee. She'd blocked his number. He tried Chris, but got only his brother's voicemail.

He pulled into the driveway fast and braked hard. The garbage bags huddled on the porch he ignored. He'd deal with what was in them later. Jon reached for his keys and grimaced. He'd left his house keys lying on the foyer table. In the heat of the moment, he'd taken Dee at her word. God, please don't let her have taken him at his! He pounded on the door.

Chris opened it. "You really blew it this time, shithead. I'm not letting you in."

Jon was too wrung-out to muster any anger towards his brother. "I have to talk to Dee."

"She's not here. After she threw your sorry ass out, she got a call to fill in a shift."

Relief hit so hard, Jon grabbed onto the door facing. If she was at work, she couldn't.... "I've got to talk to her, try to work this out. We said things we didn't mean."

"You sure? Dee thinks before she goes nuclear."

"We were so upset we didn't know what we were saying. I've got to try to make this right."

Chris stepped aside. "Good luck with that."

Jon moved past him and went straight to their bedroom. He closed the door and called the station. The woman who answered told him that Dee was out on a call. No, he couldn't wait there for her to come back. Yes, she would at least let Dee know he called.

Pacing helped him work through what he would say to her. Pacing also burned off his adrenaline dump. Jon lay down on the bed, more profoundly tired than he had ever been. He was so tired that he didn't wake when his phone began to ring in his pocket a couple of hours later.

October 21, Present Day
~ The next morning ~

Jon's Jeep sat slewed across the driveway, blocking the garage door.

"I don't believe this!" Dee stomped into the house, furious. She went straight through to the hallway. The door to Jon's study stood open, so at least he wasn't holed up in there again. Chris' snores carried through his bedroom door. She'd deal with him later.

Dee shoved open her bedroom door, letting it slam against the wall. "How DARE you come back here and crawl into bed as if nothing happened? You self-centered obnoxious overbearing patronizing ASS-hole! Get out! Get out of my bed RIGHT NOW!"

Jon rolled his head towards her, groggy and disheveled. "Lady, you got the wrong room," he slurred. "Hush up and go on before you wake up the whole house."

"Are you friggin' drunk?" Dee snapped, and hit the light switch.

Jon clapped a hand over his eyes. "Blow it out!"

"Shit, you dumbass, you are drunk." She went to the bed and jerked his hand down.

Big blue eyes, with pupils constricted to black pin-dots, rolled up to look at her. "Ain't neither. Go 'way and let me sleep, you crazed shrew."

Dee flung his wrist back at him. "I don't believe this! You're high as a damn kite! What did you take? Jon, you answer me and don't you dare lie!"

"Ain't none of your never mind." Jon listlessly shoved back the comforter and moved with a low groan, swinging his legs to the side of the bed as if he were stiff as a board.

That was when the smell hit her. Dee backed up, feeling a surge of nausea rise up as she clamped her hand over her nose. "Good lord, Jon!"

He was wearing long underwear, stained under the arms and saggy in the crotch. They had to be where that ungodly stench of stale sweat was coming from. He hadn't had time to build up that much pong since yesterday. "What have you done? Rolled a wino for his clothes?"

Jon didn't seem to register what she said. His head was swinging back and forth, taking in the room with a growing expression of confusion. "Where am I? What is this place?"

His disoriented, glassy gaze met hers then. "Who're you?"

Cold fear supplanted the nausea. "Fuck. Fuck!" Dee grabbed his wrist again, this time to take his pulse. It was slower than it should be. "Jon, listen to me. Focus! What have you taken? Vicodin? Oxy? What?"

He looked at her as if he not only didn't know who she was, but wasn't quite sure what she was.

"Nah," he finally answered, and gave a languid wave of his free hand. "Jist some laudanum, that's all."

Dee thought by this point she'd heard everything possible from the drugged, drunk, disturbed and otherwise impaired. But this confession floored her.

"Laudanum?" she echoed, "Jon, where on earth did you get that? Why would you take it?"

"Why do you keep callin' me John?"

"You stay right here." Dee planted both hands on his shoulders and pushed down for emphasis. "Don't you move!"

All she got in answer was a few slow blinks. Jon's head dropped onto his chest and he collapsed back onto the mattress.

Dee wheeled and went back down the hall to beat on Chris' door.

He jerked it open, not looking much more oriented than Jon, with his hair on end and wearing nothing but his boxers. "What? What? Is the house on fire?"

"No but I may set your dipshit brother aflame! I came home to find him back in my bed, hopped up to the gills on laudanum!"

"Jon? Take drugs? No way."

"I know opiate intoxication when I see it, you fool! Get in there and make sure he keeps breathing."

Dee grabbed Chris, shoved him in the general direction of her bedroom, then ran for her car. She flung open the trunk and unzipped her tech bag. Another two seconds, and she backed out with a small case in her hand. She slammed the trunk closed and ran back into the house.

As she rushed in, the frantic edge left her movements. She unzipped the case as she came back into the bedroom.

Chris was sitting on the bed beside Jon, gingerly supporting him in a somewhat upright position. Jon sagged against his brother as if he were boneless, nodding in and out of consciousness.

"Dee, he doesn't know me!" Chris' voice was at least half an octave higher than normal.

"Don't worry, he will soon," she said, pulling med shears out of their sheath at her hip. The sharp serrated blades sliced through the neck and down the sleeve of Jon's underwear with professional precision.

"What the hell?" Chris blurted, staring at his brother's battered body.

The massive bruising shocked her too. "He'll be able to explain himself soon." She drew up a syringe, wrapped a band around Jon's upper arm, felt for a vein.

Jon didn't seem to notice the procedure, not even when Dee slipped the needle under his skin and injected two ccs of Narcan.

The effect of the drug was always a mundane miracle. Within twenty seconds, Jon jerked his head upright with a sharp gasp and pulled away from Chris' loose embrace. He blinked eyes now lucid, their pupils dilated to a normal size.

"Welcome back," Chris told him.

Dee didn't feel quite so charitable, but she kept her professional façade in place. She crouched to put herself on his eye-level. "Jon—what happened? How did you get hurt?"

"M'horse fell on me," he muttered, then frowned. "Who are you? Why do y'all keep callin' me John?"

Dee's heart sank again. "Jon—" She reached out to lay a hand on his thigh.

He knocked it away before it made contact and lurched to his feet. He was unsteady, but coordinated once more.

"Don't you be touchin' me like that, woman!"

Jon's furious glare took in her, Chris and then the room as a whole. "I don't know who y'all are or why you brung me here but I want some answers and I want 'em now!"

"Calm down Jon," Chris began, moving to intercept his deranged brother if he lunged at Dee.

"STOP callin' me John! M' name's Tom! Tom Dorin!"

Dee slapped him. It wasn't until Jon's head rocked on his neck that she even realized she'd lashed out. Despite his confusion, despite the fact she may have aggravated a head injury— in that furious instant, she didn't care.

Jon didn't react other than to take a few lurching steps towards the open bedroom door.

Dee hurried to put herself in front of it. "No. You're not going anywhere now."

"9-1-1?" Chris asked, his voice low.

"Yes," Dee answered, her concern still tempered with fury. He was standing with his right leg on tip-toe at an awkward angle. "What's wrong with your leg, Jon?"

"I'm Tom," he snapped. "Step aside and let me pass."

"Hell no. Drop trous. I want to look at that leg."

Jon stared at her with venom she'd never before seen in his eyes.

Chris watched, phone to his ear, his answers to the dispatcher quiet, almost furtive.

"Drop your drawers or I'll knock you on your scrawny ass and cut 'em off." Dee pulled her shears back out and brandished them in his direction.

"Fine, you nasty bull-bitch!" Jon fired back. With angry movements he jerked the ruined long-johns off his shoulder and shucked them down to droop around his ankles.

Dee's vision grayed around the edges. "Chris—" The word came out a breathy wheeze. "Chris! Cancel the call."

"What?" he looked at her, confused, then glanced over at his brother. His jaw literally sagged.

"Uh… uh…," he stammered into the phone. "Sorry, you can cancel the ambulance. No, no… he's perfectly okay. He's mentally handicapped, but not physically ill. His idea of a practical joke, apparently. No, no danger to himself or others. Yes, ma'am. Yes, ma'am, I'm aware of how serious this is. Trust me, he's not going to do it again. Yes ma'am. Again, I sincerely apologize for the false alarm."

The whole time Chris spoke, Dee stared at the stranger's maimed leg. The massive scar was white with age and the thigh misshapen, making the entire leg almost two inches shorter than the left. There was no way Jon could have acquired and recovered from such a massive injury in the span of twenty-four hours. There was no easy way to fake this.

"You looked your fill?" the intruder snapped, his hands cupped over his genitals.

"Where is Jon?"

"Woman, I don't know who John is." The man struggled to pull up his long underwear, and keep himself covered and upright, at the same time.

"You're in his bedroom, dumbass. Try again!"

Chris moved behind her. Dee heard the bedside table open, heard the click of Jon's antique Colt being cocked.

The stranger heard it too. His eyes swung to Chris and stayed there. His underwear hanging on by one shoulder, the man put his hands up.

"I cain't tell you no diff'rent, ma'am, for it's the truth. I went to sleep in my own bed, down at the boardin' house. I don't know how I come to be here, I don't know where I am. I don't know you, and I don't know your John."

"At least tell us your real name," Chris interjected. He moved to stand beside Dee, the pistol trained on the stranger's chest. His hand didn't shake. "That way we'll get it right for the police report when I shoot your stinkin' ass for attempted rape."

The stranger's face went as gray-white as his long-johns. "I wouldn't never—!"

"Your name!"

"Thomas Anderson Dorin!" he said, desperation or maybe panic in his voice. "I swear to God that's my name and I never meant no harm to this woman or any other!"

"Yeah right," Dee snorted. She moved to get the phone. 9-1-1 was going to get another call. This one to the police. Angry spite prompted one last challenge.

"If you're Dorin, you tell me who kept you from having your leg amputated."

"Private Carol Lynd, Company F, 19th Tennessee Volunteer Infantry, C.S.A., twenty-fifth of November, 1863. After the battle of Missionary Ridge," the man answered with not a second's hesitation. "Carl got me away from the surgeons and bound up m' leg with pages outta his Bible."

"Holy Mary Mother of God…" Dee's lips went numb, the phone slid from her hand to clatter across the floor.

"Dee? Dee, what is it?" Chris reached out to touch her, clearly torn between keeping the pistol trained on their intruder and concern for her.

Dee made it to the bed and plopped down onto the side, feeling as if all the air had been sucked out of her lungs. "Nobody could know that. Nobody."

"What are you talking about?" Chris had decided on keeping Dorin under the gun.

Dorin stood stock still, hands spread palms out at shoulder level.

"Yesterday, right before I got called in," she said, "a package was delivered for Jon. I opened it. It was old diaries and letters. Carol Lynd's family had saved them, and they'd been up in the attic of the family home ever since. His diary entry telling about Dorin's wounding was the one thing I happened to read. I put the box in the trunk of the car. I was going to throw it in the dumpster at the station."

She looked from Chris back to the stranger with her lover's face. Her rival.

"That book probably hadn't been opened in a century. It fell apart in my hands. There's no way Jon could have known what it said. The detail about Dorin's wound being dressed with pages from a Bible wasn't in the official medical record Jon found. He would have woke me up out of a coma to tell me about something like that if he'd found it. Jon couldn't have known it. Nobody could."

"Nobody but the man it happened to," Tom offered softly.

The other man's aim wavered. The gun dropped till it was hanging at his side.

Tom eased his hands down real slow. "Ma'am, I still cain't tell you where your John is, nor how I got here, but I swear I don't mean you no harm. Let me go and I won't be troublin' you no more."

She rose and strode up to him again, tall enough to look him dead-straight on in the eyes. "What year is it, Dorin?"

The question startled him. She seemed mad as the devil and a right mean bull-bitch, but not crazy. "1873, Ma'am. Date's the twenty-first of October."

"Come on, Dee. Antique journal or not, you can't believe there's really a hundred-forty-something year old man in your bedroom." The other man studied him with narrowed eyes.

"For what it matters, I'm twenty-eight," Tom said.

They both ignored that.

"What other explanation could there be?" she asked.

"I don't know. Sick joke? Revenge? Some elaborate con?" Chris said.

Dee moved closer to him instead of answering Chris. Her hard expression softened some. "I need to touch your lame leg. Please, I need to do this. Do you understand?"

He didn't, but he did believe the conviction in her voice. Tom nodded. "Satisfy yourself, then."

She went down on one knee in front of him. Tom looked over her bowed head to lock suspicious gazes with Chris.

Dee ran her hands over his ruined leg from the crease of his groin down to his knee. Her prodding of every inch of flesh was as methodical as Doc's, and darn near as powerful as she dug her long fingers right through cloth and muscle to trace out the bone. He tried not to flinch, but whatever she'd done to him earlier had washed away the laudanum's numbing entirely.

She lifted her head and looked at Chris, her face as pale as cold ashes.

"This is no special effect. His femur's twisted and misaligned. Nobody with such a terrible fracture would be allowed to heal like this. Nobody in this century."

"Or at least, in this country," Chris countered, then blew out a long sigh and raked his free hand through his tousled hair.

"Okay," he said, "For the sake of argument, I'll go along with this guy being the genuine article from eighteenwhenthehellever. That leaves us with at least three huge problems. First, where's Jon? Second, how do we get him back? And third, what do we do with this convicted murderer in the meantime?"

The Colt was trained straight at his chest again. Tom's hands eased back up. "I ain't never stood trial for nothin'!"

"They hanged you," Chris snapped back. "So guess what?"

"Nobody hangs for killin' the enemy on the battlefield in war. That ain't murder," Tom answered, eyes narrowing. "Them's the only men I ever killed."

"What about women?" Dee asked, her voice harsh and steady.

Tom felt all the blood run out of his face, and knew with sick certainty that uncontrollable reaction had just bought him a six foot hole.

"You filthy bastard," Chris gritted. "So much for friggin' Southern chivalry!"

145

"It weren't like that," Tom whispered. He kept his eyes on Chris', expecting to feel the slam of a bullet into his chest between one heartbeat and the next.

"Then how was it?" Dee demanded. "God! I can't believe Jon threw everything away for a piece of shit like you!"

"Shoot me if you're gonna, but I didn't kill that poor woman out of malice," Tom said softly. He had never spoken before of his shameful, cowardly deed. Never once thought he would be forced to, before Judgement Day.

He looked from one to the other and knew this was likely his earthly day of judgement.

He drew a deep breath.

"I was out foragin', near Chattanooga, Tennessee. It was July, and I spied a patch of sweet corn hid away..."

He told it all, just as it happened, looking them in the eyes. Even so, it wasn't fear of death that shook his voice there at the end. "I ran and I never said nothin' to nobody. I left her layin' dead in that cornfield like a stray dog, because I'm a filthy coward."

"They hung you for that?" Dee said.

Tom shook his head. "I ain't yet been tried nor hanged for anything, so I cain't answer. All I can say is that off the battlefield, that poor woman's the only person I ever harmed in my life."

"You believe this bullshit?" Chris snapped to Dee.

"I'm lied to every day. He's not lying."

"If I shoot him, it won't matter either way. I'd rather have a harmless corpse and a hell of a carpet-cleaning issue to deal with than a confessed murderer running loose in your house."

"What if," Tom kept his voice steady and low, "When you kill me, you kill your John along with me? Seems to me we're tied together, me and him. Destroy one, maybe the other goes too."

The Colt wavered, but it didn't lower.

Dee laid her palm on Chris' shoulder. "He could be right. We can't risk it."

The Colt lowered to Chris' side. "If you even look at her wrong, Dorin, I'll blow your brains all over the wall."

"If I ever hurt this woman, I'll lay m' head against the muzzle so you cain't miss." Tom lowered his hands.

"Gee guys, thanks. That's reassuring." Dee went back to sit on the edge of the bed. Her britches-clad knees were spread wide, elbows propped on her thighs, head in her hands. "Jon's car is outside. When did he come home?"

"Around eight," Chris said.

"He left his house keys when I kicked him out. I didn't think he had another set." Dee's voice was muffled by her hands.

"He doesn't, not as far as I know. I let him in." Chris sounded a touch guilty then.

Tom eased back to lean against the wall while they talked. He paid them half-attention as the sheer strangeness of the room he was in began to dawn on him.

"What did he say?" Dee asked Chris.

"Not much, only that he'd done a lot of thinking and he wanted to talk to you again. And Dee, he wasn't high. He hadn't been drinking either. He said less than ten words to me then came in here to wait for you to come home."

"He could have left after you went to bed," she said.

Chris shook his head. "Both doors are deadbolts. He couldn't have locked them as he went out, and I know he didn't get my keys."

"I suppose he could have climbed out a window," Dee mumbled, her voice muffled by her palms. "But why? And how did Dorin get here?"

"Hey," Tom interrupted. "I got somethin' to say about this."

Chris looked his way again. Dee lifted her head.

"First of all, tell me, is this Cooper's Creek?"

"No," Chris said. "That's about thirty miles southwest. We're in Tucson."

"And, from lookin' about here," Tom gestured to include the entire bizarre room with a hand that trembled in spite of himself, "I'm guessin' it ain't 1873 no more, neither."

"Not even close. You're in the twenty-first century now," Dee said.

"Oh my lord!" Tom felt as if the earth itself dropped away from under his feet. It was his turn now to drop his face in his hands till he could get his emotions reined back in.

"And thus?" Chris prompted, his voice harsh and impatient.

Tom drew in a long shaky breath and let it out slow. When he trusted himself to speak, he lifted his head.

"I took to m' bed in Cooper's Creek about three in the afternoon on the twentieth of October, 1873, and as far as I can know, I stayed there all night. I woke up here, when you came in cussin,' ma'am. So, I'm figurin' your John went to sleep here in Tucson, somewhere 'round eight in the evenin', in this time, and he'll wake up in 1873 in my bed, whenever Miz Perkins sees fit to roust him out."

"But why?" Dee's expression was equal parts frustration, fear and anger.

"Beggin' your pardon, ma'am, but it plumb beats the hell outta me!"

Chris cocked his head. "So, if we can reverse the dislocation in space, maybe the dislocation in time will reverse as well."

"That's what I'm thinkin'," Tom nodded.

"Clothes. If we're going to be hiking, we both need clothes." Chris sounded a touch rattled, almost for the first time.

Tom was relieved to see that Colt get laid on the bedside table before Chris opened one of the smaller doors in the room.

"None of Jon's are left in there," Dee said, voice low and dull.

Chris shot her a pitying look, then nodded. "Come on, Hopalong. You can wear some of mine."

Tom scowled at the slur, but he wasn't in much position to demand any courtesy from these two. He followed after the man, his lame leg threatening to give out from the beating it had taken over the past day.

Chris went through a door a little way down the hall, into another bedroom. He opened a side door that revealed a closet. He yanked a pair of britches and a shirt off shoulder-shaped wooden hooks and flung them back over his shoulder, almost without looking.

"If your feet aren't the same size, well, tough crap and you're welcome for the blisters." He tossed socks and a pair of suede leather, heavy brogan boots at Tom's feet.

Really at his feet. Tom had to skip back, his shortened leg almost making him fall. His lips tight, he laid the borrowed clothes onto the chest of drawers and shed his ruined underwear. The dungarees were dangerously loose on his hips, the shirt just as big. Tom wasn't inclined to complain as he tucked the thin cotton into the faded, worn britches and figured out the weird interlocking hooks and sliding piece that closed the fly. He truly needed a belt, but he'd throttle himself with one before he asked for more charity from this man.

Tom sat down on the padded bench at the foot of the bed to pull on the socks and boots. They fit better than the clothes, considering, but if he had to walk very far without a built-up sole, blisters would be the least of his tribulations.

Chris pulled on his own clothes as if Tom weren't in the room. Neither of them felt the need to converse further. Dee walked right into the room without so much as a knock or a hale. She shoved a pair of crutches at him, recognizable by their shape, bizarre in their manufacture.

"Here. You'll need these."

"Thank you," he murmured. He tried them under his arms. They fit as if they had been made to measure. The relief they gave him wasn't complete, but it was no less welcome. He leaned on the soft, odd padding and waited to see what this strange pair would do next.

ଔ

As soon as they stepped outside, if Tom hadn't been convinced he was no longer when he should be, the very air would have persuaded him. It carried an oily taint he'd never encountered before. Dee's house was a not entirely unfamiliar adobe, but the hard-surfaced street and the house across the way were outside of his realm of experience.

So was the shiny, mud-colored carriage that they approached. There were no shafts on the thing, its wheels were solid and black and the boot was in the front. He hesitated, expecting one of them to open the wide stable door and bring out the horses and harness. Instead, Dee tossed Chris a metallic handful and said "You drive. I don't know where it is."

Chris went to the *left* side and got in.

Dee opened the right hand door and made an impatient gesture. "Well, get in!"

Tom went around to see that she'd folded a front seat up. He ducked into the back one and settled himself and the crutches with a grunt. She flopped the front seat back against his knees, got in and slammed the door—the thing was made of metal, not wood, he realized.

Before that had time to sink in, though, the carriage gave a roaring noise like he'd never heard and began to roll backwards. By itself. On flat ground. He shoved down the rise of superstitious fear. It was only a machine, a strange locomotive that ran without tracks. This, he could understand.

Within five minutes, the thing was moving faster than any train he'd ever been on. That would have been disconcerting enough, but the speed seemed to have an effect on his innards that was as novel as it was unwelcome.

"Y'all," he finally said, keeping his teeth close together as he could and still speak. "Y'all— I'm gittin' purty colicky."

Dee twisted around to look at him and he saw Chris' eyes catch his in the little mirror that hung on the big glass windscreen.

"Oh bleepin' marvelous," Chris groaned. "The Marlboro Man gets carsick!"

"If he goes off, Chris, so help me I'll kick your butt if you puke too," Dee told him as she snatched up the brightly colored little pail between their seats. She shoved it at Tom. "If you hurl, try to hit this."

"I can't help it, it's an autonomic sympathetic reaction," Chris whined as he pulled to the side of the road. Mercifully, the vehicle came to a sudden halt.

"Not in my car it isn't," Dee snapped. She got out and jerked the door open that Tom was pushing on. He half-fell, half-scrambled out and hurried a few strides away, his back to them both. He didn't heave, but it was a near thing. He broke out in a cold sweat, panting, and spat a few times before his guts settled back down.

"Better?" Dee asked. She handed him a clear bottle of what he hoped was water.

He took a cautious sip. It was water. It had a queer whang to it that wasn't entirely pleasant, but not bad enough to set his touchy innards off again. He'd had worse. Much worse.

"I believe so, ma'am. Thank you." He offered the bottle back.

"Keep it," Dee said, and stomped back the vehicle. This time she gestured toward the front seat. "Sit up here, it'll help. Look out the windshield, not the side window and for pete's sake, whatever you do, keep your eyes open."

"Yes'm," he agreed miserably.

She squeezed into the back seat behind Chris and closed the door, nearly catching Tom's elbow. Chris reached across Tom and grabbed a webbing belt, pulling it across his chest and lap.

"Don't bitch," Chris warned him as he clicked the belting into an odd fastener. "It's the law and I'll explain it later."

Tom nodded. Being strapped down didn't make him much more trapped than he already was. He leaned his head back and kept his eyes focused as far ahead straight down the road as he was able.

Regardless of the lack of gracious delivery, Dee's instructions were sound ones. Tom didn't enjoy the journey, but at least he didn't disgrace himself either. Soon they turned onto a road that was of a familiar sort. He couldn't well judge the distance at the speed this contraption traveled, but it was probably at least a couple of miles when Chris stopped it at the foot of a rise. "End of the line. We walk from here."

Tom suddenly recognized where he was. He'd sat atop this same ridge on Sukie, less than eight years ago. The desperate hope rose up in him that, when he got to the top, Cooper's Creek would be spread below him, bustling and unaltered, just as it had been then.

"The road's gone," he commented as he outstripped both of them up the uneven ground, despite his crutches. "It's a decent 'un, too."

"A century plus of neglect will do that," Chris reminded him.

No reminder could have prepared him for what he saw when he crested the top of the ridge. Tom eased himself down onto the ground, laid his crutches beside him. He could scarcely bear to keep looking at the desolation below, but he couldn't look away, either.

"Are you two coming?" Chris called from where he'd headed on down the ridge without them.

As he gathered the crutches to rise to his feet, Dee slipped a hand under his arm and lifted up with surprising strength. He glanced his startled gratitude but she was already hurrying away down the slope after Chris. Tom didn't try to catch up.

They started at the northeast end. The boarding house was nothing but a layer of old ash and darkened sand. The palo verde in the turn-around beside it was long dead, the ground around its weathered trunk littered heavy with dried and splintered branches.

Dee and Chris kept calling for John, stopping to search each tumble-down structure. Tom didn't waste his breath or his time.

He headed straight to the Speckled Dove. With a dread he hadn't felt since the War, he stepped up onto the warped boardwalk and approached the doorway. There was no uncanny pull at his chest, but even so....

"It's jist like I saw it," he murmured, leaning against the splintered door post.

"What? When?" Chris hurried to his side and peered into the ruined saloon.

"I saw it, jist like this, for a few seconds once. Scared the—" he glanced over at Dee, who was peering in through the broken front window. "Scared me purty bad."

"When was it?" Chris looked at him, voice and expression urgent. "Exactly when was it?"

"The seventeenth of October," Tom answered. "Jist past one."

"The same day, the same time," Chris said, his voice shaky.

"As what?" Dee moved to their side, her brows furrowed.

"When he was out here alone, Jon said he saw some sort of apparition," Chris answered. "In there. He took pictures of it, and I noticed the timestamps. He swore he saw a man and a woman. Ghosts or something."

"What did you see?" Dee asked Tom.

152

He kept staring at the interior of the bar. The sunlight played in random shafts over the ruined interior. This time, there was no lizard on the fallen beam in the center of the room.

"I felt a pullin' in the center of my chest," he began softly. "Like somebody had hooked me through the breastbone and was reeling me in, towards this doorway. When I looked inside, I seen it both like it is— I mean, like it was then, and like it is now. Like lookin' at a stream and seein' the surface and the bottom, both sharp and clear. The real got dim, like a shadow, and this got as clear and solid as it is now. Whatever was drawin' me near yanked me clean over the threshold but I jerked back against it so hard I almost fell."

He shook his head. "When I looked inside then, it was all back to how it should be, and the drawin' feelin' in my chest was gone."

"Holy shit," Chris breathed.

"Go in!" Dee blurted, and gave him a hard shove. "Go in right now!"

Tom stepped across the threshold, his heart between his teeth with hope.

Nothing happened. Even so, he didn't linger long in that unnatural ruin.

Dee passed him on his way out. "Jon? Jon! JON!"

Her voice was shrill with panic. Chris went in after her.

Tom couldn't bring himself to do so. He dropped into the chair beside the door and leaned his head back against the crumbling adobe. The thought rose that since Jon was likely back in 1873, they might come more near to finding him if they searched the graveyard instead.

The sorrowful, terrified, hopeless noise of Dee's cries for her man convinced him to keep that idea to himself for now.

ঙ

The town had never been over-large, and now there were far fewer standing structures to search. It wasn't long before Chris and Dee came back up the street to the saloon. Chris looked distraught. Dee looked furious.

Tom tensed, pulled his crutches closer and rose to his feet.

"You're still here," Dee snapped.

"Not by my choice," Tom answered.

"There's no sign of Jon," Chris said softly, his eyes scanning the ruin of the town. Tom wasn't sure if he was speaking to them, or to himself. "No tracks, nothing at all."

"I'm sorry," Tom answered any way. "I was hopin' that when we got here, it would set things to right and he'd be here for y'all."

Dee rounded on him. "What do you care about him?"

"I don't, not much, for I don't know him and I don't know y'all either. But it's likely that if he don't come back, I cain't go back. I ain't likin' this no more'n you are."

She glared at him, breathing hard, her eyes burning with malice. "I hate you. I hate you so damn much."

"I don't hate you, ma'am. I don't even know you."

"I know you. God, do I know you! I know when you were born. I know where you were born. I know every friggin' battle you were in. I know exactly when and how you die. But do you know what's the very *most* important thing I know about you?"

Tom shook his head, the hair standing up on his arms.

"I know, without a shadow of a doubt, this is all your fault!" Her voice rose to a furious shriek that woke echoes off the ridge.

Tom barely dodged the hunk of adobe she scooped up and slung at his head.

"Dee!" Chris caught her arm before she could squat for more ammunition.

"There's one more place y'all ain't looked," Tom said, wary in case either of them lit in on him as the messenger of bad news.

Chris looked up and down the street. "Where?"

"Up yonder, where the church was." He softened his voice to a respectful hush, out of courtesy. "The graveyard's just behind."

Dee made a broken little noise. She wrenched her arm free from Chris' hold. "No! He's not there!"

"We... we can't know that," Chris answered, his face gone pasty. He turned to her. "I have to look. I have to. If he's not there, then we have hope. If he is, then..." A shudder passed through Chris that even Tom could see. "At least we'll know."

"I can't, Chris." Dee's voice was tight and soft, her dread widening her eyes. "I can't."

Chris took her into a quick, hard embrace. "I understand," he murmured near her ear. "I'll go."

Stepping back, he flicked a hand towards the church. His blanched face was hardened, dangerous. "Let's go, Dorin."

CЗ

Chris examined every weathered headstone twice. Tom moved into the shade of the largest one after their first tour through.

"He's not here," Chris announced. He squatted onto his haunches and wiped his face with a bandana. "Thank God."

"I hate like ever'thing to say this," Tom answered, "But even now we can't be sure."

"Why not?" Chris glared at him. "There's no headstone for you or for him."

"But take another look." Tom nodded towards the next row. "See them gaps between the graves? Some of them was marked with wooden slabs or crosses. And the Potter's Field, jist beyond, most of them folks just had a chunk of rock set at their head and feet."

"Damn." Chris' anger crumbled into something very close to grief.

"But even so, we can't be sure," Tom stressed again. "Because we can't prove he ain't here, don't mean he is, either. Me and him's connected somehow, and I ain't nowhere near needin' a deep hole and an epitaph, so likely he ain't either."

"There's still hope."

"Yes," Tom nodded. "Believe me, I want Jon returned to you near as much as you do, because I don't like this here one bit."

"Neither do I." Chris rose and hurried out from among the graves.

Tom stayed in the shade.

Chris pulled up and turned. "You're coming too."

"I think it best to stay right here."

The gun Chris produced from behind his back bore no resemblance to any Tom had seen, but it was unmistakable all the same.

"No, it's not. You said it yourself. You and Jon are connected. Theory A: bringing you back here, didn't work. So now we go to Theory B: You showed up in his house, you'll disappear from his house. Move."

Tom wasn't sure how serious Chris took his wild bluff that to kill him would destroy his double, so he moved.

CHAPTER SIXTEEN

21 October, 1873

Jon groaned and pulled the pillow over his head to block out both the light and soft rapping. It worked for the light, but the knocking got louder.

"What?" he called back, groggy.

"Are you well this morning?" The voice was female, and unfamiliar.

Who was in his house?

"Yeah, I'm okay." Jon removed the pillow and blinked, staring around the room.

Whose house was he in? He didn't have a clue. Even worse, he had zero memory of how he'd gotten here.

It was a small room, painted a pleasant blue that tempered the late morning desert sun without casting a glare. Calico curtains hung listless at the open window.

Jon sat up, the bed creaking and rustling beneath him. The pillow he'd clutched was thin, the case boasting a faded flour company stamp on one side.

He got out of bed, crossed a small braided rug by the bedside to get to the window. He was on the second floor, and Cooper's Creek on a busy nineteenth century morning bustled along on the wide dirt street beneath.

Jon's fingers dug into the windowsill. "Oh. My. God!"

Excited anticipation welled up inside, washing away his confusion completely. The last time he felt this way, he was five and hoping for his first real bicycle from Santa. Sure, this was only a dream, but he was eager to see what his subconscious constructed from all the scattered, dry facts he had accumulated about the town and Dorin himself.

"I gotta remember this when I wake up," he mumbled.

A familiar pressure on his bladder announced itself and Jon scrabbled under the bed, delighted when he found an authentic earthenware chamber pot. He unzipped his fly and put the pot to its intended use. The scent of fresh urine filled the room instantly, heavy and sharp. It was then that he realized he wasn't quite sure what he was supposed to do with a used chamber pot. Other than clap the lid on it. Shrugging, he did just that and pushed the chamber pot back under the bed.

A shirt and pants lay crumpled on the floor, and he picked up the shirt to examine it. Most of its buttons were missing, something rusty-brown spattered it and the strong odor of stale masculine sweat rose from the fabric. Jon wrinkled his nose and dropped it.

Jon ignored the other clothing hanging on hooks and moved on to explore the rest of his dream. There wasn't much to the furnishings. The only decoration was a Currier and Ives print, *The Old Homestead*, hung on the wall in an ornate frame.

A small trunk sat at the foot of the bed, locked. A straight backed chair stood near the bed, a table beside it bearing an oil lamp and a box of matches. A pair of worn high-topped boots sat beside the chair. The sole on the right one was built up almost two inches, and a crude cane fashioned from a twisted sapling leaned against the wall nearby. Its hand grip was polished dark and smooth from handling. He leaned his weight on it then replaced it.

Jon pulled open the drawer of the small oak washstand, finding the expected male toiletries: a straight razor and strop, a shaving brush, a comb, and a folding triple mirror, obviously intended to be hung from its chain on the handy nail right above his— Tom's— eye level. One surprise was a truly barbaric looking toothbrush of bone with frazzled natural bristles. Another was the small aqua glass bottle.

The label read '*Laudanum – Poison. Medicinal use - Narcotic and Soothing. Dose. - Adults, as a night draught to allay pain and procure sleep, from ten to twenty drops, in a wine glass of water.*'

"Is that old war wound still acting up, or did you come out of the hospital with a whopping case of Soldier's Disease?" Jon uncorked the bottle and sniffed. He wrinkled his nose. "Wonder if it tastes that bad, too?"

Not inclined to find out by experience, even in a dream, he recorked the bottle and set it back into its place. A little round tin lay beside it, and when Jon investigated, he discovered it was a clever little drinking cup that collapsed and extended like a telescope. A thick, uneven bar of yellow soap rested in a saucer on top along with a shaving mug, and a bowl and pitcher of heavy, plain white graniteware. A tin slop bucket was behind the washstand's door. A sacking towel and wash cloth hung over the rail above it all.

Jon took the mirror from the drawer and hung it from its nail.

"You did travel light," Jon murmured to his reflection. "How long have you been here now?"

Jon opened the door of the room and stuck his head out. The hallway and stairs outside the room were uncarpeted, but the wallpaper was a much brighter color than he would have expected.

A faint smell of fried sausage teased Jon's nose when he reached the ground floor. An open doorway to his left led into a cluttered room with a carpet of huge cabbage roses and contrasting wallpaper with startling blue stripes. An upright piano stood against one wall and overstuffed chairs fought tall curio cabinets and knick-knack-strewn tables for space.

"Looks like somebody dragged a net through an antique mall." He glanced both ways up and down the hall then strolled into the stuffy parlor. Jon raised the cover over the piano keys and plunked out an enthusiastic version of "Heart and Soul."

A tiny brown-skinned woman rushed in with a swish of skirts. "Mister Dorin!" she gasped.

Jon grinned at her. "What, you don't like the tune? Well, I guess it is avant-garde, considering."

Her face registered utter stunned shock. Jon gave in to an impish impulse and grabbed her in a loose waltz hold.

"Heart and soul…" he sang, giving her a half-turn before she jerked away and bolted from the room as if he had burst into flame.

"That was random. Must mean I'm about to wake up," he mused aloud. "Better get down to the saloon, talk to that barmaid I saw."

He had his hand on the doorknob when the implications of the woman's shocked outburst hit him. "Oh shit— his cane!"

If he was going to be Dorin, he was going to look the part, even if this was only a dream. Jon bolted up the stairs and back into the room. He grabbed up the cane and on the way out, snagged Dorin's hat from the hook beside the door. Jon adjusted the crown's crease and settled it on his head. He couldn't resist stepping back to take a quick glance in the mirror. "Not bad."

Jon hurried down the hall and clattered back down the stairs. Another very small woman peered in, her dark eyes wide in a pale face. She rushed through the doorway and moved as if to intercept him. "Mr. Dorin, wait!"

"Sorry, lady!" Jon avoided her gesture to move straight for the front door. "Time's short. I got an id to plumb and portals to penetrate!"

He closed the door on her shocked gasp. He was stepping up onto the boardwalk before he realized that he was carrying Tom's cane, not using it. Jon slowed down to what he assumed was an appropriate limp and took in the sights as he made his way down to the Speckled Dove.

This early in the day, it didn't surprise him that he didn't hear a piano plunking or rowdy patrons from outside the saloon. His heart skipped a beat or three as he stepped onto the boardwalk and saw the same image he'd glimpsed on his last visit to Cooper's Creek.

"But of course, that makes sense. It's my dream."

Unfortunately, thanks to his efforts at authentic lameness, he also repeated his first visit by tripping over the threshold.

This time, he managed not to face-plant, thanks to that cane, but he banged his knee again. The pain of landing on the healing bruise drove a yelp out of him.

Instead of the laughter he expected from the bar's patrons, he got a burst of sympathy instead and most of them got up and headed his way. Jon stared at the oncoming men with a flash of fear. Was this dream about to turn into a nightmare?

But his rescue came in the form of a grizzled, mustachioed man in a rumpled frock coat. The man waved the others off and was at Jon's side in a few long-legged strides. He grabbed Jon's arm and bodily lifted him back to his feet.

"Thanks," Jon murmured and tried to regain his dignity along with his balance.

The man's gaze dropped down to Jon's legs, then back up to Jon's eyes, steady and inscrutable. "Tom, I'd like a word with you."

"Okay, sure. Who are you?"

That question drew another chorus of shocked outbursts from the onlookers.

His rescuer's eyes widened, then narrowed. "Doctor Hackler. Why don't we take a walk on up to my office?"

"That would be fantastic! I'd love to see how you've got it set up." Jon grabbed the man's arm and practically dragged him out of the saloon. Jon stopped in front of the two-story building that housed a barber shop. "Up there, right? On the second floor?"

"That's correct." Hackler gently disengaged his arm. "Do you remember the last time you were here?"

"Sure. Three days ago. But the second floor isn't there anymore, so I want to see what it looks like."

"Well then, now's your chance," Hackler assured him, and gestured towards the stairway climbing the outside of the building. "After you."

Jon lunged up the stairway, excitement overriding the ache from his rebruised knee. "I hope I can remember all of this when I wake up. It's great how all the things I've read are coming together."

He ran his fingers over the raised lettering on the brass name plaque nailed by the door and the key for the doorbell.

"Where have you read about 'all this'?" The doctor reached past Jon and opened the door. "Go on in, have a seat."

"Newspapers, the few surviving Confederate war records, and published letters, mostly. It's been very difficult to turn up any specific primary source material about Tom Dorin." Jon wandered in and pulled a copy of *Twenty Thousand Leagues Under the Sea* from a shelf. "Wow! Is this a first edition?"

"As it was published late last year, I assume so," Hackler murmured, then crossed his arms over his chest. "So, you think you're dreaming, right now?"

"Of course I am. This town's been abandoned for over a hundred years."

"What century is it, in that case?" Hackler chewed on the edge of his mustache.

"The twenty-first," Jon said, turning to examine a group of labeled vials in a glass-fronted cabinet. Jon pulled out one drawer after another, examining the contents of the doctor's instrument chest. "You should boil these or soak them in alcohol," he said, admiring the sharp surgical instruments.

"And why is that? Do doctors routinely cook and pickle their instruments in the twenty-first century?"

"Of course they do. You sterilize everything or your patient gets infections. And since there are no antibiotics yet, a bad infection's all but a death sentence." Jon replaced a scalpel with a shudder. "'Laudable pus,' my ass."

"I'll keep that in mind." Dr. Hackler came closer, eyes never leaving his patient. "Remove your shirts, please."

"Huh?" Jon blinked. "Why?"

"I need to examine you for injuries."

Jon considered that while studying this amalgamation of his subconscious. "Well, okay. I guess that makes sense since you're the town doctor."

He began unbuttoning his shirt. "But if this gets weird, I'm waking up."

"I certainly hope you do," Hackler murmured.

"Since it's my knee I banged up, want to see that too?" Jon asked as he tossed his shirt aside onto the narrow cot.

"If you wish." The doctor's expression had crumpled into a deep scowl.

Jon watched him warily as he unsnapped and unzipped his jeans, then let them drop around his ankles. "Well? What's your verdict?"

"Pull up your trousers," Hackler snapped. "And tell me who you are."

Okay, this had gone weird, but not in the way he'd expected, which was a relief. Jon yanked his jeans back to his waist, then reached for his shirt. "I'm Tom Dorin. Why do you think I'm not?"

"Because the only way you resemble Dorin is in the face." The doctor closed in.

"Whoa, Doc—" Jon gave an uneasy chuckle as he zipped, snapped and buttoned. Where had that been lurking in his brain? "That's way more than I need to know about you and ol' Dorin's private lives."

"Don't be obscene," Hackler snapped. "I meant nothing of the sort."

"Then what do you mean?" More to regain some personal space than anything else, Jon dropped down onto the cot behind him. He gave an experimental bounce, and frowned. "If whatever brings you to the doctor doesn't cripple you for life, this cot will."

The doctor ignored that slur to his furnishings and profession. "Tom Dorin has recent injuries, and scarring that you do not."

"Wow, what? I mean, I know about his bum leg where he got shot in the War. The man must have one hell of a killer immune system. I don't know how he survived that without dying of sepsis or gangrene or something but what else has happened to him?"

Hackler closed what little distance remained between them. "Who are you?"

Jon leaned back to meet Dr. Hackler's eyes. He realized that even if he'd been standing, he'd still have to look up. "Wonder why you're so tall? Must mean you're very important somehow," he murmured. "And I guess it makes sense that you can't tell me more about Dorin than I already know. When I—"

"I do not possess infinite patience," Hackler rumbled. "Who are you and where is Tom Dorin?"

"All right, all right. Jeez." Jon sighed and decided to go with whatever this vivid, semi-lucid dream tossed at him. "I'm Jonathan Hansen, and I guess Tom's wherever he usually is at this time of day. You tell me, you seem to be this dream's tour guide and interrogator."

"Tell me who you are and what you have done with Dorin," Hackler repeated. The stare he was giving Jon was so steely, it was hard to believe now that this sinister giant was a doctor.

"I haven't done *anything* to Dorin! He— oh for shit's sake, why am I arguing about reality here?" Jon raked a hand through his hair. Lucid dreaming meant you could tell the dream where you wanted it to go, right?

"Look, I'm going to convince you that I really am Jon Hansen and that I'm from your future. If I do that, will you let me out of here to see the sights?"

Hackler backed off far enough to settle into the straight wooden chair beside the cot. "If you can convince me of that preposterous claim, I'll show you about the town myself. What objective proof can you offer?"

Jon laughed. "More than you'll need! I've got it all right here in my pockets."

He rose and pulled out everything he'd carried that day. Cell phone, wallet, pocket knife and car keys landed on the table. Jon was elated to see the dawning of confusion on Hackler's face. He handed him the cell phone. "It opens like a clam shell."

As if he were disarming an explosive, Dr. Hackler unfolded the cell. The phone obediently played a short tone. Hackler flinched, almost dropped it. He recovered from his start quickly, and examined the device intently.

'One Missed Call' was displayed on the screen.

"What is it for?" he asked, running a big fingertip lightly over the keys.

"It's for communication over a distance. A talking telegraph, in a way. Here, hand it back a second. I'll show you, maybe."

Just in case his dream had its own logic and the nineteenth century was considered roaming, Jon hit Dee's speed-dial key. The display changed to 'No Service.' He went to stored messages, and pulled up a video text from Dee.

He hit play and handed it to the doctor.

A miniaturized version of Dee's laugh spilled out of the speaker. *"I have to show you this, Jon, it's too good to keep till I get home!"* she said, the screen showing a close up of her face as she held her phone at arm's length. The scene slid around to show an SUV backed up against the side of a house, to the detriment of both. *"Wait for it!"* Dee's voice cautioned, the camera's view lurching as she walked a few steps closer. *"Ta daah!"*

A big black lab wearing a party hat and a bandanna bounced frenetically between the front seats, his tongue lolling, his happy barks muffled. The scene shifted back to Dee's face. *"Don't ask me how he got it into reverse, why he's wearing a hat, or why they thought we needed to be called out for this! I love you, hon and I'll see you in a few hours. Byeeee!"*

The screen went blank. Dr. Hackler's face was a sickly shade.

"Too much, too soon, huh?" Jon took the phone from the doctor's unresisting grasp. "I guess showing you my driver's license would be redundant."

Hackler's swallow was audible, and his voice cracked once as he began to speak. "You've successfully convinced me, Mr. Hansen. However, that leaves me with a dreadful dilemma to overcome."

"Oh?" Jon replaced his belongings into his pockets.

"You've proven that you're from the future. However, I cannot think of any way to convince you that you are not dreaming and have, indeed, traveled back to 1873."

"Yeah, that would be tough. Anything you tell me, I could already know. Like I said, I've done a lot of research." Jon scratched his chin. "Even if I tell you something like, oh, punch me in the face and I'll believe you— and I'm not asking you to do that, by the way— that would simply be part of the dream too."

"And no proof at all," Hackler agreed. He rose from his chair and began to pace the room.

"I've never liked logic puzzles." Jon moved to stare out the rear window at a different view of Cooper's Creek, featuring an unlovely vista of the ragged row of outhouses set a hundred feet or so back behind the businesses.

"I'm quite fond of them, but this is a vitally pressing matter rather than a trivial amusement," the doctor replied. "For if you're here, then where is Tom?"

"I don't know." Jon shrugged. "Who cares? He's long dead and this is a dream."

"No, it is not," Hackler snapped. "I pray that Tom's alive and well, wherever—whenever— he may be."

Jon turned from the window, and gave the older man a wicked grin. "The answer to this logic puzzle is 'Time will tell.' I'll wake up in a few hours at most, and you and this entire town will be nothing but a fading memory."

Eager to play this dream out for all it was worth, Jon moved towards the door, but was blocked by the not inconsiderable bulk of the doctor. "Hey! You promised you'd take me on a tour."

"Answer some of my questions first."

"Screw that, old man. It's time for a scene break." He tried to step around the doctor but got a broad hand against his sternum instead.

He tried to step around Hackler again. It was as if the man's palm had grown into his own flesh. "What do you do for fun, bench-press steers? Step aside, damn it."

"Be quiet!"

It was the first time the doctor's voice had risen above a gritty rumble. Despite himself, Jon took a startled step back. The man had incredible volume. Jon took a deep breath, forced his hands to open from instinctive fists.

"Why are you so interested in Tom Dorin and this town?" Dr. Hackler stayed firmly rooted between Jon and the doorway, though he crossed his arms over his chest now.

"Okay, I guess this could be helpful. Obviously, I need to work this through, or my graduate program's gonna tank."

Jon sat down in Hackler's chair. "Tom Dorin is my inspiration, the poster boy for my Master's thesis. I was first interested in him because of this weird resemblance, of course, but as I learned more about him I became intrigued. I don't know much about his life immediately after the War, but I do know he was a Confederate sharp-shooter, in the Nineteenth Tennessee Volunteer Infantry, and that had to be especially brutal."

The doctor gave a noncommittal grunt.

Jon went on when the doctor offered nothing more. "Anyway, using Tom's life as a case study, I'm exploring how the trauma of war, untreated post-traumatic stress disorder and the destruction of the Confederacy and the entire antebellum southern gestalt led to a profound social disconnect for the survivors, tying it to possible ramifications for veterans in my time."

"So you think you know—?"

A rap on the door interrupted Hackler. "Keep your mouth shut," he hissed instead, turned, and opened the door.

Jon peeked around the doctor's rangy frame. It was one of the women from the boarding house, the second one.

"Doctor Hackler." She wrung gloved hands, her bonnet slightly askew. "I'm sorry to disturb you, but I was told you brought Mr. Dorin here. What is his condition?"

"Mrs. Perkins, that is a difficult question. If you would step inside, I'll endeavor to answer it." He moved aside and Mrs. Perkins crossed the threshold.

She paused, uncertain, just inside the door. Jon rose as Dr. Hackler closed the door again.

Hackler moved to stand between them. "Mrs. Hattie Perkins, allow me to introduce Mr. Jonathan Hansen."

"It's a pleasure to meet you," Jon smiled at her. "Properly, that is. I've wondered about you, Hattie. You really bucked your society's trends, being a successful business woman and an independent widow in a pretty rough-and-tumble environment. If I run into someone casting around for a thesis subject in women's studies, I'll be sure to mention you."

Hattie went even paler and Dr. Hackler was instantly at her side, a supportive hand at her back. "Sit down here, and we'll explain."

167

"That would be most appreciated," she managed, dropping into the chair Jon had vacated. She reached into a fold of her skirt and pulled out a small fan.

The smooth, graceful flick of her wrist as she opened and employed it captivated Jon in the way of dreams. He wondered if somewhere in her younger days, back east, she'd been a society belle. He made a mental note to research that point. Damn, he needed to get a notebook and pencil or something.

The thought made him chuckle. As if a dream notepad would do him any good when he woke up! He was glad he kept that one beside the bed, because he certainly wanted to record every second of this doozy before it faded.

"Mr. Hansen."

Jon blinked, and focused on Hackler. "Yeah?"

"Please show Mrs. Perkins what you showed me."

"Why? If ever there was information on a need-to-know basis, I'm pretty certain that qualifies." Jon looked up at the older man, curious to see what his creative dream-state would come up with as a rationalization.

"Mrs. Perkins needs to know what has become of the hired man she has come to depend upon. She also needs to be convinced that neither of us are lunatics, if the latter is possible."

"Why does she matter? I'll only be here for two or three more hours, tops. Then I'll wake up. Look, I'd much rather be exploring the town than freaking out some woman who's no more than a short footnote in my thesis!"

"Humor me. In two or three hours, Hansen, you'll be glad you did."

Hattie looked from one man to the other, and it was clear from her expression she thought both her hired hand and the town's doctor had been struck with simultaneous insanity.

"Okay, okay. You're my subconscious, so I guess you're running this show." Jon sat back down on the edge of the cot and leaned in towards Hattie.

"Here's the deal, Hattie. I know I look like Tom Dorin, and I showed up in his room this morning, but I'm not him. My name's Jonathan

Madison Hansen. I'm a graduate student at the University of Arizona, majoring in American history, the Reconstruction period to be precise, and I'm having one heck of a dream."

He shook his head with a little laugh. "Probably from an overdose of research mixed with a whopping case of stress and sleep deprivation. Dee's never going to let me live this one down."

Hattie leaned back in her chair, as if to put as much distance between her and him as possible without fleeing. She looked up at Hackler. "I don't understand... Is he deranged? Did he strike his head when he was thrown?"

"As impossible as it sounds, he's deranged only in that he considers us all to be figures in a dream. And he hasn't told you the half of it." Hackler shifted his attention to Jon. "Show her."

Jon shrugged. "Okay, whatever. If she faints though, don't blame it on me." He pulled his phone out of his pocket and held it out to Hattie on his palm. "This is a cell phone. A device for transmitting sound, images and other data across a distance. Across the planet, if you can afford the charges."

Hattie stared at it. "It looks like nothing more than an odd pill box."

"Watch." Jon brought up the same video message he'd shown the doctor. Once again, Dee laughed and the festive dog barked.

Hattie turned green-tinged white.

"And there she goes." Jon and the doctor both lunged for her as she relaxed into an odd sideways sag, limp except for her rigidly corseted midsection.

The doctor was clearly well-skilled in dealing with fainting women, so Jon stepped back and simply observed as Hackler roused Hattie. He waited with growing impatience while she regained both consciousness and a reasonable level of composure.

"Told you this was a waste of time," Jon grumbled, half under his breath.

Hattie carefully rearranged herself and her skirt on the edge of the chair. Her spine was straighter than even her corset demanded, and her chin lifted. She regarded Jon with an expression of equal parts distrust and distaste.

"For what little it's worth, Hattie, do you believe me?" Jon asked her.

Hackler handed her a glass of water. Despite her outward composure, the glass trembled in her hold. Hattie took a sip, then set it aside.

"Mrs. Perkins to you, sir." Her voice was firm, and coolly curt. She looked at Jon a long moment, then nodded. "I believe you. What I can't believe now is that I ever mistook you for Mr. Dorin at all."

"What do you mean?" Hackler asked, his deep voice quiet as if afraid to break a spell.

"The resemblance is striking, Doctor, but not complete."

"Yes, Mr. Hansen isn't lame."

"That's the most obvious difference, but not perhaps the most important one."

She fixed her attention back on Jon. He felt she was observing him more like an exhibit than as a person. Fair enough. Observation seemed to be the point of this dream.

"His entire demeanor is different. His stance is different. His speech is wildly different, in dialect and refinement and in his lack of courtesy and respect. It is his eyes, however, which betray Mr. Hansen most profoundly."

"Dorin's eyes were a different color?" Jon asked.

She shook her head, then rose and retrieved her fan from where it had fallen to the floor. Her stoop revealed a certain aesthetic grace that he had associated only with professional dancers. She turned and met his eyes as she flicked the fan back and forth.

"Mr. Dorin's eyes are the same shade of blue as yours. But one's eyes truly are the windows of the soul, and Mr. Dorin's soul is not behind your eyes."

"Good lord, I should hope not!"

She snapped her fan shut. "Where is Mr. Dorin?"

The look on her face almost had Jon taking a step away.

"I don't know." He looked over at the doctor. "Come on, do we have to go through all this again? I'll get your point when I wake up. Throw me a bone here, Id. Let me out to sight-see!"

"Mrs. Perkins, may I have a word with you outside?" Hackler asked her, ignoring Jon as if he was the one who was the figment.

"Gladly," she said, and sailed out the door in a rustle of stiff skirts and offended sensibilities.

Jon went to the door as soon as it shut. He leaned his ear against the panel. It was his dream, he'd eavesdrop if he wanted to. The stout wood muffled the sound too much. Crossing the room again, he grabbed up Hattie's glass and tossed the water out onto the floor. Pressed between his ear and the door, the glass served well enough as an amplifier.

"… severe shock, and a daunting phenomenon to accept." Hackler's voice was a rumble of vibration as well as sound through the wood.

"I'm over the initial shock, Doctor, but I suspect it will take quite some time for me to fully accept the reality of what I've seen and been told. I feel as if I may be the one caught in some fantastic dream," Hattie said.

"I understand. But even in my wildest imagination, I don't think I could conjure up that moving, talking picture." Hackler said.

"The device, perhaps, I may have conjectured… but not the image… Oh, it was all too real! The laughter in that woman's voice and that silly looking dog." Hattie's voice faded, as if she moved a little farther away from the door. "The wonder and puzzle of it all doesn't matter, not really. Not in comparison to the immediate implications. If Mr. Hansen has been abandoned here, then where is Mr. Dorin? And what are we to do with his substitute?"

"My inclination is to hire a horse, put him on it, and give the beast a hard whack across the hindquarters." Hackler's voice betrayed no hint that he was making a joke.

"Oh no! We mustn't do anything of the sort!"

"Why not?"

"'Be not forgetful to entertain strangers: for thereby some have entertained angels unawares.' If Mr. Hansen is not a stranger, then I don't know who would qualify."

"Mrs. Perkins, forgive me, but even our short acquaintance convinces me that Mr. Hansen, where or whenever he may be from, is no angel."

"Doctor— the appearance of a man from a future century, the disappearance of Mr. Dorin from his own bed— surely this is a mighty act of divine providence. Uncouth angel or lunatic sinner, we must aid him. Please, Doctor. If for no other reason than this; if something dire happens to Mr. Hansen, will Mr. Dorin be able to ever return home?"

There was a long pause, and Jon strained to hear Hackler's answer. "Then how do you suggest we manage our temporal stray?"

"I need some time—" Hattie interrupted herself with a shaky little laugh. "Some time to gather my wits and give this situation some thought. Perhaps you might be so kind as to keep Mr. Hansen here over night?"

"He thinks he'll be back where he belongs in an hour or two," Hackler answered. "Perhaps he'll be proven right. If not, I'll stop by in the morning and we'll make further arrangements."

"Thank you," she answered softly. "Would you mind escorting me home, sir? I confess I'm still quite unnerved."

"Of course," Hackler said. "I have to make the same confession of myself."

Jon's hand closed around the doorknob, but Hackler beat him to it. A key turned the lock from outside.

"Crap." Jon rattled the knob, but the lock held. He abandoned the door and went to the window. Dr. Hackler and Hattie strolled down the sidewalk, her hand on his bent elbow.

"Not that I'm complaining," he murmured to her retreating figure, "but why are you so charitable?"

The pair below crossed the wide dirt street.

"You honed in on my eyes. Dorin's eyes. Why have you been gazing into your hired man's eyes? You've got a thing for ol' Thomas, is that it, Widow Perkins?"

Frustrated, Jon rummaged through the office and the smaller adjoining room that was obviously Hackler's personal quarters. He learned a lot about the old quack, but best of all, he found a skeleton key. It fit the lock in the door.

Jon grabbed up Dorin's cane and hurried down the stairs. He was going to get as much sight-seeing in as he could before he woke up. All he had to look forward to on waking was a prolonged abject groveling session with Dee, so he was grateful for this incredible diversion served up by his sleeping brain. He was going to enjoy every second.

He smiled to himself. Everyone seemed to take him for Dorin at first glance, so he might as well put that high school drama class and all those hours watching Westerns to use. He would be Dorin for the duration. Jon gave a low chuckle as he imagined the other man's consternation if they did wind up truly eye to eye somewhere in town. After a glance up and down the street, he turned right and headed up the short end of this side, towards the bank at the end.

Almost everyone he encountered spoke a greeting and nearly as many added a remark about being glad to see him up and about. What prompted that solicitude, he had no clue. Most called him by name— Dorin's name, rather. He remembered to lift his hat and nod when greeted, and drawled a word or two each time that he assumed were socially acceptable and reasonably vague. Breaching Victorian etiquette in a dream state wasn't his highest concern, and he didn't want to sidetrack his subconscious into multiple small-talk sessions with walk-on characters.

The undertaker's establishment, Jon had no immediate desire to investigate. The era's maudlin death rituals weren't a subject of much interest to him. He passed on by, but couldn't resist hesitating at the doorway of the Sheriff's office to sneak a peek.

"Heard tell you nearly got the life mashed outta ya yesterday, Tom." The voice boomed from the dim interior of the jail.

What the hell had happened to Dorin? Oh well, fifty-fifty chance of answering the correct way... "Yes sir, I come awful close to it," Jon drawled, in his best guess at an uneducated Tennessee accent.

"Good to see ya up and about. You look better'n what I heard." The owner of the voice appeared, shorter than Jon by a head, more than making up for it in breadth of shoulder. The man resembled a humanoid bulldog, squinting up from under an overhanging unibrow. One cheek bulged with a generous cud of tobacco. "Sorry way to lose a good mount, though."

"Don't reckon thar's any good way," Jon answered. So that's what had happened; the nineteenth century equivalent of a car wreck. He was going to drag the details out of Hackler first thing. Something like this might have had a bearing on Tom's fate, if it messed the man up worse than he already was.

The man spat a brown stream into the cuspidor set near the door. "Cain't argue with that."

"Nope. Uh, I don't mean to be rude, but I need to get on down the street. Mrs. Perkins is expectin' me back."

"Don't want to keep a lady waitin'," the man smiled.

Jon assumed he was either the Sheriff himself or a Deputy, but that was a fifty-fifty guess he wasn't willing to make at the moment. He touched his hat brim and moved along. It hardly surprised him that Hackler came out of the boarding house and hurried across the street just as he got to the bank. His brain wasn't going to let him shake his over-grown id that easily, apparently.

The bank's Victorian excesses were fresh and gleaming in the harsh sunlight. Both men moved into the thin line of shade cast by the edifice.

"I distinctly remember locking you in," Hackler said with gritty annoyance.

"I let myself out. Ain't lucid dreaming a bitch?" Jon grinned back.

"Good afternoon, Doctor, and to ye as well, Mr. Dorin."

They both turned towards the woman who greeted them. Her voice was thickly Irish. Her face, and the gnarled hands lifting her faded, stiffly starched skirt, were deeply weathered and reddened. She bobbed her head, her eyes all but disappearing into sun-crinkles when she smiled.

"Good afternoon, Mrs. Finnegan." Hackler removed his hat with a hint of a bow this time.

"Afternoon, ma'am." Jon added a nod to his own hasty headgear relocation.

"It's lucky I meet ye here, Doctor. I can finally pay ye for your care of Ian."

She fumbled a little leather drawstring pouch out of a pocket, somewhere in all the yardage of her skirt.

"That's not necessary." The doctor's voice was a low purr as he held up a hand to her. "Wait until Ian has a few more pay-days and you're ahead a bit."

"Ahead?" Mrs. Finnegan's chuckle was throaty and far younger sounding than her appearance. "If it's waiting for us to be ahead ye're about, ye'll see your coin at Doomsday!"

She touched his coat sleeve then. "Please, Doctor. Consider it a salve to Ian's pride— and mine too, truth be told. Besides, even high and mighty doctors need to eat, aye?"

"Aye, that we do," he replied, a faint echo of her brogue in his voice.

She laughed again and undid her coin purse. A silver dollar, a quarter, and a tiny coin Jon belatedly recognized as a half-dime were deposited into the doctor's broad palm.

Hackler dropped the money into his coat pocket then offered his arm. He escorted her up the steps and opened the bank's heavy door. "I do thank you, Mrs. Finnegan, and I'm more than grateful to see Ian doing so well."

"Thanks to the good Lord and the good doctor, ye'd ne'r know there's been aught to trouble him," she smiled. "Good day to ye now, gentlemen, and God bless."

"You as well, ma'am."

Jon peeked into the bank as she went inside. He scowled as the heavy oak whispered shut behind her. "Easy to see where way too much of the mine's money is going. They own this bank, don't they?"

"They own the very ground we stand on, and notes on more than a few of the homes and businesses that occupy it," Hackler admitted, his tone a tad resentful as he resettled his hat.

"Monopoly's better as a game," Jon muttered and this time he was the one to set them back in motion. He'd seen all of the bank he wanted to. He adjusted his hat brim to shade his eyes.

They crossed the wide street, stepping around horse-apples and pausing mid-stream to allow a wagon and then a pair of riders to pass. They stepped back up onto the walk in front of the boarding house. It was set back a few feet from the street unlike the other buildings, behind a low picket fence. The narrow yard between fence and porch steps was bare of everything save one pathetic bush of some sort. A trio of chickens scratched and clucked in the patchy shade it provided.

Jon paused at the gate, looking up at the plain, unpainted two-story house to pick out which window was Dorin's.

Hackler took his arm and tugged. "You're not going back in there unless she invites you."

Jon moved on with the doctor, but shook off his hold with a frown.

"Say as little as possible," Hackler rumbled as they came up to the general store. A bell jangled as he opened the door.

"Afternoon, George!" he called out to the man behind the counter.

Jon started to remove his hat, but aborted when Doc didn't so much as go for his. This hat rigmarole was information he hadn't been aware of taking in, but here it was. He wondered if his confusion was connected to the same insecurity that prompted naked-in-public nightmares.

"Afternoon, Tom. Afternoon, Doc. You here for your weekly dose?"

"I am. You know if I'm a day without I start to get the shakes," Hackler agreed, sliding a coin across the worn counter.

Jon murmured a greeting back, his attention riveted on the pair as he pretended to examine a case of knives a few feet away. Was Doc some kind of addict?

Instead of an ominous bottle or packet, a plump paper sack, striped in cheery red and white, was plopped onto the counter.

"I took the liberty of gatherin' up your usual mix," George said.

"That's fine, I appreciate the thoughtfulness." Hackler took the bag.

George swept the coin below the counter. "You need anything else today?"

"No, thank you. Although, have you had any word on those books I ordered a few months ago?"

"That I have." George grinned. "They're finally in St. Louis and should be here by the end of this month, if all goes well."

"Good, good. Send Timmy around with them when they come. Have a good evening, and give my regards to the Missus."

"And hers to you both." George included Tom with a nod and then his smile dimmed a little. "You think you'll be healed up enough by

Saturday, Tom? Won't be no real hardship to me if we have to put it off a week or two."

"Uh, sure. It looked worse than it was, but thanks for asking. Our plans still stand. Good evening now," Jon gave the man a wave as he followed Doc out, with a sense of relief this time.

When the door safely closed behind with a parting jingle, Jon turned to Hacker. "Not that it matters, but I'm curious. What do Tom and George have going on Saturday?"

The doctor untied his bag, tucking the string into a coat pocket. "You're the Dorin pundit. You tell me."

He tipped the bag towards Jon. It was full of hard candy.

"Don't suppose it matters. The meter's running out on this dream." Jon chose something that looked like a peppermint. "Thanks." He popped it into his mouth. "It's good," he managed around the candy. "What sort of books have you got ordered?"

"*The Theory of Practice* by Shadworth Hollway Hodgson, and papers on the new germ theory of infection by Louis Pasteur and Robert Koch." Hackler bit off a piece of licorice. "Do either of them sound familiar?"

"The stuff by Pasteur and Koch? That's like, the sea-change of the entire history of medicine. Read it, learn it, live it. Hodgson's drivel? Use it as a doorstop. Trust me, an hour conversing with a trained parrot would convince you that guy's off his nut." He grinned. "The edition that was sent to libraries had uncut pages. On good authority, I've heard that over a hundred years later, most of 'em are still totally untouched."

The doctor made an annoyed little noise.

"Hey, cheer up. Bet it'll make great out-house paper."

"Doctor!" A man hailed from across the street. Jon touched his hat brim in the guy's direction and ambled on down the street before he could be caught up in another Victorian greeting ritual. The next shop proclaimed itself a saddlery and boot-maker, so after a desultory glance in the window, Jon moved on. It might have been fun to go in and set ol' Dorin up with a new pair of boots, but he didn't want to waste his dream on that.

✂

He was almost to the hotel when someone called from across the street again. "Mr. Dorin!"

Jon took three more strides, looking around eagerly, before remembering that he was Dorin now. He turned towards the teenage boy running across the street and met him halfway.

"You got a letter today." The boy offered it and another pair of envelopes with a grin. "Here's Miz Perkins' mail too. I was just goin' up the street with 'em. I didn't figure you'd be around to collect 'em today."

"Thanks." Jon took the mail with a rising sense of eager anticipation. "I wasn't hurt as badly as everyone seems to think." Crap, he forgot the accent!

The boy blinked, but said only, "Glad it was jist loose talk, then. See ya later!"

"Yeah, see ya," Jon replied and the boy bolted back across the street as if he had two gears, dead-stop and full speed ahead. Jon stepped off the boardwalk and leaned against the alley side of the bath house. He flicked through Hattie's mail then stuck the envelopes into his back pocket and examined the envelope for Dorin.

It was addressed simply to Mr. Thomas A. Dorin, Cooper's Creek, Arizona Territory, in a precise Spenserian script that held the curlicues to a minimum.

Jon broke the seal on the fat envelope and unfolded the pages. It seemed odd to see the old-fashioned handwriting as dark black script on paper that was bright, crisp and white.

5 October, 1873

My dear Friend,

Your letter arrived as a happy gift, something entirely unexpected but received with great joy. I think fondly of you so very often and as often have deeply regretted that we lost one another for these past several years.

It is difficult to express here how glad and relieved I am that you have finally found a place where you feel at peace and can find rest and perhaps one day full happiness again as well. Do not condemn yourself for lack of ambition, because of your present situation. As I grow older and pray God, wiser, it seems to me that contentment and happiness, and love if one can find that elusive prize, are worth far more than high social standing or any amount of wealth.

Beyond that, the plans you spoke of are sound ones as far as I am able to determine. They suit your aptitudes and your temperament, and I am certain you will find your success there and likely the more precious commodities above as well.

Selfishly, I wish your new home and my own were not separated by such a distance but I understand why our green hills are no longer the comfort and respite to you that they once were. I do miss you greatly, my friend. I would not wish to relive the years we spent at each other's side— nor, I suspect, would you— but neither would I wish them away and that almost solely because of our companionship during it all. My high regard for you is a 'spoil of war' I will never surrender. To hear that you feel the same has touched me deeply.

You asked for news from home, so I made inquiries in your behalf. Your Mother and Father both live, and are in fair health and enjoying their grandchildren. Your Father, as I understand, has somewhat softened in his demeanor over the past several years, so it may be that a message from your hand would no longer be a cause of upset, but of thanksgiving for them.

Your brother recently married a girl named Ruth Hill that I was assured you would know. As of yet, they have no children. He is now overseeing the farm and has shifted from raising fine saddle horses to the breeding of equally excellent milk cattle and mules. Your oldest sisters have married men of good reputation, all well-situated local farmers, except for Ruby who married Andrew Dothan, the son of the man who bought the farm's stallions. She is now living in a fine home near Lexington. Mary married Fredrick Harper and has two burly little boys, Caleb and Martin, two and one, respectively. Lizzie married Edwin Walthall and has three children, a boy Ellis who is three and a set of infant twin girls (not identical) named Annie and Mae. Ruby has no children, but it was hinted to me that she may be in the family way. Hannah Grace is still at home, but I hear that may not be a lasting situation as she is said to draw beaus as a bower draws bees.

As for our bunch, Malloy is almost as hard to track as you are. That particular rolling stone was last seen out near Bell Buckle, Tennessee and from reports is comporting himself as always. As far as I know he has not married and I doubt by this late date he ever will.

Dodo achieved one solitary feat of flight to wing straight home and has not stirred from his roost since. He and Pink Dress Alice were blessed with their eighth child shortly before my visit, a sturdy little fellow they christened CarlThomas, so we have a mutual godson! And yes, they say it just that way, all one word, "Carlthomas."

That part of the country may carry Shine's stamp for generations as he has exactly duplicated himself over and over as if he is a printing press. The whole lively tribe has Shine's jet black hair, long narrow face and solemn white-blue eyes. You may be amused to know that those well-traveled, well-ragged owl wings are now tacked up over his fireplace.

As for myself, I am still in single harness, but the solitude suits me. Mother is as always, so I stay close enough but far enough, as I'm sure you understand. The law firm is going well, our clientele expanding from year to year, most of it dealing with the concerns of commercial enterprises rather than those of private individuals. It keeps me busy enough to keep me out of trouble, if nothing else.

Now, my friend, I must relate something that I hesitated to tell you at all. Mrs. Beattie contacted me some time ago and asked that if I ever hear from you, to let you know that she has kept some mementos that you may wish to have. I made no promises on your behalf, as I could not be certain of how you would receive that news. I only hope it does not cause you pain to consider it. She asked me to tell you that you are still held in high regard and you will always be welcome in their home.

Tom, I wasn't quite truthful above when I wrote that solitude suits me. It did well enough, until I heard from you again. Now, I find myself quite lonesome for your company once more. It is my hope, if you are agreeable, that I may travel out your way within this year for a good long visit and 'jaw.' Please chastise me if I'm imposing on our friendship to suggest such a thing against all rules of courtesy! If you wish to have the items Mrs. Beattie spoke of, let me know and I will bring them with me if I may come or will otherwise post them to you.

In brotherly love,
Carl

 os

"Give that to me, please."

Jon almost jumped out of his skin, he was so absorbed in this incredible glimpse into Dorin's life. He was about to protest when the disappointing truth occurred to him. This was, after all, only a dream. The information in the letter was made up out of his own imagination. It didn't really exist.

Feeling somewhat crushed, he folded the sheets and handed them and the envelope over to Hackler.

The doctor glanced at the envelope and tucked the folded letter back inside. "Tampering with someone else's mail is a serious crime."

"Bite me." Jon stalked down the boardwalk, hands in his pockets.

"Tom!" Hackler called behind him.

Jon spun, but instead of Dorin what he saw was the man's cane sailing towards his face. He caught it with a scowl.

"Limp, please," Hackler admonished with poisoned gentleness. It only took about two of his long-legged strides to catch up. "Has this dream become a nightmare?" he asked, a hint of a smile lifting the corners of his mustache.

"No, only a tantalizing mirage. That letter would have been a goldmine if it was real."

It's idiotic to pout over a disappointment in a dream, but damn— Carol 'Carl' Lynd was the only one of Tom's fellow sharpshooters he'd been able to track beyond the war years, but he had gotten no reply to his most recent letter to a surviving relative. Probably that's where this bit came from. Pure wish fulfillment, the same as all the rest of it.

His stomach growled then, loudly. Like the need to use the chamber pot and the powerful smells he experienced, it was a sensation he didn't expect in a dream. Still, he'd never had one this vivid before.

"I'm hungry. Where do you get food around here?"

The doctor consulted his pocket watch. "The hotel dining room may have begun serving supper. If not, I may be able to coax Señorita Recillos to take mercy on us."

"Who's that?"

"The cook," Hackler said as they walked on down the boardwalk.

"You know everyone in town, don't you?"

"I do, or have at least made the acquaintance of the majority," Hackler nodded.

"Dang, if only you were real."

Hackler stopped short, his expression serious. "What will it take to convince you?"

"I don't know," Jon shrugged. "Never waking up, I guess. Or dying. You never feel pain or die in dreams; like when you dream of falling? You always wake up right before you hit. Have you ever noticed that?"

The expression on Hackler's face was indecipherable, but disturbing. "Then you were quite right earlier. Time will tell. You'll be convinced by dawn tomorrow."

"Dawn? I doubt you'll exist till sundown, Doc." Jon opened the door of the Hotel and stepped inside the lobby. "Huh, I wonder if eating in a dream keeps you from waking up hungry?"

Hackler shepherded him through the lobby before he had a chance to take in all the details. "Let's find out."

CHAPTER SEVENTEEN

October 21, Present Day
Tucson, Arizona
~ Later the same day ~

The trip back to the house was a morose journey. Nobody spoke. Tom was too far into his own thoughts to want to inquire into theirs. The gathering darkness outside kept him from feeling queasy again, though this time around, he would have welcomed it as the lesser of two evils.

On the way into the house, he hesitated and touched Chris' arm.

The man jerked around like he'd been stuck. "What?"

"Where's the outhouse?"

"Great," Chris grumbled. "This way."

Instead of heading out the back, Chris led him down the hallway and opened a door partway down. He pointed to a white china... thing.

"This is a toilet. You sit on it to crap and you damn well better have good aim when you piss or Dee will take your head off. You use that paper on the roll instead of corn cobs or whatever the heck you wiped your butt with back then. When you're done, close the lid and push that handle. And for cripes sake, wash your hands after, at the sink there. The handle turns the water on and off."

Chris stepped out and closed the door.

Tom expected to be shy about doing his dirt inside the house, but the cramping in his belly overcame any inhibitions. About the time he thought it would ease up, off he'd go again. He'd been costive from the laudanum for so many years, he'd almost forgotten what it was like to have roaring flux. It was one of many war memories he would never have chosen to relive.

A sharp rap sounded at the door. "Have you fallen in?" Chris asked.

Tom blushed red-hot, probably from his belly-button right on up to his crown.

"I'm sorry," he hissed back, trying to put his voice through the door but no further. "I'll try to hurry but I got the trots!"

His humiliation was complete when about half a minute later, Dee spoke through the door.

"How long have you been taking laudanum?"

"Since I was discharged from the hospital. Almost ten years now, ma'am."

"Jeez! Daily?"

"Twice a day most days, morning and evening. Sometimes a dose around dinner too. Jist depends."

"How much a day on average?" Her voice sounded tired and hard.

"Fifty, sixty drops, more 'r less."

There was a longer pause. "Twenty drops is about a milliliter— hot damn, that's a helluva habit there, Dorin. When was your last dose?"

"Probably 'round eight or nine last night."

She blasphemed fit to shame mule skinner for several seconds, winding up with, "We're going to have such a fun week."

A soft thump against the door and her voice sounded a bit muffled. "Do you know what going cold turkey means?"

"No ma'am."

"Do you know what happens when some idiot like you stops taking his drops all of a sudden?"

"Yes." He leaned back against the cool tank and closed his eyes. May the Lord be merciful and spare him from ever again having to carry on a conversation while he helplessly cramped and shat like a goose— especially a conversation like this one. "Cain't we get some tonight?"

"No. Laudanum's illegal now."

'A fun week,' his left hind foot....

ᲒᎧ

"So he's a murderer and a raving junkie. Perfect." Chris dropped his head back against the couch so he could keep the bathroom door in view.

"Stopping cold with that big a habit, he's not going to be any danger to anyone for more than a week at least." Dee set the rocker into motion with a push of her foot. "Besides, with his mangled leg, he's not much of a threat physically."

"I don't want to take the chance. We know he's killed more than once, and you don't need legs to pull a trigger or use a knife. Or hell, even to strangle someone."

"We'll lock him in my room at night. I'll sleep in the study."

"Why should you give up your bed for—?"

"Chris. Think. That's where Jon was when he vanished. That's where *he* showed up." She rose. "I'll be back in about an hour. He'll probably still be in the can."

"Where are you going?"

"To buy a double-keyed deadbolt for my bedroom door." She hung her purse from her shoulder. "You know how to use a gun. I know how to use a drill and screwdriver."

"Dee?"

She turned.

"I'll sleep in the study."

She nodded and left.

CHAPTER EIGHTEEN

22 October, 1873
Cooper's Creek, Arizona Territory
~ The next morning ~

Dee must have forgotten to close the blinds. Jon yawned, stretched, rolled over and opened his eyes.

Dr. Hackler sat watching him, arms crossed over his chest. "Good morning, and welcome to the twenty-second of October, 1873."

Jon flung aside the covers and ran to the window. The same view of the street greeted him that he'd looked down on before. When he was dreaming of this office. Yesterday.

"NO!" He bolted for the door, but the doctor foiled him once more.

"Running outside stark naked will not alter your dilemma," he rumbled. "Favorably, that is."

Jon was too stunned to argue. He flopped back down on the edge of the cot and raked his hair back out of his eyes. "This is crazy. This can't be happening. I'm still dreaming, I've got to be. This is impos—"

For a big man, Hackler could move very quickly. He jerked open a drawer of his instrument chest, grabbed a scalpel and swept it across Jon's forearm.

The blade was so sharp that a thin line of blood beaded up before Jon felt the sting. He stared down at the superficial cut and back up at the doctor.

"Do you still believe you are dreaming?" Hackler tossed the scalpel aside to clatter onto the top of the chest. "Or should I hurl you out the window so you can attest to the fact that you do, indeed, hit the ground?"

The words passed by him like wind. Jon cradled his arm. It was not much worse than a paper-cut, but the sting of it was all too real. He'd never felt pain in a dream.

"No…" he groaned, "You cut me. Why did you cut me?"

"To prove your theory that one cannot feel pain in a dream." Hackler picked up a stoppered bottle and a bit of gauze. He dampened the gauze and swabbed the seeping cut. "You also said alcohol prevents infection, correct?"

Jon hissed at the burn. He held his arm and rocked, moaning low under his breath as the realization of the impossible sank in and took hold.

Dr. Hackler sat back down, crossed his arms, dropped his chin to his chest and waited.

"What am I going to do now?" Jon managed past lips numbed with shock.

"I suggest getting dressed, for a start," Hackler said, his tone matter-of-fact as he pointed to a neatly folded pile at the foot of the cot.

"When you're decent, we will discuss your predicament with Mrs. Perkins. I spent the night pondering your plight, Hansen, and it seems to me it is in your best interests to carry on as Tom Dorin until you are acclimated sufficiently to move on."

He handed Jon the stack of unfamiliar clothing. "To do that, you must convince Mrs. Perkins that you are not a danger or a useless drain upon her resources."

Jon was still too stunned to argue, in fact, it was a life-line to be told what to do. He pulled on—Dorin's? — clothes, moving robotically. He had to suck in hard to button the waist on the trousers. Damn, did the man live on laudanum alone?

The doctor handed him his hat. Jon raked his fingers through his hair again and settled it on his head. He took up Dorin's cane and started for the door.

"Button your shirt completely," Hackler commanded.

"Why? It's hot."

"What does that have to do with it?" Hackler opened the door and stepped out.

Not having the mental energy to argue, Jon did as he was told and followed Hackler. Instead of heading right, towards the boarding house, Hackler turned left.

"I thought we were going to talk to Mrs. Perkins?" Jon asked, not able to care much one way or the other.

"We are, but I do not want to impose upon her for our breakfasts." He led Jon back into the hotel dining room.

A plate full of food was soon set in front of Jon, and though he forked it from plate to mouth, chewed and swallowed, if he had been asked between bites what he was eating, he would have had to look down at the plate to answer. The doctor didn't seem to feel the need for light conversation over the meal, and Jon certainly didn't.

Back on the boardwalk, Jon might as well have been walking from his bedroom to his living room, for all the attention he paid to the early morning bustle all around.

Hackler herded him around the side of the boarding house, and up to the back door. He took off his hat and rapped on the door.

"Good morning, Mrs. Lefler," Hackler said to the woman who opened it. The woman who Jon had swept into an impromptu waltz the morning before.

"Good morning, Doctor." She turned an obviously suspicious stare on Jon. "He doesn't look like he's from the future."

The doctor's eyebrows rose high on his forehead.

Mrs. Lefler gave a sniff. "Yes, she told me. Doesn't mean I believe it."

Her scathing gaze honed in on Jon then. "You still look exactly like the same ignorant, low-bred, uncouth Rebel cracker you always were. I believe the only thing we didn't know about you, Tom Dorin or whoever you are, is that you are the most outrageous liar that I've had the bad luck to come across."

Her ill will was a bracing slap across the face. "Wow, you do not like him at all, do you? Why? Does he call you a nigger?"

She stiffened. "No. But you just have."

She stepped to one side. "Come in, Doctor. Hattie's waiting in our private parlor."

When Jon moved to follow, Mrs. Lefler blocked his way with an arm across the doorway.

"*You* stay out here until *she* invites you in." She slammed the door in his face.

Jon shook his head.

"Dorin, if this is the impression you make on women, Dee's gonna make hanging seem like sweet relief," he muttered under his breath.

Having nothing better to do, he waited, hat in his hand, and studied the back yard with new eyes. This wasn't the backdrop for some dream refluxed up from an overdose of research. This may be his workplace for the duration of— whatever this was. Time travel? Translocation? A psychotic break? Maybe Chris was right for once.

"Mr. Hansen?"

Jon turned at the soft voice behind him. Hattie Perkins stood just inside the kitchen door.

"Yes?" he answered.

"Won't you come in, please?" She led him through a room he would have recognized as a kitchen only because of the woodburning cook stove and the pots and pans. Once in the hallway with the seizure-inducing blue-striped wallpaper, she led him through another door hung with a screen of glass beads. Dr. Hackler rose as they entered, and Mrs. Lefler eyed him with as much goodwill as she had before.

Hattie closed the door. This room was much less cluttered and over-stuffed with furniture than the parlor he'd first explored. It was bright, and even though the room looked like it should be behind a velvet rope in a museum, it felt more familiar and comfortable than any other he'd been in here.

"Please, sit down."

He settled into a rocker. Hattie perched herself on the edge of an upholstered armchair.

"I am not accustomed to subterfuge, Mr. Hansen, but Doctor Hackler and I have both come to the same conclusion."

"I have to pull off a spot-on Dorin impression," Jon interrupted. These people tended to talk like they wrote. Long winded, with sparing use of periods.

It obviously took Hattie a few extra seconds to process his colloquialisms. "Yes, that's the sum of it. Do you agree?"

"I haven't had the chance to think it through like you two," he said. "But off the top of my head, it sounds reasonable. I know a lot about this period, but it's all scholarly. I have no idea how to actually survive here, if I struck out on my own."

"Scholarly," Mrs. Lefler scoffed under her breath. "Usually another word for bone-lazy."

"Ophelia, please," Hattie rebuked, just as softly, and looked back at Jon.

"I have no need of a scholar, Mr. Hansen. I need a man who can work with his hands and is willing to do so. Do you have any experience in manual labor?"

The last thing he expected this morning was a job interview. "I've worked in construction and done some handyman work."

She rose and retrieved a piece of paper from a desk against the wall. "Will you be able to complete these tasks?"

Jon scanned the list, scheduling every hour in a long day's worth of pre-industrial drudgery. The only thing that gave him pause was milking, but how hard could that be? He'd done it once, as a kid, at the fair. "Sure, I can handle this."

Ophelia muttered something that Jon couldn't make out and Hattie apparently chose to ignore. From the way Hackler's eyes crinkled at the corners, though, he'd heard it.

"Mrs. Perkins?"

"Yes Doctor?"

"I believe Mrs. Lefler has suggested an excellent explanation for any lapses in Mr. Hansen's mimicry."

"Oh?"

Hackler looked at Jon, and this time his smile was visible beneath the overhanging lip shrubbery. His words came out in a wickedly dead-on rural Tennessee twang. "Weell, you see I hit m' head in thet fall and it done knocked me plum' crazy."

"So long as it doesn't lead to me being locked in some mental asylum somewhere," Jon said, not quite as amused. But the idea did have merit.

"That depends on your ability to pass yourself off as Mr. Dorin," Hackler said. "And refraining from offending the sensibilities of the populace too often."

"Then I'm scr— sunk," Jon amended quickly. "But I'll give it my best shot."

"It would be in your best interest," the doctor added, his tone pointed.

"And in Mr. Dorin's of course," Hattie added in her genteel voice. "When you both return to your rightful time."

Ophelia did not deign to comment, but only shook her head with a disgusted look that included them all.

23 October, 1873
~ The next morning ~

"Damn you to McDonald's!" Jon cursed from the safety of the barn hall. He rubbed his shin. "You nearly broke my leg, you mooin' shit factory!"

"You all right, Mr. Dorin?"

Jon jerked his head around, startled. Ophelia's little boy, Harold, stood at the end of the hall, an odd expression on his face. He hurried over and held Dorin's cane out.

He really needed it now, thanks to that walking waste of leather. Jon took it, grabbed the bashed-in bucket she'd kicked out after him, and heaved himself to his feet.

"I thought you and Queenie had come to an understandin'," Harold said.

"She obviously voided the contract," Jon muttered.

"Huh?"

"She's evil." Jon glared at the back end of the now placid-looking beast.

Harold giggled. "Yep!" He frowned then, looking down at Jon's right leg. "Did she hurt you bad?"

"Naw, jist stepped on m' foot then raised a sore knot when she kicked me," Jon answered, remembering to drawl. Better late than never. He eyed the boy. "You ever milk this here cow, Harold?"

"Yes sir," he answered with a frown. "You know I did. And I milked for you yesterday evening, too."

Oh crap. Jon rubbed his forehead. "Fergive me, Harold. Since I hit m' head, ever'thang's kinda all mixed up in here."

Harold flung his arms around Jon's waist and hugged tight, then backed up quick as if the impulsive affection startled him.

It certainly startled Jon. Not that he minded. Harold seemed to be a good kid.

"It's gonna be all right, Mr. Dorin," the little boy told him, looking up almost as if he were about to cry. "You'll get better real soon. I know you will."

Jon reached out and ran a hand over the boy's head. Whatever else Dorin might have been or done, at least he'd obviously been kind to this kid.

"Thanks, Harold. I will. It's jist gonna take a while, I reckon."

He looked back towards the cow, and grimaced. "But not quick enough for Queenie, or your mother. If I don't git this milk up to her purty soon...."

Harold let out a sympathetic whistle. "Want me to show you how you do it?"

"I'd be much obliged," Jon nodded.

Harold gave him a grin, and darted off to the feed bin. "Well, first you'd get her some sweet feed. You said she was too thin and this would fatten her up and keep her busy while she's milked."

He hustled back and went into the next stall, climbing up on the manger to pour it over the divider into the one in front of Queenie. "She doesn't like it if you go in on her until she's eatin', remember?"

Jon nodded.

Harold bounced back through the barn and returned with a bucket of water, a rag and a brush. "Now you can brush her, wash off her bag and start milkin', but ya gotta hurry. You see that string hangin' on her tail? You use that to tie her tail to her leg so she doesn't swat you in the face. And when you sit down, don't forget to head-bump her above her bag a few times, so she thinks you're her calf. Like this."

Harold mimed the move with a couple of backwards nods.

Jon blurted a laugh.

Harold blinked, then laughed too. A bell began to ring somewhere down the street.

"Damn it to McDonald's! I gotta get to school."

"Harold!" Jon was amused, but he assumed Dorin would be appalled.

"Well, you said damn," Harold retorted with a cheeky grin, "And shit too. I heard you."

"Yes I did, but I shouldn't have and you weren't supposed to hear me." Jon smiled back. "Don't you go repeatin' them words either, or your Mamma will flog us both!"

"I won't!" Harold promised as he ran out of the barn. "At least, not where she can hear me!" he added over his shoulder.

"Careful, I suspect she's omniscient," Jon muttered, and turned back to his other nemesis. "Okay, Hamburger. Let's try this procedure again, shall we?"

Queenie lifted her tail and deposited her opinion in the dung channel.

CHAPTER NINETEEN

October 26, Present Day
Tucson, Arizona
~ Six days later ~

Dee unlocked the bedroom door and opened it cautiously.

The hesitation was unnecessary. Dorin lay curled into a tight fetal ball in the center of the bed, his body twitching with violent shivers. He was wet with sweat, the bedclothes a tangled mess around him.

"Tom?" She moved closer and set the cup down on the nightstand.

He lifted his head.

There was no doubting the veracity of his misery. His pupils were dilated, and he squinted up at her, trying to focus through red-rimmed watering eyes. His nose was bloody-raw, the skin chapped almost off by constant running and wiping. She could see his quivering jaw muscles clenched, his face blanched whiter around the lips, signs of serious pain borne stoically.

"I suppose asking you how you feel would a pointless question."

"Yes'm," he mumbled, and dragged sweat-soaked, tangled hair away from his face with a trembling hand. He pushed himself up to sit hunched over, and reached for the sheet.

Dee helped pull it up around his shoulders. "I'm not going to badger you into the shower today."

"Thank you."

She waited for a minute or so, long enough for him to close his eyes. When he didn't speak again, she touched his shoulder. "I brought some broth. You need to try to drink it."

"Not sure it'll stay down, but I'll try."

She handed him the cup. As he slowly sipped at it, she moved around the room and the bathroom, refilling his water mug, changing the bag in the pail by the bed, setting out another box of tissues for his eyes and nose, gathering a clean set of sheets for him.

The whole time, she kept glancing over. He simply sipped his broth, silent. When she laid the sheets at the foot of the bed, he set the cup aside.

"I'm sorry, ma'am. If I drink any more right now, it's jist gonna come right back up."

"Okay, but try to sip on it some more as you can. You need the nourishment. Do you think you can get up so I can change the sheets for you?"

He nodded, and slid to the edge of the bed.

Dee draped his arm around her shoulders and supported him to sit in the chair drawn up close to the bed. He wrapped his arms around his midsection and curled up.

Once he was settled back into the fresh bed, Dee smoothed the sheet over him.

"Thank you," he whispered, eyes closed again, the helpless, emotionless tears of withdrawal seeping from under his lids. He wiped his cheeks and his nose with the tissue in his fist.

Dee went into the bathroom and got some petroleum jelly. She swabbed it over his raw nose and cracked, scaling lips.

Tom gave a little sigh. "That feels better. Thank y'."

"Tom?"

He opened his eyes and lifted his head. "Yes'm?"

"Why haven't you asked me again for laudanum? One dose would make all this go away."

He grimaced. "I know. But you said it was illegal now. I don't want to break the law for a bit of relief and I sure ain't gonna ask you to do it for me."

He laid his head back down.

She could imagine the stiffness and aching in his muscles, the cramps in his gut. Misery so intense that most who suffered through it were certain they were dying. "Try to sleep if you can. I'll be back to check on you in an hour or so."

Tom nodded and curled himself up tightly again.

Dee stepped out of the room and leaned back against the closed door, eyes squinted hard. She didn't lock the door when she moved away.

CHAPTER TWENTY

1 November, 1873
Cooper's Creek, AZT
~ Twelve days later ~

Doctor Hackler had just dismounted after making his rounds when a rider came into town at a frantic gallop, scattering chickens and children and more than a few startled pedestrians caught in his path.

He pulled up in front of the livery, his horse roaring and foamed with sweat. "Don't bother unsaddlin', Doc!" he called out as Lem stepped out.

"What's happened?" Doc swung himself back into the saddle of his ugly, ill-tempered gray.

"Accident up at the mine. Fella got his arm crushed. It's broke bad. Bones is stickin' out."

Hackler turned to the wide-eyed boy watching from the end of the sidewalk. "Buck, run up to Mrs. Perkins and tell Dorin I'm on my way with a horse. I want him to go with me."

"Yes sir!" Buck all but saluted, impressed with the urgency of the call. He darted out of the stable at his own version of a full gallop.

"I'll saddle Punkin for ya, Doc. Seems Deuce favors her lately." As he spoke, Lem hefted a saddle from the rack. "Johnston, take him on into the corral. I'll cool him off and rub him down. Go ahead and harness the team to the buggy."

The messenger nodded and dismounted, leading his exhausted horse into the enclosure.

"Thank you, Lem." Hackler guided his horse carefully past the stableman, and loped towards his office.

He swung down at the foot of the stairs, flipping a rein over the flimsy banister. Deuce stood obediently in place. The gelding was an intractable biter and a shameless kicker, but he was content as a stone to stand tied.

∞

Buck ran over to Mrs. Perkins house and pounded on the door with all the enthusiasm and authority mustered by the emergency.

"Why are you beatin' on Miz Perkin's door, Buchanan Hatch?" Harold demanded with some self-importance of his own. "You got some bad news?"

"Doc's bringin a horse for Mister Dorin to go with him out to the mine for a 'mergency." Buck responded airily. "So guess you better go get him!"

"I reckon," Harold grudgingly agreed. "You stay here. Miz Perkins doesn't need you trackin' in with your dirty bare feet." He turned and hurried through the house.

He went straight through and out to the back, where poor Mr. Dorin was having all kinds of trouble splitting kindling.

"Whoa! What's up Harold?" Sweating profusely, frustrated, Jon was glad for the break. "Someone chasing after you?"

"No sir, not 'xactly. More like they're after you. Buck says Doc's bringin' a horse for you. There's a 'mergency at the mine."

"What?" Jon looked at the boy, confused. "Why would Doc want me?" Still, he picked up his hat and followed Harold.

"I dunno. Buck didn't say." Harold sniffed. "Buck doesn't ever say anythin' that he doesn't absolutely have to, like he's one of those new telegraph things. He thinks he's some big frog, 'cause people send him with messages and he helps deliver the mail. He knows everything that goes on around here and keeps most of it to hisself."

"He has to. Private messages should be kept private."

200

"I'm not gonna tell nobody," Harold retorted in a slightly offended tone. He trotted ahead to burst through the kitchen doorway.

"Mamma! Miz Hattie! Doc's gonna take Mr. Dorin up to the mine! There's a 'mergency, Buck says!"

Jon met the taciturn Buck at Hattie's front gate. "Harold says Doc wants me?"

"Yes sir, he's comin' with a horse." Buck pointed down the street to Dr. Hackler, riding towards them at a fast lope, leading a saddled horse.

Following Buck, Jon called up to him, "Why do you need me?"

"Mount up, we're wasting time," Hackler said as Buck darted back down the street.

Jon looked apprehensively at the horse, then awkwardly swung himself up into the saddle.

Harold watched from his sentry-post on the porch.

Hackler urged his horse into a fast canter. "Your first day with us, you spoke as though you know more about medicine than I do. If that isn't the case, I sincerely hope you will not allow your pride to overshadow your knowledge."

Jon yelped as his horse sped up to keep up with the doctor's. "I dunno. Maybe I do. What's the emergency?" he gasped, struggling to keep his seat.

"Open fracture," Hackler replied. "So we need to make time, or our patient might be rude enough to bleed to death before we get there."

Jon raced through what he could remember. "Uhm. You need alcohol, for preventing infection. Uh... pins?"

"Alcohol I have in quantity, per our discussion on infection control and the contributions of Koch and Pasteur," the doctor nodded, but then gave him a quizzical scowl. "Pins? I'll be suturing flesh, not piecing a quilt."

Jon closed his eyes and hung on tight as his horse bounced over a gap in the road. "Hardware pins, or screws maybe. They put them in my brother's arm when he broke it. I guess they screwed the broken ends together or something. I don't remember exactly."

"That's a shame," Hackler grumbled, "Because what you describe is an entirely novel process. A pity you can't recall the details."

"Dammit, Doc, I was thirteen, my brother was screaming his head off, I was afraid he would die and I'd get blamed for it. I'm a historian! Not even a medical historian. Cut me some slack."

"This town has no need of historians." Hackler gave him a measuring look, "But anyone with medical knowledge is an asset."

The doctor kneed his horse closer, and caught the bridle of Jon's horse. "Let us hope you make a better apprentice than you are a horseman. Give me your reins and hang onto the pommel, boy. I want to get there before nightfall!"

Jon handed over his reins and Hackler touched his own horse with his spurs. The big gray sprang into a gallop as they passed the last dwelling on the main road.

Jon gulped, grabbing leather and a handful of coarse mane, hoping the beast would follow the doctor's horse and not dump him in a ditch somewhere as he frantically searched his memory for anything left behind by a 'History of Medicine' undergrad class, a Red Cross First Aid/CPR class and Dee's offhand comments when she studied or talked about her shifts.

When they came within sight of the mining camp, Hackler handed the reins back to Jon. "Think you can keep your seat the rest of the way in?"

"Go. If I fall off, I'll walk in," Jon replied. "If the bone's sticking out, infection is the worst thing. Sterilize it with boiling water, alcohol, or heat."

"I do remember your opinion of laudable pus," Hackler nodded and slowed his gray to a lope as they passed through the narrow, crowded 'street' through the center of the mining camp.

"I'm trying to remember! Jeez, I'm not a doctor. I don't even know enough to fake it."

"You know more than a miner," Hackler pointed out.

He headed up towards the main shaft, where a crowd was gathering in the unmistakable configuration of tragedy.

Jon followed the doctor, wincing as he heard the shrill scream of a very young man or a child. Either option chilled him.

"Stand aside!" Hackler bellowed and all but shoved his way in with his horse's broad forequarters and snapping teeth. He swung out of the saddle and dropped the animal's reins. The big gray instantly relaxed, though he would still lay back his ears and snake his ugly head towards anyone who got too close. Hackler slung his saddlebags over his shoulder, tossed his kit-bag to Jon, and made his way towards the screams.

Still confused as to what his role was to be, Jon caught the bag and slid off his horse.

The injured miner was barely out of childhood. His cries of pain were forced out through jaws clenched in desperate, premature machismo. His right arm lay at unnatural angles, darkening blood and pulpy flesh visible through tears in the boy's sleeve.

The doctor made his way to the injured boy, who'd been laid on a makeshift table formed from planks held up by barrels.

"Anybody got hot water, I need it," he informed the crowd at large, then laid a gentle hand on the boy's forehead. With the other, he grasped the lad's injured hand. It was blue-tinged, and lax.

The boy's face was pale, his skin clammy. Jon realized the kid was slipping into shock. They didn't have much more time.

"Loosen the tourniquet, Ian," Hackler instructed the man holding a loop of cord twisted tight around the boy's armpit and shoulder.

As the ligature slackened, bright fresh blood welled up from the wounds to join the sticky darker puddle on the wood, but the hand did not pink.

"Move your fingers for me, son," Doc said.

"I can't," the boy moaned. "I can't even feel 'em."

"Tighten the tourniquet again," Hackler instructed curtly, but his voice softened as he spoke to the boy. "You're going to be all right, Sean."

He glanced over at Jon.

"Cut away his sleeve," Hackler ordered. "Then get out the chloroform. It's in a small leather case along with a mask. Soak the mask's sponge with chloroform and for the lord's sake, don't breathe the fumes."

"I'm gonna lose it, aint I?" Sean gasped out.

Jon took the straight razor in the kit and cut off the boy's sleeve. He turned away quickly, blanching at the sight of exposed bones and mangled flesh. Jon opened the bag the doctor had tossed to him and found the case, preparing the tin mask as he was instructed.

"Here," he offered the implement to Hackler, avoiding the boy's eyes.

"Most likely," Hackler confirmed to Sean, his voice calm, though his expression was saddened. He began to examine Sean's arm, ignoring Jon's offer other than to say, "Put it over his mouth and nose. Sean, you breathe slow and even. Don't fight the fumes."

"I can't do without my arm, Doc." Sean said, his voice strained but stoic.

The ravaged limb was limp as a sock from shoulder to elbow, the flesh crushed, and the bone shattered into at least four or five pieces. Hackler shook his head.

"Son, you won't be able to do anything with it, either. It's useless to you now."

"Then take off the band." The boy shuddered. "Let me bleed."

"Losing an arm's better than losing your life. Breathe deep and try to be calm. Tom, apply the mask. Now."

Jon lowered the mask over the boy's face. "Dammit, Doc, can't you do anything?"

Sean twitched and began to toss his head back and forth, his eyes wide, his pupils constricting.

"I am doing something, Mr. Dorin. I'm doing my best to save this boy's life. You, and you! He's going to thrash as he goes under the chloroform. Hold him down."

The two burly men the doctor conscripted took a leg each. The first man, who was holding the tourniquet tight, leaned his weight against the boy's uninjured shoulder.

True to Hackler's prediction, Sean began to buck and squirm against their holds, reflexively struggling as the vapors disconnected mind from body. His shouts were unintelligible. His scream was all too clear.

Unfazed, the doctor spread a clean towel and opened an amputation kit atop another barrel. Needles threaded with silk sutures rested in a bottle of alcohol. A bowl of steaming water was set nearby, and Hackler used it and the soap and nailbrush in his kit to scrub his hands. He lifted Sean's ruined arm and laid it on another drape.

Jon blinked, and a tear dripped onto the tin inhaler. "He's just a kid! He should be playing video games! He should be plotting how to get Ellie Mae out of her drawers."

The doctor showed no sign of hearing that. He cleaned Sean's skin above the ugly wound with swabs and alcohol. "Now find his pulse and keep a watch on his pupils. If they dilate, his pulse slows, or if his breathing becomes shallow, lift the inhaler and sing out."

Sean gave one last inarticulate yell from beneath the mask. His straining body went slack against the planks.

"Sean! Can you hear me?" Hackler called near the boy's ear.

Sean did not respond. Hackler checked the boy's pupils then waited for a minute or two longer. Seeing no further movement from the boy, he glanced at Jon. "He's deeply unconscious. You may lay the inhaler aside now."

The doctor moved swiftly, his motions sure from skill and practice as he began the task of dismembering Sean below the deltoid muscle. For all his precision, the process resembled more the work of a fastidious butcher than the careful ministration of a compassionate healer.

"There's got to be a better way. God, Doc, he's just a kid!"

"Contain yourself, Tom," Hackler rumbled, almost absent-mindedly.

The sound of the saw against bone undid him. Jon upset the bottle of chloroform as he turned away, gagging. One of the spectators grabbed the bottle before it emptied itself.

Hackler didn't spare Jon a glance. "Kick my assistant aside, Harper, and take over watching the boy's pulse and breathing. I shouldn't be more than four or five more minutes."

The doctor's voice was as calm as if he was discussing the price of apples. He laid the detached arm aside as if discarding a stick of firewood, then began to rasp the cut end of the bone to smooth the edges.

Jon stared down at the horrible object. It seemed sacrilegious, almost, to leave the arm abandoned, its fingers curled palm-up, as if pleading for help. But he didn't have the spine to pick the thing up, either.

Hackler secured flaps of muscle and fat over the end of the stump and, neat as a seamstress, closed the skin back over it.

Jon pulled his morbid gaze from the severed limb in time to catch Hackler's skillful repair of the stump. "This is... wrong."

"There's no help for it," the man holding the tourniquet told him. His voice shook, and his face was white beneath the dirt on his face. "If he didn't take me son's arm, we'd be burying the whole of him."

"Finnegan," one of the spectators asked the man in a hushed tone. "My Nora will see to your Missus when Johnston brings her in."

God, oh god— Ian Finnegan! The washerwoman's husband. Sean's father. Sean Finnegan, his friend Joe Finnegan's great-great grandfather from Cooper's Creek.

Jon felt sick now for an entirely different reason. He grabbed one of the towels from Hackler's bag and picked up Sean's severed arm. It felt heavy and cold. He wrapped it as if the rag was a burial shroud.

~ *Later that evening* ~

After a couple of months of sedentary scholarship, and the past week of relentless nineteenth century manual labor while wearing Dorin's lopsided boots, plus getting kicked by a cow, plus today's precarious horseback ride to the mining camp, Jon found himself wracked with spasming pain in his lower back and stiff muscles everywhere else.

He considered bribing Moz at the bath house for a whole barrel of scalding hot water, but was pretty sure he wouldn't be able to get himself out of one of those high-sided tin tubs. That is, if his stoved-up back would let him lift a leg high enough to get in.

Aspirin, he sadly recalled, wouldn't be available for at least another twenty years.

He slowly made his way up to his room and went to the washstand. That little aqua bottle, a quarter full of brown fluid, had more than historical appeal now. Jon picked up it up. Laudanum. It certainly trumped aspirin on the fast and sure pain relief scoreboard. He read the label again.

206

The word 'Poison' was off-putting. The word 'Narcotic,' touted as a virtue, wasn't much more reassuring. He turned it in his hand, watching the fluid shift, measuring his misgivings against his pain.

Somewhere below his open window, a cat screeched. Jon flinched. The creepy noise signaled feline lust, not pain, but it set off echoes of another shrill scream in his memory. Between his aching body and his reeling brain, Jon knew that sleep would only come tonight if pharmaceutically induced.

"It's not meth, idiot," he mumbled. "You aren't going to turn into an addict from using it just once."

He filled the little tin cup with water from the pitcher. Very carefully, he measured out six drops from the bottle. He swirled the cup to mix the fluids. As he lifted it to his lips, he caught his own gaze in the mirror.

"Cheers, Dorin." He saluted his reflection with the cup, then swallowed the dose.

CHAPTER TWENTY-ONE

October 29, Present Day
Tucson, Arizona
~Eight days later~

Withdrawal, as Dee called it, had brought one mercy amongst its torments. Lying curled into a shivering, aching, cramping, goose-fleshed, snot-streaming, sweating ball of misery for a week had kept him too occupied to fret about the greater predicament he was in.

Last night he'd finally slept for more than a restless hour, and this morning he felt like he was on the mend. Tom stretched, working out a few kinks down his back, and looked out the window. The sky was beginning to lighten and the house, except for Chris' snores, was quiet.

Tom gathered his crutches and went over to try the door. Dee must have unlocked it sometime while he slept.

He went back and got a clean set of the clothes they had given him. Dee had forced him into the shower nearly every day. He hadn't yet learned to like the sensation for it was too much like standing naked in a driving rainstorm, despite the warmth of the water. But that tub in the other bathroom was a fine one indeed, and the anticipation of a long hot soak propelled him down the hall.

He came to an abrupt halt, seeing Dee standing at the sink, cleaning her teeth.

She spat froth and rinsed her mouth. "So, you're ambulatory this morning."

"I reckon," he answered, not knowing what he was answering to. Agreement seemed least likely to cause upset.

Her clothing puzzled him. It was obviously some sort of uniform, with badges and a nameplate and a webbing belt hung with pouches, buckled around britches festooned with a multitude of pockets. "Ma'am, forgive me for bein' forward... but are you a soldier?"

The thought was unsettling, but he had heard of a few such. Of course, any woman in uniform he'd heard of was passing herself off as a boy. Dee's uniform didn't in any way conceal her gender, and she had her long brown hair pinned up on her head in a very feminine plaited crown. Tiny studs sparkled in her earlobes.

Dee shot him an odd look then glanced down at herself. She gave a little chuff and shook her toothbrush dry.

"First of all, would you please drop all that obsequious ma'am malarkey? I'm no older than you. Calling me Dee is fine and keeps you from sounding so much like some hick goober. And no, I'm not a soldier, and I'm not a police officer."

That last occupation hadn't even entered his head.

"I'm a paramedic. But you wouldn't know that word. I'm a—" she paused, tilted her head and thought a second or two. "A civilian ambulance driver and doctor's field assistant."

Tom was surprised by that on several levels. Then she added a few more.

"And since my morning sickness finally stopped this week, thank God, I'm going back to work while I'm still able."

She glanced at the tiny watch she wore on her wrist. "Crap. Hope traffic's light."

"Goodbye, Dee," he murmured as she brushed past and hurried away.

Morning sickness, that was a term he hadn't heard, but he knew what it meant anyway. His poor mother had suffered terrible sickness in the morning every time she was in the family way. Dee was working a man's job while that way. John was soon to be a father. What little optimism the day had brought evaporated like dawn mist.

Tom turned on the water in the tub and sat down on the edge to wait for it to fill.

Somehow, he had to figure out how to set things back right for them all, and soon. Lord only knew how her John was getting along, back in Cooper's Creek. A man used to hot and cold running water, free-roaming locomotives, ambulances driven by women in a delicate condition and all the other changes of this age must be as confused and bewildered by the nineteenth century as he was by the twenty-first.

❧

Soaking to his chin until the scalding water started going cool soothed his body but did nothing to soothe his mind. When he stepped back out into the hall, he smelled cooking and realized all of a sudden that he was half-starved.

Chris looked around from the white porcelain cook stove. "You look better."

"I am," Tom said. His nose led him to a glass pot of strong coffee. He filled one of the mugs that hung nearby and dropped into a kitchen chair. The first sip was always pure heaven, but this coffee tasted better than any he'd ever had.

"Milk's in the fridge," Chris offered. "That big white metal cabinet against the wall. Sugar's in the bowl on the table."

"I apreciate it, but it's fine as it is," Tom savored another sip, feeling the warmth spread out in his empty belly.

Chris set a plate in front of him of fried eggs, sugar-cured ham and grits. "I heard you and Dee up and around earlier. I thought you might be ready to eat when you finished marinating in there."

"Looks good, thank you."

"De nada."

Nothing more was said between them until Tom got up to refill his mug.

Chris sopped up the last of his egg yolk with a bit of toast, stuffed it into his mouth and held his mug out.

Tom obliged him, and sat back down.

"Chris, if I knew how to get your brother back here, he'd already be home." Tom kept his eyes on his mug.

"I know." Chris leaned forward, shoved his plate away to make room for his crossed arms. "I've been giving that a hell of a lot of thought while you were in the throes of d-i-y detox."

"You come up with anything? 'Cause I admit I'm beat six ways from Sunday on this 'un."

"Nothing solid— time travel is considered fiction, not science, at least by anyone not wearing a tin-foil beanie. But we've got some strong clues to go on."

"The visions me and Jon both seen in the Dove?"

"Exactly," Chris nodded, "and the über-creepy physical resemblance between the two of you. Okay, here's what I'm thinking."

Chris took another slug of coffee as he gazed past Tom's shoulder, eyes unfocused, clearly getting his mental ducks in a row. "Do you know what a tuning fork is?"

"Sure."

"Okay, you know that if you strike one fork to make it hum, and bring another one set to the same note near it, the new fork will start humming without being touched, right?"

"I ain't never done it, but I've heard tell it's so."

"They will," Chris said. "So, my thought is, that for some reason, because you and Jon are obviously extremely similar physically, when you were both at the same point in space, on the same day in the year, maybe even under the same atmospheric conditions, you both started vibrating to the same frequency, made a connection without contact, like those forks."

Tom took that in. "I can sorta see that, but what happened to us, it'd be like if I set a fork to singing on this table and you brung one in a century later and it rung even though the first was long gone and silent. And then them two forks switched places."

"Yeah, there is that." Chris sighed.

His expression was so grieved that Tom couldn't bear to keep his eyes on Chris'. He looked down at his mug instead, turning it. It had a picture of a cat with a huge toothy grin and as he twisted the cup, the cat faded in and out of view, leaving only that menacing smile behind.

"I think we're on the right trail," he offered. "For him and me both to see the same thing at the same time, that cain't be chance. It would be easier to figure if we'd exchanged places then and there, but it was three days later."

"Maybe there was a link, a connection, created at the Dove that day, but it wasn't triggered until later." Chris said.

"Like a long fuse?"

"Exactly. But what set it off?"

Tom thought back to his last day in Cooper's Creek and grimaced. "Cain't be pain. I was hurtin' bad but your brother weren't."

"No, he wasn't in physical pain. Emotionally I'm sure he was a wreck."

"Why? What happened?"

"He and Dee fought over her pregnancy. He said something incredibly stupid to her and she kicked him out. When he came back later that evening to talk to her, I could tell he was really torn up about it."

Tom's head came up. "Despair."

"Yeah.... Wait, you're saying that's what triggered it?"

Tom dropped his eyes again. "Maybe."

"Why? What happened to you? I thought you had a riding accident."

"I did," he agreed. "But the bruises weren't the worst of it. Sukie…"

Tom had to stop, afraid his voice was going to break.

He felt a hot rush of shame and clenched his jaw. "Dammit, she's jist a worthless little scrub mare, but… the truth is that she's the first livin' creature I let myself care about for more than ten years. She broke her leg when she fell and I had to blow her brains out and leave her layin' for the buzzards and coyotes."

Chris made noise that might or might not have been sympathetic.

Tom didn't dare look up at him. He pinched the bridge of his nose hard and stared blindly at the grain of the tabletop until he felt he could trust his voice again. "I laid in my bed that day feelin' like everything I touched turned to dust and ashes."

"The lowest point of your life," Chris offered, almost under his breath.

Tom shook his head, lips tightening in a wry twist. "No, not the lowest, but way down there amongst 'em, for certain."

"I'm pretty sure it was that way for Jon, too." Chris blew out a long breath and dragged his hands down his face as if he were wiping away water. "So, you're both under incredible emotional stress, both exhausted physically. You were in tremendous physical pain as well, and got doped out of your mind. You both go to sleep, I'm betting at about the same time. Something about being asleep, in that condition, triggered the exchange."

Both of them sat silent for a while after that. Chris tapped his fork against his plate in a nervous tattoo.

"Helluva key to have to turn, to make it happen again." Tom finally said. "Maybe I should go back out to the town, keep a watch on the Dove in case that... vision... comes back."

Chris looked like he was going to agree, then he shook his head. "We've been over and over that, Dee and I. As much as we'd like to dump your sorry ass out in the desert, we keep coming up against the same strong hunch that you'll go back where you came in, probably in your sleep again."

Tom lifted an eyebrow. "I kinda doubt Dee'll go along with me sleepin' in her bed from now on."

Chris pulled a face. "I do too. But that's more likely to happen than you surviving out at that ghost town for any length of time. There's no water there anymore. That's what nailed the lid shut on that town."

"So what do you suggest we do?"

"Hope," Chris offered softly. "Pray, if you believe in that sort of thing."

Tom replied only with a huff of breath.

"Feeding you and talking with you doesn't mean I trust you. Do we have an understanding?"

Tom nodded. "Never expected you did. Trust has to be earned."

Chris finished his coffee. Tom toyed with his empty mug, watching that eerie cat disappearing, reappearing. He wondered why it smiled.

A few seconds later, Chris slapped the table, startling Tom.

"So! Enough of this for now," Chris said in a forced hearty tone. "It's time for Twenty-First Century Technology 101. First class: common household appliances and how to use them. Let me give you the guided tour."

CHAPTER TWENTY-TWO

17 November, 1873
Cooper's Creek, AZT
~ Sixteen days later ~

Jon moved the wheelbarrow down the barn hall to the cow-stall, hefted the manure-fork and went to work. He didn't understand why Hattie demanded such strict sanitation in her barn. Her cow probably had a cleaner bed than a good part of the human population. And how did Queenie repay that kindness? By covering as much of the fresh bright straw with flops as possible, every night. He wondered if Hattie was even aware of that fact.

"SOOOOPERSTISHUS!" sounded behind him, and "CLAPtrap!" as a small body landed in the straw pile.

"Gonna be 'skewered carcass' if you don't have a care, Master Harold Lefler," Jon scolded, hefting the manure fork menacingly, though he couldn't help but be amused by the boy. "What if y'd landed on this thang?"

"I'm too careful! I can leap like a mountain cat!" Harold swiped claws toward Jon. "Rawr!"

It felt good to joke with the boy, and let everything else slide for the moment.

Jon gave a little yelp of ersatz fright and 'threatened' Harold with the fork. "Don't you come no closer, you mean ol' lion!"

"RAWR!" Harold advanced on Tom. "I'm mean n' nasty and you can't scare me! I'll eat you all up!"

"Oh no! I'm doomed for sure!" Jon lamented, backing up down the hall. "A mountain lion stalkin' me and no gun, no rifle, nothin' but a flimsy ol' fork! Is there anythin' I kin do to talk you out of it? I'm real scrawny and tough as a boot, y'know. I'd probably jist stick in your craw and choke you to death."

"I'm gonna eat up Arnie Ledbottom, then, 'cause he ripped up the lizard I catched for Annie Marshall. RAWR!"

"Now that was right mean-spirited of ol' Arnie, and sad for that po'r lizard, so I cain't blame you for that." Jon planted the fork and leaned on the handle. "Now, though, I'm bettin' Annie Marshall would appreciate a flower or somethin' better'n a lizard. Girls are funny that way."

"But you can pick flowers anywhere when it rains... I had to catch that lizard!"

"True enough, and it don't make no sense, but there ya go all the same. Fact is, Arnie likely done you a favor despite himself. I'm bettin' if you'd come up to Annie with that big, fine lizard, she'd a screeched like a train whistle and took off runnin'."

"He's mad cuz she likes me better," Harold asserted. "She let me carry her books last week."

"That's a good sign, but even so, y'd do better with a flower than a lizard." Jon chuckled. "Don't want to lose your advantage over ol' Arnie, right?"

"Ma says I should let her alone," Harold pouted. "Let Arnie carry her books instead of me."

Jon suddenly realized the underlying import of the otherwise amusing little situation. Harold was black, and all the rest of his schoolmates were probably white. The fact that he was allowed to attend the school on equal footing was more a measure of how very few 'coloreds' there were in the Territory than a sign of enlightened public policy. If Harold, even at this innocent age, started paying affectionate attention to a little white classmate? Jon suppressed a shudder.

"Always good to listen to your Mamma, especially about such things as this," Jon nodded solemnly. "'Sides, girls ain't nothin' but trouble, you mark my words."

"Hmph," Harold looked up at Jon. "Mamma says you're a barefaced liar and I oughta stay away from you and Obie Elmslee says you're devil-rid but Doc says that's sooperstishus claptrap. Most ever'body else says you've gone plumb crazy."

Harold's expression wavered between indignation and hurt. "But I know you ain't gone crazy like everbody's saying, you're still just all mixed up from hittin' your head. And you ain't mean so you can't have got a devil in you. And I know you ain't lyin', like Mamma says. You never lie, you said so yourself, right Mr. Dorin?"

Lovely. Just friggin' lovely. If even a kid had heard this kind of gossip, he was in deep manure already and the cow had nothing to do with it. He turned away and attacked the stall. "No, I'm not crazy and I'm not lying, and I'm certainly not demon-possessed. That's what devil-ridden means. It's strong words to say someone's devil-ridden, for folks that believe that sort of thing. Your sayin' they're likely damned to Hell."

"Well, then it sure ain't right for Obie to go around sayin' it, either. I'll pop him in the mouth if he spouts it again." Harold mulled it over in his head and came up with his other authority figure. "Sooperstishus CLAP-trap!" he pronounced, goosing Jon.

Not in the mood to play around any longer, Jon simply shifted away from Harold's prodding fingers. He decided it would be best for the boy to reinforce the status-quo rather than get into his own eclectic belief system and futuristic civil rights.

"I wouldn't say that neither, if I was you." He flung a forkful of fouled straw and manure into the barrow. "Most folks hereabouts believe the devil's as real as God, and that he does torment folks. And don't go punching Obie in the mouth. That'll get you and probably your Mother too into more trouble than you can imagine."

"I won't," Harold muttered, kicking at a clot of straw. "But it don't mean I'm not gonna want to all the same. It's not right for folks to say what they do about you. It makes me madder than *hell*. I wish I could give them all a good thrashin'!"

"Well, I truly appreciate you wantin' to take up for me like that." Jon patted Harold's shoulder. "You're a fine, true friend. But you'll help me best by stayin' outta trouble and watchin' your language. If your Momma hears you cussin' she'll likely think I've taught you, which I likely have, and she'll thrash both of us."

He hefted the wheelbarrow and moved out of the barn to dump it on the muck-heap.

"Mister Dorin," Harold ran up to him as he dumped the manure. The boy threw his arms around Jon's waist and hugged tight. "I know you ain't crazy or devil-rid or nothin' of the sort. You're my best friend, Mr. Dorin."

Jon had to blink a few times to clear his vision. "Your my best friend too, Harold." He rubbed his hand over the boy's back.

"HAROLD CURTIS LEFLER!" pealed out across the yard.

Harold cringed, hearing his mother's summons.

"Better go quick," Jon urged. "It's never good when they use all three of your names!"

"Yep. Never good when y'answer, neither," Harold muttered, trudging across the yard to meet his doom.

It was a great effort, but Jon managed to stifle his chuckle till the dejected little boy was out of earshot. No, it always went from bad to worse at that point.

He put the wheelbarrow and fork away, and then went to the woodpile. The realization his own situation was going from bad to worse sobered him. If these people became convinced he was a dangerous psycho, his fate could be a lot worse than a long drop on a short rope.

October 29, Present Day
Tucson, Arizona
~ Later the same day ~

By the end of his first convalescent day in this new century, Tom felt that he and Chris had achieved, if not yet an armistice, at least a wary cease-fire.

220

Tom sat out on the back veranda, leg propped up, sipping a tumbler of cold tea and watching the sunset fade. Chris looked haggard in that unguarded moment, staring out at the sky. Tom knew nothing he could say would make the man's loss any easier to bear, nor the uncertainty more certain. None of them knew how to undo this strange curse laid on their lives.

Tom frowned. This wasn't his fault, no more than any of theirs. It was high time to quit cringing and saying sorry every other word to them. Past time to lift his head, show them a grown man with some pride instead of a whipped boy. Start again now with them both as he meant to go on.

"How does she know so much about me?" he asked.

Chris looked over. "Jon studied you. Dug up your enlistment record and stuff like that. He talked to Dee about you, a lot. More than he should have."

"Why? I ain't nobody important."

"Look in the mirror."

It took another swallow of tea before the strangeness of that reply hit Tom full on. "Wait, you're sayin' he took an interest in me because I look like him?"

"Yes." Chris looked at him odd. "That's why I said, look in the mirror. It's not as if this hasn't come up before, like from the first friggin' second we laid eyes on you."

Tom leaned forward, startled that it hadn't dawned on him before. "How could he know?"

"Huh?"

"How could he know what I look like?"

"The picture," Chris answered, an unspoken 'you idiot' loud to hear in his tone.

"Picture?" Tom felt as confused as the village idiot, that was sure.

"Daguerreotype, tintype, graven image, whatever. You know— black box, steal soul?"

Once again, it felt like the earth dropped out from under him. "Chris, I ain't never had an image took in m' life."

"But... it's *old.*" Chris protested, his own expression stunned. "You had to have."

"No. I never did. Not even when I enlisted and a lot of fellers were havin' 'em took. I didn't want to spend the money then and I never had no reason to want one afterward."

"But..." Chris suddenly jerked his hip up to dig something out of his pocket. He poked at it with a forefinger then put it to his ear. "Dee Collins, please," he said to the object. "It's urgent."

Tom watched, newly resigned to silently riding out bouts of random mystification like this.

"Dee— where's that picture of Dorin? Look, I'll explain when you get home. Just tell me where it is. How'd it get there? Oh. Okay. No, nothing that won't keep till you get home. Later, kiddo."

Chris stuck the device back in his pocket. "Come on. We've got to move a sofa-bed."

Tom followed Chris into the room they called the study.

The sofa was incredibly heavy, and didn't want to slide over the grooves between the tiles, but with some grunts they budged it out a couple of feet.

A cheap wooden tintype case lay in the clotted dust behind it, the cover broken free from the back.

Chris picked it up and wiped off the image with his shirt tail. "The time-swap scrambled your brains, because somebody caught your best side." He handed it over.

Tom looked down at the image. His own gaunt face looked back, obviously riled enough to tear bloody hunks out of somebody. "This cain't be me."

"But—"

"I never had a image took. I never owned that shirt or that neckerchief. That is not me." He handed the eerie thing back.

Chris took it, looked down at it and back to him. "If it's not you," he whispered.

"It's your brother."

"Oh God— no! Jon said this was taken the day they hung you!" Chris' voice shook and he dropped down onto the couch as if his legs wouldn't hold him up any longer.

Somehow, Tom wasn't rattled, even though he could far too well imagine the feeling of a rough hemp noose around his throat. He propped his hip on the arm of the sofa.

"I say it's him. But maybe it is me and I jist don't know it now. Time seems to be movin' in lock-step for me and him, past and future, since back at the Dove. Whichever of us is there in that image, it ain't happened yet for the feller on that tintype. Not for another five months. A heck of a lot can happen to a man in five months."

CHAPTER TWENTY-THREE

25 November, 1873
Cooper's Creek, AZT
~ Eight days later ~

Jon forced his attention back to old Gus Hopkins' running dialogue, an unending stream of random info like the scrolling headlines across the bottom of the screen on a news channel.

"...Bank manager's new bride is supposed to be arrivin' on this week's stage. From back East."

Hopkins' tone said volumes about what he thought of Easterners. "Hope she ain't the kind to wilt in this heat. Now my Florence - she was a strong woman and a good one - none of those faintin' spells that those young women seem to take to nowadays. Place is startin' to be a reg'lar boomtown. I remember when—"

Mr. Hopkins rose from his seat with a grunt and lifted his hat to a woman stepping up onto the boardwalk. Jon rose and removed his hat as well, the action almost a reflex by now.

Not even the era's voluminous clothing could conceal the fact that the young woman was heavily pregnant. Jon was mildly surprised that current uptight social mores even allowed her out of the house.

"Good afternoon, Mister Hopkins." she said, inclining her head with regal grace. Her voice was breathy and girlish.

"Afternoon, Miz Ferris," Mr. Hopkins smiled. "How're you t'day?"

"I'm fine, thank you."

Jon didn't speak, remembering a stern etiquette lesson from Hattie. A gentleman does not speak to a passing lady unless spoken to. But wow, this woman could give Marilyn Monroe voice lessons.

Jon had an instant, incongruous mental image of Mrs. Ferris vamping 'Happy Birthday, Mr. President' to Ulysses S. Grant.

Perhaps she had been distracted by greeting Hopkins, or simply mis-stepped, awkward with her burgeoning belly. The heel of her shoe caught in the boardwalk and she lurched forward directly into Jon.

Dropping his hat, Jon caught her under her arms, but not before his hands encountered the surprisingly firm, rounded flesh at her calico-swathed waist. The sensation made him hesitate a moment before he brought Mrs. Ferris to her feet.

"Oh!" she squeaked as she stumbled, and stiffened in Jon's lingering hold, looking up into his face with wide, startled eyes. "Thank you, Mr. Dorin. You may release me now," she gasped.

"Of course, Ma'am," he mumbled, and drew away his hands.

"Oo!" she whimpered as soon as she bore her own weight, and started to sink to the dusty boards.

Jon caught her again. By the elbow this time.

"My—" She blushed despite her discomfort. "My shoe heel is trapped, sirs. I fear I've done myself an injury."

"I'll go find Doc. You know where your Billy is, Miz Ferris?" Mr. Hopkins asked.

"I believe he may still be at the freight yard," she replied, distracted, and leaned down towards her skirt hem. "Ooo!"

The little wail sent Hopkins scurrying off like an arthritic cockroach.

Jon knelt at Mrs. Ferris's skirt hem. "Ma'am, if y'd allow me, I might kin help."

She looked at him again, and bit at her lip as she leaned as far away from him as her trapped foot allowed.

Afraid, he suddenly realized. She was afraid of him. The town crazy was way too close for comfort.

Pain over-rode fear, though. "You may try, Mr. Dorin."

She reached down and drew up her skirt far enough to reveal a pair of sleek, dusty little high-button boots, with heels that sported their own pinched waists and broad bottoms; one of which was wedged out of sight through a knot-hole in the plank.

"I'm gonna have to touch you to free your boot, but I don' mean no disrespect 'r nothin', ma'am," he drawled as a precaution.

"I understand, Mr. Dorin." A sheen of sweat was standing out on her upper lip now. "Pleasem I'm in pain."

Jon closed his hands around her foot— not much bigger than a child's— and gave a hesitant, gentle tug.

Mrs. Ferris squeaked again, but the boot didn't budge.

Jon studied situation another second. Using any more force on her foot was going to injure her ankle even more. "I'm sorry, ma'am, but looks like I'm gonna have to take your boot off to free ya."

Mrs. Ferris reached down to run her fingertips over the row of shiny black buttons. "Oh dear. How? I have no buttonhook with me, of course!"

Crap. Pulling his knife to cut the buttons off would probably frighten her into hysterics. Or labor. "I reckon they's one in the store."

Jon looked up at the curious audience gathering around them. "One of y'all wanna go in and ask Hudson?"

"I will, sir," a young woman volunteered and darted into the store. Another opened a parasol over Mrs. Ferris to shade her from the sun.

"I think I seen Doc down at the Hotel," a little boy offered. "I'll run fetch him."

"Billy's at the—" The male speaker somewhere behind Jon self-edited in midstream. "I'll tell Billy he's needed, Miz Ferris."

"Here now, Mr. Dorin. Step aside and I'll assist Lissie."

The buttonhook volunteer brandished the tool and sank down to take the place he'd occupied at Mrs. Ferris's feet. She gave off a cloud of lilac perfume and sweat.

Jon rose and moved back. The female bystanders closed ranks around the pregnant woman then, clucking and cooing and patting. It was obvious he was now superfluous and entirely forgotten.

"You're so welcome," he muttered to himself, touched his hat brim to all concerned and moved off down the street. "My work here is done. Hi ho Silver, away."

Speaking of work— Jon glanced up the street in the direction of the boarding house. Now that siesta was past, he was expected to be hanging around, awaiting evening orders.

Jon interrupted his reluctant pace to pause at the doorway of the Speckled Dove. Like the hat rituals, that momentary inspection was becoming a reflex by this point.

Everything looked normal for late afternoon in 1873. The lunch regulars had left, and the night owls hadn't crawled out yet. The interior was shadowed and quiet.

Jon glanced back up the street.

Screw it. They could blame well wait on him for a change.

He went inside. Fred wasn't in sight, but the door into the back opened and a woman stepped out. She yawned and tucked a wayward strand of dark hair back into her careless upsweep.

His heart went into instant overdrive. This was the woman he saw in the doorway of the ruined saloon, five weeks ago. Almost a hundred-fifty years from now.

Jon crossed the threshold into the welcome shade of the room, still almost unable to believe she was real.

"Afternoon, honey," she murmured. "What can I do for ya?" Her voice carried a faint New England nasality.

"One-and-one," he answered, laid one of the coins from Dorin's trunk on the bar and sat down at one of the tables. The woman brought a mug of beer and a shot of whiskey over and set them in front of him, then settled herself into the chair beside him.

"I haven't seen you around before," he commented after swallowing his shot and chasing it with a gulp of lukewarm beer.

"I've seen you plenty of times," she teased. "Peeking in the door like you're afraid to come in." She shrugged. "But I've not been here long. When Ada up and ran off back east to live with her sister or somebody, I decided to try my luck here."

"Too much competition up at the mine?" Jon grinned.

"Too much dust." She grinned back, and helped herself to a swig from his mug. "Besides, water, men, and money all roll downhill, so I don't see much point in meetin' any of 'em at the top."

Their hands brushed as he recaptured his beer.

"What's your name, sugar?" she asked.

"Tom."

"Tom," she echoed. "Wouldn't be Tom Dorin, now would you?"

"I am."

"Aw, I've heard some things about you," she purred, leaning closer.

"Nothing good, I bet."

"Huh! When is it ever?" She took another sip and licked her lips. "But at least it's interestin'."

"What should I call you?"

"Catherine Marie," she said.

"That's a touch high-falutin' for a whore, ain't it?"

She bridled, but a sly amusement played around her lips. "Maybe it is, or maybe I'm looking to raise the tone of this establishment, *Thomas.*"

"It'll take more than classy name-callin' to do that, sweetheart."

"You're probably right," she conceded with a chuckle and stole another sip of beer. "So I reckon Kay will do well enough for now."

She pushed the mug back to him. "But here's a word of friendly advice, Tom. Don't go teasing the woman who can spit in your drink."

"Don't see it matters much," he drawled, "Since you're already drinkin' outta my mug like it's the town dipper."

"Only trying to be friendly."

"Friendly's good," he nodded, "So long as you leave me the lion's share."

She took that as an invitation to slide from her chair into his lap. "Oh, I'll make sure you're satisfied when you leave here."

"I just bet you will," he murmured as she draped her arms loosely around his neck and gave an expert little wiggle on his lap.

"Mr. Dorin?"

They both looked towards the doorway.

Kay's professional sensuality disappeared in an instant, her face going sharp and her voice shrewish. "Get away! You've got no business here botherin' your betters, boy!"

Jon shoved her off his lap without caring if she hit her abandoned chair or the floor.

"Shut up!" he snapped to her, but softened his voice to the boy. "What is it, Harold?"

"Miz Hattie wants you. She's pretty riled up, Mr. Dorin."

Harold glanced warily from Jon to Kay, who was glaring at the boy while she flicked and yanked at her skirts, much like a cat will groom after falling off a windowsill.

"Great." Jon stood up, chugged the last of his beer. "Oh for thirty-six, the string continues."

Kay stepped away. "You come back and see me when that mealy-mouth and her pet nigger is done workin' you like a rented mule, and I'll stiffen up that limp pride of yours, Thomas."

Jon didn't dignify that with a response. He laid a hand on Harold's shoulder in silent apology and went up the street without glancing back.

October 30, Present Day
Tucson, Arizona
~ The next day ~

Chris was working on his laptop when she came home. Tom was sprawled on the couch, dead asleep, his face relaxed and peaceful. She could understand why he may have been reluctant to go back into that bedroom, considering the past ten days.

"Good morning," Chris greeted her softly and closed his laptop. He rose and took the box from her arms. "What's this?"

"Shh!" She jerked her head towards the hallway and Chris followed her out. "Set it in the bedroom, please."

"What is it?" Chris asked again as he set the box down inside the door.

"Books." Dee rubbed her temples. "I don't know how to break this to Tom."

"Dee, please. Break what? I'm dyin' here." Chris looked back at the box.

"It's his life. Including what will be his future. What happened to his family, his friends. I didn't read much of it, but from the amount of stuff in there, I'm pretty sure his friend kept a diary every day of the War and maybe for years afterwards."

"Good lord. That's going to be a boot to the head."

"It's given me a headache to think about it. It's all happened, they're all dead and gone—but they're not. Not for him, not for them either, if he gets to go back."

"Cripes, you're right." Chris' face brightened then. "Wait! If that's his future, our past, then it's proof this will all work out and he'll get back to where he belongs. We'll have Jon back and can forget this whole Twilight Zone episode!"

"I'm still not sure if we should—"

"Hey, ya'll," Tom shambled down the hall, looking drowsy and concerned. "What's goin' on?"

"How are you feeling?" Dee laid her hand on his forehead and gave him her best 'I care but I don't think your condition is grave' smile.

"Much better, thank you. I'm on the mend now." His expression looked a little startled when she touched him, but he didn't pull away.

"Good. Have you eaten?"

"Yeah, not too long ago." He looked a touch suspicious.

"That's good. Take it slow for the rest of today." She decided to delay the inevitable until she could think of how to break it to him gently.

"I was just asking Chris why he called me at work to ask about the tintype. What's that all about?" She went back towards the living room as she spoke.

"You may want to sit down first, Dee," Tom suggested.

"That'd actually be a good idea," Chris added.

"Urgh, that sounds ominous." She curled up in her favorite chair.

Interesting. They both sat down on the sofa, the center cushion between them like no-man's land. A somewhat united front.

Chris leaned forward, his mobile face drawn into lines of genuine dismay. "Tom says the picture isn't of him."

"Why?" she looked at Tom, feeling dread knot in her stomach.

"I never had a image took in my life."

"At least, not in your life so far." Hope mingled with the dread.

"That's so," he conceded. "Chris and me, we come to the same conclusion. I never had no image made, but that don't mean I might not yet, if I get put back."

Her head was about to split now. "I feel like we're all stuck in a house of mirrors. I hate those things. We have five months to find our way out. Damn, I hope it doesn't take that long."

She laid a hand on the firm little bulge below her navel. "By then, I need all this crazy crap to be just a bad memory."

Tom's expression told her that she wasn't the only one having uncomfortable epiphanies that morning.

Yeah, do the math, big guy. "Tom, since you're already sitting down, there's something I have to tell you, too."

"What's that? What's happened now?"

Very apprehensive. Understandable. Considering all he had been through in the past ten days, a lack of anxiety would indicate serious brain damage.

"Remember when I said I read about your leg in Carol Lynd's diary?"

He nodded, a flicker of sorrow darkening the blue of his eyes. "Chris said 'dumpster' meant you threw it in the rubbish and it's gone."

"I meant to throw the box away into the trash, yes, out of angry spite at Jon. But when I got to work, we were so busy I didn't get the chance and forgot about it. It was still in the back of my car. I put it in your room, if you want to look at it."

He was up and limping down the hall before the last few words were out of her mouth.

"How do you think he's going to react?" Chris asked, as the bedroom door closed in the hallway.

"You're the one with the writer's imagination, although I would think a minimal level of compassion would be enough to give you a clue."

"Is that what this morning's performance is about? A minimal level of compassion?"

"Just say it, Chris. My head hurts too much for word games."

"Okay. Why have you gone from screeching 'I hate you, this is all your fault' and chucking rocks at his head, to cooing and feeling his forehead and acting like you're his mommy?"

"Get me a couple of acetaminophen first, will ya?" she grumbled, laying her head back and putting her feet up.

He did, but he didn't drop the subject. He barely paused it long enough for her to swallow the pills. "He's still dangerous."

"I don't think he is."

"Dee, he's a murderer! He shot a defenseless woman. He said so himself!"

"That was an accident."

"So he says. Why in the world are you suddenly trusting this guy?"

"I didn't say I trust him. I said I don't think he's dangerous."

Dee held up a hand to ward off the protest about to burst out of his mouth. "When someone is in great pain, especially for an extended period, their bedrock personality comes out. Most junkies, as soon as they start to sweat and shake, they would sell their souls and their sainted mothers for a fix to ward it off. The whole time he was going through utter hell, he never once asked for a dose. I asked him why, and he said he didn't want to break the law or ask me to, either. You know what else?"

Chris shook his head, obviously not swayed.

"All that time, he never complained. Never whined. Never got angry. He just... suffered. And thanked me for taking care of him, even though I would have been more nurturing to a sick dog."

"Big deal, so he can suck it up."

Dee snorted. "Says the man who whinged and whimpered for a week over a head-cold."

"I didn't shoot an innocent woman in the guts and call her a bitch while she died."

"Okay. Right. You be the suspicious watch-dog then. I'm tired, Chris. I'm confused, I'm hurting and I don't think that man is a danger to anyone but maybe himself."

"Dammit." Chris rubbed his eyes. "I can't trust him, Dee. I can't because every time I look at him I lose Jon over and over again."

Dee went to him and put her arms around him. It was a toss-up who was holding onto who to keep from shattering into a thousand sharp shards.

03

It was an ordinary pasteboard box. Tom looked down at it for a long stretch of time.

Nothing ominous from the outside. Marked only with Jon's address, and the return from someone in Farragut, Tennessee, there was no hint of what an unnatural object it truly was.

It held his future and it held his past, all at the same time.

Tom eased himself down onto the floor, laid his crutches aside and drew the box closer. He opened it with caution, as if something vicious lurked inside, crouched to spring at his throat.

Did he really want to know his own future? Wasn't knowing the future the sole prerogative of the Almighty? If he saw his own destiny written down as certainty, would he be allowed to survive long enough to fulfill it? If he didn't like what he read, could he change it?

He hadn't had his heart between his teeth like this since the War, when everything would go slow and so extremely clear in the midst of battle, like time itself slowed out of respect for the deadly peril of the situation. His hands were steady as he unfolded the flaps, despite the cold dread in his guts.

Nothing demonic leaped out at him with an unholy screech. There was nothing, in fact, more frightening than a letter lying at the surface, a few short paragraphs written in a shaky feminine hand.

Dear Mr. Hansen,
I'm sorry I have taken so long in replying to your request, but this was a difficult decision for me to make. Even after so many years, my family still told stories about my Great-Grandfather Lynd as I was growing up, and I always felt a special affection towards him. But, as I am the last of the blood relations, I feel it is my duty to both my ancestor and to history to begin sharing this remarkable record of his life and the times he lived through.

I have included everything in his effects that dated from the Civil War up through the year of 1874, to be sure it includes any possible interaction with Dorin. My sole caveat, as we discussed previously, is that copies of the journals become the property of the history department of Arizona University, with the originals returned to me once you have completed your thesis this year. I will be donating them, along with the rest of Grandfather Lynd's effects, to the Confederate Memorial Hall in Knoxville, Tennessee.

The ebony box and its contents you may keep or donate as you see fit. They originally belonged to Thomas Dorin and have no connection to our family other than through the friendship Dorin and Grandfather Lynd shared.

I hope you find in this material what you seek, and that it helps you succeed in your ambitions.

Sincerely,
Denise Lynd-Caywood

Tom laid the letter aside with an odd mingling of elation and bereavement. Sounded as though Carl had a long life, and a good one, for his family to remember him that fondly well over a century later.

There were scattered journal pages under the letter, and he carefully gathered them up. He recognized the battered leather cover instantly. It was the journal Carl kept through the first part of the War, which explained the book's crumbling condition.

How many times had it been soaked with rain, or with sweat, dropped in the mud of a camp or handled with filthy hands when there had been no water to spare for washing, even with Carl's nervous inclination?

His touch reverent, Tom tucked the scattered, stained, brittle leaves back into the book. He traced his fingers over Carl's neat script, and huffed at the sight of his own sloppy scrawl on the facing page.

Thanks to this first lesson and several others, his spelling had improved greatly, but sadly, his penmanship hadn't. Not by much.

Several pages had been cut out, past that. He knew why. He had carried them for ages, until they were soiled past legibility.

He turned through the book to where the spine had broken apart. The entry Dee had read. The part that described how Carl saved his life once, and now most likely twice. As he read on, Tom pressed a knuckle against his teeth so hard he almost cut through his skin.

He had suffered so terribly from his wounding, he hadn't given a thought to what Carl had gone through. Now, he knew how much it cost his dear friend to see him at the point of dying. To give in to his desperate plea to be rescued from the surgeon's saw, even though Carl was certain he was killing his friend by doing as Tom wanted, as surely as if he'd pressed his pistol to Tom's head and pulled the trigger.

How much it hurt Carl to march away, when the War moved on and left the battle's wounded behind. That Carl felt as though he now fully understood the love between David and Jonathan, and like those other long-ago young soldiers, in the midst of war's horrors Carl had found more than a friend, but a true brother.

Tom carefully closed the fragile little book and laid it aside. He pressed his fingers against his burning eyes, and blew out a long, shuddering breath.

When he reached into the box again, his hand closed around a tooled leather tintype case. Now, his fingers trembled as he undid the clasp.

Carl gazed up at him, appearing a bit uncertain in his new, stiff uniform, though his grip on his rifle was one of experience.

"Dear lord, Carl," Tom breathed. "We was both jist children, certain we was men."

He blinked, sending tears rolling down his cheeks. He wiped them away against his shoulder, then touched Carl's face with a gentle fingertip.

"I love you too, though we never said it. Wish I had. You're more my brother than my own bone and blood kin ever were."

He laid the photograph aside, though he couldn't bear to close the case again. Tom swallowed down the massive lump in his throat and began lifting out the other items. All journals, of one size or another, all marked on the cover with their dates in Carl's neat, precise hand.

He laid them all aside in careful stacks, until he came on the one dated 1873. He paged through it, skimming across the lines until his eyes were arrested by the sight of his name.

Carl was writing about getting his letter, the one he had written and mailed off two months before his whole world and time itself turned inside out.

Carl had taken the trouble to track down Shine and visit, and to seek out Tom's own family. Tom could easily imagine Shine's brood, and little Carlthomas.

The entries stating that his family was doing well soothed an ache carried so long that he recognized it only by its relief. It hurt ten times more to realize that, had this curse not fallen on his life, he would have gone home himself, if he had been allowed to receive the letter Carl was planning in his journal to write in reply.

He wondered what mementos Beth's mother had intended to give him. He wondered if he would have accepted them, if he'd gotten Carl's letter.

Then he read words Carl had surely meant for no one's eyes. Words describing his attraction to Hannah Grace, hesitant words that conjectured how Tom would react to him having fallen in love on first acquaintance too, but to his best friend's favorite sister.

"I'm glad you did," Tom whispered. "I hope she sees you for the fine man you are. I couldn't hope for no better for her than you…."

He closed the book. "I cain't read no more, Carl. It's jist wrong, with you not here to tell me different."

Another box had been covered by the journals. A wooden one this time. Smooth ebony, with a brass clasp gone brown and green with age. He lifted it out and set it in his lap, then unfastened the clasp and raised the lid.

Letters.

His letters to Beth.

Even the plaintive one he'd scrawled on a scrap of ragged wallpaper. The one that had likely arrived after she fell ill.

All his futile words of friendship and devoted, desperate love, wedged tightly inside the box, tied together with a faded ribbon that had once been the color of ivy.

He tipped the little ebony casket to drop them out, afraid they would crumble if grasped too tightly.

An emerald-colored silk bag slipped out from beneath them, landing in his hand with a slight, shifting weight that felt yielding and almost alive. He untied the tarnished gilt drawstring and turned the bag up.

A long, heavy braid of hair, so astoundingly red it was truly orange, slithered out into his palm. Bound at each end with bright ivy-colored ribbon, little curls sprang defiantly free all along its length.

⛃

The wail was low-pitched, but even though a solid door and plaster, the long, drawn-out cry conveyed such agony and anguish that the hair rose on the back of Dee's neck and goose-pimples shivered down her arms.

"Holy crap!" Chris exclaimed. "And I was about to say it was way too quiet in there!"

Dee sprang to her feet and hurried down the hallway, Chris almost treading on her heels. She could hear weeping now. The painful, harsh sobs wrenched out when a stoic man is utterly broken.

Chris laid his hand on hers as she grabbed the doorknob. "Leave him alone. This is private."

"I can't. He needs to know he's not alone." She turned the knob. Chris stepped back.

Tom sat on the floor, a small jewelry box upended beside him. He held something cradled to his chest, something small he curled his body around. As he wept, he rocked, devastated into that instinctive motion of self-comfort.

Dee sat down beside him and put her arms around his shoulders. His rocking stilled, the only sign that he was aware she was there. Over his shoulder, she saw what he held.

Hair. It was a braid of hair he clutched and wept over.

⛃

"Thank you, Dee," Tom said, his voice thick and hoarse. He wiped his tear-streaked face with the damp cloth she'd offered. He laid it aside then, his face set once more into its usual somber lines. Only his reddened eyes and nose gave away the fact that he'd broken down.

"These books need to go back to that woman in Tennessee," he said. "She asked for them back, and I'd jist as soon Jon not go rootin' through my life any more than he already has."

He shot her an uneasy glance, "Meanin' no disrespect, of course."

"None taken. I'm not so sure I like the idea of anyone reading a diary I'd written, to be honest."

She picked up the bundle of letters he had laid out of his lap when he regained some control and started to tuck them into the box.

"Not those," he said almost sharply.

"I'm keepin' those," he added in a milder tone as he took them from her hand. "They're mine, that little black box there too. Carl was gonna bring them to me. They got nothin' to do with his family. That Miz Caywood said so in her letter."

"Okay," Dee nodded. "I'll write her a thank-you note."

"I appreciate it." He picked up a photograph then and stilled, looking down on it with an expression she couldn't name. "I don't have no right to keep this, but I don't want to let it go, neither."

"Is that Carl?"

Tom nodded and handed it over.

Dee looked down into the photo's earnest face. "He was so young, it breaks my heart," she whispered.

"We didn't think so then," Tom said.

"You were very close, weren't you?" She handed the image back.

Tom closed the case as if he were closing a coffin. "He was more my brother than my own brother ever was."

"I'm so sorry." She put an arm around his shoulders again, and this time he leaned into her touch, just enough to feel the shift in his weight.

"Me too," he said softly, his voice sounding choked again. "Carl was gonna come out and see me, but then—"

Tom swung a hand to take in the bedroom, the entire twenty-first century.

"Wait," Dee said as his gesture ended with the tintype held over the box. "We can make a copy of that photo before we send it back."

"You can? I'd be more grateful than I can say." He laid it in her hands.

239

He picked up the braid of hair from his lap, coiled it and gently slipped it into a silk bag, every touch a caress.

"Who was she?" The words escaped before she could stop them.

"Sarah-Elizabeth Beattie," he said, as he tied the bag shut and closed the ebony lid over it. "Beth."

His fingertips traced the ornate clasp. "We was to be married."

"What happened?"

Tom's eyes were as dull and flat as his voice. "She caught typhoid and died, durin' the siege of Richmond."

Dee put her arms around him again, this time embracing him as she would a grieving friend. He wrapped his arms around her in return.

"I know it's not enough to say," she murmured near his ear, "But I am so, so sorry. About Beth, and everything else."

He nodded, his cheek against her hair. "So am I, for your Jon and all you're goin' through."

The sharp rap on the door startled them apart. "Is everything okay in there?"

Dee jumped up and jerked it open. "No, not okay, but holding together."

"You sure about that?" He peered past her at Tom.

Suddenly nervous, Dee glanced back at him too.

Tom ignored them entirely, moving to set the ebony casket and Carl's picture on the bureau.

"Not good news from the old folks at home, I gather?" Chris asked under his breath.

"How could it be? Geez, Chris—do you have any tact whatsoever?"

"No, I left it in a taxi in New York."

"Chris," Tom said, catching his eyes in the mirror rather than turning. "Would you get that box freighted back to that woman who sent it?"

"Sure." Chris stepped inside and picked up the box.

Dee followed him out and closed the door. "Do not think you're going to read those journals."

He stopped dead and gaped at her. "You're kidding, right? Dee— this stuff will tell us if Jon gets home! Don't you want to know?"

"Of course I do!" she snapped. "But those books won't tell use anything we don't already know— someone calling himself Tom Dorin was hanged on March 13, 1874. We still won't know whose neck was in the noose!"

Chris' crestfallen expression would have been amusing if it wasn't followed by a grief as raw as her own. "When he gets back, will you try to work things out?"

She shrugged, and bit her lower lip to keep it from trembling. "I was, I still am, very hurt and angry at him. But he's in danger. I can't turn away and not try to help, no matter where our relationship stands."

∂

For three long hours, he waited past the time Dee and Tom went to bed. Chris left his room, silent on bare feet. He retrieved the fateful box from the kitchen counter.

Once back in the study, safe behind a locked door, Chris slit the fresh packing tape on the box and dug out the diary dated 1874.

His hands shook as he quickly flipped through the little book, scanning for nothing but the dates neatly inscribed at the top of each page.

NO!

He stared down at the page that should have been March third. A spill of ink had obliterated the entry and seeped through the rest of the pages leaving them marred, wrinkled, and empty save for a notation on a small unstained spot on the inside back cover.

'1874 will continued in a new volume. The hotel cat is henceforth banished from my room.'

Chris dropped the ruined journal and dumped all the rest out onto the sofa beside him. Despite his half-spoken pleas to dead Carl, old Ms. Caywood and whatever deity might be listening, the second journal for 1874 wasn't in the box.

The journals scattered across the floor, flung across the room. Chris kicked each and every one of them for good measure as he cursed that clumsy cat and the universe at large.

CHAPTER TWENTY-FOUR

29 November, 1873
Cooper's Creek, AZT
~ Four days later ~

Damn that Kay. Jon stepped on the broom handle, pulled up on the chicken's feet and the bird went limp. He flopped it onto the stump and swung the hatchet as if he were beheading the hateful bitch instead of a hapless chicken.

He handed the corpse over to Harold to hang up like ghastly laundry so the bird could bleed out. Jon grabbed his next squawking victim from under the crate that held Sunday dinner's main course captive. He was so angry, the loathed chore didn't turn his stomach as it usually did.

Kay's casual cruelty towards Harold was only part of his anger. This wasn't the twenty-first century, it was the nineteenth. Bigotry was taken for granted. He didn't have to like it, but he did have to accept it as unavoidable. What really pissed him off, he decided as he dispatched another cockerel, was that despite her blithe hatefulness and the fact she was as discriminating as a bus station urinal, he still found his mind drifting towards the possibility of taking her up on her offer.

Mrs. Ferris kept haunting his unguarded moments too, but for an entirely different reason. It was as if that fleeting, inadvertent grope of her pregnant belly had burned the sensation into his nerve endings. It kept him thinking about Dee.

She was probably showing now, too. Not as much as Lissie, but enough. Rounding out with his son. If she'd kept the baby. He doubted she followed through on his stupid demand, though. She already had enough Catholic guilt laid on her over them living together. Even if she'd considered it, Chris would have talked her out of it.

"She's not bad, little bro. Shortchanged on the tits, but I can see why you fell for the eyes. And I sure wouldn't mind having those legs wrapped around my—"

Jon yanked up on another chicken's feet, getting a twinge of satisfaction as he felt the neck bones separate.

Oh yeah, Chris would have talked her out of an abortion all right. Jon had no doubt at all Chris kept right on talking until he talked himself into Dee's bed. He could see it all too clearly. Wasn't like it hadn't happened before with other women. Only this time, Chris would soon be playing Daddy to his son as well as banging his girlfriend.

The hatchet bit so deeply into the stump that Jon had to jerk and rock it to free the blade.

"You all right, Mr. Dorin?"

"Huh?"

"You seem like you're mad about somethin' today." Harold deftly tied the last bird to the line to bleed out. "I ain't done nothin' wrong, have I?"

"Nah, it ain't you."

November 12, Present Day
Tucson, Arizona
~ Fourteen days later ~

Tom was restless, in both senses of the term. His leg and back throbbed with unwelcome but familiar pain. The pills Dee gave him scarcely took the edge off, though he was grateful for even that much relief.

He shifted in bed again, trying to find a more comfortable spot, a better position, anything that would woo sleep. Even when his body showed signs of cooperating, his brain wouldn't hush and close shop for the night.

Tom threw the covers aside and got up. He limped over to the bureau. Carl's image was invisible in the dark. He touched the thin, brittle leather of the case. "I wish you were here with me. Between us, we'd figure out what to do. You might even like it here, have yourself a high ol' time. I know you'd like how clean it all is, and there's enough books in this house alone for at least two or three schoolhouses."

His hand drifted over to caress the smooth top of the little ebony box. "Wish you were here too, Sarah-Beth. If I had you beside me, lookin' up with them tip-tilted green eyes and that little imp smile, I wouldn't care much about where or when we was. Seems like my whole life ain't been worth wet powder since you got took out of it."

Tom opened the box and lifted out the silk bag. He hobbled back to the bed and propped his aching leg.

He cradled her hair on his chest, the silk cool over his heartbeat. He stroked it like a kitten, closed his eyes, and counted his breaths to quiet his mind.

☙

The door opened, and the light spilling in from the hall woke him out of his hard-won sleep. Tom looked over and saw Dee standing there. Her hair fell loose all down around her shoulders and the light behind traced her slender body through her gown as if she were clad in only a veil.

"What is it?" he asked, sitting up. "Is somethin' wrong?"

She put a finger to her lips and glided closer, silent as a spirit. She came right up to the bed till her gown brushed the edge of the mattress. She pulled a tie at her throat and the gown fell away with a whisper.

"Dee?"

She smiled, and put a knee on the bed, climbing in beside him even as she put her arms around his shoulders and lowered her head to kiss him. He laid a hand on her side to pull her closer, feeling the curves of lean ribs and tight muscles beneath skin softer than rose petals.

☙

Tom's eyes opened as their lips began to touch. His heart was going at a gallop and he had broken out in a sweat.

He was alone.

He sat up abruptly. The silk bag slithered down his belly and was cool against somewhere else altogether.

He rescued it from his lap and laid it on the pillow beside him, then pushed back to lean against the headboard, his head dropping against the wood with a hollow thump.

He sighted down along his midline with a scowl. "You there can lay right back down and go back to sleep. I got enough to worry over without you perkin' up all of a sudden."

That part never had much good sense, so it showed no signs of paying his admonition any heed.

"I gotta find some work," he grumbled as he settled back supine and did his best to think only high, pure thoughts.

"Hard work in the hot sun to tire us out good so I don't lay around and fret all night and you don't raise up and make trouble. I done kept my word for more than ten years, I ain't about to go breakin' it now."

CHAPTER TWENTY-FIVE

1 December, 1873
Cooper's Creek, AZT
~ Two days later ~

"It sure wasn't anything you've done here, Dorin." Jon left his bed and stretched. "Unless you're going to go crazy and bash somebody's head in from utter screaming boredom."

Nobody had a bad word to say about Dorin in town. At least, not predating his own arrival and imperfect imitation. Even now, the worst gossip was that he'd lost his marbles. He might be in danger of being locked away in some hellhole of an asylum, but Dorin wouldn't face a noose for that.

Nothing in Tom's trunk gave a hint of any past misconduct. There wasn't anything even of value in it, other than Dorin's money pouch and a holstered cap-and-ball Colt.

The rest was only a leather wallet of personal papers. Sappy love letters from some teenage girl named Beth who died from contact with someone else's filth. Emotionally ambiguous letters from Carl Lynd, frequent while Tom had been in Newsom hospital, sporadic thereafter.

"Did they hang people for being a closet bisexual? Because that's the only possible transgression I can pin on you from this pathetic pile of crap, Dorin."

He turned back to the bed to clear off the papers. He tapped Dorin's folded discharge document against his palm. "Of course, who knows what you did before you got knocked off the big game board, huh? Or after. The next nine years of your life were a big black hole of nothing, as best I could determine. You killed somebody at some point. Wish I knew the details, so your homicidal indiscretion can't spring up to bite me in the ass."

Jon stretched out on the bed, hands laced behind his head and one boot propped on the toe of the other. He thought the situation through.

"Then again, the details don't matter because his crime can't be pinned on me. I can easily prove I'm not Tom Dorin. Doc might not testify for me if he's pissed, but there's no way Hattie would perjure herself by saying I'm Dorin on the stand, so there's at least one upstanding corroborating witness. If worse comes to worst, I'll whip out my cell phone again. Damn, hope the battery will hold out that long. Wonder if I can trickle-charge it with wires and a couple of potatoes? Or I can rig up a Baghdad battery, maybe."

He chuckled. "Moot point, though. Dorin hangs. I'm not Dorin, and I can prove it beyond a shadow of a doubt to even these mouth-breathing hicks."

Jon grinned and stretched. "So, that's air-tight proof that sometime between now and March, I go home and he winds up back here in Cooper's Crack, AZT. I think that happy epiphany deserves a drink."

Jon rose to retrieve Dorin's money pouch. "Or what the hell, a drink and a screw. Why should I live like a monk while Chris and Dee are humping each other? And I'll be back in the land of penicillin before crotch-rot can take hold."

He stuck sufficient coins in his pocket, settled his hat on his head, and strolled out of the boarding house into the deepening night, whistling.

December 11, Present Day
Tucson, Arizona
~ Twenty-nine days later ~

"Would you like anything while I'm up, Dee?" Tom picked up her empty water glass as he passed the end table.

"Yes, more water, please."

"I could use a refill too." Chris rattled his tea glass.

"Your legs ain't broke," Tom shot back and hobbled off to the kitchen.

"Neither are hers!" Chris called after him, and rolled his eyes at Dee.

She shook her head and pretended to become absorbed in her web-surfing again.

Now that she was conscious of the difference, Dee wondered how she'd been blind to it for even an hour. Chris would periodically ask if she needed anything, and if she said yes, he'd do whatever she asked. If she said no, he'd go on his merry way and not give her another thought till he passed back through the room, three minutes or three days later.

She could probably count on one hand the times she'd had to ask Tom for something, and in fairness, most of the remainder were requests he couldn't have anticipated.

Otherwise, it was as if he did anticipate what she might want, or need, or even what would simply be a nice thing to do.

As soon as she came in, she had doors opened for her, things carried. Mail and pillows handed to her, the ottoman pushed closer, the remote was laid within easy reach and she never had to refill a glass or hardly ever wash one anymore.

Dee's lips quirked.

If he could hop up and pee for her every five freakin' minutes, he'd probably do that too. She had no doubt all this chivalrous attention was due to her 'delicate condition,' which was more than a little condescending… but she had to admit, it was a brand of condescension that felt quite cozy in practice.

Tom set her glass back on the coaster, filled to the brim with fresh ice and seltzer water, just like she liked it.

"Thanks."

"You're welcome." He settled back into the rocker he favored, propped up his leg and went back to the history book he was devouring a decade at a sitting.

What didn't feel so warm and snuggly was comparing Tom's solemn solicitude to Jon's happy-go-lucky indifference. Dee sipped her water, savoring the tingle of the bubbles followed by the faint bitterness of the seltzer.

Jon hadn't ignored her from the beginning. If he had, she would have never fallen for him. Certainly wouldn't have let him move in. But as their relationship changed from casual to committed, it was as if his attention had altered from deliberate daily affection to random bursts of charm or the occasional grand gesture, like that trip to Vegas.

She sighed, staring at the computer screen without taking in a single word.

This past year, especially, she had felt as if she had become nothing more than a meal ticket or worse, a constant irritant to him, rather than a lover and a life-partner.

She looked over at Tom again, somehow mesmerized by the slow motion of his rocker as he pushed it gently with his good leg.

Funny that he favored rockers, but got sick in the car....

Dee shook her head. There she went again, avoiding an unpleasant train of thought.

Maybe Jon loved her, maybe he didn't. Maybe she'd been deluding herself the whole time, desperate to fulfill her parents' expectations even though she rebelled at the same time. Maybe she was hormonal, and this all was a crock of crap. Regardless, she was certain Dorin didn't care for her any more than he would any woman he considered helpless and his responsibility.

She gave a little sigh. She was sure he took very good care of the horses he used to ride, too. She wondered if he ever smiled at them.

"Great, now I'm jealous of a horse," she muttered under her breath. "Gotta be the hormones."

"Huh?" Chris said, and Tom glanced between them both.

"Nothing, talking to the baby."

~ *The next day* ~

It was still dark out when he gave up on further sleep. Tom dressed and left the room, careful to keep as quiet as crutches could be against the tile. He was at a loss for what to do with himself with no cows to milk, no wood to split, no horses to school nor crops to tend or even a flower bed to weed.

Regardless of how far he was behind the times, there was only so much reading a man could bear in a day. He needed to work, not lay about like some invalid.

The rub was, he didn't have much of an idea how anyone in this century earned their daily bread. Dee's job he understood somewhat, though he was as capable of helping her out there as he was of lifting off into flight.

Chris was an author, and he understood that too, but there was no chance of anyone wanting to read what little he would have to say.

Tom searched as quietly as possible through the closets till he found a broom and dust pan. At least they hadn't changed much over the decades.

He swept that house like it was the day before the Second Coming, but even teasing out and gathering up every last dust-clot and fleck out of every corner didn't take him till much past the first light of dawn.

He went outside when he could see good. Tom walked around the house first, noting a cracked roof tile that needed mending and a patch of plaster off the house corner that should have been repaired before the rainy season set in and got to the adobe. The front lot needed to be raked clean and the whole place could use a coat of whitewash and some fresh paint about the doors and windows.

He went around the side of the house. He wasn't sure how far Dee's property went back, but he'd know once he walked the fence lines. After a quick rummage through the garage, he stepped out armed with a hammer tucked under his belt and a generous handful of ring-shanked nails in his shirt pocket. He strolled the fence, in no particular hurry.

He moved a branch off the opposite side. The board was loose beneath. Tom unhooked the hammer from his belt and drew a couple of nails from his pocket. A few quick blows and the fence rail was secured again. The neighborly thing to do. He stuck the hammer back under his belt and walked on.

He made note of a couple of patches of milkweeds that he'd grub out before the sun got too high. Dee wasn't running any stock now, but there was no reason to let the land grow up with poisonous trash, either. He made his way down the fence, reaching out to shake any board that was bowed or possibly loose. When he skirted around a fallen palo verde that had broken down part of the fence, he stopped in his tracks.

Just past the dead tree, a sorrel mare lay on her side, shoulders and neck lathered with sweat, straining in hard labor. He eased himself down so as not to spook her, and watched to see what kind of problem she was having.

She lifted her head and blew a loud breath at him, a sharp challenge of identity.

Tom blew back, softer.

She gave another, milder huff.

Tom answered again, softer yet.

The mare laid her head back down, satisfied he was mannerly and most likely harmless.

He slowly rose and approached her on a narrowing parallel course, till he could kneel by her head. "Hey there, gal. You havin' some trouble?" He cupped his hand near her nose, so she could get his scent.

She inhaled calmly enough, then lifted her head as if to swing herself back up.

"Whoa gal, easy..." Tom pressed his hand against her neck to keep her down.

"Easy now," he crooned and moved to her hindquarters, sliding his hand along her hide. As soon as he got to her rump, she obliged by giving a hard contraction. One tiny hoof poked out of her birth canal then disappeared again as she relaxed.

"Got a leg folded back, does he?" There was only one thing to do. Tom stripped off his shirt, then ran his hand through the fluids oozing from the mare's body, using them to slick up his right arm.

"I know we ain't been introduced," he informed the mare conversationally as he stretched out at her fanny, "But desperate measures for desperate times. Easy now..."

He waited for a relaxation and slid his hand into her wet heat, pausing every time she bore down. Her muscles felt as though they were going to crush his arm.

He heard another horse approaching, and craned his neck up. A young woman rode up on a splashy paint. The sun was behind her, so all he could see of her was her shape and the sun's glow off the edges of dark red upswept hair.

"What the hell do you think you're doing, Jon Hansen?" the woman demanded in a low voice. As soon as she slid off her gelding, her demeanor changed.

"Hey Sass," she cooed in a throaty singsong. "Hey pretty girl. Are you having trouble? Is this pervert being mean to you?"

She made her way slowly to the mare.

Tom gritted his teeth through another fruitless contraction for the mare. At least this time, he could feel a tiny muzzle.

"Foal's got a leg turned back. She cain't pass it." He took advantage of the relaxed instant to work himself deeper, till his chest and shoulder were up against her haunches.

"I can almost... argh... There!" He persevered through another contraction as the foal surged towards him, sliding his hand along the little neck and shoulder and down. He grabbed hold around one slender cannon before the mare heaved again. This time, Tom pulled as she pushed.

The woman crouched, stroking the mare's neck. "I hope you know what you're doing, Jon," she challenged, in that same singsong. "Or you're in more trouble than she is."

"I done this before," Tom crooned back, closing his eyes to concentrate on touch. That little mislaid leg came forward and Tom gripped it and the other leg, the foal's small pasterns between his fingers. "Come on, mamma— you're almost finished. Jist one or two more, darlin'."

Another valiant shove from the mare's insides as he pulled, and Tom's arm and a dark foal reappeared in a gush of fluid. Tom cleared the remains of the sac away from the foal's hindquarters.

When the little animal didn't immediately move or breathe, he put its muzzle to his mouth and sucked in hard enough to get a mouthful of birth-fluid. He spat it out with a grimace and scrubbed the foal's side with his knuckles.

It gasped, sneezed and then lifted its head.

Sass lifted hers too, and looked back at her infant. The foal lay still for a worrisome long few moments, then began to struggle, long legs going in four confused and contrary directions.

"Oh! Good baby!" The woman enthused. "Come on baby, stand up now."

It took several more minutes, but Tom didn't mind the wait, because this show never got old.

Sass levered herself to her feet, careful of her foal lying at her rear. The cord broke. She licked her newborn as the baby thrashed, all gangly legs and raw determination. The foal got halfway upright and tumbled back down in several false starts but soon got her legs reasonably spread under her and managed to stay up.

Tom wiped off his arm best he could and shrugged his shirt back on. The young woman stepped back from the mare as Sass nudged her wobbly offspring to her teats.

She flipped open her telephone. "Mom? I found Sass." She paused and laughed "Yeah, she decided to wander off to deliver again."

While the woman talked, Tom caught the mare's forelock when she looked as though she was considering moving away with her foal. A natural urge, to get away from the blood-smell, but he didn't want to chase her. He waited, sharing breath with the mare, letting her rub against him and get his true scent, mingled with her own and the scent of her foal.

"Where else are we going to go, Mom?" The woman rolled her eyes as she flipped the phone closed.

"I can walk 'em back," he offered. "She's in good shape and the foal's done had her first feed."

"Yeah, but Mom will want to do her amateur veterinarian act, so we might as well wait. Sass seems to have an aversion to delivering in a nice foaling stall. Except for her second, she's always early or late, just enough lull us into letting her out on her own. And she's a real Houdini at finding a way out of a fence. You're difficult, aren't you, honey?"

She tugged the halter and lead out from under her belt and handed them to Tom. "It's kinda weird, huh, that you live right next door to my parents, and we never realized it."

"Reckon it jist never come up," he shrugged, hoping to bluff through this awkward conversation with vagueness as he slipped the halter onto Sass.

"True, and considering that your live-in didn't come up in conversation until the very last possible instant, I suppose it's not that weird after all." She cocked her head and studied him. "Okay, I know I'm rude, but I have to ask. What's up with the accent, and what happened to your leg?"

"It's a long story," he shrugged, hoping to avoid a lie, no matter how necessary.

"We've got nothing else to do at the moment. You sound completely different."

"So I been told," Tom nodded, taking care to speak with proper grammar at least. "I can't remember what I sounded like before. I guess nobody really knows how they sound."

"Before what?" She smiled, and batted her eyelashes up at him. "Come on, Jon. Don't keep me in suspense."

"I had a bad accident," he answered, trotting out the excuse Dee and Chris had hammered out and hammered in. "On a four-wheeler. I tore up my leg and bashed my head. The doctors call it a closed frontal lobe injury. I'm told it's what give me this drawl in my speech and changed my personality and knocked some memories clean out of my head entirely."

Her kittenish, teasing expression fell away instantly. "Oh no! That's terrible! Jon, I'm so sorry. When I realized I hadn't seen you around campus in a while, I assumed you weren't interested in being friends with me any more. I never dreamed it was anything like this, or I would have visited or called or something."

"It's all right," he shrugged. "Wasn't exactly like I been in any shape to look up friends and acquaintances." He decided he'd have to do it sooner than later, so he added, "I hate to have to ask— but what's your name?"

"Callie," she offered, her voice sounding a little small. "Callie Darger. You don't remember me at all, do you?"

He shook his head. "I'm sorry, but no, I don't."

"Wow. I'm sorry about that, too. But hey, the bright side is, we got to make another first impression on each other, right?"

"There is that," he nodded.

"Well, then let's do this properly. Hello, I'm Callie Darger. You'll forgive me if I don't offer my hand?"

"Nice to meet you, again, Callie." He glanced down at his soiled right hand. "No need to ask forgiveness. I sure understand, considerin' the circumstances."

"It's not that I mind gross!" she protested. "It's that I'm supposed to be meeting someone. Then Sass decided to wander off."

"Well, that part of a horse don't wash off too easy, so I cain't blame you," he agreed. "If you need to go on, I'll wait with 'em." He scratched under the mare's jaw. "We seem to be gettin' along right well."

"Which is surprising. She's usually skittish around strangers when she's close to foaling."

He shrugged. "I've always been partial to mares, and they seem to take to me purty easy."

"Oh, really?"

Engine noises drew closer, too quickly for Tom to frame a response. A woman, older than Callie and with light brown hair, sprang out of the vehicle and hurried to the mare and foal.

The second passenger climbed out more slowly, his features much like Callie's but of a different race. "Mister Hansen?"

"Yes, sir?" Tom replied, one hand on the mare's lead rope, the other curved over her nose, in case she got nervous. He hoped that Jon didn't know this man well, even more, that they weren't on the outs.

"What happened here?" Mr. Darger asked, looking at his wife checking the nursing newborn, and his daughter.

"The foal had a foreleg bent back. Jon straightened it out," Callie answered.

"She was havin' a hard time. From the way she was lathered and how she paddled up the ground, she'd been strainin' quite a while." Tom added. "The foal wouldn't have lasted much longer. She'd already broken her sac and was purty dry."

"Which leg?" Mrs. Darger asked Tom as she straightened.

"Near foreleg, ma'am."

"Hm. She's not favoring it. And she seems to be nursing okay. She's a bit early, but Sassy's never been predictable. So, Callie, what's her name?"

"Jon delivered her, so according to the family rules…." Callie's impish grin took in both her parents.

"I guess you can name her, Hansen," Mr. Darger decreed. "But please, not something that will make us have to deal with copyright or trademarks?"

Tom studied the foal, who was presenting her narrow behind to them at the moment, her fluffy tail flicking fast as an over-wound pendulum as she nursed. Then, she looked back at him and bobbed her head, beads of milk spangling her whiskers.

"Sukie's Shade," he said.

"Sukie?" Mrs. Darger asked.

"Something about her head, and the set of her ears, reminds me of the best horse I ever owned," he said.

"I didn't know you'd ever owned a horse, Mr. Hansen," Darger added.

"It's been a number of years, sir. Long before I lived here." Tom looked towards the foal again, and couldn't resist calling softly. "Sukie! Hey, Sukie-gal!"

The filly glanced over at him and flicked her ears before returning to her mother's teat.

"See! She already responds to it!" Callie laughed.

"Yeah, I can see she's real impressed with me."

ɔ

"Good mornin' Dee," Tom called out as he came back into the house.

She looked up at him blearily from where she leaned against the counter, staring at the burbling coffee-maker. "What's good abou—Jeez! What is that stench?"

She straightened in a hurry, frowning at him as she sidled away, hand capped over her nose. "Is that blood?"

Tom looked down at his gore-streaked hand. "Yep. There's a good bit of horse-manure, too."

"What the heck have you gotten into already? It's not even eight o'clock."

"A mare's foal-bed, about shoulder deep."

Dee gaped at him.

He turned on the water-tap and grabbed the bottle of soap. That brought her back to herself in a hurry.

"Not in the kitchen sink! Jeez, Tom! Go to the bathroom. Better yet— go outside to the hose!"

He headed for the bathroom, and fired back over his shoulder, "I got me a job out of it, if that makes me smell any better."

"Not by much."

She followed him as far as the bathroom doorway. By this point, he was somewhat over his natural modesty, seeing as how she and Chris both lounged around more or less half naked most of the time. He took off his shirt without much of a qualm to scrub the worst off his arm at the sink while he ran the tub. If he was going to have to wash to the shoulder and across his chest, he might as well soak his leg and back in the bargain.

"Dare I ask why you had your arm shoved up a horse's ass, and how that led to a job offer?"

"The Dargers had a mare get loose last night. A dead tree on your side had took part of the fence down and the mare got over on your land. She was havin' trouble foalin'. The Darger girl, Callie, showed up right before I got 'er straightened out and delivered. She called her folks, we talked for a bit, and Stephan Darger offered me a job at their place. I start tomorrow mornin'."

"Wow. I'm happy for you," Dee answered. "I know you've been bored, sitting around the house."

"I never been idle in m' life," Tom shrugged. "Found I don't take to it too well. At least this is somethin' I know. Horses cain't have changed much, nor cattle either."

"Well, they run a dude ranch, so that's going to be an eye-opener. Think you can handle giggling city folks playing cowboy without losing your cool?"

He wasn't entirely certain he understood what she was getting at, but he took a stab. "Don't figure they'll be stickin' me right out with the payin' public, not at first. Probably I'll jist be rakin' out stalls or haulin' feed to start, but don't matter to me so long as I get paid."

He lifted an eyebrow at her. "Besides, I weren't a cowhand but for one drive, anyhow. That was enough for me to figure that there had to be a good hundred better ways to earn a livin,' so if it's a cowboy they're wantin', I'll be play-actin' right along with them."

Dee laughed. It was, he realized, the first time he'd heard it. For such a rangy, raw-boned woman, her laugh was a right pretty, feminine sound, a sound he'd like to hear again.

The thought sent a flush up his neck, and he turned his attention to the tub, turning off the taps.

"There is one other thing," Dee said. "You know Stephan Darger is black, and his wife Paula is white, right?"

Tom turned back to her. "I did take notice of that when I met 'em."

"Does that bother you?"

Tom shrugged. "Who folks marry is their business, not mine."

"So you're willing to obey orders from a black man?" Her eyes were intent on his face.

"I'm willin' to obey orders from any man who pays my wage. Dee, I figure men is like horses, and a good horse ain't ever a bad color. How me and Mr. Darger get along ain't gonna have nothin' to do with the color of his hide or mine."

He gave her a steady look of his own. "Why did you think otherwise?"

"Uh, an incomplete understanding of the South, apparently," she answered with a wry tilt to her mouth. "But if I take time right now to summarize the entire history of race relations in the US, you'll stink up the whole house. Toss me that shirt. It needs to go straight into the washer.

He scooped it up off the floor and lobbed it towards her. Dee caught it with two fingers and a puckered-up grimace of distaste. She closed the door then, leaving him to soak the stench off in privacy.

CHAPTER TWENTY-SIX

5 January, 1873
~ Thirty days later ~

Jon presented the bucket with a grin and a slight bow. "Good morning! I can guarantee that there's no hair in this milk today, Mrs. Lefler."

Ophelia lifted an eyebrow. "And how can you be so sure?"

His grin widened. "I filched some of your clean cheesecloth off the line and milked through a few layers."

"So that's where it went," she muttered, then took the bucket. "I have to give credit for a clever idea where it's due, I suppose."

"Mark it up to Yankee ingenuity if it helps."

"You said you were from Tennessee."

Jon shook his head. "Dorin's from Tennessee. I'm from Cincinnati, Ohio."

"Hmph," was all she had to say about that. She started to close the kitchen door.

Jon blocked it with his hand, and she scowled at him. "Mrs. Lefler, I know you're busy, but if you could spare a moment of your time, I'd appreciate it."

Her scowl didn't lighten, but she did hesitate. "I suppose I could spare a few minutes, if you'll help peel and slice carrots. You do know how to do that, don't you, city boy?"

Jon chuckled. "Yes, that I can handle. My Mom taught me how."

He could tell she was biting back a choice comment on that, but instead she took a seat at the work table. He found a paring knife, sat down across from her and raked over a portion of the small mountain of carrots. He peeled and sliced a few to make sure he met her standards, and then he broached the subject.

"I know we got off on the wrong foot. Some of that is Dorin's fault, but a good part of it's mine, too. I want to apologize for my thoughtless words when we first met. I didn't intend to offend you, but I did and I'm sorry for that. I'm sorry too that my incompetence has made your work harder these past couple of months. That was never my intent, either."

She looked surprised for an instant, with suspicion following hard on its heels. "What's prompting this sudden attack of contrition, Mr. Hansen?"

"It's not sudden," he shrugged. "More like, shamefully delayed by misplaced masculine pride, I guess. And you can call me Jon."

"Ummhmm." She chopped through a carrot like an executioner with an ax. "It still smells like you want something in exchange for that pretty apology."

"Well, yeah," he agreed. "I do. A less hostile working environment, for starters. And I could use your help, if you're willing."

Her suspicious expression shaded to scornful. "What could I possibly do for you?"

"Help me with Mrs. Perkins."

"The only help you need with Mrs. Perkins is to learn some decent manners and give her a full day's work for your pay."

"That's not what I meant. She's in danger."

Ophelia's hands stilled. "How?"

"From Tom Dorin."

Her hand closed tighter around the heavy knife she was using. "From you, then."

"Aw, come on!" Jon leaned back in his chair. "What's it going to take to convince you I'm telling the truth about who I am? I'll show you my watch and my driver's license, but I'm not going to risk draining down my phone."

Ophelia laid the knife down, but kept her hand over it. "Why do you think Hattie's in danger?"

Jon leaned forward. "Look, you and I both know she doesn't think of Dorin only as the hired hand, right? That she's got… let's call it, um, a more personal interest in him? In the most chaste way, of course. No offense."

Ophelia's hand moved away from the knife. "Go on."

"She's a very kind woman, and I owe her huge for taking me in. But to me she seems kind of naive and way too trusting to be in this business. I don't want to see her get hurt, not emotionally and certainly not physically. I can't give you details, because I honest to God don't know much more than I'm telling you now— but Tom Dorin's dangerous. I mean, really dangerous. And by March thirteenth, everybody's going to know it. I'm not going to be around then, but she needs to be kept as far away from Dorin as possible."

"I'll do what I can," Ophelia nodded. "I never trusted that jaybird." She picked up the kitchen knife again and gestured towards him. "I don't trust you, either, Jon Jackanape."

"Ah, but the enemy of your enemy is a friend, right?" Jon smiled.

She almost smiled back.

CHAPTER TWENTY-SEVEN

December 29, Present day
~ Eighteen Days Later ~

As soon as the garage door came down, Tom stepped through the kitchen door and opened her car door for her. "Welcome home."

"Thanks." Dee smiled. "Have you had a good day?"

"So far it has been." His voice was always warm and kind, but as usual, he didn't smile back.

When she stepped to the back of the car and opened the trunk, he followed and helped her lift out the groceries.

She tried another smile on him. This time she got a nod before he turned to hobble back into the house. He held the door for her, despite his own load and the hindrance of his cane.

"Wow, it smells good in here," she commented as she stepped into the house.

"Hope it tastes it too," he said, setting the groceries on the counter beside the refrigerator. "At least you can testify to Chris that I didn't scorch ever'thing or set the kitchen afire as he predicted."

"He's a big one to talk. All he can manage is eggs and bacon. I wouldn't have guessed you could cook, though," she said, lifting the lid on the bean pot to peek in.

"I had to learn a little or starve. Not sure I'd say I can cook though," he shrugged, putting away what he could. "It's jist soup beans and fried 'taters and cornbread. And I ain't none too sure about that cornbread. I'm used to cookin' over a fire, not on a stove. 'Specially not one I don't have to stoke."

"Hey, it's food, and I didn't have to fix it, so you won't hear any complaints from me even if I have to drink that cornbread." She dropped into a chair with a weary sigh.

"Don't think it'll be quite that bad," he drawled back, his tone droll and his face somber, then pulled it out of the oven. It looked done enough on the outside, anyway.

She started to get up and he shook his head.

"Rest yourself, Dee. I'll get it, I'm already up."

"Thank you." She smiled again as he set a full plate and a glass of cold tea in front of her.

She got a soft "You're welcome," but no smile in return. She was beginning to wonder if he knew how. It was becoming a challenge.

"Aren't you going to eat?" She asked as he moved towards the back door. Automatically, she assessed his gait as he walked away. He still had a slight limp, probably from pain, but those new boots with their massive lift got him off crutches, at least.

"Nah, not here. I got to help with the sunset ride tonight, so I'll eat then."

"Okay, have fun." Dee tried a bite of the potatoes, rich with tender onions, fried crisp and brown in probably way too much bacon grease.

"This is good, by the way!" she added around the mouthful as he went out the door.

Tom gave her an almost shy glance back over his shoulder and a flick of a wave.

Dee watched out the window as he mounted up on the horse he must have ridden over from the ranch when his morning duties were done.

His movements were so natural, so smooth as he settled into the saddle and loped away down the field, that it was hard to remember in that moment how physically disabled he was, how painfully awkward in most other ways.

Dee shook her head and blew on a spoonful of beans, watching the skins break and curl under her breath. The Dargers had no idea how genuine a cowboy they had hired. She bit into the cornbread and chuckled. It was, indeed, a bit damp still in the middle. No need for a straw, though.

That's when it hit her.

Chris was gone for a couple of days. Tom knew he was going to be helping with the sunset cookout when he started this meal. For her. He went to this trouble, only for her....

January 10, Present Day
~ Thirteen days later ~

Television normally held no appeal for Tom, in fact, he said it gave him a headache, but Dee could see that this commercial held him transfixed.

"Hey, that might be fun to watch again," Chris commented as film clips from Ken Burn's Civil War documentary flared and scrolled across the screen. "Dorin can point out all the inaccuracies."

Tom shook his head hard, and Dee wasn't sure if it was in answer to Chris' question or an involuntary return to awareness at the end of the commercial.

"I would think he's seen all of it he wants to," she chided Chris, but kept her eyes on Tom.

"Aw, come on," Chris protested. "Even in his day, it was almost ten years later. That's gotta be enough time for the worst to wear off, right? After all, it's not like he shows signs of having post-traumatic stress disorder or anything. This is history, it's important to everybody. It's not like I'm asking him to—"

"I'll thank you both to talk to me to my face when I'm in the room." Tom said. He looked at them with no expression at all on his face, despite the heat in his voice.

Dee was startled by that curt request, and Chris scowled.

"I'm sorry, Tom," Dee said, feeling herself blush under Tom's stare. "We were inexcusably rude."

"Don't apologize for me!" Chris snapped, but kept his scowl turned on Tom.

Tom pushed himself to his feet and started out of the living room. He glanced back over his shoulder. "Yeah, don't ever apologize for him. Let him take claim of his own boar-hog nature for once."

Chris lurched up but Dee grabbed his arm. "Leave him alone, Chris."

"After that crack?" Chris yanked free and took a stride towards the hall.

Dee grabbed him again.

"Oh meow." She rolled her eyes. "Chris, after all the digs you've made at him, that one shouldn't leave a mark. We were rude first after all."

"How was asking about the war rude?" Chris flopped back down in his normal boneless sprawl, only his scowl marring the impression of congenital indolence. "Geez, Dee, aren't you a little curious? We've got a freakin' time-traveler here!"

"Ugh, are you really that dense? We were talking around him like he wasn't there. Rude in any century."

She sat down on the sofa again. "Asking him about the war isn't exactly rude, but it is insensitive. Haven't you noticed he never talks about it at all? Pushing him on it is, I dunno, kinda like pestering me to talk about the goriest calls I've ever been on or something."

"I thought it helped to talk about trauma," Chris answered, his scowl turning to something more petulant.

"It does with someone who can empathize and help you through the fallout, someone you know has been through the same kind of situation," Dee answered, her voice softer.

"You watch that film again, Chris, but this time put yourself in it. Then you decide if ten years is enough time to get past that enough for casual discussions with smart-ass strangers." She rose, having lost all interest in what they'd been watching.

"Why am I always the bad guy here?" Chris whined as she started out of the room.

"You're not. We all are. None of us are. This all sucks." She hurried away, not sure exactly where, though the bathroom was always a good idea.

"Not gonna argue with you about that," Chris grumbled, almost too low for her to catch as she walked away.

બ્ય

The next afternoon, Dee stepped into her bedroom and saw an odd packet lying on the bench at the foot of the bed. It was a stack of folded, yellowed papers, tied with a faded green ribbon.

Beside it was a sheet from the pad in the kitchen. She picked it up. Tom's bold scrawl marched across it in lines that tilted up from left to right.

Dear Dee
If you want to know what I done in the War read these. If you got questions after only ask and I will tell you all you want to hear. You got a right to know what sort of man I am and what I done as you are sheltering me under your roof. Chris can go bark up a tree. I aint telling him nothing.
~T

Dee chuckled at that last, but felt a quiver of anticipation too. Chris was right, she was curious about Tom's past. She sat down and unknotted the fragile ribbon.

As she opened the letter on top, she expected to see a woman's ornate Victorian penmanship. Instead she saw Tom's handwriting, and such atrocious spelling that she had to sound out many of the words to figure out his meaning as she read.

21 June 1861
Deer Beth
I was most pleesed to git yor leter to day an if i draown in thim i wil go undr the see of ink with a big grin on my face.

I hope you hav a good eye doktor in mind becaus you wil shorly need one after readin my skrawl. My hand is turrible i no an my spellin is worst an it is no fawlt of my Ma for she tryd her verre best to teach me but it were a task akin to makin silk purrsis frum sows ears....

By the time she got to the end of the last letter, Dee realized she was straining to see. Not only because the sun had left the windows, but because the page wavered from the film of water in her eyes. As she read, it was as if she became the person Tom had been writing to, and she longed to answer him between one letter and the next.

"No wonder he still grieves for you," she whispered to the woman who'd read those letters first. "You were the only one he could open up to. The only one he trusted to understand without thinking he was a coward or weak somehow."

Dee wiped her eyes on the hem of her t-shirt and carefully bound those precious letters again with Beth's hair ribbon. She went to the desk and sat down, pulled over a notepad and pen.

Tom,
Thank you so much for trusting me enough to let me read these letters. You don't owe me anything at all, much less something this personal, but I am so honored and grateful that you trust me enough to let me see into this painful, difficult but precious part of your life.

I am so thankful you had Beth to talk to, and so grieved that you lost her. After reading your letters, I feel like I know her too.

This time and this crazy situation has to be so hard on you, maybe as hard as the war. I know it's hard on me— understatement of any century, right? The truth is, Tom, I could use someone to talk to about it all sometimes myself.

Maybe by talking to each other like this, we'll find some way to get through all the craziness without going crazy.

~D

Before she could think about it too much and chicken out, Dee folded her note, grabbed up the letters and deposited them both on Tom's nightstand. He'd see them when he came in from work.

CHAPTER TWENTY-EIGHT

19 January, 1873
Cooper's Creek, AZT
~ Fourteen days later ~

"Mr. Hansen?"

Jon banged the back of his head against a beam in the low barn loft as he turned. "OW! What?"

Rubbing his abused skull, he glared at Hattie. He immediately tried to smooth his expression into something less antagonistic, but it was clear his effort was too late for a mollifying effect.

"I thought you might like to have your pay," she began in that cultured voice that could cut like a razor, "Before you go off to— Wherever you go in the afternoon."

Like she didn't know every friggin' step he made in this dust-riddled terrarium of the damned. She held out her hand, the money wrapped in a scrap of paper.

He'd given up wondering if that was a weird etiquette rule, or a neurotic quirk, or just her charming little passive-aggressive way of pointing out that she didn't want to risk touching his skin as she passed the coins over.

Didn't matter. Immediately after getting the first of those little monetary kiss-offs, he'd worked out that Dorin was earning a little more than a buck a week, plus room, board and clean clothes once a week.

Dorin was a gullible idiot with no personal life at all, or Hattie was one hell of a wildcat when those skirts of hers were flipped up over her head. Not that he'd know, since she'd not favored him with as much as a flash of ankle, which led him to lean towards the former conclusion.

"Thank you," was all he said, and made a point of letting his fingers brush hers as he took the coins.

"I expect you back promptly this afternoon. You've been trying my patience with your tardy returns."

"Sure," he shrugged, and stuck the money into his pants pocket. "I'll cut my drinking and whoring short today, just for you."

Hattie's nose wrinkled like she'd caught a whiff from the outhouse but she turned without a word and sailed back into the house.

Jon smirked at her retreating stiff back before he strolled off for the lower end of town.

One thing was certain. The modest little cache in Dorin's money pouch wasn't cash he'd saved up from this job. And that money pouch was a lot lighter in his pocket than it had been three months ago. If he carried on in even the piss-poor manner to which he was becoming accustomed, he would run through that surplus long before he was translocated or zapped or whatever back to when he belonged.

The prospect of unrelieved boarding house servitude was too gruesome to dwell upon. But where in this dump could he find a better job? He certainly wasn't going up to the mine and risk ending up like Finnegan's ancestor, or worse. The problem was, other than at the mine, the unemployment rate appeared to be zero.

He was a third of the way to the Speckled Dove when it dawned on him that the narrow mindset of these provincial hayseeds had rubbed off on him and he was running short on time for grabbing an opportunity that was quite literally once in eternity. The realization stopped him like he'd smacked into a wall.

Right now, right in this very decade, the western world stood on the trembling brink of the technological revolution. Oil lamps would go electric. Horses would give way to steam, steam to the internal combustion engine. Iron would be supplanted by steel and wood by plastics. Paper would bow to silicon chips. And he was positioned to take advantage of it all, with compound interest rates like God's own bank account and insider info to make a Wall Street shark feel like plankton.

Jon's grin felt avaricious even to him. He tugged his hat brim down and kept his eyes on the boardwalk to shut out social distractions as he went on to the Dove. He knew with fair accuracy who he should contact, which businesses to invest in. With careful planning through a long-lived bank or investment company, he'd return to his own century so rich, he could hire Gates as his personal tech monkey.

As he followed the thought out, Jon realized he couldn't make himself wealthy before this little blast to the past, because, well, if he'd had a small country's working capital to operate on, he wouldn't be poking around Cooper's Creek on the fateful day. Set up a time paradox and there'd be no space-time hiccup and no chance for long-term financial planning. Very, very long-term. Too, depending on when in his past his largess arrived, he might not even take an interest in history or meet Dee… or knock her up.

His forward motion paused for another few beats as he thought that through. No, he'd set it up to arrive well after he got back. Despite everything, he did want to be with her, and of course he wanted to raise his own kid.

Chris would crap a brick.

The look on his brother's face would be worth having had to skate along for the first third of his adult life right above bankruptcy. Of course, to do any of this, he'd need a heck of a lot more ready cash than he had now. He added up the scant funds on hand and made a rough guesstimate of compound interest alone. Dorin's remaining stash would accrue to a little less than three thousand bucks over the intervening years. So a simple savings account was out.

He needed ten or twenty thousand to invest in coming attractions, at the very least. Damn, around here, only the mine had that kind of cash floating around. It wasn't that disheartening thought that smacked the breath out of him at the doorway of the Dove, though.

IT was back.

He felt like his ribcage was going to be ripped out right through the skin, the pull was so strong this time.

"NO! Not yet!"

But he wasn't given a choice about it. The pull was inexorable, drawing Jon towards the threshold, even though he resisted every millimeter, his body straining backwards against the pull at an impossible angle.

Kay sprang up and came towards him. "Tom!"

The instant she crossed the threshold, the pull vanished.

Jon fell as instantaneously with no chance to catch himself. The impact knocked the breath out of him. He saw stars from the whack on the back of his head against the boards and tasted iron in his mouth. He'd bitten his tongue.

"Tom! Are you all right?" Kay knelt beside him and gave him a little shake.

He caught her wrist, and wheezed till he could regain enough breath to speak. "Yeah, I'm okay. Just let me lay here a few seconds."

She pulled her hand free of his loose grasp and laid it on his forehead instead.

Less in a hurry, as he was about everything, Fred leaned against the door post. "You need Doc, Dorin?"

"Nah." Jon sat up, spat a bit of blood, and didn't protest Kay's help in hauling himself back onto his feet. "I jist took some kind of turn there."

"One helluva turn if you ask me," Kay said. "But you ain't feverish."

Fred grunted, satisfied with that, and went back to the bar as Kay shepherded Jon to his usual spot.

"What happened?" she asked.

"I dunno," he shrugged, then decided what the hell, the whole town thought he was nuts anyway. "Doc said I might take spells for a while after that bad knock. Reckon this was one of 'em."

Kay gave a sympathetic cluck. "Sounds to me like you could use a drink. You're still white as cake flour."

"Yeah, a drink would be good." Jon leaned forward to rest his throbbing head on the heels of his hands.

He owed Kay big. If that pull had taken him all the way inside, he might be back in the twenty-first century, still flat-broke. He began to shake, the after-effect of a massive adrenaline dump. Yeah, he needed that drink, badly.

"Here ya go, honey," Kay crooned as she sat a full shot and a bottle down in front of him. "First one's even on me."

"You're a saint, darlin'," Jon drawled and picked up the shot glass.

"Our lady of perpetual panderin'," Fred commented from where he was leisurely clearing away the remains left by the dinner rush. "And it ain't on me, Saint Catherine, so you owe me two bits."

Jon's chuckle delayed his intake of the liquor long enough for a thought to make it through his addled haze. He set the glass back down as if he'd been about to imbibe battery acid. "I cain't," he blurted out.

"Huh?"

"Likker," Jon answered. "I ort not to drink after that spell. It makes me groggy, and it's dangerous to sleep after you whack your head hard. I need somethin' that'll keep me awake all night."

"I reckon there may be some coffee still in the back," Kay frowned. "But it's stone-cold and prob'ly tastes like stale cat-piss by now."

Jon shook his head. "It ain't enough to keep me awake, no way."

Kay tilted her head for a few seconds in thought, then grinned. "I know what you need. Give me a dollar."

"A blow ain't gonna keep me awake neither," Jon grumbled.

She gave him a playful tap of her fingertips on the side of his head, careful to avoid the lump on the back. "That ain't what I'm talkin' about, you lecher. Gimme a dollar and I'll go to the store for what you need."

Jon handed over the coin and she hurried off upstairs. A couple of minutes later, she was back down, buttoning a calico shirtwaist over her skirt that looked far more prim and proper than anything she ever sported at the bar.

"Now, don't you look like some rancher's sweet young wife?" Fred grinned.

"Shut it, Ezell," she snapped and hurried out the door.

"What the hell do you do to her?" Fred drawled when Kay was safely out of earshot. "She's like butter on a hot biscuit, whenever you step through the door."

Jon chuffed. "She ain't that soft on me, she ain't never give me nothin' for free." He tapped the shotglass of whiskey. "Hell, I'll be payin' dear for this snort, one way 'r another."

"Damn straight on that un," Fred nodded like a sage.

Neither of them felt the need for further conversation after that. Just as well, his head was throbbing. Jon rested his head against a forearm and gingerly fingered a lump on the back of his head that was the size of half an egg. He might have a concussion. Falling asleep any time soon probably wasn't a good idea even if he didn't intend to avoid waking up back in his bed in Tucson.

Kay was stripping the paper wrapper off a bottle as she came back into the bar. She plunked the brown bottle in front of him with a triumphant grin. "Here's whatcha need, sugar."

She downed his complimentary shot herself as Jon picked up the bottle. It seemed odd, still, to see such things bright and new, the label not tattered or half-missing.

'COCA WINE' it declared in a proud nineteenth century font. A slow grin spread over his face.

"Oh heck yeah, this'll do the trick." He pulled the cork with his teeth.

"Want a glass?" she offered the empty shot.

He answered that with a long swallow right from the bottle neck. The stuff probably had more sugar in it than a milkshake, because it was only faintly bitter going down.

Jon hoped that the promise of cocaine content wasn't a blatant rip-off.

January 19, Present Day
~ Nine days later ~

Tom stared out the windshield at the desert landscape rushing towards him faster than a locomotive. The stark vista and the awesome speed had long past lost any novelty and charm.

It was always a miserable trip out to Cooper's Creek. The least of it was that he had to make it there without the motion-sick medicine Dee usually gave him before they went anywhere. They were all afraid its effects might keep... whatever it was... from happening again. Not a one of them dared hint that it might never happen again, whether he was a touch groggy or more than a touch colicky.

So far, it hadn't seemed to make any difference either way. Nothing ever happened. After the first few times, Dee stopped going. It upset her too much and he and Chris both worried about the effect on her and Baby.

He missed her. Not that she was so pleasant to be around when they were out here, with every sight and every discomfort reminding her how bad the situation was. But without her tempering presence, prickly as she was, Chris was at his worst.

At home, with Dee around, Chris restrained himself to sly digs and outright insults. The second she stepped outside the door, Chris went surly and sullen and usually locked himself in the study, coming out only for food and drink and insults.

Out here, though, surly turned downright mean. More than once, Tom wondered if both of them would walk back over the ridge when the sun started to drop below noon's peak.

He didn't have much care lost on Jon Hansen, from what he knew of the man, but Tom had not one doubt that the only thing keeping himself alive was Chris's fear over what harming him might do to his brother.

So here they were, going through the drill again. Arriving at the same time in the early morning, him sticking close around the saloon while Chris did whatever he did.

ॐ

Tom drew breath to holler Chris back and give up for the day, but something besides a shout jerked the air back out of his lungs. Tom wrapped an arm tight across the horrid, drawing pain in his chest and stared into the Dove.

There was no mistaking the weird double-time vision now. He could see Fred, clear as day, eating his lunch. Ezell's black-haired whore sat at the same table, looking out like she could see him, puzzlement on her face.

"Chris!" Tom's shout came out more like a breathless wheeze.

Swaying from the relentless tug, he forced in a deep lungful past the pain and tried again. "CHRIS!"

Tom's next step was a running one towards the doorway. The pull vanished the instant his feet landed on the other side of the threshold. The saloon looked just the way it had every other damn time they'd been out here.

Ruined.

Deserted.

Tom went to his knees, his cane clattering to the warped floor, his fists slamming against the rough wood. He let out a raw scream, rage and loss too deep for even the worst blasphemy.

The scream hung in the air, took on a different timbre.

It was the second scream that had him scrambling to his feet and hurrying up the street. "Chris? CHRIS! Where are ya?"

"Bank!" Chris' voice was shrill and tight.

Tom went up the cracked steps as quick as he could.

Chris lay inside the door, sickly green-white as old milk. He clutched his left leg. "My foot went through the floor. I think my leg's broken!"

Tom carefully skirted around the rotten spot and lowered himself down to sit beside Chris' left leg. "Gimme your knife."

"Like hell! You're not going to do some crazed frontier surgery on me!"

"You stupid ass, I cain't see your leg through your britches. Give me your damn knife."

His breath short and high in his throat, Chris managed to dig through his pocket. He handed over a small jack-knife.

Tom split the leg of Chris' britches to right above the knee. The joint was skinned up, but Chris didn't come off the floor when he gave it a tentative shove sideways, so it wasn't broken or torn loose.

Chris' shin, though, that looked nastier. The long slim bone had a kink in it that God didn't put there, but he couldn't tell through the blood if the bone had come through the skin. Tom wiped at the blood with his bandanna.

Chris let out a yell and took a slap at his head.

Tom ducked it. "It's broke, but it don't look too bad. You're jist cut up some from a nail or something, but the bone ain't pokin' through."

"It feels like it is! Look again!"

"It ain't, I'm tellin' ya."

Bad break or no, Chris' foot was likely to swell up till getting that boot off would be a trick later. Tom unlaced it and tried to tug it off as gentle as he could. Chris let him know, loudly, it wasn't gentle enough.

He pulled the sock off too, then rose and quickly scrounged for some likely strips of wood. The town was so dried out and brittle, it didn't take him long. He padded the rough stuff with strips of Chris' britches leg, and then used strips of Chris' sock and the bootlace to tie on the makeshift splint.

"Shit. SHIT," Chris panted, leaning back on his elbows, pale and a touch greener about the mouth. He looked like he was about to go out of it when Tom eased the unlaced boot back on.

Tom touched his shoulder. "Chris, you need to settle yourself down. You ain't gonna die from this, but gettin' yourself all worked up about it is jist gonna make it worse."

"Easy for you to say."

Tom rose with a pained grunt of his own. "Yeah, it is, you mollycoddled son of a bitch. You think you can walk if you lean on me real heavy?"

"Don't have a choice, asshole," Chris muttered.

"Sure you do. Graveyard's jist up the street."

Chris gave him a venomous look, then reached up. Tom took his hand and crouched, wrapping Chris' arm around his shoulder as he heaved them both up.

"Good thing it's my left leg," Chris gritted.

"I been told I'm one helluva lucky bastard," Tom answered. "Must be rubbin' off on you."

"Remind me to thank you for that when I'm not about to puke."

As they stepped off the boardwalk, Tom didn't notice the lizard that darted away right in front of him. The little creature got out from under his boot with its life, but left its sacrificed tail writhing in the dirt.

CHAPTER TWENTY-NINE

19 January, 1874
Cooper's Creek, AZT
~ Several hours later ~

It was probably almost eleven. The house had gone quiet over an hour ago. Jon paced his room on bare feet, four strides from the window to the door, three from wall to wall. The restricted range of motion made the small room more and more like a cage, so he forced himself to stop. His random halt was in front of the wash stand. He looked at himself in the mirror. Despite the lamp's glow, his pupils were wide glittering black holes swallowing the blue.

Jon grinned. The coca wine was performing exactly as advertised, though its mellow lift had been augmented by the sharper buzz of a large pot of coffee brewed so dark it was almost too bitter to drink. No danger of falling asleep any time soon.

"I gotta think this through," he muttered. "I gotta figure something out. A hundred bucks isn't enough to do it, even with more than a century of interest. I gotta make some solid plans."

Dorin had a pad of writing paper and a pen and pencil, but there was nowhere to hide plans like these in a public room like this. The last thing he needed was for Hattie or Ophelia to stumble across them and start asking awkward questions.

He made another fretful circuit of his room and his flicking gaze fell this time on the print, the room's only ornament. Jon grinned and lifted it off the wall. He flipped the frame over, untied the piece of string it hung from and removed the back.

"Perfect."

The lamp table and the print's frame became a writing desk. Jon scrawled figures on the writing pad. No, there was no way his meager funds would accumulate with normal interest to more than about two thousand bucks, no matter how generous the estimate. Earning any significant addition to that wren-sized nest egg was as impossible as booking a flight out of here. Not in three days. Not if he spent the rest of his surely miserable life in this dust-bucket under Hattie's domination.

The parlor clock, and his brain, ticked on as he searched for a solution. There were always a limited number of options for acquiring a large amount of cash quickly. He wasn't going to earn it, certainly wasn't going to inherit it or find a briefcase full of bills on a subway seat. He pretty much sucked as a gambler, too many tells, and Las Vegas wasn't even a one-horse town yet.

The parlor clock struck one and he was left with one viable option.

Steal it.

That got him pacing again. The last time he'd heisted anything, he was seven and pocketed one of those little electronic watch games from a friend's birthday party. The reaction of his parents, and the humiliation and shame of apologizing to his friend and returning the toy made the intended impression. He never stole again.

If he didn't overcome that early inhibition, he'd land back in his own time with nothing but an insane story to tell. He knew he couldn't forgive himself for that. He'd be reminded of it every time a bill was due or the checking account ran low.

Jon dropped back onto his chair. This was his only chance, but these people would have a lifetime to make up the loss. Heck, he might even be able to make restitution some way. Start a charitable trust or drop some cash on a distant descendant or something. That would even the cosmic books, surely.

He rocked the chair up onto its back legs and propped his heels on the bottom shelf of the lamp table as he considered his expanded set of possible funding sources. Hattie had some cash on the premises, working capital. Not much, but more than he had. That, he decided, would be a last resort. He didn't want to bite the hand that fed him unless he had no other choice.

Hackler appeared to be paid in pocket change. He had to have a cash reserve, the man obviously wasn't penniless. Whatever the doctor had stashed, though, he kept in the bank or somewhere else outside his quarters and office. Nothing to tap there.

Nothing to tap anywhere else, for that matter. A few of these hicks might have a canning jar of silver dollars buried out back somewhere, but there didn't appear to be real wealth anywhere in this part of the Territory.

Except the bank, and the mine that fed it. He didn't have any problem picturing himself wearing a bandanna mask, hat pulled down low to hide his betraying eyes. Pulling Dorin's pistol on some pale and quaking poindexter behind the teller's counter.

He didn't have any problem picturing himself promptly shot full of holes on exiting the edifice, either. The James-Younger gang, with all their larcenous experience, would soon be blasted to tatters in Northfield, Minnesota after knocking over a bank. Jon had no delusions that he'd do any better on his own in a town where every man, woman and dog recognized him at first glance.

Jon dropped the chair back onto all four legs. He rolled the stubby pencil back and forth through his fingers as he considered the quandary.

"I need a con," he muttered. "Some kind of fast-acting scam."

Nothing came to mind. Rather, about a thousand things came to mind, but his brain was in hyperdrive and he couldn't follow any one line of thought for more than a few seconds before haring off on a tangent.

One of those tangents was Kay. With his body's enthusiastic approval, that was a line of thought he was able to fixate on. Jon laid his pages of scrawled figures on top of the print, replaced the backing board, and hung the picture back on its nail.

Jon slipped out of the boarding house, boots in his hands. He sat down on the bottom porch step to put them on, then hurried down the boardwalk to the Saloon, the only building in town still spilling light out onto the street. He limped only because Dorin's built-up boot forced him to.

January 19, Present Day
~ Two hours later ~

"Oh God," Chris gasped when they finally got over that cursed ridge. "I've never been so glad to see a car in my life!"

He fumbled around in his pocket and brought out his cell phone. "Dammit! Still no bars."

That led to another pocket digging, though this time he dropped the keys, hit by another bout of nausea. Tom tried to keep them both upright as Chris heaved. He didn't try to get out of the way, resigned by this point. They were both covered in sweat, dirt and puke.

Instead, he managed to haul Chris over to lean on the side of the car, and hurried off to grab the keys. "Don't you dare fall on me again," he growled. "I couldn't hardly get you back up the last time."

Chris didn't say anything, but gave him a look of utter misery. Tom handed him the keys and Chris pushed the button that unlocked the vehicle's doors.

"You drive," Chris muttered, shoving the keys back into Tom's hand.

"I don't know how."

Chris already had the right hand door open, half falling again. "Today you learn."

It was a near thing when he lifted Chris' splinted leg in, but the threat of being stranded out here kept Chris conscious. Barely.

"WAKE UP! Tell me what to do." Tom yelled and jabbed Chris' shoulder.

"Yeah, yeah. Push down on the left floor pedal and keep it down until the engine starts." Chris twisted around to stab one of the keys at the wheel. He gave it a turn once Tom helped him get it in the slot. The engine roared.

"Okay…" Chris wiped his face against his shoulder. "Don't touch anything yet. The left pedal on the floor is the brake. It slows and stops the car and the right one is the accelerator that makes it go. The harder you push either of them, the faster you stop or the faster you go. The wheel steers it left or right."

Chris swallowed hard. Tom offered him the water bottle. Chris took a sip, laid his head back again. When he spoke, his voice was raspy and strained.

"Put your foot on the left pedal, push down and keep it there while you push that button on the lever between us and pull it down to D, that's drive. Then take your foot off the left and ease down on the right. The car will go forward."

"Sounds easy enough." Tom put the lever to D, turned the wheel away from the base of the ridge, took his foot off the brake and pushed the right pedal.

The car lurched forward like a hornet-stung horse, flinging rocks and dirt up in the air. Tom jabbed at the brake and nearly threw them both against the front of the thing. Chris let out a squall like a rutting cat.

"We're both gonna die," Chris moaned, scrabbling for the webbing harness to strap himself into his seat.

"Shut up," Tom gritted, feeling fresh sweat break out over his forehead and under his arms. "I'll figure this out."

Chris groaned.

The car lurched and shied and almost bolted and gave a groan or two of its own, but they made it back down the rutted road and up onto the paved one at a speed somewhere between a trot and a gallop.

Driving was easier, somewhat, on the smoother surface. Tom gave the thing a little more rein and worried more about keeping the monster between the broken yellow line in the center and the solid white one on the right side than about keeping it from running away with them.

Chris kept checking his cell phone every few seconds and cussing it between moans of pain. "I've got bars! I've got bars! STOP!"

Tom slammed a pedal to the floor. The vehicle roared and shot forward.

"THE OTHER PEDAL!"

Tom stomped the other one just as hard. The car squalled and skated around itself till it wound up crossways of the road, facing the other way.

Chris had his eyes screwed tight shut and he wheezed like a bellows. Tom didn't feel much more composed, his knuckles tight on the wheel.

Chris cracked one watering eye open, enough to give him a side-long look. "Okay, Speed Racer. Very, very slowly, get us off to the side of the road."

With extreme caution, Tom managed to make the recalcitrant machine ease off the pavement with a bump, onto the gravel and dirt at the side. As soon as they rolled to a halt, Chris popped the lever to P, and turned the key to kill the engine.

"Cripes, how do driving instructors survive?" Chris muttered as he dialed his phone.

"I need an ambulance," he said into it. "I've got a broken leg. My shin." His voice slid into a pathetic range then. "I had to walk on it for over an hour."

Tom got out of the car while Chris was telling where they were. He sagged down onto the dirt, his sweaty back against the hot metal, and figured he'd sit there and let himself shake until Chris hollered for him again.

20 January, 1873
Cooper's Creek AZT
~ Late night ~

"You ain't gettin' tired of me already, are you?"

Jon's fingers tightened in Kay's hair at her crown. He lifted her head from his chest, the pull gentle but brusque. "What're you talking about?"

Kay jerked free of his hold. "You're in my bed but you sure ain't been here with me for a good while."

He scowled at her. One of the things he appreciated about purchased sex was that he didn't have to talk about a single damned thing afterward. "Why do you care? You get paid all the same."

"Just curious. You usually ain't much of a deep thinker, seems to me." She stroked down his body. "If I'm borin' you, I'll have to try a few new tricks. I kinda like havin' you around regular."

"If I tell you what I'm thinking about, will you show me one of those tricks? Even trade."

Kay gave that proposition serious consideration. "Well, it's been a slow night." Her smile turned sly. "And ever'body else is asleep or passed out, so, you got a deal. You tell me what has you wool-gatherin' and I'll give you a treat."

Jon laced his hands behind his head. Kay rolled onto her belly and propped herself on her forearms like an erotic sphinx.

"I was thinking about what I'd do if I was a billionaire," he said.

Kay's eyes widened, then she laughed. "I can answer that real quick— you'd do anything you damn well pleased." She flopped down onto her pillow in a graceless sprawl. "I don't think that's worth a treat. You might as well be musin' about takin' a stroll on the moon. It's more likely to happen for ya."

He gave her bare behind a smack.

"Hey!" She yelped and sat up with a scowl of her own. "You gonna start that business, it's gonna cost you double!"

Jon chuckled. "Just had to get your attention, sweetheart."

He sat up, shoved his pillow against the thin iron bars of the headboard. "What would you say if I told you I had a way of making at least a quarter-million happen within the next ten years?"

"I'd say I'm wonderin' why you're shovelin' cow shit for room and board if you're so almighty smart." She crossed her arms over her chest.

"Lack of seed capital, that's all." Jon shrugged. "I know where to invest and how much. Sure propositions, if only I had cash to work with. Things are going to change, Kay. We're on the edge of a whole new world. You wouldn't believe me if I told you what you'll see in the next twenty years."

"You talk like you're some kind of prophet."

Jon merely cocked his head at her.

She laughed again. "You're crazier than everybody says you are!"

"No, not crazy, but if I try to explain you'll think I am."

"And that right there sounds real crazy all by itself." Kay reached for her robe hanging on the bedpost.

"Go on home, Tom. And for god's sake, lay off that damned coca-wine and get some sleep before you really do go crazy."

"Come on, Kay—"

She cut him off by throwing his clothes across his face and chest.

ℂ

Jon slunk back into the boarding house and up the stairs. Dawn and the start of another day of menial servitude wouldn't come for another couple of hours. Sleep was not an option.

He fidgeted, at a loss to keep himself occupied. A random thought drifted through his brain and he seized on it with a grin. After retrieving Dorin's writing supplies, Jon sat down at the lamp table.

Since all this was very real, then that letter from Carl had been real. He could talk face to face with the best friend Dorin ever had. After all, Carl had all but invited himself out on the next stage.

Jon dipped the steel-nibbed pen into the ink bottle and did his best to replicate Dorin's uneducated scrawl. When he felt he had it right, he started on a fresh sheet.

Dear Carl,
I was most pleased to get your letter and there is nothing I would like more than a chance to see you again….

January 19, Present Day
University of Arizona Medical Center
~ Later the same day ~

"Okay, you want to tell me what happened out there?" Dee asked.

Tom looked at her, definitely worse for wear, but not as haggard as she felt. "It happened again, that weird double-time thing."

Tiredness vanished in a flash of adrenaline. She straightened.

"I seen 1873, Dee. It was so clear. My time was showin' more real than the Dove looks now. I tried to jump right straight in and home. 'Course, you can plainly see it didn't work. That's when I heard Chris screamin' and run to see what'd happened."

"We don't know that it didn't work," she said.

He frowned a little at her.

She touched his shoulder. "Whatever this is, it didn't take you at the saloon the first time either. It was when you were asleep, three days later."

"You're right! Lord, how could I be so stupid to forget that?"

"Well, you've had a lot on your mind today."

"How's Chris doin'?"

"He's going to be okay. They had to put him to sleep to reduce the fracture, that's why it's taking so long. But we'll have him home in a couple of hours."

"And I can go to sleep," he murmured.

"Yes." Her voice was not much louder than his.

He surprised her by reaching out to take her hand. She laced her fingers with his and looked down. Her hand looked refined and even delicate, engulfed in his callused, scarred and deeply tanned one.

"Dee, I know you'll be overjoyed to get your Jon back. And I'm gonna be real glad to be back where I belong. But... I'm gonna miss you."

"I'll miss you too." Dee looked into his eyes, and a chill of dread slithered down her spine. "Tom— don't forget what's supposed to happen to you, when you get back. Don't you dare stay in that town!"

"I promise you, as soon as my boots touch the dirt back there, I'm headin' out on a bee-line for Tennessee and I ain't slowin' down for nothin' nor nobody."

"You do that. Go way back into the mountains if you have to. Even change your—"

"Pardon me."

They both turned towards the stranger's voice.

"Ms. Collins? Mr. Hansen is asking for you," the nurse told her.

"I'll be right there." Dee turned back to Tom with a smile that felt a little wobbly and gave his hand a squeeze.

He squeezed back before he let go. "You tell him I said to buck up and dwell on them pretty nurses instead of his leg."

She gave a little chuckle. "Sounds like good advice. I'll pass it along."

24 February, 1874
Cooper's Creek, AZT

The rustle of furtive movement roused Jon from a pleasant post-coital doze. He cracked one eye, checking to make sure Kay didn't have her hands in his pants pockets.

She sat in her chair close by the open window, a small leather pouch in her lap. She poked at something she held cupped in the palm of her hand, oblivious to his covert observation.

When she poured the objects back into the pouch, something reflected the afternoon light with a fleeting, weak glimmer.

"What have you got?" he asked.

She looked up with a wry expression. "River rocks, I suspect, and one expensive lesson against trustin' a smooth-talkin' stranger."

"You, trust? He must have been a master of eloquence to suck you in." Jon extended a hand. "Lemme see."

Kay came back to the bed and tossed him the little pouch. Jon loosened the drawstring and poured out a tablespoon or two of yellowish, glassy stones.

"There's got to be one whopper of a tale behind these for you to take them in trade," he commented as he poked at the rocks.

"He was such a handsome fella, a real charmer to boot," she sighed. "Said he had business at the mine, travelin' on his company's line of credit. That's why he bartered these for a lay."

She picked up one of the stones and rolled it between her fingertips. "He told me they're raw diamonds."

"Diamonds, huh? You're good Kay, but you're not that good."

She stuck her tongue out at him. "I'm good enough for you to beggar yourself every week to have at me. He said these aren't real fine ones, but swore they're diamonds all the same."

"Industrial diamonds?" Jon held a stone up to see how much of the light passed through it.

"Maybe," she nodded. "He said they used them in factories to cut stuff and polish things, but that these would still make me a pretty necklace if a jeweler shined them up or whatever they do to make diamonds look nice."

She shook her head. "I'm thinkin' I gave him a long hard ride for a pinch of river trash."

As Jon watched the muddy sparkle of a sunbeam refracting through the little stone, a memory surfaced. A scrap of history pursued one morning for its inherent interest rather than its relevancy to his thesis.

He popped the stone into the air with his palm like a child's jack and caught it again. That article certainly held relevance now. "No, I think you made the best trade of your life."

Jon sat up and dropped the stones back into their pouch. "If these are diamonds, even worthless industrial crap, I know a way they can make us both rich. We'll need someone else to partner with us, though, someone with business connections to people a lot higher than a shit-shoveler and bar-whore."

Kay's expression turned slyly smug. "There's a fair few gentlemen at the mine and the bank who know me better than they'd care to admit."

"That's a good start. Would any of them be more interested in making a pile of money than in sticking to a strict rendition of the truth?"

She laughed. "I can think of one or two."

Jon lay back, pulling her down with him. "Tell me about them."

January 24, Present Day
~ Five days later ~

"Mornin', Chris." Tom said.

There it was again, that hopeful glance at him, wilting into disappointment. "Yeah, morning."

"You need anything?" Tom asked.

"Nah, I'm good." Chris stumped on down the hall to the bathroom, still awkward on his crutches.

That exact scrap of conversation had become an uncomfortable routine, but the worst part of it was yet to come. Tom leaned against the kitchen counter, waiting. The shrill bell always made him flinch when it went off. He lifted the receiver, dread in his belly. "Hello?"

"Hello," Dee's voice replied, and then there was an awkward pause. "Tom?"

"Yes. I'm sorry."

"Me too," she sighed. "But Tom, I'm not only sorry because Jon's not back. I know how much you want to go home."

His hand tightened on the smooth grip of the phone. "Listen, I think tomorrow I'm gonna get up proper and go on back to work."

"NO!"

He winced and pulled the phone away from his ear.

"No, please, Tom," she continued, her voice softer but no less urgent. "Don't give up yet. Please, give it at least a couple more days, okay? We told the Dargers a week, right?"

Tom closed his eyes. "Two more days ain't gonna matter. If it was gonna happen, I'd done be gone."

He heard a sharp gasp.

"Don't say that!" she snapped.

Tom's jaw tightened and he couldn't help but rub at the ache in his temples. "I'm sorry, Dee. I am. More than I can say. But not admittin' the truth won't make it go away."

An almighty clatter made him pull the phone away from his ear again. "Dee?"

Nothing but a mechanical hum answered him. Tom hung up the phone. Most of the day was still left. He'd go on over and see if the Dargers could use him. At least they were always glad to see him.

ဆ

The house was dark when he came back after sunset. The only lights on were the tiny green and red ones that glowed from the various machines scattered about the place. It was quiet too, or as quiet as it ever got with those machines humming and the cars passing on the road.

Chris' room was open and dark. Dee's door was closed and no light shone from underneath. Tom walked light to keep his boots from clomping on the floor as he went back to the kitchen after his exploratory circuit. He got a beer from the fridge and stepped out onto the veranda to enjoy the early evening before the night's chill set in.

"Where were you today?"

The terse question from the darkness surprised him. He looked over to see Dee huddled up under a jacket on the swing.

"I was at work," he answered, sitting down in one of the chairs. He hauled his leg up onto the footstool.

"We agreed on a week," she said, her voice low and gritty.

"You insisted I take a week," he amended after a swig of beer. Still couldn't quite get used to beer cold as ice. "I waited five days, for your sake. Like I told you yesterday, two more days weren't gonna make no difference."

"You don't know that!"

"You don't know that neither, and you need the money."

She went quiet then for a long stretch, though he couldn't see her face well enough to figure her state of mind.

"You promised, you sonuvabitch!"

Well, that cleared his doubt right and proper. "I didn't," he answered. "I quit arguin' with you about it and you took it for me agreein'."

"Don't you tell me what I was thinking!"

"Fair enough, and I apologize for presumin' such." He turned in his chair to look at her straight on. "I decided that after three days and two more, waitin' around on what weren't gonna happen was a waste of my time, the Dargers' good graces and money we sorely need. That's what I was thinkin'."

Another long stretch of silence. Dee crawled up further under that jacket she had thrown over her like a blanket. "Like going to work isn't a waste of time for you too," she muttered. "What a joke."

Tom set his beer bottle down and looked at her again. Now that his eyes were adjusted to the dark, he could see the terse, hardened line of her mouth below the shadowy hollows of her eyes. Lord, but the woman was far too thin, especially for her being in the family way. "Beg pardon?"

"You're a dead man where you sit," she snapped. "You've got forty-two days. That's all. I know it, you know it, and I'm damned sure Jon knows it." She sat up, shoving away the jacket.

As it fell to the paving stones, he recognized it. It was the short leather jacket that hung in the hall closet. John's jacket.

"You know what I think?" she said.

"No," he answered, his own voice coming out hard and clipped. He softened it. "Course I don't. Tell me your mind, Dee."

"I think you're still here because you want to be. I think you've decided you like it here, and hell, if I was standing in your boots I sure wouldn't be in any hurry to get back to a sure-fire date with a noose."

"Dee, that ain't—."

"Don't interrupt me!" she rapped. "Look, I can't blame you for not wanting to go back. No matter what you did back then, or you'll do when you go back, I can understand not wanting to wind up on those gallows. You'd have to be crazy or suicidal to want to go back and face that."

She went quiet again. Tom watched and waited.

"I don't want to hang. I admit that," he said after the silence stretched out long enough he figured she'd said her piece. "When I get back, I'll do ever'thing in my power to avoid it. But I do want to go back. I don't want to be here, and I sure don't want to be takin' John's place in any way."

Dee made an odd, pained little sound. "You are taking Jon's place."

"Dee, I don't mean to," he said.

"I know," she answered, coming to her feet with an abrupt grace despite her unwieldy belly. She bolted into the house and by the time he got to his feet and followed, her bedroom door was closed.

"Dee?" he called, and rapped softly.

"Go away, Tom." Her voice was thick and muffled. "I don't want to talk about it anymore. Just… leave me alone."

Tom turned from the door. As he limped back through the dark house, he realized that away and alone were what they were all afraid of the most.

☙

With nothing else to do, Tom settled onto his bed. He picked up the book on the nightstand, but after staring at the same page for lord only knew how long, he laid it aside.

His conscience was nagging at him too loud to let him read. Tom pulled a notepad out of the nightstand drawer and a pen, then drew the book back over for a makeshift writing desk.

I'm sorry I made you mad and hurt your feelings. I did what I thought was best but I didnt think about how you would see it. I do want to go back I swear that to you. I dont belong here no more than John belongs back in Coopers Creek. Us swapping times and places like we have done aint right nor natural. If Gods will for me is the noose then so be it. If I can get back to my own time I will take whatever comes with it even if it is to hang. At least I will know you have your John back and your suffering is over. There is nothing you have done to deserve any of this curse. Knowing you has been the bright spot in this for me and always will be come what may.

Tom folded the note, stepped as quietly as he could across the hall, then slid the paper under her door.

C3

The next morning, there was a sheet of pale blue paper lying just inside his room. Tom picked it up and unfolded it.

I owe you an apology too. I'm always mad and my feelings are permanently hurt these days. You catch most of the fallout, and usually for no reason but wrong place, wrong time.

Tom, please don't talk about God's will and the noose in the same sentence. There's no way a loving God will allow either of you to hang for something that was no one's fault but His. I know you want to go back to your own time, and I want that too, but promise me when you go back you'll do everything possible to keep yourself safe.

You're the bright spot in this mess for me, too, and I'll never forget you.

I'm going to stop now before I cry. Again. As if you haven't noticed, I do a lot of that lately, too.

Oh, and I don't know why it bugs me, but it does every single time, so I'm speaking up. Besides, you need to know in case you have to sign something. It's not J-O-H-N, it's J-O-N, short for Jonathan. His full name is Jonathan Madison Hansen, but he never uses his full first name, so sign anything Jon M. Hansen, okay?

Tom folded the blank end of her note and tore it off the sheet, then picked up his pen.

Thank you for forgiving me. You be mad glad or weepy as much as you like for it dont matter to me as long as I am in your good graces. I will do my level best to keep myself in them. As for the last I will remember to spell his name proper if need be. I hardly never use Thomas Anderson Dorin neither. The last time was when I signed up for the War.

γ

Dee woke up late in the morning, feeling grungy and hung-over from yet another night of sleepless crying till dawn. She stumbled to the door to go to the bathroom, but paused to pick up the little slip of blue paper lying on the floor.

Even now, his scrawl made her squint. "Anderson, was that your mother's maiden name? I wonder if that's something else you have in common with Jon?"

Rhetorical question for now, she realized as she tucked his note into a dresser drawer. She'd have to remember to ask him when he came back from the Dargers'.

CHAPTER THIRTY

January 30, Present
~ Six days later ~

Tom looked over at Callie. "I apologize for you havin' to do the drivin' on this trip."

She glanced at him, her eyes hidden by those odd-shaped smoked glasses that reminded him far too much of some kind of big bug, like a praying mantis.

"Hey, no apologies necessary," she said. "I understand. Besides, even someone who can drive a car or a pickup might not be able to drive this rig."

Her smile flashed bright, and impish dimples formed in her cheeks beneath those unnerving glasses. "So you can relax. You haven't lost any manhood points here."

Tom could feel his cheeks heat up, but her bold, open spirit always seemed to embolden him too.

"Glad to hear it," he drawled, giving her a sidelong glance. "For I ain't got many to spare these days."

"Huh. Doubt that. But you're earning a good handful by coming out with me on such short notice. You have no idea how glad I am you showed up. I've never had to buy horses at an auction before. I felt like I'll be buying a trailer full of pigs in a very big poke."

"So long as we get there in time to look 'em over good, I can promise you that we won't head back with any pigs in the trailer."

"I trust you on that," she said. "I'll never hear the end of it if I come back with some nag with a dozen horrible vices."

"Nah, you seem to be a good judge of character."

Callie shrugged and gave him an unreadable look through those tinted glasses. "Of men, yeah. Of equines, a little shakier there."

Tom wasn't quite sure what to say to that, so he settled for, "You'll do fine," and took a cautious sip of his bottle of water to keep his gut calm.

"You doing okay over there?" Callie asked, her tone a lot more sympathetic than Dee's or Chris' ever were.

He nodded. "I am. Surprises me really, but I'm glad of it." He gestured towards the windshield. "Somethin' about bein' higher up like this helps."

Tom wondered if it was because it was more like being on a train, though he'd never been on one that went near this fast. Nor was any train this comfortable; his experience with trains was limited to flat cars and crowded box cars fit more for hauling livestock than men.

"Good! I hate feeling queasy, it's the worst." She gave him another dimpled smile, and then turned back towards the road.

Tom chuffed. "It ain't the worst, but it sure ain't no fun."

A mile passed in comfortable silence, ticked off by those little numbered signposts along the edge of the wide, smooth road.

"Jon," Callie said, and pushed her glasses up on top of her head this time before she glanced over. "How are you doing, big-picture? You've seemed... more subdued... lately. Troubled, even."

Tom looked down at the water bottle he held, turning it in his hand, feeling the odd clear stuff it was made of flexing and springing back against his fingers.

Callie laid a hand on his thigh and his head jerked up to stare at her, startled. She drew it back like he'd gone red-hot.

"I don't mean to pry into your life," she blurted out, then slowed. "But I know that even before your accident, you and Dee had some real strains on your relationship. How's she handling all the changes? How are you dealing with it all?"

That soft tone of kind sympathy cut him deeper than cruel scorn. Tom swallowed hard against a sudden lump in his throat. He opened his mouth to brush her concern away with some vague assurance that he'd be fine, that Dee was fine.

"She's havin' a real hard time puttin' up with me," came out instead. He clamped his jaw tight, but it was too late. The words seemed to hang in the air between them.

"Oh Jon, no! Why do you think she feels that way?"

"Why wouldn't she?" he shrugged. "She misses the Jon she knowed. She blames me for takin' him away. She keeps me around only because she thinks I might be able to bring him back someday."

The water bottle crackled in his grip. "I thought at first maybe I could bring him back to her. too, but now— well, ever' day that passes, both of us is more afraid he's gone for good. It's him she grieves for, and I'm nothin' more to her than an unwelcome stranger who wears his face. I can't blame her for how she feels. I don't hold it against her."

Tom passed a hand over his mouth to still a sudden trembling. "I'm livin' with a stranger too, way too close to some other man's woman, and I got no right to be there."

"But Jon," Callie protested, her voice low. "You're still the same man. Yes, there are changes and even I can see that they're profound ones. But no matter what happens to you, you're still Jon Hansen."

"No, I ain't. I ain't him in no way." Tom looked down at his lap. His stomach roiled. He brought his head back up and stared straight ahead. He wasn't sure why he'd told her all that. Some weakness unlocked by an aching need for someone to understand, someone who didn't look at him with disdain because he wasn't someone else.

"Do you love her?"

Tom could hardly force the words past his clenched jaw. "God's truth? I mayn't be so sure of what I feel for her, but I'm damned certain the Jon she's pinin' for didn't love her like he should."

Callie sighed and dropped her glasses back over her eyes. "Look, I know I can't fully understand everything you're going through— but if you're both so unhappy now, you don't have to stay. Call it a brave try by all and move on. Both of you can get closure on this and make new lives."

"I can't," he said.

"Why?"

"There's the child to consider," Tom said. It was easier, somehow, to talk to her like this, both of them looking ahead, her eyes hidden by the darkened lenses. "A baby needs a father, and a baby won't care if I'm Jon or Joe or Rip Van Winkle, so long as I'm there to love him and take care of him and his Mama."

"Where was this archaic chauvinism hiding in you before?" she huffed. "Gah! Sometimes I think it must be embedded in the Y chromosome! Dee is well able to take care of herself, and that baby. Don't get me wrong, it's all kinds of honorable and appealing that you're not running away from your responsibilities, but because you have a child with someone doesn't mean you have to live with that person to be a good parent."

She gave an almost equine snort. "Trust me, I know. If my mother had stayed with my father, I'd be twenty kinds of deeply messed up because I'd have grown up watching them scream at each other, hating each other's guts. I was far better off bouncing between them, no matter how much I bitched about it at the time. He's a good dad, and she's a good mom, even though neither was around twenty-four-seven, and Paula really is my second mother. I consider myself especially blessed, truthfully."

Tom swallowed the last gulp of lukewarm water along with that revelation, and twisted the cap back onto the bottle with unnecessary force. "I'm glad it went good for you and I ain't sayin' it's wrong, but it ain't the way I was raised up to think."

"Well, word of advice from the trenches. Leave that kind of thinking back in Hooterville or Mayberry or whichever backward little town it came from, and step into modern reality, before that mindset buys you and two other people a world of hurt that'll last lifetimes."

Tom didn't know what to say to that, and she was content to let the silence be. Three more miles passed beneath them.

"So!" Callie said.

He startled, but she wasn't looking at him to see it.

"We need to be looking for at least one good roping prospect," she said. "You have any experience training roping horses?"

Tom relaxed, more grateful for the change of subject than he would ever confess.

February 8, Present Day
Tucson, Arizona
~ Nine days later ~

Dee settled into the desk chair and opened Chris's laptop. The conversation she'd had with the hospital's orthopedist had thrown her mind into overdrive. Her curiosity wouldn't let her completely disregard the possibility that Tom's painful disability could be corrected with a bone-lengthening procedure.

A scant half hour later, she closed the laptop and rubbed her eyes. "Why am I even sitting here? This is crazy. Jon's coming back in within thirty-three days, and even if we had enough time, we can't afford it."

She heaved herself to her feet and shoved the chair back under the desk. "I don't know why Tom's here, but obviously, it's not for corrective surgery."

The baby kicked and Dee patted her belly. "One good thing about pregnancy, Little Bit," she sighed. "I can talk to you instead of to myself!"

ℭ

Chis scowled at the web page that came up on the screen when he woke his laptop. "What the...?"

He looked through the recent browser history, feeling sicker by the click. "Hey, Dee, can you come here a minute?"

"Sure!" she called back cheerfully, and soon appeared in the study doorway. "What's up?"

Chris gestured her over to the desk, then turned the laptop so she could see the screen. "Surgery for that sorry asshole? Does this mean you've given up on Jon?"

"No! Of course I haven't! But I don't see how hoping Jon can get back means I can't also look at something that might help Tom."

"Why did you even bother?"

"What do you mean?" she frowned.

"Oh, I don't know. Maybe I'm the one out of line here for wondering why you're researching a twenty-thousand dollar operation for a guy who's gonna be *HUNG* in a month!"

"We don't know that's going to happen!"

Chris felt his face blanch. "You want it be Jon's neck in that noose?"

"I don't want it to be either of them!" she protested.

"On March thirteenth, Tom Dorin hangs. Indisputable fact. Recorded history. We can't change it. It's either going to be that stupid bastard out there playing cowboy, or my little brother. You tell me, Dee — what's your choice? Because it's sure sounding to me like it's Jon's neck you want to put in that noose."

Dee jerked back as if his words were blows. "I never really wanted him dead!" she burst out, and ran for the door. "It's not my fault! It's not!"

ଓଃ

The noise of Dee's weeping was heart-wrenching. It sounded pretty hysterical, too. That couldn't be good for her. She hadn't closed her door.

Chris groaned and scrubbed his hands over his face. He might not be able to stay married past the half-life of a banana, but all the attempts made him fluent in Fight. That open door and those noisy tears were a demand for solace that could not be ignored. His awkward hobble down the short hallway felt like the green mile.

She was curled up into a tight fetal ball around a bed pillow, and didn't appear to notice when he sat down on the bed behind her and rubbed her back. "Dee, I know this isn't your fault," he told her softly, past the huge painful lump in his own throat. "You didn't cause this. You couldn't, no matter how you feel about Jon."

All that did was provoke a harder bout of crying.

"The last thing I said to him," she managed, the words broken into halves and thirds by choking sobs, "Was drop dead!"

An instant mental image assaulted him: A wooden trapdoor falling away beneath dusty boots.

Chris was wracked by a shudder and when he managed to speak, it was through a throat pinched tight and dry with dread. "You didn't mean that. Nobody ever means that."

He lay down behind her and put an arm around her waist. She wiggled back to spoon tight against him, and her hands clenched onto his as if she were drowning. They were both shaking now.

"But it was the last thing." Her voice was so thin, so soft, he would have missed the pitiful words if his cheek wasn't against her hair.

"He knows you didn't mean it." Chris closed his eyes tight against the burn, but tears rolled out to slide into her hair anyway. "And it won't be the last thing. I won't let it be the last thing."

February 28, Present Day
Tucson, Arizona
~ Twenty days later ~

"Any preferences on dinner?" Dee asked from the open doorway of the study.

Chris looked up from his laptop with that double-blink that always reminded her of a groggy owl. "Yeah. Roast duck at The Arizona Inn."

Dee felt her eyebrows lift. Dinner there would buy groceries for a week. "Who is it you're trying to impress this time? Some movie mogul, or potential wife number...uh...six?"

"I suppose I deserve that dig— but tonight it's neither. I've made reservations for us."

"Us as in you and me?" Dee asked.

Chris nodded.

It was Dee's turn to blink. "Why on earth do you want to take me out there?"

"See, you asking that answers the question." Chris gave a flick of his hand. "I want to do something nice for you, okay? Something special. Life's crappy right now. I can't change that, but you're still brewing up your first baby and that's a Very Big Deal that's once in a lifetime. Come on, Dee, if you don't deserve some pampering now, when will you ever?"

He must have seen her hesitation on her face and spoke again before she could put together an answer.

"You do realize if you're about to pull out that tired old 'but I have nothing to wear' excuse, I'll drag you out the door right now to the nearest maternity dress shop," he said. "They have those, right?"

That charming Hansen smile was back, and it was impossible not to smile back.

"Yes, they do, and no I wasn't." Even though the thought had crossed her mind.

"So, why the reluctance?" Chris pressed, his expression softening along with his voice.

Dee felt her cheeks flush. "I don't know, Chris, it seems... too much. Why couldn't you take me out to Longhorn's or something?"

"We can do that," he agreed with no hint of annoyance at all. "I'll cancel the reservation at the Inn. Moderation isn't my first instinct, but the last thing I want is to put you on edge and make you uncomfortable."

His grin flashed again. "Kinda negates the whole pampering intent, after all."

Dee nodded and gave him a smile of her own. "So, what time were those reservations?"

"For eight. That's not too late for you, is it?"

"I think I can stay awake that long," she agreed.

"So, Longhorn at eight then?"

"It's a date," Dee agreed, finding herself actually looking forward to getting out of the house on a non-work or errand-related basis.

؃

He made her laugh. Chris found himself pulled along into it with her. Then neither of them seemed to be able to stop, even though what set them off wasn't that hilarious.

It was nothing more than mutual stress-relief, he knew that logically, but as they wound down he couldn't help but relish the light in her eyes and the flush in her cheeks.

Dee looked happy in that fleeting moment, and he hadn't seen that glow in her since their first meeting, seven months and a lifetime ago in Vegas. Not all his own warm glow was from the fireplace that crackled across the room. Was the same true for her? Before he thought it through, he reached across the table and took her hand.

She gave it a gentle squeeze then drew hers away. Chris wanted to kick his own shin under the table as he watched the amusement in her eyes evaporate.

"Thank you for taking me out tonight. I really needed this," she said.

"Don't mention it," he shrugged, decided to hell with it, and laid his hand over hers again.

"I don't mean anything by this," he gave her hand a squeeze again, "Except that I care about you and I'm glad to see you at least a little happy for a change."

Dee blushed. "I'm sorry. I know you don't, but I'm so wound up, I feel like I'm going to fly apart if I have to handle one more thing."

"That's understandable. I know I'm all over the emotional map on any given day. I can only imagine how much harder it must be for you. I'm missing my brother, but you're missing the father of your child, the love of your life."

She bowed her head for a long moment, and then spoke so softly he had to strain to hear her. "I was a fool to love your brother."

She lifted her head and what shone in her eyes now was teary anger. "I threw him out, Chris, remember? I can forgive the way he treated me there at the last, but what he said to me about our baby, the look on his face? I don't care if he meant it or not, I can't forgive that."

Chris snatched his hand away. "So you want him to hang," he snapped.

"No!" she burst out, drawing looks from the diners around them. "No," she repeated more softly, but no less intensely. "Of course I don't. Jon's an asshole, but he doesn't deserve to die. I want him back here safe as much as you do, but don't expect some happily ever after fairytale on his return."

"Why not?" Chris pressed. "Why can't there be a happy ending for you both? We don't know what Jon's going through back there. I understand my brother even better than you do. He can be a jerk, sure, but he's not some rotten to the core monster either. People change, Dee, and no matter what else this craziness means, it's gotta be the attitude adjustment he's needed all his life. When he comes back, promise me you'll give him another chance?"

Dee wiped her eyes with the corner of her napkin, and her face became a cool blank mask. "I hope you're right, Chris, but I can't make any promises. Jon's had chance after chance, and he blew through them all."

"So you're replacing him with that antique gimpy imitation, expecting to do better?"

Dee flung her napkin onto the table and stood. "I could do worse," she hissed. "I could choose you!"

She turned and stalked off towards the front of the restaurant. Chris threw some cash on the table and followed.

"You planning on walking home?" he asked when he caught up.

She didn't turn around. "I'll call a cab."

"Don't be such a diva. I brought you, I'll take you home."

He made her laugh again, but her scathing chuckle wasn't one he wanted to hear a second time. "So gallant. Fine. Let's go."

❧

As Chris started the car, he glanced over to Dee. She was rigid, staring out the side window.

"Relationships aren't ruined by one person," he said, "And I sure as hell can testify to that. Whatever went sideways with you and Jon? It's not all about Jon. You can be a real—"

"You actually want to go there?" Dee's voice was sharp and even.

No. No he didn't. What would be the point? Chris pulled out of the parking lot, suppressing the urge to squeal the tires. Don't goad the angry pregnant lady.

Chris stole another glance. Yes, she could be a bitch, but it took one to stand up to him, or to Jon. Maybe she had learned a lesson through all this too, because she seemed resolved to not let Jon or anyone else walk all over her ever again.

Chris wasn't sure if her hard-won self-assurance would doom a happy ending when Jon found his way back. He refused to consider how he felt about it either way. The only certainty was that his little brother was a blind jackass where Dee was concerned, but Jon deserved one last chance.

March 1, Present Day
~ The next day ~

"Jon!"

The gelding Tom was currying snorted and tossed its head, shying in the cross-ties. Tom had to side-step fast to keep his toes safe from the gelding's hooves.

"Sorry, sorry," Callie apologized in a lower voice as she came closer. "I should know better than to yell near the barn."

"Not me you owe an apology to," he commented, looking over the gelding's back at her. "But I suspect Badger'll forgive you if you talk sweet and give him a scratch under his jaws."

"Badger, huh? I thought his name was something like Barsfield Marcos. He's one of the one's we bought at the last auction, right?"

"He is, and he's gonna make your Ma a fine roper. But that name's a mouthful for royalty, much less a horse."

"I suppose so, and a rose is still a rose." She gave him a smile and the gelding a scratch along the backbone.

"And this rose still smells like a sweaty horse," Tom teased.

"Good thing I don't mind that smell, huh?" she retorted, and picked up a dandy brush to flick away the dirt and loose hair the curry comb lifted. "I was wondering if you had any plans for lunch?"

Tom shrugged. "I was gonna eat over by the spring, that's all."

"Care for some company?" she asked, pausing her brushing to look him in the eyes.

"I'd like that fine," he nodded. "Want to head off as soon as I get this fellow back in the stall?"

"Sure. I'll help," she smiled and moved around to his side of the horse, their shoulders almost touching as she followed his currycomb with her brush. Not the usual way of doing the task, but Tom wasn't of a mind to protest.

ଓ

"May I ask you an intrusive personal question?" Callie asked as she felt around in the bottom of her potato chip bag for crumbs.

Tom looked over at her, seeing mostly just the top of her curly auburn hair. "Since when have you held off long enough to ask permission first?"

Her head snapped up, eyes wide, and she studied him.

"You're teasing me," she concluded. "You are, right? Or do I owe you an apology for being an obnoxious jerk?"

"You don't owe me an apology for anything," Tom assured her. "You ain't never out-right rude."

"But sometimes overly curious?" She smiled.

Tom shrugged. "Truth is, it's good to know you care enough to ask."

"I do," she said softly. "Very much."

It was Tom's turn to look away. "So what do you want to know?"

"Two things," she answered. "First, I know you still have a sense of humor, so why don't you ever smile any more?

"Haven't had much to smile about in a long time," Tom answered. He tossed a pebble into the small pool they sat beside.

"No, I suppose not," Callie sighed, wrapping her arms around her shins. "I don't know whether I feel sorrier for you or Dee the most, but I do know I miss your smile."

"I'll start up again, eventually," he shrugged.

"When, Jon?" she persisted. "What are you waiting on? You're miserable, Dee's got to be miserable. Why not make a drastic change, a clean break with the past? It could hardly make your situation worse."

"Change is coming," he answered under his breath, staring at the constant ripples on the pool, stirred by unseen forces deep underneath. "March thirteenth, ever'thing's gonna change, for me, for her, for good."

"Is that when the baby's due?" Callie asked.

"Is that your second question?" He put a teasing lilt in his voice. Much as talking with Callie eased his mind, he wasn't about to try to explain why that date was the most momentous one in his and several other lives.

"Ah ha! Look at that! Your eyes crinkled at the corners!" she exulted. "Not a smile, but I'll take it."

She gave him a playful shove that rocked him on his haunches. "No, that's not my second question! I'm not going to waste it on that. I can talk to Dee and find that out on my own."

Tom didn't comment on that. She had every right to speak to Dee about anything she pleased, but the thought of it made him uneasy and he wasn't certain why. "What do you want to know, then? Sun's movin' on."

Callie blew an impatient chuff. "Okay, okay, Mr. Punctuality. My second question is, would you have dinner with me? Not here, on the ranch, but somewhere nice where we can talk as long as we like and get to know one another again? Kind of a date, you know, just between friends, like we used to?"

"I'll think on it," he answered and got to his feet. He offered his hand.

She took it and pulled herself up. "When? Come on Jon, I'm not the patient type, unlike you now, which gets to be really annoying sometimes I must say."

"March eighteenth," Tom answered and turned away towards their tethered horses.

"Why then? Why not tonight, or next week?" She put her foot in the stirrup, mounting as easily as any man.

"Uh-uh. You asked for two questions, you got two answers." He turned his mare towards the ranch buildings and kneed her into a fast lope.

"Gah, you're literal!" Callie laughed and flicked her gelding with the reins to catch up. "Race you back?"

"Go!" Tom called, and put heels to his mount's sides. It felt real good to be on a horse galloping full out, running fast from nothing at all, towards... nowhere much.

PART TWO

CHAPTER THIRTY-ONE

28 February, 1874
Cooper's Creek, AZT
~ Three days later ~

The stage rumbled to a stop in front of the hotel, the horses blowing and stomping, harness chains jangling and a portentous choking cloud of dust settling over the whole scene. The small knot of curious spectators gathered who greeted the stage every time it rolled into town.

Jon coughed into his sleeve, nerves making his gut a little uneasy.

The driver climbed down and opened the passenger door, folding down an iron step. A man emerged who had to be Carl. He was shorter than Jon by several inches, and even swathed in one of the baggy suits of the day, he looked slightly built. His drooping mustache was blond. His sunburned face was lined with weariness and travel dust.

After a second of hesitation to make sure that the woman emerging behind him was being properly assisted by the driver, Carl stepped away from the stagecoach and turned towards Jon. His wide smile instantly erased the aging effects of days spent jouncing along, shoulder to shoulder, with up to eight strangers in a rolling box smaller than most garbage bins.

Jon met him halfway, and shook the hand Carl offered.

"It's so good to see you again, Carl," Jon drawled. He hoped any flaws in his accent would be chalked up the erosion of time and travel. "It's been way too long."

"Too long indeed," Carl answered, still beaming, his eyes never leaving Jon's face. "I had almost given up hope of hearing from you again, my friend."

"Same for me," Jon nodded, limping beside Carl up the steps into the hotel. "It's took me a good while to light in one place long enough to pass letters back and forth again."

He gave Carl a pat on the back that raised a cloud of sandy grit. "I'm real grateful to you for comin' out all this way."

Carl paused then, a few feet from the front desk, and turned to take Jon into a hard, quick, one-armed hug with a clap on the back. "I would gladly have traveled a great deal farther to see you again, Tom."

Jon blinked and stole a quick glance towards the desk clerk and other passengers. None of them appeared to be paying them the slightest attention.

Stepping back a little as Carl released him, Jon looked down at the slighter man, his mind grabbing for traction as he tried to come up with a way to respond to that. "If I hadn't run out of travelin' cash and landed up here, you might have had to go clean on out to California."

Carl stepped up to the desk, taking his place in the short line beside his even dustier luggage. "I wouldn't have minded at all. If you were in California, I could take the train the whole way!" He laughed and gave Jon a wink.

"I'll keep that in mind for the next visit," Jon teased back. He gestured to Carl's bags. "Would you like for me to walk you to your room?"

Carl shook his head. "Thank you, but you needn't put yourself out. The bellboy will see to it. I'd like to clean up and rest a bit, but would you be free to have supper with me here and make a late night of catching each other up?"

"I'd like nothin' better," Jon smiled and meant it. Despite the strain of keeping up hick appearances, talking with Carol Lynd himself was a stroke of cosmic fortune he'd never have again. There was no way he wouldn't get his Masters' with this sort of data to work with.

"I'll see you at seven, then." Carl nodded and stepped away to sign in.

"I'll be here," Jon agreed and left the hotel lobby. Hattie had semi-graciously granted him the rest of the day off, so he'd spend the time till dinner re-reading those hospital letters between Tom and Carl. After he had a glass of coca wine. He'd backed off the stuff enough to sleep again, but he missed the sharp agility of mind attached to the insomnia price tag.

He needed to be on top of his game with Carl, and the man himself said they had a late night ahead of them. Jon whistled under his breath as he headed for the boarding house.

❧

"Don't you dare stick your fingers in that butter, Jon Hansen!" Ophelia swung at his hand with a big wooden spoon.

Jon jerked his fingers out of range of both butter and spoon. "I wouldn't have to if you didn't keep the silverware under lock and key."

"I keep it under lock and key so coarse mannered morons like you don't go wandering off with it to pick your teeth or scrape manure off your boots."

"Which is why I'm driven to sticking my fingers in the butter instead of using a proper knife," he countered with a grin.

"What do you want with a lump of butter anyway?" She dropped the spoon back into her mixing bowl and pinned him with a matronly frown, fists propped on her hips.

"To grease my boots." Jon lifted a shod foot in demonstration. "I know raising a shine on these is an impossible dream, but some oil or something would darken them up so they don't look so scuffed."

"You use lard for that, Future Man," she said, and reached for the can near her mixing bowl. After plopping a tablespoon or so out onto a saucer, she offered it to him.

"No, you use lard. We use proper shoe polish, but mostly we don't wear leather boots and when our shoes get dirty we throw them into the washing machine."

"From what I've seen of washing machines, they look to be more work than the wash-pot."

Jon smiled at her. It astounded him that of the three who knew his secret, Ophelia was the only one questioned him about things to come. Maybe it was because she knew her Harold was the one with the most to look forward to.

"Not those crank ones. Those are as obsolete as your wash-pot. Ours run by themselves on electricity. They do everything automatically except fold the clothes and put them away."

"Hmmph," she sniffed, turning back to her baking. "Machines like that go a long way to explain why you're so soft and lazy."

"That's an accusation that's still being thrown around about the whole western hemisphere more than a hundred years from now, so you may have a point." Jon saluted her with the saucer. "Thanks. I'll get out of your way and your saturated animal fats now."

"One more minute won't matter, since you're already here and pestering," she countered, looking over her shoulder at him. "Who's this man you're all fresh shaved and polished up to meet, if you don't know anybody in this century but us?"

"Carl Lynd," Jon answered. "An old war buddy of Dorin's. His best friend, as far as I can tell. I'm going to gather some insider information for my thesis."

Ophelia faced him with a lifted eyebrow. "You truly believe you can pull the wool over this man's eyes, a man who waded through blood and fire beside Tom Dorin every day for four years?"

"I think I've got a good chance at it." Jon opened a cupboard and grabbed a cleaning rag for his boots. "Ten years changes everybody. A head injury can transform a person's personality overnight. I'll make him buy my story, you'll see."

He glanced at the clock ticking on the opposite wall. "But I don't want to be late." He waved the rag at her like a hankie as he exited. "See ya!"

"I almost feel sorry for Tom Dorin," she commented to the cake batter, and loudly enough to carry to Jon as he headed down the hall. "If his life wasn't in a shambles around his feet before, it surely will be if he

314

comes back. Lord, lord— that man's going to have to flee the Territory and everyone who ever laid eyes on him."

"Oh ye of little faith!" Jon fired back from the front hallway then sprinted back up the stairs as fast as Dorin's lopsided boots would let him.

CЗ

The waitress cleared away their dinner plates.

"Excuse me a moment, Tom?" Carl asked.

"Sure," Jon nodded. "Take your time."

Carl rose, placing his napkin neatly by his plate. Jon watched as he crossed the dining room, heading for the back door. Carl's effusive, affectionate friendliness had cooled, one tiny increment at a time, as they talked over their meal.

Thinking back over the conversation, Jon couldn't pick out a single thing he said or did that was an obvious screw-up, nothing that could have tipped Carl off that his 'friend' was an impostor.

Maybe Carl had built up Dorin's memory to a level that made the real thing— or at least, the passable facsimile— disappointing?

Had he missed some signals Carl was sending out, like that startling display of public affection out in the lobby?

Maybe his act was convincing but Carl was discovering that their years apart had changed them past compatibility?

Jon took a sip of coffee and shook his head. Hell, for all he knew the two had some secret Confederate handshake. So long as Carl was willing to talk to him, he'd keep trying to weasel out bits of unrecorded information.

CЗ

Carl paused on the dim path between the pool of lantern light at the hotel's back door and the one glowing in front of the outhouse. He smoothed his mustache with nervous strokes then drew a handkerchief from his pocket and wrung his fingers in the fine cotton.

He hadn't been so naive as to expect Tom to remain unaltered after ten years. Considering Tom's state of mind at their last parting, Carl wouldn't have wished his friend to stay entrapped in that misery.

Changes he had expected, but to find the familiar face across the dinner table transformed into a total stranger was a blow he hadn't anticipated. Tom told him tonight about receiving a hard strike to his head not long ago.

Carl folded his handkerchief and tucked it back into his pocket. Perhaps Tom's mishap, tragic as it was, explained everything.

He turned and went to wash his hands at the bowl and pitcher set out by the hotel's rear door. As he dried his hands, Carl wondered why his friend's new mental aberration turned every subject of their conversation into something like an interrogation.

1 March, 1874
~ The next afternoon ~

"Mr. Dorin?" accompanied the sound of pounding bare feet from behind him.

Jon's shoulders hunched. The arrival of Bucky Buchanan at a full gallop hadn't boded well for him the last time. He turned from the garden row, using the hoe as his cane. "What're you here for today, Buck?"

Dorin's hick drawl came out naturally now, an unwelcome habit that grated on his ears, unrelenting as the ache in his lower back and the blisters from the man's lopsided boots.

"Got a message for you." Buck offered a folded sheet of paper.

"Thank you." Jon unfolded it, glanced down to see a few surprisingly legible lines from Kay. He smiled. Good news for a change.

He looked up again to see Buck still standing there, practically vibrating with impatience. "What're you waiting on?"

The boy's bare feet shuffled in the edge of the garden's looser soil. "Uh, she said you'd pay me a nickle for bringing it."

Figured. Nothing ever came for free from Kay. Jon stuffed the note into his pocket. "Two cents, for I didn't make that deal."

Disappointment showed on the boy's face, but he didn't protest. "Yes sir."

"Wait here." No need to have the boy trail him into the house and raise a bunch of questions from Hattie the Nag or Ophelia the Omniscient.

Jon limped to the back door and hesitated, leaning towards the open doorway to listen for a few seconds. Not hearing any activity beyond, he stepped inside and hurried through the house towards the stairs.

He made it to his room, retrieved a couple of oversized copper cents and headed back out with all the stealth of a lamed ninja on a raid. The kitchen was still empty. He was going to make it this time.

"Mr. Dorin!" Hattie's testy summons came from somewhere near the front parlor.

Shit. So close. Jon blew his brains out with a finger gun.

"In a minute!" he snapped over his shoulder and went through the back door without slowing down.

Bucky was still waiting, though he'd moved into the shade cast by the house.

"Think fast." Jon tossed the coins at him.

Bucky snatched them out of the air with a flick of the wrist almost too fast to follow.

"Thanks!" the boy grinned, then took off like a sprinter out of the blocks. Too bad all that natural talent would go to waste out here.

Jon didn't pause this time to admire the kid's effortless strides and speed. With much less grace than Bucky but almost as much hurry, Jon headed out the back gate in his wake. Kay hadn't allowed him much time to get down to the hotel and the meeting she'd arranged.

☃

Carl heard footsteps outside his room, the unmistakable halting tread of a lamed man using a cane. He opened his door and there was Tom, coming down the hallway.

Before Carl could call out a greeting, Tom stopped at a door closer to the stairwell and rapped once, paused, rapped twice, paused, then once again.

A clandestine request for entry. Carl drew back, closing his door enough to avoid detection. From his vantage point on the opposite side of the hall, he could see the man who answered Tom's knock.

Tall, portly and well-groomed, the occupant of that room was obviously at his ease, in snowy shirtsleeves and a bright paisley silk waistcoat that indicated an excess of money and a modicum of taste.

The man didn't speak as he stepped aside to let Tom enter; a dusty day-laborer in patched, faded trousers and a sweat-stained collarless chambray shirt. A man who obviously didn't have two dollars to rub together.

When the door closed behind Tom and Carl heard a key turn in the lock, he stepped out of his room and crept down the hall. He took great care to move silently across the uncarpeted floor.

Carl inclined his head towards the stranger's door, alert for anyone entering the hallway or coming up the stairs. As he listened to the the muffled voices on the other side, his eyes widened, then narrowed.

A heavy tread in the stairway sent him away from the door before he heard much more of their suspicious conversation. Carl retreated to his room. A conversation with the town's doctor was in order before he next encountered Dorin.

☘

The polished brass plate on the door read 'H. R. Hackler, Medical Doctor.' Carl turned the doorbell key.

A sonorous voice within called "Come in, please."

As Carl opened the door, the doctor rose from his desk and met him with an extended hand. "I'm Dr. Hackler. How may I help you, sir?"

Carl's own hand was engulfed like a child's in the taller man's grip, but the doctor's hold was gently firm, not challenging.

"I'm Carl Lynd, sir. Might I have a moment of your time? My concern is not for my own health, but for that of my friend."

"Tom Dorin?" Dr. Hackler said.

"Yes, sir." Carl wasn't surprised by the doctor's accurate supposition. Cooper's Creek was very small, and it was not an exaggeration to presume that half of the population had seen his arrival and the other half had heard of it by this point.

"Please, sit down. I'll answer what questions I may, but do understand that a doctor is much like a priest in regard to the confidences entrusted to me."

"I do, indeed. As an attorney at law, I am under similar ethical constraints." Carl sat in the chair in front of Hackler's desk as the doctor retook his own behind it.

Hackler nodded. "What are your concerns?"

Carl forced his hands to stay still by spreading them over the ends of his chair's arms, willing his grip to remain light. "I find his current state highly alarming."

"In what way?"

"Doctor, how well do you know Tom?"

Hackler's hands were loosely laced on the desktop, at ease to all appearances. "I consider him a friend."

"As do I," Carl said. "A very dear friend. That is why I am so unsettled by his actions and his demeanor now. Doctor, the man I see today is far different from the Tom Dorin I served beside, and even different from the man who wrote the letter I received recently, renewing our friendship after a silence of some years."

"What manner of aberrations do you observe?" Hackler leaned back, moved his hands to his own chair's arms. His grip was tight enough to slightly blanch his knuckles.

Carl had thought on little else since that disturbing dinner and spent the night after sleepless, herding his vague misgivings and solid suspicions into an orderly list in preparation for this moment. Even so, a lingering uneasiness set him to smoothing his mustache with a folded knuckle.

Hackler's eyes followed the motion for an instant before rising again to meet his own.

"The man I knew," Carl began, "Is lacking in formal education but is highly intelligent. Tom's nature is one of idealism, optimism and gentle humor, though last I saw him that happy natural state of mind had become one of disillusionment, somberness and melancholy due to the hardships and sorrows he endured."

The memories of Tom's first transformation overcame him for a moment. When Hackler nodded in the pause, Carl retrieved himself from the past and continued.

"After a particularly cruel tragedy, he became embittered, perhaps even vengeful for a time, but even then he was amenable to appeals to his better nature. Above all and despite all, Tom Dorin was a kind man, an honorable man, who carried himself with an innate dignity and inborn courtesy towards all that surpassed the facile posturings of formal society."

"You speak in the past tense. Do you no longer find him so?" Hackler straightened in his chair. His hands clasped once more on his desktop, their interlacing tightly closed.

Carl shook his head. "The man I see now is rude in conversation and in manner, prying, glib and flippant, sometimes to the point of irreverence. He cannot recall much of his past, and worse, rather than admit the defect, he confabulates while his mannerisms betray that he is knowingly attempting to deceive. Even his very physical carriage has changed from a natural noble posture despite his lameness to a careless slouch that has him sagging into every chair like a half-filled sack of grain. Worst of all, he appears self-absorbed, entirely uninterested in any subject of conversation that does not directly relate to himself."

Hackler lifted an eyebrow and leaned back once more. "Are you aware that Tom received a severe blow to the head recently?"

"He told me of it on the evening of my arrival, yes."

"It is not unknown for victims of such an injury to survive with little to no physical ill effects, while suffering more or less profound mental aberrations afterward. Perhaps you're aware of the somewhat infamous 'Crow-bar Case' involving a railway worker in the late 'forties?"

Carl shuddered. A cousin had seen the poor fellow's remains on exhibition in the Warren Museum a few years back. His vivid mental image of that injury, as Roderick described the impaled skull, had turned his stomach.

"I have heard some little about it in passing, yes."

"One of the victim's friends stated that 'Gage is no longer Gage,'" the doctor continued. "A distressing loss of decorum and an increase in impulsive actions and inappropriate outbursts were noted by those who had known the man before his accident."

The doctor's interlaced hands drew back to rest on his midriff. His mobile face went still. "The alterations you describe in Dorin can be attributed to similar effects from his own cerebral insult."

"If I am not mistaken, Doctor, Gage's personality became... infantilized, in some ways. He lost many of his social inhibitions and tended to act impetuously, driven by the baser animal impulses."

Hackler sighed. "Yes, that is true in Dorin's case as well."

"But did Gage become larcenous?"

That made the doctor draw back against his chair.

"I am not aware of such an alteration in Gage's moral character, nor in Tom's." Hackler leaned forward once more, his hands going to the arms of his chair with a clawed grasp. "What have you observed?"

"Something... quite disturbing, but somewhat ambiguous," Carl said. "I am not at liberty to say more until I discuss my suspicions with Tom."

"I understand," Hackler answered with a rather curt nod. "I do urge you to come to me with any ongoing concerns you may have, when you feel free to confide them to me."

"I will do so, you may be sure." Carl rose and the doctor did as well. "I won't impose upon your time further today, however."

The doctor shook his hand again, his grip tighter this time. "It is no imposition, Mr. Lynd. Allow me to see you to the door."

Hackler stepped out onto the landing with him, and Carl could feel the man's gaze pressing hard against his back all the way down the stairs.

He wondered if the doctor also saw what he did, up the street. Tom Dorin, who he knew not to drink due to pure dislike of the taste of alcohol and its effects, stepping up to the doorway of the saloon. Tom Dorin, who had kept himself chaste after receiving a horrifying, grisly warning of the wages of sensual sin, greeting a bar-wench in that same doorway with a laugh and a slap to her satin-clad rump.

Carl strolled across the street in that same direction. He wasn't certain about the cause of Tom's abrupt degradation into this distasteful stranger who usurped his friend's face and name, but Carl was certain of one fact gained today; Hackler was withholding information, if not outright lying.

When he heard the doctor's door close behind him, Carl turned and went back up the sidewalk, towards the boarding house.

CB

A little Negro boy on the boarding house porch appeared to be fighting off a gang of swordsmen with his broom, any sweeping being merely incidental to the desperate fray.

Carl paused on the walk and watched him for a moment. The boy was so absorbed in his fantasy, Carl could almost see the pitched battle himself. He found himself almost reluctant to interrupt.

"Ho there, brave D'Artagnan," Carl called. "Dare thee suffer those ruffians to escape for the nonce?"

The boy almost dropped his sword but on finding it only a broom in his grasp once more, leaned it against the side of the house.

"They can't escape from me forever," the child called to him with ferocious scowl of righteous wrath. "I'll have my revenge!"

That savage scowl vanished as Carl stepped up onto the porch beside him.

"Are you wanting a room, Mister?"

"No, thank you," Carl said. "I'm here to visit a friend of mine, Tom Dorin."

"Oh!" The boy's smile widened. "You must be Mr. Lynd! I'm Harold Lefler, pleased to meet you."

"Likewise, Mr. Lefler. How do you know of me?"

"Mr. Dorin told me about you. He was real excited that you was coming all the way out here from Tennessee." The boy frowned then. "But he isn't here right now."

"Oh, that's a shame. Do you know when he's expected back?"

"Any minute now." The boy's bare feet scuffed on the porch floor. "He's um… he's sorta late today. He doesn't eat his dinner here anymore."

"I see. Well, may I be allowed to wait here for him?"

"Sure, that's fine. Come on in the parlor." Harold opened the door for him and stepped aside like a miniature butler.

Carl glanced toward the comfortable parlor occupied by a couple of residents, then squatted down to put himself at the boy's eye level. "May I ask you a favor?"

"Maybe," the boy answered. "What is it?"

"Promise you won't laugh?"

Harold nodded.

Carl dropped his voice to a conspiratorial murmur. "At the risk of sounding like a wilting milksop, I'm afraid I am not used to this sun and heat. I find myself exhausted and with a nasty headache."

"Oh! I'm sorry. You want a cool towel for your forehead? That always helps Miz Hattie."

"No, thank you, but I know if I can lie down somewhere quiet, it will ease." Carl filled his glance back towards the parlor with blatant pathos. "I hate to ask anything of you on such short acquaintance, Harold, but I cannot bear the thought of having to hold polite conversation with everyone in the parlor while my head is pounding so. May I lie down in Mr. Dorin's room instead?"

The little boy's face drew up. "I'll have to ask Miz Hattie first."

"Of course, of course. Would you do that for me please? I'll wait here."

Harold nodded and hurried towards the rear of the boarding house. Carl took in his surroundings. The place as clean and pleasant, its décor reflecting the haphazard acquisition of comforts here in the Territory more than the mannered formality back east.

Within moments, Harold returned. "She said she supposes it'll be all right for you to go up, since you and Mr. Dorin are friends and all."

"We're very dear friends indeed," Carl assured him. "For more years than you've been alive."

Harold exhaled an impressed breath. "That is a long time. Mr. Dorin's my friend too, for ever since he came here."

"Even after he hit his head?"

Harold's concerned little frown turned into a moue of sadness. "Yes, even after that."

He reached out for Carl's hand. "Come on, Mr. Lynd. I'll take you up to his room so you can rest. It's on the east side of the house, so it's nice and shady in there now."

"Thank you," Carl answered, and gave that warm, trusting little hand a squeeze. "That sounds very restful and restorative."

Cઇ

"You want me to come wake you when Mr. Dorin comes back?" Harold asked after opening the door of one of the upstairs rooms.

"No, that won't be necessary. Just send him up. I'm a light sleeper, so I'll wake as he comes in."

"All right, you feel better real soon, Mr. Lynd," Harold answered and went back towards the stairs.

"I will," Carl promised, and closed the door. When he heard little bare feet galloping down those stairs, he turned to inspect Dorin's quarters.

They were reasonably tidy, but spare. Other than the clothes hanging on hooks and a dusty saddle lying in a careless heap in one corner, there was no sign of an occupant at all.

Carl was sorely tempted by the drawer in the washstand and the smaller one in the lamp table, but he resisted his unseemly curiosity. The small trunk at the foot of Tom's bed inflicted no added enticement, for it appeared to be locked.

He went over to the washstand, poured a little water into the bowl and rinsed his face and hands. A reflection with troubled eyes met his gaze in the mirror.

Carl sighed, dried himself with his handkerchief then sat down in the room's chair. His line of sight fell on the room's only adornment, a print by Currier and Ives.

He could see why Tom had chosen it. The prosperous farm in the image bore a passing resemblance to Dorin's own home place. But, it hung crooked on its nail.

Carl managed to ignore that imbalance for almost five minutes. He huffed a sigh then, got up and straightened the thing, ashamed anew of the foolish relief the pointless action supplied.

As he turned away, the picture crashed to the floor. Carl flinched and turned back. The picture lay face down on the floor, glass shards spread out around it, the frame broken apart at the corners. The frayed twine that served for picture wire had given up after that one last slide against its rusty supporting nail.

"Aw, blast it all!" He picked up the ruined mess, hoping the print at least had survived the fall. There was more in the frame than the print. Between the print and the backing board, several sheets had been tucked away out of sight.

Carl sat down in the chair and began to read the closely packed handwriting that marched across them in an educated but unusual script.

There were several rows of Dorin's signatures, for forgery practice, apparently, as the last was a close imitation of Tom's scrawl. Other sheets held monetary figures, including estimations on the liquid assets of Mrs. Perkins, Doctor Hackler and others, columns of prestigious and unknown names and companies, and most damning of all, rough plans for a scheme that appeared to involve salting a desolate location with industrial diamonds to woo the greed of potential investors.

Carl flung the sheets onto the bed and went to the trunk. He put his side to it and kicked backwards, striking the hasp of the lock a sharp blow on its edge with the heel of his boot.

The hasp popped free of the flimsy lock. Carl knelt and opened the lid. Spare undergarments and socks were on top, along with a couple of bottles of coca wine. Two bundles of letters lay underneath, one of them the letters he'd written to Tom during his friend's convalescence and afterwards, the other containing those cherished messages from Tom's beloved Beth. Carl laid the clothes aside on the floor, the letters carefully balanced on top.

He lifted out Tom's Colt, hidden beneath it all, and drew the weapon out of the holster, careful not to touch the trigger. He remembered how Tom filed down the action on his rifle until not much more than a harsh look was enough to fire its load.

Carl had no desire to find out if his friend had modified this pistol in the same manner, by accidentally punching a .44 caliber hole through the side of Mrs. Perkin's house.

The condition of the weapon drew a frown. Corrosion spotted the bluing of the barrel, and the grease over each round looked and smelled rancid. Even more inexplicable was that sixth capped round, under the hammer. Even in the War, Tom never carried his sidearm on a live chamber.

Carl laid the weapon aside on the bed, well away from an accidental jostle. He turned back to the trunk. Now that it was emptied, a new strangeness was revealed. He leaned back to check his hunch against the outside of the trunk.

One push on the corner of the thin sheet of wood was enough to get his fingertips in far enough to lift out the false bottom. What was underneath seemed mundane at first glance. Only clothing.

When he drew it out, he realized that it was clothing such as he'd never seen before. A shirt made of oddly patterned fabric, with small round pairs of metal devices up the front edges in lieu of buttons and buttonholes. Blue dungarees of an outlandish cut with inexplicable metal pieces in the fly. Soft fabric shoes with flexible soles, striped with bright color, bearing the word "Nike" on the top of their tongues.

What the Greek winged goddess of victory had to do with shoes was as much an enigma as the shoes themselves. When he tipped one up to examine it, a folding pocket knife and something entirely unrecognizable fell out. He shook the other one and got a recognizable wallet and what he could only assume were keys.

Carl laid the shoes aside with the rest of Dorin's belongings and opened the wallet. Inside was a brightly colored miniature portrait of a smiling woman, a brightly colored photograph, he assumed, for no artist could capture a likeness so true and vibrant with mere paint and brush.

There were small bills in various denominations, currency that claimed to be American but was like none he had encountered. Several calling cards were imprinted with words whose language was English but whose sense was largely nonsense.

The most astonishing of all was a stiff card behind a clear window. Over a remarkable image of blue desert sky and arid red hills was another vivid image, of Tom, smiling, his hair cut short and strangely.

But it was the text that stunned him most. 'Arizona Driver License' 'Jonathan M. Hansen' and an unfamiliar form of street address for somewhere in Tucson.

The rest, well, he had to silently mouth the rest to force his mind to accept the numbers. 'Expires: 3-15-2050.' 'Issued: 3-15-2005,' 'Date of Birth: 7/31/1985.'

Carl tossed the damning, baffling card onto the odd clothes then reached out for the last object. Smooth and rounded, made of nothing he could name, it was shaped like a clamshell or pillbox, with what appeared to be a hinge at one end.

He opened it. Square, ugly letters marched across a square of illuminated glass, spelling out 'No Service' with a firefly glow. Then the device gave three shrill peeps and the message changed to one that held steady for a few seconds before vanishing, leaving the glass dark and black. 'Low battery.'

He closed it with a snap, tossed it onto the uncanny pile, then scrubbed his hands against his thighs. He reached out for the bundles of letters, somehow comforted a little by the familiar sensation of old, worn paper against his palms. He tucked them inside his coat pockets.

The door opened behind him.

Ꮆ

Jon opened the door. Everything inside him sucked away into a cold, sickening vacuum.

He strode towards Carl, standing there by his bed. By his stuff. All his stuff.

"What the fuck are you doing in here?"

"Learning the truth," Carl answered. His voice was as fierce as his face. "What did you do to Tom?"

"Nothing! Get out of my room!" Jon sidestepped around Carl towards the pile of clothes. His real clothes. His wallet. His cell phone. Oh god, his cell— the battery. The incriminating papers from the picture frame.

"You stupid sawed-off cock-sucker! You've ruined everything!" He spun, his fist lashing out towards Carl's face.

Almost before he saw the man move, Carl knocked aside that swing, Jon's fist only grazing the side of his head.

In the same instant, Carl closed in and grabbed him by the collar, twisted tight enough to choke, shaking him hard. "WHAT HAVE YOU DONE TO TOM DORIN?"

Jon jerked at Carl's wrists, tried to break free from that strangling hold but only managed to turn them both in a tight circle. *Fuckin' little queer is gonna kill me—*

Jon's lungs burned, everything in him screamed but no sound leaked out past the chambray garrote tightening around his throat.

Carl shoved him backwards. The backs of Jon's knees hit the edge of the bed and buckled.

Carl shoved harder. Jon's spine bowed backwards. New agony flared through his body.

Gray fog ate away the edges of his vision.

Jon's hands dropped from Carl's wrists, blindly slapped against the quilt.

An instinctive reflex, a last grasp for air.

For life.

One palm struck smooth curved wood, cool steel.

Jon swung the Colt up, into Carl's face.

The man flinched back, his retreat faster than the release of his stranglehold, pulling Jon upright with him as Carl tried to put himself out of the line of the muzzle.

Wheezing, Jon swayed on his feet but didn't fall. He shook all over as he cocked the pistol. "Keep your damned mouth shut and get out of town before I kill you."

"Like you killed Tom?"

A scream rang out from the doorway. Carl spun away from him. Jon jerked all over, startled.

The Colt spewed a cloud of flame and smoke and deafening noise.

It was as if time stopped, life freeze-framed. A pall of blue-white smoke hung between him and the door, but it wasn't thick enough.

It didn't keep him from seeing Hattie in the doorway, her face white and twisted in terror.

It didn't hide the pulsing, weakening spurts of bright red blood that spread across the lavender of her dress.

He clearly saw Ophelia and Harold staring, stunned and blanched, at Hattie as she crumpled to the floor.

Then everything happened at once.

Carl twisting the Colt from his hand. Ophelia wailing, dropping to her knees to gather Hattie into her arms. The other boarders shouting, running down the hallway and up the stairs.

Harold looking up at him, too hurt for tears. "Why'd you do it? Why'd you do it, Mr. Dorin?"

"I didn't mean t—!"

Carl's fist slammed into Jon's temple, silenced his remorse.

~ *Later that evening* ~

Carl sat down on his hotel bed. He drew his bag over, opened it, and tucked Tom's treasured letters in beside a thickly wrapped bundle.

He lifted it out, unwound the protective swaddling. He cupped his hand over the curved lid of the small ebony jewel casket within as if it were a beloved friend's shoulder.

Carl closed his eyes. "I am certain you are with her again, my friend," he whispered. "Rest easy. I swear to you, I will not allow this impostor who sullied your honor and stole your life to take from you anything more."

He lifted his head, rose and went to the washstand. The lip of the pitcher chattered against the edge of the bowl, splashing droplets across the marble top of the stand.

Carl set the pitcher aside. Wrung his hands in the lukewarm water, already gone gritty with the ruddy dust that tainted everything in this town. He dropped his head to avoid the mirror.

Carl's wet hands slid on the cool marble as he planted them on either side of the washbowl, suddenly bent double by a harsh, broken howl bursting out of his mouth, straining his throat, scalding as vomited poison.

ଓ

She wasn't sure what time it was. Stopping all the clocks was the first thing she did after Hattie was carried away by the undertaker.

Ophelia glanced out the window at the stars. It was late, that's all that mattered. Well after midnight, well before dawn. She went out to the summer kitchen, careful to close the back door silently behind her.

She opened the firebox on the stove. There were still glowing coals, she'd been careful to ensure that would be so. Ophelia took the poker and prodded the coals, blowing on them to coax them to hotter life.

Little by little she fed them tinder, then kindling, then pitch-wood until the fire burned so fiercely that the stove lids rattled and the heat from the open firebox shrank the skin of her face against her bones.

Kneeling on the floor in that scorching glow, she unwrapped the bundle she carried. One by one, everything went in.

His shirt. His trousers.

His shoes, one after the other.

The worthless money from his wallet.

The calling cards, the license for driving, the bright image of the smiling woman, the leather case itself.

The strange keys, the pocket knife.

Last of all she cast in the thing he called a cell phone.

Some of it burned, some of it shriveled. All of it blackened and gave off an acrid stench that had her covering her nose with her apron.

She didn't close the door on the firebox until all of it was unrecognizable.

Ophelia went back into the house then, to her room to wash off the horrid stench of Jon's proof and change her clothes before she began the preparations for Hattie's wake.

10 March, 1874

The only place in town big enough to hold the expected crowd was the Belknap and Horner Freight Company's yard. The partners agreed to suspend business for one day to allow their warehouse to be pressed into service as a makeshift courtroom on the arrival of the circuit judge.

That august personage sat behind Belknap's ink-stained and match-scorched desk, the whole lot given judicial gravitas by the height of a packing box platform.

Carl studied the judge surreptitiously, attempting to divine the man's general demeanor before the trial began.

Judge Clarence Schaefer was a stocky man, his head glossy and hairless as a china doorknob, that hirsute oversight compensated by a flourishing ginger mustache. Already, the judge perspired heavily in the morning heat, darker swatches marring the underarms of his suit coat. The dominant impression Carl received was jaded weariness compounded by the understandable desire was to be somewhere cooler and quieter than this warehouse.

A chair was placed beside the judge's perch, its lonely and vulnerable position marking it as the witness stand.

The jury of twelve sat to one side of that, the second six chairs elevated on lumber risers. The jurors scratched and fidgeted, murmuring among themselves and periodically firing tobacco juice into strategically placed spittoons.

Horner's longer desk served as the counsel table for the prosecution, which would be the town's sheriff, and the defense. As the town proper boasted no lawyer and Carl was of no mind to come to Hansen's legal aid, the man would be representing himself.

A few rows of motley chairs behind the legal bench held favored spectators and the witnesses, himself among them, along with the town's newspaper owner, with his pencils and notebook at the ready.

Carl forced himself to maintain a posture of respectful ease, willed his hands to lie still against his thighs. The effort cost him dear already, he felt as if his nerves were watch-springs all wound to the snapping point.

Mrs. Lefler sat beside him, straight-backed, head held high. Her gloved hands lay still against the lap of her austerely elegant black dress. She was without the shelter of a mourning veil, though her eyes were swollen and red. She looked neither to the right or left.

Harold perched on the chair beside hers, his little polished boot-toes scarcely touching the floor. He chewed his bottom lip and looked around the room, furtive as a young rabbit caught in the open. His eyes were dulled, his face set in a saddened cast just the dry side of tears.

Carl feared the child would never again feel the joyful innocence he possessed on the day they met, swinging a broom handle sword, those few short moments before his trust shattered forever. Harold sniffled and Mrs. Lefler reached out, without turning her head, and enfolded his hand in her own.

Carl had to look away to maintain his own composure. He turned his attention to the crowd thronging every open space in the building and those outside it. The whole of the populations of the town and the mining camp appeared to be either inside the warehouse or encircling it, turning the atmosphere within stifling despite the building's open windows and wide loading doors.

The constant rustle and roar of impatient humanity swelled to a dangerous pitch. The accused had arrived.

Freshly appointed deputies shouted and shoved, flanking Sheriff Doyle and Jonathan Hansen, protecting the man from those more interested in swift punishment than due process.

Hansen stared straight ahead, his eyes aimed at the judge but likely seeing nothing. Doyle's hold on his manacled arm seemed more support than restraint. As they passed through the spectators, men spat and hissed, women gasped and drew their skirts away.

The trial hadn't begun, but it was clear Hansen was already convicted by his peers. In this case, at least, public ire and unquestionable guilt were in double harness. Carl smoothed his mustache and straightened his lapels.

When the pair reached the bench, Sheriff Doyle herded Hansen to his chair and pushed down on the man's shoulder. Hansen folded onto the seat as if he were a jointed doll.

The judge banged his gavel until a reasonable approximation of quiet fell over the court. "The United States Territorial Circuit Court is now in session in the matter of the People versus Thomas Dorin. How does the defendant plead?"

Doyle jabbed Hansen in the ribs, and the man lurched to his feet.

"Not guilty, your honor, and my name is not Thomas Dorin! I'm Jonathan Hansen! You've got the wrong man! This is his trial, not mine. I'm from the future— I can prove it. I can prove it!"

The sheriff yanked Hansen back into his chair so hard that Hansen's head bounced. The judge banged his gavel until the crowd's outburst ceased as well.

"The normal procedure is for each side to give opening statements, but in light of the defendant's display, I feel it necessary to first ascertain that this man is sane and fit to stand trial," the judge said. "Sheriff Doyle, can you provide such assurance?"

"Yes sir, I can. We figured Dorin would go off on this again. He's hardly shut up about it since I put the cuffs on him, down at the boarding house."

The judge cleared his throat and the Sheriff nodded. When Doyle spoke again, his voice was far more formal.

"If it please the court, I call Doctor Hackler as witness to Dorin's fitness to stand trial."

"The court so grants. Doctor, please take the stand," the judge answered. As Hackler came forward, the judge addressed Doyle once more. "You may be seated, sir, until I make this decision."

"Your Honor, I know this sounds insane but you have to believe me!" Hansen burst out, coming to his feet again. "I can prove it. It's all in my room! Send someone to get it out of the trunk at the foot of my bed. There's a false bottom, it's all there. It'll prove I'm not crazy, I swear to god!"

"Sheriff, please remove the prisoner," the judge responded, then pounded his gavel as Hansen was hauled back out and through the threatening crowd. Hansen struggled this time, keeping up his claims of innocence and temporal misplacement.

"I will have order in this court!" The judge shouted over Hansen's hysteria and the crowd's catcalls and aspersions.

Once some measure of silence was restored, the judge turned to Doctor Hackler, who sat in the witness chair as if he were in his own parlor.

"Doctor Hackler, have you examined the defendant?"

"I have, on occasions some months past and on the evening of the tragic incident before the court, after the defendant was incarcerated."

"In your learned opinion, is the defendant Thomas Dorin sane or insane?"

"Sanity is a difficult determination to make," Hackler answered. "The defendant makes wild and extravagant claims which any reasonable person would deem fantasies at best, insane ravings at worst."

He steepled his fingers and fixed the judge with his gaze as if they were the only two in the room. "But a belief that one is a castaway from another century, or even the rather common delusion of being another person, does not necessarily legally preclude this man from being deemed fit to stand trial. I am no lawyer, but my understanding is that the legal definition of inculpable insanity excuses only those persons incapable of judging right from wrong, or those who have no more control over their actions than a wild animal."

"Those are the accepted standards," the judge agreed with a nod. "By those standards, is Mr. Dorin insane?"

"By those standards, your Honor," the doctor answered, his voice as grave and solemn as his expression, "Mr. Dorin, also known as Jonathan Hansen, is as sane as you or I. He understands the rules of morality and he acts with forethought and awareness of consequence."

Carl noted that the doctor shifted then in the witness chair, changing his posture to slightly turn his shoulder to the jury. The first sign of indecision he had displayed.

"As for the defendant's claim that he is not Thomas Dorin, but is indeed Jonathan Hansen," Dr. Hackler said, "I cannot confirm nor deny that claim under oath, due to the sworn vow of confidentiality between a physician and his patient."

"So noted and recorded by this court," the judge proclaimed, then turned to the jury. "Gentlemen of the jury, the true identity of the defendant is irrelevant to the crime of which the defendant is accused. Please make your determination of guilt or innocence solely upon the testimony given pertaining to the death of Mrs. Harriet Perkins."

The judge then gestured towards one of the deputies acting as bailiffs. "Tell Doyle to bring the prisoner back in, and stand guard. Keep the defendant quiet and in his seat."

☙

Ophelia gave her testimony first, the anguish in her eyes and the slight quaver in her voice more moving than gallons of tears.

The judge was admirably gentle with Harold, patient as he drew out the boy's testimony, soothing Harold's nerves but never steering the child's words.

Carl took the stand next. Hansen lifted his head, and there was never a moment in the War when Carl met that much hatred and venom seething in another man's stare.

He returned both to Hansen in full measure.

"Please tell the jury what happened on the night of March first, Mr. Lynd," Sheriff Doyle asked.

"I was concerned about the behavior of my friend, whom I hadn't seen in several years." Carl began. "I went to call upon him at the boarding house and was allowed to wait for him in his room. I straightened a picture on the wall, and in so doing, it fell. The frame broke and I discovered within it documents detailing plans to steal from Mrs. Perkins and others, as well as detailed plans describing a scheme to commit fraud on a grand scale."

"Shocked beyond propriety, I then searched his belongings. In lifting items out of his trunk, I came upon his revolver and laid it aside on the bed. Mr. Dorin returned to the room and assaulted me. We struggled together until Dorin got his hand on his pistol, cocked it and aimed it at my head, declaring he would kill me if I spoke of his plans. That is when Mrs. Perkins screamed from the doorway. Mr. Dorin turned towards her and the gun went off, the ball striking Mrs. Perkins in the chest, causing her death almost instantly."

The effort cost him dearly, but his honor forced Carl to add, "I do not know if Dorin fired intentionally."

"You hear that, Judge? You hear that? It was an accident. I didn't mean to shoot her. I'm innocent!" Hansen burst out before the deputy grabbed the back of his neck and shook him hard.

The noise rose to a level just short of deafening. The judge banged his gavel until the spectators quieted their exclamations.

"Are you confessing before this court that you did indeed shoot to death Mrs. Harriet Perkins?" the judge asked Hansen.

Hansen lifted his manacled hands to wipe them over his sweating face. "Yes, I did shoot her and dear God, I can't even express how sorry I am that she died but it was an accident. I swear I didn't mean to hurt her. All I wanted was for Carl to back off and get out of my room. He was trespassing, going through my private property. He's the only one who broke the law that day. Nothing on those papers means anything, it's not a criminal offense to write something down, no matter what it is. I haven't acted on any of it. I haven't done anything wrong."

"Did you strike Mr. Lynd first?"

"I admit that, yes. I took a swing at him but I didn't grab the gun until he was choking me. I was about to pass out, I had to defend myself or he would have killed me!"

The judge turned to Carl once more. "Did you have permission to be in the room rented to Mr. Dorin?"

"Yes, I did."

"Was that permission granted by Mrs. Perkins or Mrs. Lefler?"

"I don't know, your Honor. Mrs. Ophelia's son Harold let me into the house, then left my presence to request permission for me to stay. He guided me upstairs afterwards."

"Miz Hattie told me Mr. Lynd could stay up there, sir, 'cause he had a headache. Mama was there, she can tell you that's so," Harold piped up.

"Thank you, Harold. That will be all," Judge Schaefer answered, and not unkindly. "Mrs. Lefler, did you witness Mrs. Perkins giving permission for Mr. Lynd to be in the defendant's room?"

"Yes sir. I was standing right by her side when she said it," she answered.

The judge turned his attention back to Carl. "Did you search through his personal possessions?"

Carl's hands tightened on the chair's arms despite his will otherwise. "Yes, but only after finding the suspicious documents that Sheriff Doyle now has in his possession. I considered I had due cause at that point, considering the implicit threat to Mrs. Perkins' property described in those documents."

"Did Mr. Dorin strike the first blow?"

Carl reached up to touch the blue bruising on his cheekbone. "Yes."

The judge made a noncommittal throaty noise and nodded. He fixed his attention on Hansen once more. "Do you have anything further to say in your own defense, Mr. Dorin?"

"What defense? I don't need a defense. It was an accident. She startled me when she screamed, I flinched and the gun went off. It's horrible that she died but it's not my fault. And I'm not Dorin, I'm Hansen. This is supposed to be his trial, not mine!"

He turned around in his chair towards the other witnesses, "You know it's true, both of you!"

Turning back to the judge, Hansen leaned forward, eyes glittering, his face scarlet red. "They know I'm telling the truth, Carl does too but they're all lying! Hackler perjured himself under oath— he knows who I am. Hattie did too. They hate me now because she's dead but it's not my fault. I'm Jonathan Hansen, not Tom Dorin and I'm not guilty of anything!"

"Enough!" Judge Schaefer punctuated his annoyance with a resounding slam of his gavel that likely left a permanent dent in Belknap's desk top.

"Mr. Dorin, as I stated to the jury in your absence, your true identity is irrelevant to the matter on trial. By your own words, before this jury, you have confessed to committing physical assault with intent to do bodily harm. You committed this assault upon a person who had lawful permission to be in a rented room you occupied. While in the commission of that assault you caused the death of Mrs. Harriet Perkins. If a death occurs during the commission of a crime, the perpetrator of that crime is deemed guilty of murder in the first degree, regardless of the lack of murderous intent and malice aforethought."

Hansen seemed to sink, to draw back into himself, his face going bone-white in an instant. "That's not fair," he said, almost in a whisper. "It was an accident."

The judge ignored that protest, turning to the rather stunned appearing jury. "The defendant has confessed his guilt in open court. Gentlemen of the jury, you are dismissed from your duty. Please keep your seats."

Carl drew out his handkerchief and wiped his face, almost sickened by profound relief. This rough-hewn, frontier courtroom lacked decorum and many of the traditional formalities, yet justice was served here today for poor Mrs. Perkins, and to some degree, for Tom.

"Mr. Dorin, or whoever you think you are, please rise and face the bench," the judge commanded.

This time, Hansen had to be bodily lifted to his feet and it was clear that only Doyle's strength kept the man's knees from buckling.

"By the power invested in my by the United States Territorial Court, I hereby sentence you to hang by the neck until you are dead, such sentence to be carried out before noon on the thirteenth of March, in the year of our Lord eighteen-seventy-four. May God have mercy on your soul."

"Why do we gotta waste good wood on a gallows when there's a fine hangin' tree up the street?" someone yelled from the back of the room.

The judge slammed his gavel down. "Then build a trapdoor platform to ensure a humane execution and hang him from that tree. So long as you don't lynch this sorry soul before the thirteenth, I have no objection to the method used to suspend the rope. Sheriff Doyle, please remove the prisoner and hold him in custody until the appointed time of his execution."

"But this isn't right!" Hansen struggled, writhing against Doyle's grasp as deputies closed in. "It was an accident! I can't hang for this! I'm not Dorin! I'm not Dorin!"

"Dorin or Hansen or the man in the moon, you confessed to murder and you're guilty as sin," the Sheriff boomed as Hansen was lifted off his feet.

Carl thought he caught, from the corner of his eye, Judge Schaefer nodding subtle agreement to that.

Hansen was hauled back out through even hotter public disapproval than had greeted him on his arrival.

The judge waited until the hue and cry began to die down, then hammered the crowd back to order.

"This court is now dismissed."

∞

That evening, Judge Schaefer walked up the street to Sheriff's office. He knocked then stepped inside. "Sorry to interrupt your supper, Mike."

"You didn't interrupt, Clarence, I was about finished up anyway. Have a seat." Sheriff Doyle pushed a chair towards the judge with his foot then set his plate aside and wiped his mouth. "You come to see Dorin?"

"No."

"Good, because that crazed jaybird has finally quit yellin' his head off and I don't want him all riled up again. I'd like to get some sleep tonight."

The judge huffed agreement and settled into the chair Doyle had offered. "But I do have questions about him."

"Not thinkin' of overturning your own rulin' are you?"

"No, but I'd like to be certain I've recorded the correct name of the convicted in the court records."

Mike Doyle leaned back with a screech of chair springs and propped his feet on his desk. "It's Thomas Dorin, far as I know."

"He claims he has proof otherwise."

"He also says he's from the future, so I wasn't surprised there wasn't anything in that trunk of his but some spare clothes and a bit of cash."

"So you did take a look."

Mike nodded. "Day after the shooting."

"Why? Surely you didn't believe his wild assertions."

"Nah." Mike shook his head. "But I've been lied to by enough low-life types that I figure I can tell the difference when I hear the truth. Crazy as he sounds, Dorin sounds like truth when he says he's this Hansen fella. So, to ease my mind if not his, I went over there and had a look for myself. Nothin' in that whole room that you couldn't buy for yourself at Hudson's store. Guess it's true that crazy people sincerely believe their own crazy babble."

Clarence glanced towards the darkened doorway leading to the office's pair of cells. "Do you think it was really that blow to his head that unhinged him?"

"No way of knowin', I reckon," Mike said with a shrug. "He seemed sane as me or you, before. I am sure of one thing Him and everybody else would be better off if he'd dashed his brains out when his horse went over on him last October. Mrs. Perkins, God rest her sweet soul, should never have kept him around the place when he first started going loony, but none of us knew how bad he'd get. Not even Doc." Mike sighed. "Reckon we're all guilty of her death that way, a little."

He bent down and pulled a couple of shot glasses and a bottle out of his desk drawer. "Want a drink?"

"Yes, thanks."

Mike poured two measures and passed one to the judge. He lifted his own. "To Mrs. Hattie Perkins, God rest her."

"To Mrs. Perkins."

CHAPTER THIRTY-TWO

13 March, 1874

He sat on his bunk in the jail cell, his face turned towards the slight breeze that found its way through the barred window. The sky was beginning to lighten past dawn into day.

A bustling clatter outside his cell temporarily drowned out the exterior sounds. He ignored it.

"Stand up!" the Sheriff barked.

He rose and turned. A camera stared at him, the town's photographer beside it holding a flash pan. Behind stood the Sheriff, a pair of deputies, the town's newspaper owner with his notepad at the ready, and the little puke who caused it all.

"Move to the corner, please," the photographer said, "And hold very still."

He sidestepped as requested. Resistance would be a waste of time.

The flash powder went off with a blinding burst of white light.

He blinked away the spots in his eyes, went back to his bunk and turned his face back towards the window.

"Do you have any final words for the public?" the newspaper owner asked in an avid voice.

He raised a fist, extended his middle finger.

The sheriff grabbed that arm and yanked it down behind him while the deputy pulled the other wrist to meet it and bound them together with cord.

He didn't bother to flex his fingers against the restricting burn.

He didn't struggle when they grabbed an arm each and marched him out of the jail, up the street through a crowd.

He heard nothing around him, saw nothing ahead of him but that high, raw timber platform under the silvery-green palo verde.

The noose hung from the heaviest limb swayed a little in the morning breeze.

Twelve steps up, the thirteenth the last.

A lizard lay on the edge of the sixth step, bobbing its head, its swollen throat a vivid orange.

He took each stair at a steady pace.

The lizard darted away.

His boot sole pressed down where it had lain.

The wooden platform thumped hollow under his feet. The sharp, fresh-sawn scent of it filled his head.

He stopped on the trapdoor in the center of the platform, allowed himself to be turned to face the crowd looking up from below.

So many faces.

He stared out above them all, out into the clear morning sky.

His arms were bound tightly to his sides and a rope was cinched around his ankles.

The air wavered in front of him.

Formed itself into a familiar phantom.

Dorin. Staring right at him with horror in his eyes.

"DORIN!" He struggled against the ropes, the crushing grips of the men around him. "I see you, you worthless son of a bitch! You're supposed to hang, not me! I'm innocent!

A black hood came down over his head.

"Tell them who I am! Tell them! Dorin! *TELL THEM!*

The noose dropped around his neck, a sinuous weight pulling tighter.

"Do you wish to pray, my son?" The meaningless words of a preacher, maybe a priest, at his cloaked ear.

He shook his head.

Straightened his shoulders.

Lifted his hooded head.

The trapdoor fell away beneath his feet.

One flash of searing pain

13 March, 1874
~ Late afternoon ~

"Is anyone here likely to claim the body?" Carl asked the undertaker.

Hansen's body lay between them, draped with a sheet.

"No," the man shook his head, his face set in morose lines that Carl suspected were a permanent occupational effect. "I suppose he'll be given a pauper's burial in the church-yard. Do you know of any next of kin who should be notified, Mr. Lynd?"

"No." Carl looked at that still, draped form and felt the gnawing of one last doubt, an implacable final misgiving. "May I view him for a moment?"

"Of course." The undertaker stepped out of the room, back into his front office.

Carl lifted the sheet over the corpse's right leg. The bare limb was blue-tinged and waxen from death, but as straight and unmarred as his own.

He dropped the sheet and went out into the undertaker's front room. "Embalm him at my expense."

PART THREE

CHAPTER THIRTY-THREE

March 13, Present Day
Tucson, Arizona

In Tom's life, he'd endured more than a few nights that aged him years instead of hours. This was proving to be one of the longest of them all. He glanced over at the clock again, its squared-off numbers glowing cold green in the near-blackness of the bedroom.

Two minutes after midnight.

Hanging day.

A slight motion dipped the mattress as Dee leaned past him to check the clock yet again. She made a little soft noise and he reached out to touch her hand. She drew it away and sat back against the headboard once more. Less than a foot of space between them, but it might as well be a mile.

After another long while, she spoke. "What time did they hang people, back then?"

Tom waited for Chris to answer, but when the silence stretched out, he looked towards her shadowy figure. "Usually at full dawn, but sometimes at noon."

"When do you think they'll—?" Her voice choked off, and this time when Tom reached for her hand, she clutched his own with the strength of the drowning.

"I don't know," he answered, just above a shamed whisper. "Depends on how many folks have gathered to watch, I reckon."

"God!" Chris snapped, invisible in the darkest corner, like an outraged ghost. "Shut up, Dorin!"

"Do you think anything he can tell me will make this worse?" Dee's voice was thick with tears.

Chris moved to sit on the edge of the bed beside her, put his arms around her. Tom pulled his fingers free of hers. He rose and moved to the chair Chris had abandoned.

"He didn't have to paint you a fuckin' picture," Chris gritted.

Dee began to sob openly. "I don't love him anymore, but I don't want him to die!"

"I know, sweetheart, I know," Chris choked out as he pulled her closer.

"I so sorry!" she sobbed, her wail muffled against Chris' shoulder.

"I know," he answered between his own sobs. "I am too."

"It ain't dawn yet," Tom told them, as every sound from the pair seemed to rip at his soul. "There's still time for him to come home."

The only answer was the sound of grief. Tom leaned his head back and set his eyes on the window, the glass still inky black.

ᨃ

He hadn't fallen asleep, he was sure of it. Tom blinked, but nothing changed. He was still on a new-made platform, in the shade under the palo verde, facing a phantom vision of himself standing on the trap door, his twin's arms bound tight to his sides, legs bound at the ankles around dust-covered boots.

Everything around Tom wavered, transparent, the bedroom window glowing with dawn's light behind it all.

Past and present playing out at the same time once more.

Tom tried to turn, to bolt down the gallows steps, to leave this borrowed bedroom.

He couldn't move. He couldn't look away, because everywhere he turned his head, there was Jon.

As trapped as his double, Tom had no choice but to stare straight into the man's hollowed eyes.

Jon blinked, his glazed gaze suddenly focusing sharp on Tom, his eyes widening. Jon's mouth opened, his neck strained with the force of his shout, but Tom heard nothing, even though the other phantom figures on that gallows seemed to hear whatever Jon yelled.

Jon futilely struggled against the Sheriff's hold, still shouting as the hood was pulled over his head. He went still as the noose tightened around his neck.

The sheriff stepped back as the preacher came to Jon's side and said something to Jon. Asking for last words, most likely.

Jon shook his head, straightened his shoulders, lifted his hooded head. The trap door fell away beneath his feet.

Past and present exploded in one flash of searing pain.

؃

"It's dawn," Dee whispered, still huddled in Chris' arms. He shuddered, and she felt his nod against her hair.

Tom sat stock-still in the chair across the room, the growing light spilling across his chest, creeping up towards his face.

"Tom?" she called softly.

He didn't move. His eyes were wide and staring, fixed on the window.

"Tom?" Dee pulled back from Chris' embrace, unfolded her stiffened legs.

"Surely that cold-hearted sonuvabitch isn't aslee—" Chris groused as he helped her onto her feet.

Tom's paroxysmal gasp cut Chris off as Tom flung himself out of his chair, his hands flying to his throat.

As abruptly, he fell face first onto the floor, seizing.

Dee forgot about her tingling feet as she ran to kneel beside Tom. "Help me get him onto his side!"

Chris was only slightly slower, and with his help Dee got Tom rolled onto his side and held there, despite his helpless thrashing.

When Dorin went limp, Dee rolled him onto his back. His face was pale, lips blue-tinged. She felt for a pulse as she held her cheek near his nose and mouth.

"Is he dead?" Chris asked. "I don't think he's breathing."

Dee's movements were automatic, almost reflex as she tipped Tom's head back and lifted his jaw.

"He's in full arrest." She blew into his mouth, watching for the rise of his chest.

"Do you know CPR?" she demanded over Tom's body as she put the heels of her hand on his sternum and started compressions.

"Uh… yeah… I think so."

"Then give him a breath. NOW, Chris!"

Her rational mind counted compressions and breaths while the emotional side of her psyche screamed hysterically in some distant mental corner.

After three rounds, Tom sucked in a ragged breath on his own, and his skin lost that ghastly bluish pallor.

"He's back," she whispered, sitting back with an ungraceful thump. She shook out her aching arms.

"Should we call an ambulance?" Chris rose to grab for the phone.

"Only if he has broken ribs." Dee rolled onto her knees and reached out to shake Tom by the shoulder. "Tom! Tom—can you hear me?"

Dorin moaned, the first sound of pain she'd ever heard him utter, then his eyelids twitched.

"Come on!" She shook him harder. "You're not going to die on me too!"

"Then stop shakin' me so hard," he slurred, and opened his eyes.

Chris gasped.

Dee flinched in equal shock. Tom's eyes were blood-red, the whites obscured by burst vessels. "Can you see?"

"Yeah, I can see. My chest hurts, though."

"I'm sure it does. Do you have pain when you take a deep breath?"

Tom drew a long one in, let it out and shook his head. "Jist sore here," he mumbled, rubbing his sternum.

Dee explored it with her fingertips, and though Tom's jaw tightened, he didn't make a sound.

"I don't think anything's broken or torn," she told him.

She looked over Tom to Chris. "Help me get him up and into the bed."

"I'm all right," Tom protested, pushing himself up to sit. "I can manage on my own."

Even so, it took the pair of them to help him stagger the short distance to the bed and to ease him down on it. It was only then, looking down at his ravaged face, that reality hit her full force.

She buried her face in her hands. Tom sat up and stroked a hand down her bowed back. "I'm so sorry, Dee. Chris. I'm so damned sorry."

"Dee, I can't stay here." Chris bolted out of the room, but not even walls and doors could entirely enclose the sound of his weeping.

CHAPTER THIRTY-FOUR

March 18
~ Five days later ~

There was only him and Chris in the house that morning. Dee had gone in to work. He worried about her doing even desk work, with her heart so heavy and Baby so near to being born, but Tom couldn't fault her for wanting to get out from under the heavy cloud of despair in the house. He understood her need to escape for several hours to somewhere normal and sane, normal at least for her.

That left him alone to avoid Chris and to try to find something to keep himself occupied until her return. There wasn't much to do. He'd already burned through all the work outside the house during the anxious days of waiting. Tom grabbed a broom and went out to sweep the patio again. He'd hardly started when he heard the telephone ringing. He ignored its shrill noise just as he ignored the shrieking of a scrub jay in the tree that shaded the space. Chris would grab the thing up soon enough. He always did.

Either way, the ringing soon stopped. A couple of minutes later, the patio door slid open. "It's for you," Chris said.

"What?" Tom turned, leaned the broom against a post.

"The phone call, Hopalong. Is for you." Chris enunciated each word very precisely, as if speaking to a half-wit.

It would have been more of a shock at this point if the man had spoken with a civil tone and used his true name. Tom passed him, certain that the impact of their shoulders in the space wasn't an accident of his own aim. He let that slide off his hide too.

Chris followed, almost close enough to tread on Tom's heels, all the way back to the phone in the kitchen. Then Chris stopped in the doorway, leaning against the frame with a smirk on his face.

Tom decided to ignore that annoying human jaybird too, and picked up the ear-piece of the phone that was lying belly up on the counter. "Hello?"

"It's March eighteenth," Callie answered.

Tom started as her disembodied voice spoke out into the room instead of only through the ear-piece as he'd always experienced before. He glared at Chris and got another smirk in return. Chris planted himself more firmly in the doorway.

A half-second's reflection on knocking that jeering look off the other man's face was enough relief to let Tom turn his back to Chris instead.

"That it is," he answered Callie. "My day off this week."

"Which worked out perfectly, didn't it?"

He couldn't see her teasing smile, but he could hear it, and with the phone blaring her words at a near shout, so could Chris.

"Worked out perfect for what?" he hedged.

"Aw, Jon..." The playful glee was gone from her voice. "Surely you haven't forgotten about our date?"

He'd no more forgotten than she had, but he ignored the strong temptation to take the easy way out with a lie. "No, I ain't forgotten."

"You just don't want to keep it, right?" The light tone of her voice had an edge to it now.

"It ain't that. I keep my promises, and besides, I enjoy your company," he answered, because to explain was far beyond what he could confide in her or anyone else.

"Then what's going on?" Callie's voice sounded more concerned that annoyed. "Talk to me, Jon. Please."

352

Tom glanced over his shoulder at Chris. The man lifted an eyebrow and flicked a hurry-up gesture towards the phone. Tom scowled at Chris to no discernible effect and turned away again.

"No," he said, then quickly amended that curt syllable before she thought he was angry with her. "I can't. Not right now."

"Eavesdroppers?" Callie asked.

"Pretty much." He cut his eyes at Chris, who beamed like she'd paid him a compliment.

"Ah. Okay. We'll talk tomorrow. No excuses, no holding back this time." Her voice was soft, almost a whisper. As if that made a difference, with this betraying machine.

The thought of talking to her about all this put a leaden lump in his gut but there was some hope there, too. She was level-headed, forthright and sharp as a briar. She could look at this mess from the outside, maybe see something the three of them couldn't.

"Sure, Callie. See you tomorrow."

As soon as he replaced the earpiece, Chris spoke up.

"So you made a date with your girlfriend for after the thirteenth. Good to know you were never serious about wanting to go back to where you belong." Chris no longer stood in a mocking slouch.

Tom forced himself not to mirror the man's aggressive stance. He didn't owe Chris any sort of explanation of his thoughts, but he'd give over this last one. "Wantin' to go back to where I belong is exactly why I put her off on it. I figured I'd be gone by now."

"You're long overdue to be gone, one way or another."

"That may be so, but I ain't gonna turn tail and leave Dee alone to fend for herself."

"She's not alone. She has me." Chris took a step closer, chest swelled out and chin held high.

"You?" Tom sneered. "You'll hang around till you're tired of playin' house, then you'll run off after some passin' piece of strange tail, like you done with all five of your wives— or was it six?"

"My ex-wives all knew what they were getting, and so did I." Chris shrugged.

"Yeah, and so will Dee. Now there's some real security for her," Tom snorted.

"This is different. Dee's carrying my brother's baby. You think I'm going to let some stranger waltz into her life and raise Jon's child, much less a busted-up homicidal relic who can't even operate a toaster without detailed instructions?"

"From where I'm standin', she could do a far sight worse." Tom looked Chris over as if assessing a suspect horse, then stared into those shifty green eyes.

"You anachronistic moron. Stow your moldy Victorian moral code and I'll set aside my overpowering urge to kick your ass. Let's think this through with cold hard logic, for Dee's sake."

Chris went back to his casual slouch against the door frame. "You'll make what, ten, twelve thousand this year shoveling horseshit and babysitting tourists?"

"Near twelve." Tom felt a touch of pride.

"A small fortune in your day, I admit," Chris went on, "But now? It won't cover the mortgage."

Tom steeled himself against the jolt of that. He should have expected it, considering the prices he'd seen on everything else. "What is the lien on this place?"

"I'll show you." Chris straightened. "And it's not only the mortgage to worry about; there's everyday expenses, insurance, taxes. And you'd better have a plan to start saving for college for Baby. Even now, a year's tuition at a decent school is twenty-five grand or more. God knows what it'll be in eighteen years."

Chris even sounded a bit awed there at the end.

Tom felt stunned. "I want to see these figures of yours."

"Don't trust me, huh? Good. I don't trust you either. Come on. I can show you bills, tax returns, the sad and sorry budget they were running on when Jon—"

Chris snapped his teeth closed on his brother's name, turned on his heel and strode down the hallway towards his study.

Tom followed. At least Chris trusted him enough now to have him at his back. Tom wasn't sure he held the other man in that much regard still.

Chris flung himself down into the desk chair and pulled a bunch of papers out of a drawer. He began to spread them across the desk, sparing Tom the slightest glance. "Grab a chair."

℃

An hour or two later, Tom looked down at the damning figures as all his plans and hopes shriveled like paper in fire. Chris had proven his point. Even at the best Tom could expect to do, he'd be nothing but a monetary millstone around Dee's neck and a blight on Baby's future.

Chris shuffled the sheets back into order, ignoring Tom as if he'd vanished from the room.

Tom slapped his palm on the desk. Chris met his eyes, startled and wary.

"You damn well better keep your vows to her sacred, Hansen, or I swear to God I'll bury your sorry ass so deep not even the worms'll find you."

For once, Chris' gaze was neither mocking nor malevolent. "I'll never do anything to make her unhappy. She and the baby will have my best, I give you my word."

He offered his hand, and Tom grasped it in a brusque, hard shake of mutual grudging agreement.

Looking into Chris' eyes, he had no doubt the man meant what he said, at least in the here and now. Tom levered himself up onto his feet, stiffened from sitting so tensed up. "I'll be out of here in the mornin'."

Chris accepted that with a nod, then a sly grin spread across his face. "You might want to call the Darger girl back and keep that broken date. I'm sure there's a more comfortable place to sleep over there than the bunkhouse if you play your cards right."

Tom didn't dignify that lechery with an answer as he left the room, Chris' wicked chuckle at his back. He didn't have any faith that Chris' sworn word to be good to Dee would hold up any longer than this cease fire between them had— but Tom's vow to the man was bedrock certain.

March 19
~ The next morning ~
355

"You don't need to pack a duffel bag to move across the hall, y'know," Dee said.

Tom looked up to see her standing in the doorway, her hands resting on the swell of her belly. There was a teasing smile on her lips and dread in her eyes.

"No, but I'm movin' a good bit farther than across the hall," he answered.

Her smile vanished, leaving only the dread.

"Tom, there's no reason for you to leave." She came into the room and sat on the corner of the bed, shoving his bag aside. "Besides, where will you go?"

There were a lot of reasons for him to leave, most of which he didn't want to talk to her about right now, with her baby pressing hard to be born and shadows of sleepless nights darkening the skin around her eyes.

"The Dargers will let me bunk out there," he said. He picked up a pair of dungarees, a pair he'd bought with his own pay, to lay them in the case.

Dee's hand closed on his wrist, stopping the movement, her grip strong as any man's. "Tell me why you've decided to leave so soon." She loosened her hold, and her voice softened. "Please, Tom. Talk to me."

"I figure there ain't no point in lingerin'." He shoved the britches into the bag and eased down onto the mattress beside her. He laid a hand over hers, still encircling his wrist.

"No good can come of me bein' here now. Seein' me all the time pains you and Chris, and keeps him riled up till he can't work. Dee, he's the one who can best take care of you and Baby. I ain't never gonna have enough to even keep food on your table. It's high time for me to stop presumin' on your charity and make my own way."

Her grip tightened instantly, short nails digging into his skin, then she flung his wrist away, drawing up like a hissing cat. "So without so much as a word, you've decided what's best for me?"

Tom nodded. "For you and for Baby, yes. Chris, he said—"

"Fuck Chris! This isn't about Chris."

Tom blinked, that powerful profanity from her lips still a shock. "S'long as we're all under the same roof, it is."

"This isn't Chris' house," she snapped, "and if anyone's overdue to move out, it's him."

"He don't see it that way, and I reckon he's right." Tom's jaw tightened with frustration and shame. He looked down at his hands, laced them to keep them from forming fists. "He's done resolved himself to take care of you and Baby. I got no part in that plan."

Dee wiped a hand down her face and blew out a breath. "Okay, Chris and I are going to have a long talk very soon, but right now I want to keep this between you and me."

Tom looked back into her eyes. "Fair enough. I ask your pardon for decidin' to leave without speakin' with you first. So, tell me, Dee. Why do you want me to stay?"

She shook her head. "First, I have to ask you something else. Is there another reason for you to go to the Darger's, besides working there?" Her chin lifted a degree. "Callie called me a few weeks ago, after that road trip you two took. She didn't come right out and say it, but I got the strong impression she wouldn't shed a tear if you decide to leave me."

Tom felt his jaw go slack and tightened it again so he wasn't gaping at her like an idiot. "Callie's been a friend to me, sure."

He decided to out with it all. They'd had enough of minding words and holding silence. "And yeah, she's willin' to be more than a friend and right quick, if 'Jon' cuts ties with you."

"How do you feel about that? Do you want her to become more than a friend?"

"Ain't never let myself think that way about her." Tom spread his hands. "But even if I had, as a friend or otherwise, she ain't interested in me, Tom Dorin. She only knows me as Jon Hansen, the friend she knew from the university, but all crippled up and half-demented now, and that's who she's drawn to, for lord knows why."

"She and Jon were friends, before?"

Tom nodded, "From what I gather, real good friends."

"Funny, he never once mentioned her." Dee's eyes narrowed. "So they were *very* good friends, I'm sure."

"Either way," he reminded her, making his voice soft and gentle to cool the heat of her belated jealousy, "It don't matter now what might have gone on with the two of them. This here is still about just me and you, ain't it?"

Dee nodded and looked away.

Tom waited, giving her peace, till she straightened her shoulders and looked back into his face.

"So tell me why you want me to stay," he urged, his voice still soft. "I can't be Jon for you neither, Dee, no more than I can be for Callie."

"You think that's why I want you to stay?" Dee frowned. "Do you think I want you to be a substitute Jon?"

"That pretty much says it, yeah." Tom answered. "You've been so angry with me, blamin' me for all this from the first, but so heartsick over him bein' lost, and me here lookin' like his twin— what else do you expect me to make of all that?"

"Nothing, I guess," she murmured, then dropped her face into her hands, fingers digging into her hair. "But it's not what I really want. Ugh! This is all such a tangled up mess!"

This time, he didn't stop himself from reaching out to her. Tom stroked his hand over her bowed back, slow and steady, the same as if he were gentling a skittish foal. "Then it's high time we sit here and tug on the strands till we get it all unknotted. You want to do that, Dee?"

"That's about all I'm sure I want," she mumbled into her palms. "You must think I'm a lunatic."

"Nah," he answered, still stroking her back. "Just almighty confused and heartsick. Anybody would be, put where you've been forced to stand lately."

A sob jerked her body. Then she stiffened beneath his hand and he heard the grinding of her teeth.

"It's all right, Dee," he murmured. "Them tears, they gotta come out."

"No." She lifted her head, her eyes watery but determined. "I've cried enough. Crying's not going to help any of this."

She turned under his touch to lay her hands on his shoulders. "I owe you a major apology. I did blame you for this at first, and even when I stopped, I still took out a lot of my anger and fear and hurt on you, and I was wrong to do that. None of this is your fault. Hell, none of this time-twist craziness is Jon's fault either."

She paused, her teeth clamping onto her lower lip.

Tom held his hand still against her back, her heartbeat racing beneath his palm. "I thank you for that, Dee," he murmured. "I wouldn't have brought this on you and Jon for the world."

"I know. I don't think we'll ever understand how or why this happened— there's no blame in this part of it for anybody, except God maybe."

Her hands squeezed at his shoulders, then dropped to her lap. "But there is blame here, and it's all on me and Jon. Our relationship was finished before he got kicked to 1873. Even if none of the rest of this happened, I wouldn't have let him back into my life.

"I thought you love him."

"I did, for a long time." She sighed. "But I shouldn't have. I don't think he ever loved me, not really. Things between us started going downhill fast more than a year ago, but what he said to me the last time I saw him, well…."

Dee's hands clamped around her belly. "That made how he honestly felt about me crystal-clear. So yes, I was angry at him for being a coldhearted, self-centered asshole, and angry at myself for being such a deluded fool, and I was hurt and I was glad he was gone and at the same time I felt guilty, because he was gone *that* way and I was so scared and worried about him, because I still cared enough about him to not wish him dead."

"I didn't want him to die neither," Tom said. "I weren't eager to stick my head in the noose, but I'd rather done that than for him hang in my place. I expect neither you nor Chris to ever be able to forgive me for that."

She shook her head. "You and Chris will have to come to terms about Jon's death on your own, but as far as I'm concerned, that's not your fault either. I believe you about what happened out in that cornfield.

That poor woman's death was tragic, but it was an accident. Hanging someone for an accident is a horrible miscarriage of justice, and you don't deserve to die for that any more than Jon did. I can't forgive you, because you've done nothing that needs forgiveness."

Tom felt tears sting his own eyes. He blinked them away. "Thank you, Dee. Knowin' that's what you think about it means a lot to me."

He looked into her dark brown eyes, eyes that still glittered with wet sadness. "So, why do you want me to stay on?"

"Because I can't bear to deal with one more change right now," she said, the words coming out shaky. "Please, Tom, stay, at least until Baby's born." She reached out and touched his hand. "Knowing you're here, watching over me, taking care of me, it makes me feel… safe. Secure." She sighed. "I haven't felt that way for a long time, even before Jon disappeared."

That confession went straight to his heart with a pain like the twist of a blade. "I'll stay," he assured her. "For as long as you want me around. Dee, I swear to you and to God, I'll do everything in my power to keep you and Baby safe and happy."

Dee's arms went around him in a tight embrace. "Thank you," she whispered against his shoulder, then hiccupped a sob. "I'm sorry. It's the hormones."

"Don't matter what it is," he answered, wrapping his arms around her as she pressed so close that he felt Baby squirming between them. He stroked her back, threaded a hand into her hair. "There's no shame in a woman's tears."

Those words, softly spoken, opened the flood-gate. Dee's fingers clenched in the back of his shirt and her whole body shook with the force of her sobs. Tom held her tight, rocking a little and crooning comfort as best he could. For as long as the storm raged around her, he'd do his best to shelter her from the worst of it.

He'd better, because when Chris cut out on them, his own back might soon be the only shelter Dee and Baby would have

CHAPTER THIRTY FIVE

March 19
~ Early evening ~

As soon as he stepped inside, the sound of voices drew Chris farther into the house. He stopped in the hallway, looking in at the two in the master bedroom, unaware of his presence.

"You take the high screws and I'll take the low ones and maybe, just maybe we'll have the crib together by the time I go into labor," Dee said from her perch on a low stool.

"If we're lucky." Tom shook his head and exchanged the screwdriver for the instruction sheet. "Don't people read no more? Why's this all in pictures?"

"The crib's made in Sweden, so maybe an artist who can draw tools and chubby naked people is cheaper than a good Swedish-to-English translator?" she said.

"Actually, it was done that way so even someone who's barely literate can get the thing together," Chris commented.

Dee and Tom turned towards him with startled glances.

"Once someone explains a hex-key to him, anyway," Chris continued. "Hopalong, a word?"

The meaning of the glance that passed between Dorin and Dee was entirely without translation, pictorial or otherwise, but Chris didn't like it.

Dee nodded and Tom limped out into the hall.

"Outside," Chris hissed under his breath and Tom flicked his hand in an 'after you' gesture. The rattle of paper and wood behind them assured Chris that Dee was occupied again with the crib assembly.

When the patio door closed behind them, he glared at Dorin. "You gave me your sworn word!"

The man shook his head, his expression inscrutable. "No, all I swore was to bury you if you didn't keep your word. All I agreed to was to do what's best for Dee."

"Which we both know includes you being Somewhere Else," Chris answered. "Today."

Tom scratched at his stubble. "Now see," he drawled, "The hitch in that plan is that we both passed right over askin' Dee what she thinks is best for her— and she didn't take well to the oversight at all."

"Dee's bereaved and pregnant. She doesn't know what's best for her right now," Chris snapped.

"Care to explain that to me slowly, please, in small words so my pathetic bereaved and pregnant brain can keep up?" Dee's voice, low and mocking, came from behind him.

Chris turned to see Dee standing just outside the door, her fists on her hips. He spun back to Dorin. "You knew she was there."

Dorin simply shrugged.

"Tom, if you'd give us a moment?" Dee asked.

"Sure," Dorin nodded and hobbled back into the house.

Dee closed the patio door behind him, then rounded on Chris. "Sit. This is going to take a while."

"Dee, I didn't—"

Dee snapped her fingers and pointed to the chairs. Damn, but he was already feeling a little sorry for the baby. Chris sat, and Dee took the lounger facing it, putting her feet up with a little moan.

"Are you alright, kiddo?" he asked.

"I'm a helluva lot better than you think, obviously," she snapped. "Pregnancy isn't a disease and it's not a mind-altering state. I'm perfectly capable of making decisions about my own life, all by myself."

"Dee, that's not what I meant."

"Oh really?" Dee scoffed. "Y'know, for a successful author, you seem to have terrible trouble expressing yourself."

"Writing gives me time to think through what I intend to say," he answered with a sigh. "It's talking that gets me into trouble. Not enough time between impulse and speech for my internal editor to kick in."

"I want to hear what you think before that internal editor takes over." She laced her hands over her swollen belly. "You can give me a revised written statement later."

One last shot. "Dee, I don't want to upset you—"

"Then don't," she snapped. "But we're having this conversation, Chris. Now."

"Okay, okay. So, where do you want me to start?"

"How about starting with why you convinced Tom to leave without saying a word to me first?"

"Why do you want him to stay?" Chris frowned.

"Chris—" Dee warned.

Chris leaned back, forced himself to relax against the cushions. "I don't see any reason he should stay. We know he's not going back where he belongs, so he doesn't have to stick around. He's still a stranger, Dee. Maybe a dangerous one."

She drew a sharp breath and he held up his hand before she could speak. "You want me to explain myself, so hold all objections till the end of my confession, please."

Dee nodded.

"Dee, you don't need an anachronistic boat anchor around your neck, and that's what Dorin's going to be. I'm not saying that's his fault, but it's not something that's gonna change any time soon either. He barely makes above minimum wage out there at the ranch. I know what you're making. Unless you plan on going back on the ambulance full-time as soon as the cord's cut, you'll be going down for the last time under a sea of red ink before the end of the year."

Dee lifted her chin, eyes narrowed. "And if Tom leaves, then I won't have what little income he brings in, so I'll be drowning in debt even more quickly."

"Not necessarily," Chris leaned forward, hoping he looked as earnest as he felt about this. "Dee, in every way but the official paperwork, you were my brother's wife. My only brother— the last family I had left."

His voice broke and he had to stop to take a few deep breaths. Dee looked at him with sympathy, but stayed silent.

"You're carrying Jon's baby," Chris went on. "Don't you realize you're both very important to me? I'm not going to leave you in the lurch and I'm certainly not going to step aside and let some stranger take over raising Jon's child."

"I will be raising 'Jon's child.'" Dee hugged her abdomen. "This is my baby too. No one is going to 'take over' raising my child. Not Tom, and not you."

"I know, but what I mean is—"

"Rephrasing isn't necessary," Dee interrupted, her tone softer. "I think I understand what you mean." She rose and moved to the chair beside his.

"What I don't understand," she went on, "Is what your expectations are. When you say we're important to you, and you're not going to leave us in the lurch, what exactly do you mean? How do you see that working out in practice?"

This was too important to rush. Chris looked into those beautiful brown eyes that had so entranced Jon from the first, and searched for the right words to explain to her what he hadn't yet fully explained to himself.

Dee waited, studying his face as intently as he watched hers.

"I don't know, exactly," he admitted. "I mean, I don't think you need me in the next room twenty-four-seven anymore, but I want to stay close. Dee, I never got to be the brother to Jon that I wanted to be. Yes, I screwed up some, I did some things I shouldn't, but the distance between us started with Jon. He would never let me get close. He wasn't the partner to you he should have been, for a lot of the same reasons. I want to make up for both of those shortfalls, with the baby and with you."

He stopped, unsure what to say next or how she was taking what he'd spilled out. Her vaguely sympathetic expression gave him no clues.

364

"That sounds like a heavy-duty commitment," she said. "What do you mean exactly by wanting to make up for Jon's shortcomings with me?"

Chris shook his head, still pinned by her steady, gentle gaze. "I don't know, exactly. I figure we'll work that one out as we go along. I care for you Dee, I deeply care for you."

He wiped his palms on his thighs, then wanted to kick himself for that giveaway gesture. Maybe she'd take the statement at face value and move on.

"Deeply care for me like a sister-in-law or like a lover?" she demanded.

Damn. He forced himself to keep looking her straight in the eyes. "Did you ever interrogate Jon like this?"

She drew away, deeper into her chair. "No, and I should have. I may make monumental mistakes in my life, but Chris, I don't repeat them. Can you answer my question?"

"I haven't tried to dissect this, y'know," he retorted. "Yes, in some ways you're like a sister, but in other ways what I feel for you is very much not a sibling sort of affection. Am I 'in love' with you? No. Not yet, anyway, but I'm not ruling it out either. Dee, we've both been dragged through so much crap lately it's a wonder we're still somewhat sane. So why don't we take whatever's between us now one day at a time and see how it goes?"

She reached and took his hand. "I can't do that, Chris."

Her words sent a sharp, startling twist of pain through his chest. "Why not?"

"Because I'm already sure how I feel about you. You're Jon's big brother, and now in my heart you're my adorable, annoying, happy-go-lucky, over-protective big brother too. I know you'll make a fantastic uncle to this baby."

She sighed and squeezed his hand.

"But...?" Chris asked, not caring that his voice sounded a bit choked.

"I do like you being here, in my life. I hope you'll want to stay a big part of it, and Baby's. Heck, even if you wanted to build a house on the back acreage or something, I'd be all for it. But, as much as I love you now, I know I'll never be in love with you. I'm sorry."

"Yeah, me too," he murmured under his breath, then caught her gaze again. "Are you in love with Dorin? Is that why you want him to stick around?"

"I don't know. Maybe. Maybe not." Her lips crimped into a hard line and something not so warm and fuzzy sparked in the depths of her eyes. "I haven't tried to dissect this, y'know."

He heard his own flip intonation echoed back at him, and it stung. "For cripes sake, Dee, at least tell me what you see in that—"

"That what?" she snapped.

"That man," he amended quickly. "I'm not asking why you're giving him a chance and not me. I'm asking why you're giving him a chance at all." He drew his hand out of hers.

"I've been watching him," she answered, her voice soft and steady again. "And I've seen that he's a very kind, very moral, very honest man."

"Who just happens to look a helluva lot like your recently dead sig-other," Chris ground out.

"Yes," she admitted, very low. Dee dropped her eyes to her belly and began rubbing a pulsing spot that made the fabric of her top ripple. "It's possible that I'm deluding myself and making another huge mistake, but Chris, I've thought about that and I'm certain I'm not trying to remake Tom in Jon's image any more than I would do that with you."

She chuffed, her face going hard. "Although I will admit that Tom's more like the man I thought Jon was, when Jon and I first got together. But, I know he's not Jon and I know Tom's not perfect either. I'm willing to take Tom as he is, time-lost and uneducated and all the rest, because of *who* he is, in his own right."

"Sounds like love to me." The words were bitter in his mouth.

Dee shook her head. "No, not love. Not yet. Right now it's respect, and trust."

"Which implies you don't trust and respect me."

"I didn't say that."

"No, because you're kind and you have an ounce of tact," He straightened from his slouch and leaned towards her. "I don't and I've got enough of a mean streak to say what I think. You're making a huge mistake here, and I ought to walk out the door and let you go down in flames, but I won't. I care about you and this baby too much to abandon you like that."

"I don't need your charity," Dee snapped.

"Yeah, kiddo, you do," he fired back. "But it's not charity when it's from family."

"Then what do you want from me in exchange, Chris? To lie to you about how I feel while I bleed you dry like all the rest of your bimbos?"

Geez, now she looked like she was going to cry. So much for not upsetting the pregnant lady.

"What I want," he said slowly and very gently, "Is for you to be happy and secure, so you and this baby can enjoy your lives without worrying about anything."

Dee nodded and wiped her fingers across her eyes. "That's what everyone wants for the people they care about. I want it, you want it, and if you ask Tom, I'm sure he'll say he wants it too."

She looked at him, her gaze damp but steady. "So, between the three of us, do you think we can work out a way for all of us to get what we want?"

"I'll do my part," Chris answered. Dorin could damn well answer for himself. "I'll start by spoiling this baby rotten at every opportunity."

Dee gave him a shaky smile and a tiny chuckle. "You're going to be an epic uncle, y'know."

"I'll have to be, to stand out in the mob of uncles, aunts and cousins this kid's gonna have. How many is it at current date?" He gave her a grin in agreement that the heavy discussion was over for now.

"Exactly? I'll need a calculator for that," she answered with a roll of her eyes.

CHAPTER THIRTY-SIX

March 20
~ The next afternoon ~

Hat in his hand, Tom rapped on the ranch office's door. His mouth was dry, despite his certainty about what he'd come to say.

Stephan opened the door, a rush of cool air and a warm smile reaching out to greet Tom. "Hello, Jon. What do you need?"

"If you can spare a minute or two, I'd like to talk to you, sir."

"Of course, come on in. I've got nothing pressing right at the moment." Stephan stepped aside to allow Tom to enter. "Please, have a seat."

Tom lowered himself into one of the chairs in front of the desk, and Stephan took the other.

"What's on your mind?" Darger asked.

"I'd like to talk to you about changin' my duties, sir. I feel I'm better suited to workin' with the horses than with the cattle or the guests. You've got a lot of young stock comin' on, and I'd like nothin' better than to help start 'em off right."

Stephan nodded slightly at Tom's every sentence, as was his habit. Tom had learned to wait for the man to speak, though, before assuming that habit meant agreement instead of only thoughtful interest.

"Paula and I have taken note of your horsemanship and equine management skills," Stephan began in that slow, rich voice of his.

"Frankly, if you hadn't come to me today, we would have spoken to you about this soon. Tell me more about your experience and training."

"As you know, sir, I've had no formal school trainin' with horses." Tom shifted in his seat, more to ease his leg than out of nerves. "I grew up on a stud farm out near Benton, in east Tennessee. I had a natural interest and a natural skill too, so my Pa put me to use right young."

Stephan smiled. "I put Callie in the saddle as soon as she could sit up and hold on."

Tom nodded. "I been told that Pa had me in arms on a horse as soon as my Ma would let me out of her sight that long."

"Which breed did your family focus on?"

Tom hesitated for a split second to remember the modern names. "Saddlebreds, for the most part, though we had a line of Hackney crosses that was well thought of in those parts."

"Were you involved in showing them?"

Tom shook his head. "No sir, I wasn't. My interests was more with the breedin' and trainin' side of the operation."

"I certainly value experience over untested education, and you've given every sign of knowing what you claim to know." Stephan steepled his fingers. "We've watched the way you've worked with little Sukie, and frankly, we're impressed. You've proven yourself an excellent colt-starter, so we'll begin with that duty and go on from there, if that's agreeable."

"Yes sir, it is. Thank you."

03

Tom left the office feeling some pounds lighter across the shoulders. The raise he'd negotiated wouldn't meet Dee's needs, not by a long shot, but every dollar helped. At least now, he knew he was doing the best he was able to take care of her and Baby.

He headed for the tack room to get a colt-halter and lead. He'd be working with all the young stock, but now he had the Dargers' official permission to train up little Sukie like she was his own, and that gave his spirits a lift too.

March 23

~ Three days later ~

Tom grabbed his jeans, using the cloth as a handle to lift his leg up onto the ottoman.

Dee was pretty sure she heard a soft grunt forced out between his teeth too. "The ibuprofen isn't helping much, is it?" she asked.

"It helps some." Tom looked at her, and she was struck by the deepening lines around his mouth and his solemn blue eyes. He might even be thinner. She could kick herself for not noticing earlier, too wrapped up in her own misery while they'd all waited for some certainty.

"Not enough, though," she answered. "Not with you working like you've been."

He shrugged. "A man's gotta work, Dee."

"But you're in pain, Tom."

Again, that resigned shrug. "It ain't signifyin' anything that can be fixed, so might as well grit and go on with what I need to do."

"What if you didn't have to grit and go on? What if it could be fixed?" she asked.

Tom straightened, and his eyes widened. "You mean, not take it off, but make it right?"

"No, no doctor now would take it off. You've obviously got decent blood flow and nerve connections down through the leg, so there'd be no reason to. The only time they amputate anymore is if the leg is dead anyway."

Tom was silent a moment, the lines deepening in his face. He looked away then reached down and rubbed his thigh. It was one of the very few times he let her catch a glimpse of the extent of his chronic pain.

When he met her eyes, his expression was stoic again though his voice was soft and awed. "I never hoped to be healed of it this side of the grave."

"Tom, it's unlikely that they'll be able to fix it completely. You've obviously lost some muscle, and I can't know how much healthy bone is left. I'm going by what I read about the original injury in the surgeon's report. You may always have a limp. But I'm certain that it can be repaired to function better than it does now, and the difference in length corrected to some extent."

He was quiet so long that she began to become concerned, but before she spoke, he did.

"Before I say yes to this, do you know how many die from it? Half? A third?"

"Oh my god, Tom! You're willing to even consider a surgery with a fifty percent mortality rate?"

"From what I've seen, it's purty much the goin' rate," he shrugged. "I jist need to know, to weigh the pain against the chance of dyin'."

"I'm sorry, that's... barbaric. I'll have to look up the exact statistics, but the biggest potential problem with the surgery itself would be the chance of infection, which we can usually knock out pretty quickly with antibiotics, or maybe an embolism, so I don't know, maybe one in ten-thousand or fewer? The anesthesia itself can be a problem, but since you're healthy and young, that mortality risk is probably around one in twenty- thousand or even lower. Doctors now don't do surgery with the kind of mortality rates you're used to, unless the patient's going to die anyway without it. That's like, I don't know, opening up someone's chest in the ER to get their heart going again."

He looked a bit slack-jawed. "*One* in ten thousand? Or less? With them kind of odds, I'd charge a brigade with a buggy whip!"

"It'll be a long painful process though, and you'll have to do several months of physical therapy afterward." She pursed her lips against a stab of unearned guilt. "That's why I haven't mentioned it to you, well, before now."

"Dee, if it can be made even a little better, so I can work easier, I don't care how long it takes." He looked away, then back at her. "It can't hurt no worse getting' fixed than it did gettin' broke.

The desperate hope was so raw in his eyes, it was her turn to look away and close her eyes to hide strong emotion. The couch dipped as he sat down beside her, and the gentle touch of callused fingertips on her cheek startled her eyes back open.

"Why do you look so sad all a sudden?" he murmured.

She shook her head, and gave him only half the answer to his question. "There's something else I have to tell you before you get your hopes too high. It's a very expensive operation."

The light died out of his eyes.

"Wait, it's not impossible because of that. It's only that there's a catch, a requirement. I have health insurance that will pay for at least eighty percent of it all. But for you to be covered under my insurance, we have to be legal spouses first."

"Married?"

She nodded. "There's probably some sort of waiting period after, too, I'm not sure. But definitely married first."

She had no idea what he was thinking as he drew away.

"I'm not saying you'll have to be chained to me forever," she hurried on, "Not till death do us part and all the rest. If you'd rather, it can be…" she hesitated, searching for a term he might know. "A marriage of convenience. Just to satisfy the rules."

His only reply was a harsh chuff. He rose and dropped back into his rocker, lifted his leg back onto the ottoman, flat stoicism shuttering his expression once more.

"I know you don't like this, Tom. I don't like it either. But the surgery and everything else will cost thousands of dollars without insurance. There's no other way."

"Yes there is," he gritted, not meeting her eyes. "We can leave my leg as it is."

"No. That is not an option. There's no sense in you suffering when there's a solution. If a sham marriage is the price I have to pay to see you healed, I'm willing to pay it."

A muscle in his jaw worked.

"What if I ain't?" He met her eyes with a gaze as hot as blue flame. "What if I'd rather stay lame than settle for a sham marriage?"

"It's not like it'd have to be for life!" Dee insisted. "Once the procedure's completely over, you could—"

"I could what?" he snapped, his voice furious for the first time. "Walk out on my solemn vows to my God and my wife, leave Baby behind, cryin' for Papa? If you think that's the kind of man I am, Deidre

Collins, then you ain't been payin' attention or I ain't been behavin' the way I oughta around you!"

Dee realized she was pressed back into her chair, cringing away from the intensity of his outburst.

"It's nothing you've done," she burst out, then swallowed and started again. "You're always a perfect gentleman. I... I underestimated your convictions, I suppose. I didn't think people from your day married for love all that often anyhow."

"I can't speak for ever'one else, but I would never marry for any reason but love," he answered, his demeanor softening. "I sure won't marry for dishonest gain."

Dee winced, her own conscience giving her a hard, if belated, pinch. "It would be technically dishonest, I guess. I didn't allow myself to think about it that way, because I want this for you so very much."

Tom moved to sit beside her again. He reached out and stroked his palm over her bowed head. "Don't fret, Dee. Now that I know what's possible, I'll find a way to make it happen someday."

That gentle, caring touch soothed a gnawing ache deep inside. Dee allowed herself to luxuriate in the comfort for a long moment, eyes closed.

"What if it isn't dishonest?" She looked up at him again. "Us marrying, I mean."

His hand stilled, curved against the crown of her head. "Are you sayin' you love me?"

"I could," she whispered, and licked lips gone suddenly dry. "I'm already more than halfway there— but I'm scared."

"Tell me your fears," he urged, his voice almost as soft as hers.

She closed her eyes again, hiding from the uncomfortable intimacy of his earnest blue gaze. "I was so sure Jon was the man I'd be spending the rest of my life with, and look how that turned out. I... I'm afraid to trust what I'm beginning to feel for you, to trust my own judgment about anything again."

"Give yourself time, Dee," he urged, stroking her hair again. "Time to grieve and time to heal. As for you trustin' your own judgment, well, I can't claim to know one way or the other on that, but you can trust I'll always treat you right. You got my sworn word on that."

Dee looked back up into his face and she didn't doubt the tenderness and concern she saw there. "Do you love me?"

"I could. I'm a good piece more than halfway there." His hand left her hair to rest lightly on the curve of her abdomen. "I already love this baby as if it's my own."

Dee straightened and Tom drew his hand away. "Tom? Would you… hold me? Just for a little while?"

He nodded and opened his arms. Dee leaned against him, rested her head against his chest. His arms were warm and strong around her, his heartbeat steady and slow beneath her cheek.

Maybe this would be enough, for now, for both of them.

April 9
~ Seventeen days later ~

Tom glanced up as Chris stepped into the garage from the house, then went back to seating the sixth ball into the cylinder of Jon's Colt revolver.

"Why don't you unload that relic and hang it on the wall?" Chris asked. "That's pretty much all it's good for now."

Tom shrugged and began to seal each of the rounds with grease. "Jist because somethin's old don't mean it can't still serve its purpose."

Chris resettled his bag's strap on his shoulder and gestured towards the gun in Tom's hand. "I suppose that's true. Hey, I've been too proud to ask and too distracted to look it up, but what the heck's the grease for?

"To keep the gun from chain-firin' if a spark blows back when it goes off."

"You mean all the chambers can go off at once?"

Tom nodded.

"Yikes. Even more reason to get rid of it. Besides, it was obsolete even in your day, right? Didn't pretty much everyone have metallic cartridges and smokeless powder by the time you went 'poof?'"

"Not smokeless powder, but metal cartridges, yeah." Tom picked up the capper and quickly set percussive caps onto five of the six nipples, leaving the one under the hammer uncapped. "But until I get real familiar

375

with that slick little pistol you bought for Dee, I'd ruther keep this one ready and close to hand."

"This isn't the Wild West anymore, Hopalong, so keep it in your pants."

Tom lifted an eyebrow as he slid the Colt into its holster. "I ain't the only one who ought to heed that advice around here."

Chris gave a curt laugh. "No, probably not. But there too, I suspect you'll be judged the better man."

He hit the button to raise the garage door. "Whether you 'ort to' be or not."

Tom let him have that last word, turning his attention to disassembling the sleek modern firearm that still seemed foreign to his hands.

Chris backed his car out, then stopped halfway down the drive. Curious, Tom squinted against the bright light outside.

A young man was on the edge of the driveway, someone Tom hadn't seen around the area before. Something about the stranger, the way the boy moved, raised the hair on the back of his neck. Tom laid the magazine of the new gun aside to wrap his hand around the familiar grip of the Colt.

Chris was already sliding the window down on his car. "Can I help you?" he asked the boy.

"Yeah, man." The boy stepped closer. His right arm made a suspicious dip. A shiny muzzle pointed right at Chris's face. "Get out of the car."

"HEY!" Tom yelled at the same instant, the Colt cocked and aimed before the word was out of his mouth.

The boy spun towards him.

Tom's finger started to squeeze, the muzzle aimed solid right between the boy's eyes.

There was a split-second, the space between heartbeats, before that slight pressure on the trigger let the hammer drop.

"Help me!" The high-pitched whimper was pathetic, choked with pain and terror. "Please, mister… help me! Help… me…." She fixed on his face, her eyes already going glassy and distant.

The Colt spewed a cloud of flame and smoke and deafening noise.

The little bastard squalled and clapped his hand to his ear, his pistol flying out of his hand to skitter across the hood of Chris' car.

"That weren't a miss," Tom growled, the Colt already cocked on a fresh chamber. "Get on the ground or guess where the next one's goin'!"

The boy dropped onto the pavement so fast it was a wonder he didn't bust his own nose.

"Nice shot, cowboy." Chris said from the car, his voice shaky.

"Some things, a body don't never forget," Tom shrugged, keeping his eyes and the Colt trained on the quaking, cussing young man flattened against the driveway. "You all right there, Chris?"

"I think I may need to trash these slacks, but yeah, I'm okay." Chris began dialing his phone as he slid out, juggling phone and crutches. "I need the police." he said into it after a second or two. "Someone tried to carjack me in my own driveway. He's being held at gunpoint right now."

⋈

Calling in the law after a scuffle was a far more worrisome and drawn-out process in this century than it had been during his own. It was well after dark before he and Chris could head for home.

Chris hadn't said half a dozen words to him once they were let out of the police station. Tom studied him out of the corner of his eye. Chris seemed tired and grim, but not angry.

"I'm sorry I took a shot," Tom offered into the heavy air between them in the car. "I didn't have time to think it through, considerin' the situation."

"I'm not," Chris said. "That worthless little punk might have killed me. He's obviously no stranger to the police department. I am glad you didn't shoot his damn head off, though. That would have made this a lot more complicated."

"Think I'll see the inside of a jail cell over this anyway?"

Chris shook his head, attention back on the road. "You shouldn't, since you only made his ears ring. Imminent danger to your life or the life of someone else, that's legal justification for using deadly force in Arizona."

Even in the car's dim light, Tom could see the shudder that ran through Chris's body.

"Having a .45 shoved into my face surely counts as imminent danger," Chris said.

"If it don't, then there ain't no justice anymore," Tom answered.

"There's as much as there's ever been." Chris's voice was tainted with bitterness. "So I suggest neither of us get too complacent."

Tom let that hang between them for a while. He turned away from the window towards Chris again as they neared the house. "I'll be real sorry if this brings trouble and distress to Dee, but however this falls out in the end, it would have brung her far more grief if you'd stopped a bullet with your brains."

"You sure about that? She might consider it good riddance."

"You're so full of shit it's a wonder your teeth ain't brown. You're dear to her as a brother and you damn well know it," Tom said.

"Yeah, I damn well know it," Chris snapped as he pulled the car into the garage. "That's the problem for all of us."

"Nah, just for you." Tom met Chris's stare with a steady one of his own. "You want to start a battle for Dee's affections, then you make sure your powder's dry. I ain't backin' down on this."

The air between them seemed to heat up. "Do you love her?" Chris asked, his voice tight and hard.

"Yes, I do." A knot tight in the center of Tom's chest slid loose as that confession came out. "Do you?"

Chris looked away. "It doesn't matter. It's not me she wants."

"You two done talked about this?"

Chris nodded. He gave a chuckle as bitter as quinine. "She made it clear that I'm permanently in the 'brother' category as far as she's concerned."

"Ain't no way that weren't tough to swallow," Tom said, feeling genuine sympathy for the rogue. "Think you can abide by her wishes enough to stay in the picture? Dee and Baby need all their kin, and me and you can stay out of each other's way."

Chris rubbed a hand over his mouth. "I don't have a choice. Dee wants you, and now I owe you my life."

"You don't owe me nothin'. You'd have done the same if it'd been me on the business end of that little shit's pistol."

In the darkness inside the car, Tom couldn't read the expression on Chris's face before the man turned away again and started out of the car.

Chris spoke over his shoulder. "I'll tolerate you, Dorin, if you marry Dee, but that won't make us family."

"Fair enough," Tom answered. He gave Chris a head start before following him into the house.

CHAPTER THIRTY-SEVEN

April 10
~ The next day ~

Absorbed in hammering out the details of the latest tribulation of Marshal Maxx Starr, Chris ignored the doorbell the first time it rang.

The second time the chime pealed through the house, the slight echo reminded him that Dee was at a doctor's appointment and Tom was at the Dargers'. Chris clicked Save, temporarily abandoning Maxx to his fate atop a sinking riverboat.

"I'm coming!" he yelled towards the front door and whoever might still be on the doorstep. One glance through the peephole at the pretty, curvy woman with a wealth of auburn curls made him glad the visitor was the persistent sort.

He grinned as he opened the door. "Good morning!"

"Hi!" she smiled back, and juggled the wrapped gift she held to offer her right hand. "I'm Callie Darger, from the next place over. I brought something for Dee."

Her voice was a sensual purr, an almost startling contrast to her Pollyanna appearance.

"Ah ha! So you're the mysterious Callie. I'm Chris, Jon's brother."

"I thought you must be, there's a family resemblance," she said.

"Since you're friends, I won't tell him you said that. Come on in." He stepped back and gestured towards the living room.

Callie followed him inside and discreetly looked around.

"Make yourself at home," Chris said. "Dee's in town, but she should be back any minute now."

"Oh, then I shouldn't stay. I was going to drop by for a minute anyway." Callie offered the package. "A baby gift, y'know. From the family. Mom would be here too, but she's at an event this week."

Chris took the pastel package and set it aside. "Thanks, but come on, don't rush off. I was getting a case of cabin fever this morning with nothing but my keyboard to keep me company. Stay long enough to have a cup of coffee, at least?"

"Sure, I can do that," Callie said with a smile and followed him into the kitchen. She settled at the table as Chris poured out the last of the morning's pot.

"I have a confession to make," she said.

"What's that?" Chris sat down across from her.

"I didn't come by only to drop off a gift for the baby. We heard about that awful robbery attempt, on the news. Jon said everyone was all right, but I wanted to make sure for myself."

"Why?" Chris cocked an eyebrow at her.

Callie blinked, then a sensual little laugh rippled out of her, dimpling her cheeks. "I was concerned, though honestly? I have to admit to some morbid curiosity too, I suppose. What really happened? I asked your brother, but you know how Jon is now, a man of few words and short on the details."

Chris flicked a dismissive hand. "Not much to tell. The punk stuck a gun in my face and told me to get out of the car. Jon was in the garage cleaning guns, saw what was happening and fired a warning shot. The little coward wasn't about to go up against an armed opponent, so he surrendered and the police took him in. That's pretty much everything. I'm surprised it was considered exciting enough to even get mentioned on the evening news."

"That's awful! I'm glad no one got hurt." Callie nodded towards Chris' cast. "Looks as though you've barely had time to heal up from your last misadventure."

"Let's not talk about that one," Chris said. "I'd rather not reveal myself as a complete idiot on first meeting."

"That humiliating, huh?"

"Don't go bumbling into abandoned buildings without checking the floor first," he answered with a sage nod. "And that's all you need to know."

"Okay, consider the subject changed." She tilted her head. "Since I've already confessed to being a shameless snoop on first meeting, would you mind me asking you something about Jon and Dee?"

"Not at all." He shrugged. "No promises that I'll answer, though."

"Fair enough." Callie fidgeted with her mug. She closed her hand around the Cheshire cat on the side, obscuring its persistent grin. "What's your take on Jon and Dee's relationship? Jon's almost a different person now. I'm having a harder time getting a read on his emotions than I once did, but I can tell he's been unhappy most of the time since he's been working at the ranch."

Chris leaned back in his chair, studying her face as he considered how to answer, or whether to answer her at all. "Since the accident, Jon and Dee have had to deal with some drastic changes. The way Jon is now, well, it's as if he and Dee are having to get to know one another all over again."

Chris shook his head. "Their relationship was shaky before Jon got hurt, so they're having to work through that baggage on top of everything else."

"Geez, and her pregnant, too," Callie murmured in a throaty whisper. She looked into his eyes with concern and sympathy in her own. "I realized they had to be struggling with all of this, but it's staggering to try to fathom the extent of it."

She reached out to touch his hand. "How are they dealing?"

Chris shrugged. "It was pretty bleak between them for a while, but they're doing better than I thought they could. I think Dee's come to terms with Jon not being the man she knew, ever again. They seem to be working out a new relationship. A fresh start for them both, I guess."

"That's good," Callie said, "I wish them the best." Her fingers curled lightly around his hand. "How are you dealing with it all, Chris?"

He felt his jaw tense. They'd just met. He should brush her intrusive concern off with some flip answer. But her question, and the way she asked it, got way too far past his defenses.

Besides, who could he talk with about this mess? Not Dee, and sure as hell not Tom. His agent? A party buddy? One of the assorted exes? Some random fan?

Chris shook his head. "I'm dealing, that's about the best I can say."

"Are the changes in Jon that disturbing for you too?" Her fingers squeezed gently around his own.

Chris drew his hand away and clenched both of his around his mug. "Sometimes I think it would have been easier to take if Jon was killed that day, back in October."

Callie's eyes widened.

"I don't really wish my brother dead," Chris added quickly, and looked down into his murky coffee. "It's that Jon, well, I look at him and I'm seeing my brother's body, but there's someone else looking out of his eyes. Someone that I'm not certain I even like."

"And you don't know how to reconcile your love for your brother with that confusion and alienation," Callie ventured, her voice gentle. "You're lost for a way to get some closure on your old relationship and uncertain about building a new one."

Chris looked up to meet her eyes again. "Are you a psych major?"

"No, organic chemistry. Why do you ask?"

"Because you've nailed it. That's exactly what's going on for me." He shook his head. "And I've never spilled my guts to someone on first meeting like this. I'm usually the one listening to true confessions over a cup of coffee."

Callie gave a soft, breathy laugh. "If it makes you feel any better, I've been accused of having 'tell me your troubles' etched across my forehead. Besides, sometimes it's easier to confide things to a complete stranger than to someone close to you. There's a whole lot less risk."

"No offense, but what I just said to you feels pretty damn risky in retrospect."

She took a sip of her coffee and shrugged. "None taken. Don't worry about it, Chris, I don't gossip. And it's not as if you confessed to murder or something, after all. You're dealing with an incredibly tough situation, and everybody needs a friendly ear now and then."

"Thanks." Chris shoved his cup of coffee aside. "Hey, since I'm being recklessly candid, I have a very rude question for you."

"Oh? I'm intrigued. What do you want to know?"

"Are you and Jon gettin' it on?"

A gasp and a swallow of coffee are two actions that shouldn't occur at the same moment. Callie spluttered and coughed, her eyes watering from the heat.

Chris handed her a napkin and waited until she caught her breath. "Sorry, I didn't mean to almost drown you with that."

"S'okay," she croaked, then cleared her throat again and gave a shake of her head. "And people tell me I'm painfully frank!"

"So are you?" Chris asked.

"Am I what?" she asked, followed by a raspy chuckle. "Painfully frank or doing Jon?"

"Answering the second will answer them both," Chris said with a shrug. He rose and poured her a glass of water from the fridge.

"Thanks." She took a long sip of the cold water before she answered. "And no, I've never screwed your brother. That frank enough for ya?" Callie wagged a finger at him. "Not that I didn't try, before his accident, but he backed off in a hurry when I came on to him."

She tilted her head and gave him a tiny, wicked smile. "Although the moment he brushed me off was the first time I heard anything at all about Dee, so draw your own conclusions there because I sure did. Anyway, after that, I didn't see him or hear from him again until the day he delivered that foal."

"What about now? He spends most of his time at your parents' place."

"Look, I can't say that I wasn't still interested in more than friendship when he started working for us, but he's kept me at arm's length. He's determined to be a good father to his baby, and that includes keeping Dee in his life, if she's willing."

"She is. I almost wish she wasn't, but she is," Chris said.

Callie gave a shrug. "I don't think it's a good idea for them to stay together either, but I'll never be a home-wrecker, Chris. There's way too many single men out there to cause that much pain to another woman. Besides, I figure that if a man is willing to cheat on his partner with me, he's going to play around on me too, as soon as the new wears off the relationship."

"So you and Jon are just friends now, with no benefits?"

"Not even a dental plan."

Which had him almost strangling on his own swallow of cooling coffee.

"Friends were all we were before his accident, and it's all we'll ever be," she added.

Chris looked across the table into her gray eyes and believed her. "You can do better than Jon, anyway."

"Way to stand up for your brother there, Christopher!" she said with a laugh.

"Hey, we're still being brutally frank, right?"

"Always," she nodded. "So, you have someone more suitable in mind, do you?"

Her sex-kitten purr survived the scalding coffee. No wonder Jon bolted when she put the moves on him. Callie Darger was way too high-octane for his little brother, Dee or no Dee.

"Let me check my contacts list and get back to you," he answered with a wink.

"Do that," she nodded and rose. "You know where I live. But right now, I should be going. I have a late class today."

Chris rose as well. "I'll walk you to your car."

"Just in case?" she asked.

Chris lifted his shirt tail, revealing the butt of a semi-automatic holstered inside the waistband of his jeans. "Yes. Just in case."

C３

The sporty vintage Mercedes convertible sitting in the driveway was completely unfamiliar to Dee. She pulled in beside it just as the front door opened and Chris walked out beside a pretty redhead.

Well, that explained the car, but if he thought he was going to start 'entertaining' in her house, then they were going to have a serious discussion as soon as his flavor of the week left.

"Hello," she called to the woman as she got out of the car. "I don't believe we've met."

"Hi Dee," the woman said. "I'm Callie Darger. I'm sorry it's taken me so long to come by and say hello in person."

Dee recognized the woman's voice instantly. She would never have matched this fresh-scrubbed face to the dial-a-porno voice she knew from their earlier phone conversation. She shook Callie's uncallused hand. A bitter taste clenched her teeth behind her smile.

"No problem. I haven't exactly been a model neighbor either."

"We should fix that," Callie answered, with a wider smile.

Dee couldn't bring herself to agree. Or smile back.

Before the pause became too awkward, Callie shook her head. "Anyway, I shouldn't keep you standing on your walk any longer. I stopped by on my way to class to drop off a baby gift. Mom sends her best wishes. She had an event today or she would have come by too."

"Thank you. Please tell Paula I said hello," Dee answered, feeling a bit more friendly. "She and Stephan are welcome to stop by any time."

"Sure," Callie nodded. "Take care." She moved past Dee towards her own car. "It was nice to meet you, Chris!" she called back with a wave.

"You too," he answered. "Don't make yourself a stranger."

Callie pulled away and Dee stalked— well, waddled like an annoyed duck in a hurry— to confront Chris as he retreated into the house. "What was she really doing over here?"

Chris pointed to the festive package with a rattle tied into the bow. "Dropping off a baby gift. Why are you so upset?"

Dee picked up the package. "I think she and Jon had something going on."

She gave the package a savage shake that set the rattle clicking.

"Not according to her," Chris answered.

"Oh, of course not." Dee plopped the box back onto a side table and went into the kitchen. "How did that subject come up, anyway?"

"I asked her if she and Jon were getting it on."

Dee rounded on him, mouth gaping. "You said it like that?"

"I don't have a transcript, but yeah, pretty much like that." Chris rubbed his chin. "I do recall using that exact phrase."

Dee rolled her eyes and got a glass of water. "Well how did you expect her to answer? Oh yeah baby, three times a week and twice on Sunday?"

"Nice scheduling," Chris muttered and returned a wink to her scowl. "Callie strikes me as a candid to a fault. She certainly didn't try to make herself come out better in the telling."

"What did she tell, then?"

Chris came closer and put his hands on her shoulders, rubbing them gently. "The takeaway is that she and Jon were friends, maybe inappropriate friends, and she came on strong with him. He backed off fast, told her he loved you, and didn't have anything else to do with her until Tom was hired."

That bitter taste was back in her mouth. "What does she think about 'Jon' now?"

"She says that since he's been at the ranch, 'Jon' has kept her at arm's length, and she's given up."

"And you believe her."

"Of course. Why wouldn't I?" Chris drew his hands away from her shoulders and stuck them into his pockets.

Dee cut her eyes at him. "Because she's pretty and has a voice like Mae West?"

"Give me a little credit. Dee, her words were 'He's determined to be a good father to his baby, and that includes keeping Dee in his life, if she's willing.' She said she has no interest in being the other woman in anybody's relationship. So yeah, I believe her."

"Tom said that?" Dee said.

"According to her."

She didn't even realize she smiled until Chris spoke again.

"Oh, so now you believe her."

"No," Dee's smile grew. "I believe Tom."

April 12
~ Two days later ~

"Tom? Can I talk to you for a minute?" Dee asked.

Tom looked up from his book, laying it aside on the end table. "Of course. What do you need?"

"Well, nothing, really," she smiled as she sat down on the ottoman beside where he rested his maimed leg. "I picked up something today that I thought you might be interested in."

She handed him a manila envelope.

Tom drew out the name-change forms within, and after a moment, looked up at her with a hint of surprise on his face. "You won't be hurt by me doin' this?"

"No." Dee shook her head, a wave of dull sadness rising and falling within her. "Jon's never coming back, and it's time I fully accept his death, so I can move on, so we can all move on. I know how much your own name means to you."

She reached out to touch his hand that gripped the forms. "This way, you can legally call yourself Tom Dorin again."

Tom laid the papers in his lap, smoothed his hand over them. "Thank you, Dee," he said almost in a whisper. "I don't know how to tell you how much this'll mean to me."

"It's all right," she murmured. "You don't have to explain." She stroked her fingertips along his cheekbone. "I can see it."

The front door opened.

"I hope nobody cooked!" Chris called out. He stepped into the living room bearing take-out bags and a cloud of rich, hot fragrance.

Dee's stomach growled and she rose with a little chuckle. "Your timing's perfect. I was about to get something started."

Tom slid the forms back into the envelope and tucked it under his book.

ა

One week later, a nervous 'Jonathan Madison Hansen' stepped into a judge's chambers, Dee at his side. Less than ten minutes later, he stepped out as Thomas Anderson Dorin.

"Cain't hardly believe that's all there is to it," Tom said as they went back down the corridor in the Courthouse.

"Me either, but wow, isn't it great?" Dee smiled up at him as they headed for the Clerk's office to pay.

"I ain't gonna let my guard down till we're back out on the street."

He opened the door to the County Clerk's office for her and they joined the queue.

❣

Standing in line to pay the fee took longer than the hearing had, but even so they were at the counter before either Dee's feet or bladder began to complain.

Her hand tucked in the crook of Tom's elbow; she kept him from moving down the hallway once they left the office.

"Somethin' the matter?" he asked, the relaxed lines of his face altering to ones of mild concern.

"Nope." She shook her head. "But I have a proposal for you."

"What do you propose?"

Even though she'd planned this moment, she still had to take a deep breath to push the word out past a sudden flurry of internal butterflies. "Marriage."

He looked so stunned, and stood there silent for so long, Dee forced out a chuckle to shore up her crumbling confidence. "I know that's not at all romantic, but if I go down on one knee right now, it may take a fork-lift to get me back up."

"Ain't I the one who's supposed to be on bended knee for this, anyhow?" Tom sounded as rattled as she felt. His tan was blanched a little around his mouth.

"I don't think kneeling is a good idea for either of us, so why bother with any of the other conventions?" She drew a deep breath, let it ease back out. "I'm serious about this, Tom. Would you like to marry?"

"Today?"

"Why not today, if we're going to?" Dee stroked a hand over the top of her belly.

Tom's gaze dropped from her face to her hand. His expression softened, but then his lips took on a grim tightness. "Is that the reason you want this? To give Baby a name?"

"No! I wouldn't marry you or anyone else for that reason alone. It's stupid!"

Tom cocked his head and narrowed his eyes.

"I'm not saying *you're* stupid." She groaned and scrubbed her hand over her face. "Good lord, I couldn't possibly make this worse if I tried!"

"Come here, Deidre," Tom urged as he took her hand. Leading her over to the bench in a nearby stairway alcove, he sat down beside her.

He kept her hand wrapped in his. "I told you a while back that I wouldn't marry for any reason but love. I love Baby already like this child's my own, but a man and woman need more than the love of a child between them to make a proper go of it. Do you love me, Deidre Collins?"

"Yes. I love you very much, Thomas Dorin. Do you love me?"

He lifted a hand to her cheek, his fingers curving to cradle her face in his palm. "More than anyone, in this time or any other."

Dee gazed into his eyes, so blue and still shadowed, even now. "Kiss me?" she whispered.

The pad of Tom's thumb brushed over her lips, a subtle caress somehow more intimate than a kiss.

"We're so close now. Whyn't we wait till we're pronounced man and wife?" he murmured.

"You're impossibly old-fashioned," she muttered with no complaint at all, leaning in to wrap her arms around him.

He cradled her against his shoulder. "And I never know what you're gonna do next, so we got some interestin' days ahead of us."

"Understatement." She smiled.

His hand smoothed over the back of her head and she sighed in contentment.

"Dee, are you sure about doin' this right now? Are you certain you don't want to hold off 'til your folks can be here, or your friends can stand witness with you?"

Dee shook her head. "No. Today is for me and you. My family and friends can wait a while longer. After Baby's born, we can throw a big celebration and have a formal ceremony then if we want."

"So long as you're certain." Tom's arms tightened in a hug. "Since this is the only time you're gonna be married, 'least for as long as I'm around to have any say on it, I want everything to be as you want it."

She nodded against his shirt. "Would you mind though, if I call Chris? I'd like for him to be with us for this, if he's willing."

"I was gonna ask for that, if you didn't," Tom agreed. "He's a part of this new family we're makin'. It'd be heartless to not say nothin' to him about this till we get back to the house."

Dee sat up and reached into her purse for her phone.

~ Later that day ~

Tom hefted one of Chris' suitcases into the back of his car. "I don't want you to go thinkin' you ain't welcome here any time you care to come back through."

"I know," Chris answered, his normal sly amusement nowhere in sight. He closed the trunk. "And I may take you up on that soon, but right now you two need time to be newlyweds before you become a family."

"You're still part of this family, Chris." Tom loosely crossed his arms over his chest.

Chris swiped at a dusty spot on the sleek vehicle's red paint. "I know that. Sorry it's taken me so long to come around."

Tom shrugged. "You have a lot on you. I ain't got no hard feelin's."

Chris looked up. "Neither do I, not anymore." He rubbed a hand over his hair. "Look, I know I've been a major asshole for months and—"

"You're done forgiven, Chris," Tom interrupted. "That's what havin' no hard feelin's means."

Chris lifted an eyebrow and that impish little smirk of his played about his lips again. "Okay, since an actual apology isn't expected, would you at least tolerate an explanation? Confession being good for the soul and all?"

"Since when are you worried about your soul?" Tom mirrored Chris' lifted eyebrow right back at him.

Chris grinned. "I'm going to take it as a compliment that you think I still have one. Let's get out of the heat for the rest of this."

Tom followed Chris back into the house. They went into the spare bedroom that was now Chris' again.

Chris dropped onto the foot of the bed and Tom propped a hip against the bureau.

"So what do you need to explain?" Tom asked.

"Why I've treated you like shit," Chris answered. He leaned towards Tom, his hands laced between his knees. "I loved my brother, I still do. But we were always angry at each other for a hell of a lot of reasons, and when I came out here, I got angrier because he was too bull-headed to take responsibility for what he was doing to Dee. The last time we spoke, I was so furious with him I barely let him back into the house. Then he vanished, and I was still angry, even though I was terrified I'd never see him again, never get to make things right."

Chris hesitated, his gaze going down to his hands. Tom simply nodded, waiting to see if Chris would go on.

"When we knew he was never coming back, I was devastated— he's my little brother, the only family I had left. I was still angry, enraged, but with grief and guilt on top of it."

Chris looked into his eyes again. "I took all that out on you like some spoiled brat kicking the family dog and I'm sorry. You're not my brother, and no matter what you've done in your past, you're not the reason he's dead."

"I had only one brother too," Tom told him, "And me and Joshua, we rubbed each other bleedin' raw from the day I was out of the cradle. We hardly had a kind word between us even on the day I run off to the War. I know some about that kind of anger, and the guilt and pain of never gettin' to make it right. But I have learned one thing about family, since I left home."

Tom laid a hand on Chris' shoulder. "A man can have more than one brother, and not all of 'em have to be born of the same mother."

"You think that's where we are now?" Chris' voice was low as he looked up, without the heat of a challenge in his tone.

Tom gave Chris' shoulder a squeeze then drew his hand away. "I think that's where we can be, if we're willin'."

"Got any suggestions on how to get there?"

Tom rubbed his jaw, studying on that a moment. "For a start, you can pull your gear out of your car and stay a while longer."

"Nah, you and Dee need some privacy," Chris said.

"Then settle somewheres close then. We can't hardly learn how to be family, you and me, if you're wanderin' around over half the country."

"Okay, I'll give you that. I'll get a hotel tonight and find a real estate agent in the morning."

"There ya go." Tom said, "There's our start. There's one more thing, though."

"What?"

"You call me Hopalong one more time, I'm bustin' your mouth."

Chris laughed. "Aw, come on! Hoppy was a cowboy hero, beloved by children of all ages. He earned millions just from putting his face on lunchboxes."

"Yeah, well I ain't never met the man. I'm just a gimp who hops along, and I won't never see nowhere near a single million even if I live to be as old as I really am, so I don't take to it kindly."

"Okay, okay." Chris held his hands up in playful surrender. "No more nicknames."

April 26
~ One week later ~

"So," Chris flung his arms wide. "What do you think?"

"It's gorgeous, Chris, but there's an echo!" Dee giggled and the merry sound bounced around the room.

"Hey, there is!" Chris chuckled. "Well, once I get some furniture in here, it'll sound less like an auditorium."

"You plannin' on runnin' a boardin' house? This is a lot of territory for one man," Tom asked, only half teasing.

"Have you seen Dee's family?"

Tom shook his head.

"Neither have I, but they're legendary. You'll need to borrow this joint when it's your turn to host the big annual shin-dig. Besides," Chris pointed to Dee's belly. "Do you think she's going to stop at one?"

"Chris!" Dee gasped, turning scarlet.

Tom felt his own face go hot. He couldn't help that, but he sure wasn't going to do anything to spur Chris along that line of conversation. "Don't see how that has anything to do with the size of *your* house, but however many we're blessed with, we'll make room for."

"Somehow," Dee sighed.

"Which reminds me," Chris said. "I've had an idea I need to discuss with you, Tom."

"Am I included in this negotiation?" Dee asked.

"Sure," Chris nodded. He led them back through the house to his office. It and his bedroom were the only two rooms that were furnished.

Dee sat down on the chaise end of the plush sectional, putting her feet up with a sigh of relief. Chris and Tom settled into the other corners.

"Okay," Chris began, leaning towards Tom with an eager expression. "You know I write Westerns, right?"

Tom nodded. He'd read a couple that were on Dee's bookshelves. They were barely a step above dime novels in his estimation, but there's no accounting for folks' tastes in such things. They'd certainly made Chris a wealthy man and he had to respect that.

"Jon was always after me to make them more realistic, to work in real history instead of making it up as I went along." Chris shook his head. "I told him that Starr's fans don't want history, they want the Wild West fantasy. I still believe that."

"But that doesn't mean it's not time to branch out into another genre." Chris motioned towards Tom. "After all, you're living history, sitting right on my sofa. You've lived through the most tumultuous, momentous times our country's ever faced. There's got to be at least one best-seller in your life story."

Dee looked at them both with wide eyes.

Tom shook his head. "Chris, I thank you for that regard, but there weren't nothin' of interest in the first part of my life, and I weren't no storybook hero in the rest of it."

"That, my friend, is why I'm a best-selling author and you're a ranch hand," Chris said, but there was no scorn in his voice. "You're too close to your own life to see the literary gold. Besides, what have you got to lose? If the book bombs, then all you've risked is some time. If it does well, I'll give you sixty percent. I'll absorb all the costs, either way."

"That's a very generous offer, Chris. More than generous. But lost time's worth more than lost gold for anybody." Tom looked towards Dee.

She reached out and took his hand. "Do this, Tom. Not for the money, but to tell your story. Your real story, without holding back. I think you need that whether the book sells a single copy or half a billion."

"Are you sure?" Tom watched her face. "Some of my story is your own to tell."

"I'm sure," she whispered, her fingers closing around his in a secret hug.

Tom nodded and looked back at Chris. "So how do we start this book-writing procedure?"

"At the beginning, of course," Chris grinned. "When and where were you born?"

"September twentieth, eighteen-forty-five, a few miles northeast of Benton, in Polk County Tennessee."

As Tom spoke, Chris rose and went to his computer. As keys clicked, he looked at them over the screen. "So you didn't live in a named town?"

"No, it's jist farmland," Tom answered. A chill ran down his back. "Or at least, it was then. For all I know, Benton ain't there no more."

"Oh, the town's still around," Chris assured him, attention back on his screen. "Towns do come and go, though. Sometimes counties too."

"But," he gestured them over. "Does any of this look familiar?"

Tom moved over to stand behind the desk. Dee went with him, sliding her arms around his waist and resting her cheek against his arm.

Tom leaned in over Chris' shoulder. He gave a low whistle.

"Benton's a far sight bigger than I remember it, and most all them roads was laid after my day. But if the center of town's still where it was then, our farm is about here." He pointed at the screen. "You think there's any trace of it left?"

"Hard to say," Chris enlarged the map to its highest level. "There's still a house there."

"How'd they get a map this fine?" Tom was awed by the image on the screen. "Any closer and you could read a newspaper over somebody's shoulder."

"They take pictures from outer space," Chris said with a casual shrug.

Tom's surprise and suspicion must have been plain to see.

"From. Outer. Space," Chris emphasized, "With a floating camera, sort of, way up above the atmosphere. I'm not yanking your chain this time, ask Dee. Anyway, do you think this is the place?"

Tom studied the image. "The land looks right, but the house ain't quite where I remember." He gestured towards the machine. "Can you find out who owns the place now?"

"Not without a modern address to go on. The surest way would be to go out there and check the property tax records at the courthouse. We could track it all the way back to your parents' deed, that way."

"Uh, guys, before that train of thought leaves the station?" Dee broke in. "Nobody's going on a cross-country road trip and leaving me behind any time soon."

"I wouldn't leave you behind, sweetheart, not even for Tennessee and all the rest of the world rolled up together," Tom promised with a hug.

Chris lolled his head back to look up at them.

"The state's been around since the early eighteenth century," he assured them with a cocky grin. "It'll still be there after the munchkin's hatched."

He closed his computer and rose. "That'll give you time to learn to drive, too, John Wayne. That's your last big prerequisite for joining the twenty-first century as a fully functional adult human being."

"Oh yeah?" Tom shot back, game for the needling now that the malicious edge was blunted. "I done learned all I needed to when you busted your leg. I drove you then just fine while you puked and squalled like a scalded cat."

"No, we *survived* your attempt at driving when I was incapacitated by agonizing pain. I had to make the choice between putting our lives into your clueless hands or slowly dying out in the middle of jump-off nowhere. You didn't drive, you somehow kept from crashing for several miles."

"Guys," Dee groaned. She divided a half-serious quelling scowl between them. Chris ignored that and Tom did too.

Tom lifted his chin and folded his arms over his chest in mock challenge. "Then if I'm to learn to do it proper, somebody's gonna have to teach me. You volunteerin', scribbler?"

"Dee can tea—"

"Dee will do no such thing," she interjected. "As much as I love you, Tom, there was no way on God's green earth I'm going to sit in the passenger seat while you learn to drive."

"Reckon that leaves you, now don't it?" Tom drawled, lifting an eyebrow in Chris' direction.

"There are driving schools." Chris' voice held the amiable tones of sweet reason.

"Which we can't probably can't afford," Tom retorted.

Chris opened his mouth.

Tom cut him off at the pass. "And which you ain't payin' for."

Dee looked between them both, a slight smile on her face even as one foot tapped the floor in a testy rhythm.

Chris had best never play poker. Tom could almost hear every thought that left its trace in the man's expressions.

"Okay, okay!" Chris threw his hands up in a quick gesture of surrender. "I'll pick you up tomorrow at ten. I want to have strong coffee and a good breakfast under my belt before I stare Death in the face. Repeatedly."

"I'll be waiting and ready," Tom agreed with a nod. "But there's one other thing."

"What?" Chris asked.

"Who the thunder is John Wayne?"

April 27
~ The next evening ~

They were laying around after supper like two lazy cats, nestled up together on the big sofa. The sink was still full of dishes, but Tom was too full of food and contentment to care right then.

"I need to ask you something," Dee murmured as she lifted herself up from his side with a soft little grunt.

"What's that?" Tom sat up as well. Whatever came out of Dee after an opener like that one was sure to be diverting, and sometimes astounding.

"Would you like to be with me when Baby's born?"

This one edged on astounding. "I never thought about you wanting me with you right then, much less what my druthers is."

"Men didn't stay with their wives when they were giving birth?" She cocked her head at him, all curiosity.

Tom gave his head a shake. "I reckon some did if there weren't no woman around to do what has to be done. I know all my sisters was brung into the world by Granny Meacham."

"Was that your mother's mother?" Dee asked. "I assumed her maiden name was Anderson, since it's your middle one."

"Ma was born an Anderson," he assured her. "Naw, Miz Meacham weren't a blood-relation but everybody called her Granny because she was a granny-woman, Dee. She delivered most of the babies and doctored a lot of the sick around those parts."

"Oh! A midwife!" Dee's face brightened. "And sort of a nurse-practitioner, I guess. We still have those, but now they have to go to school and get licensed, and nobody calls them Granny."

"Let me ask you something then," Tom ventured. "If there's still mid-wives, why do you want to go all the way over to the hospital when your time comes? Seems to me it'd be easier on you here, in your own bed, without a lot of strangers millin' around."

He slid his arms around her again as a chilling thought rose up in his mind and out of his mouth. "Is there somethin' wrong with you or Baby that you ain't told me?"

399

Dee gave a little gasp and looked up into his face, eyes wide. "No, honey! Everything is fine, perfectly normal. When I first found out I was pregnant, I thought about having a home-birth, but I decided I wanted to go to the hospital so I could have pain-relief if I want it and so I'll be right there where all the doctors are if anything goes wrong."

Before he could ask, she answered. "I'll be fine, I promise. So will the baby. It's extremely rare for a woman to die from childbirth now. It mostly only happens when the woman is very ill going in, and you know I'm as healthy as one of the ranch horses."

Tom felt as if an overloaded pack dropped off his shoulders. "Thank God! Thank God! I been sweatin'over this and prayin' for you since I found out you was carrying."

"Oh honey!" Dee wrapped her arms around him and kissed him, quick and hard. "I'm so sorry! I never thought to talk to you about it."

"And I couldn't bring myself to ask," he murmured, holding her close. He stroked the side of her swollen belly. "Superstitious, I reckon. Afraid if I spoke of that devil, it would appear."

"Well, this century's spawned other devils to take its place, but that one's well and truly slain. Nothing bad is going to happen to me, and Baby's going to come out healthy too."

"Even so, I won't rest easy till it's all over and I can see you're both hale and hearty for myself." Tom laid his cheek against her hair and closed his eyes to hide his lingering worry.

"So, does that mean you'll want to be with me?" Dee pulled back enough to look up at him, her eyes soft.

Tom looked down into her tanned face with its sharp bony lines and those big sweet eyes like a doe deer's, and realized that some time, somehow, she'd become beautiful in his sight. "Every moment that you want me there, I'll be by your side."

Her smile seemed to light up her face and half the room besides. "That makes me so happy! I was hoping you'd say yes."

"I can testify already that sayin' no to you about anything ain't gonna come natural for me."

She gave him a little laugh and a peck on the cheek, then struggled to get off the couch.

He helped lift her to her feet. "Where you off to in such a hurry?"

"Guess," she groaned, then spoke again over her shoulder as she hurried towards the bathroom. "There's some stuff you need to look at, too."

Tom spent those few moments of solitude steeling himself for what was to come. It didn't matter how many mares he'd help foal, a human birthing was a far more portentous event and despite Dee's assurances, for him it was one fraught with mortal peril for mother and child.

He hadn't praised God lightly when she told him that few women died from childbearing now. Since the War, Tom hadn't prayed for much of anything, but he'd bowed his head for Dee and the baby many times since landing in this new century.

Tom lifted his head when he heard Dee come back in the living room. She was still smiling, a stack of glossy, colorful papers in her hand. After settling back close beside him, she dropped the sheaf into his lap.

"This is a lot of information, but you need it. Labor and delivery can be overwhelming even for a man who's used to modern medicine and has been inside a hospital more than once." She handed him a map of a group of buildings and pointed. "Okay, when it's time, we'll go in the southeast entrance."

CHAPTER THIRTY-EIGHT

April 30
~ Three days later ~

A vague, almost subliminal discomfort woke Dee from her morning nap. She assumed it was her bladder that disturbed her sleep, but she was too relaxed and drowsy to get up until it complained again.

Then a low drawing pull spread across her lower abdomen. A sensation vaguely like a menstrual cramp, but unique in its strength and duration. Her eyes flew open and she reached down to rub the spasming muscles.

It had to be a contraction. Dee lay perfectly still, waiting, her eyes on the clock. Several minutes later, another contraction gripped her belly.

After the third one, she was certain. They were regular, she was in early labor. With a smile on her face and a flutter of nerves in her stomach, she eased herself off the bed. Contractions or not, her bladder was demanding its own share of her attention.

She would wait to call Tom. There was no reason to send him into a panic until she had to.

 CB

It was time. The contractions were three minutes apart. Dee set down the clock and picked up her phone. "Hello, Paula, it's Dee Dorin. Is Tom anywhere nearby?... No, nothing's wrong, but it's time to go to the hospital.... It's not an emergency... yes, I'm sure."

She gave a little laugh, and a contraction cut it short. "Paula, I'm fine, I swear. I'm a professional, remember?... Thank you so much... We'll call as soon as we have news."

It couldn't have been much more than ten minutes later when she heard hoofbeats coming up fast behind the house. She waddled to the patio door in time to see Tom pull his horse to a sliding stop that would win a buckle in a rodeo. Stephan Darger rode up at a more prudent speed behind him. Tom bailed off and tossed Darger the reins. "Dee! Shouldn't you be off your feet?"

"I'm only in the first stages, sweetheart," she teased. "The baby's not going to fall out on its head."

Tom didn't look convinced by that as he hurried over to put his arms around her.

Stephan laughed, obviously the veteran of the three of them. "You should be so lucky that it will come so quickly. Callie made us wait twenty-six hours. We'll be praying, but I'm sure everything will go beautifully."

"Thank you, sir," Tom answered as he put his arms around her as if her knees might fail at any second. "I appreciate them prayers."

"Thanks, Stephan. Pray it won't take twenty-six hours while you're at it, ok?"

"I will," he chuckled and turned his horse. "Call when you can!" he called over his shoulder as he kneed his mount into a trot.

"Come on, love, let's get your bag and get you out to the car," Tom crooned and moved towards the patio door as if he were guiding a frail invalid.

"Tom, this isn't an emergency. You have time to take a shower." She gently extricated herself and opened the patio slider before he could do it for her. "Besides, I need to call Chris to take us over, and I need to call my doctor to let her know this show's on the road. And I need to pee. Again."

"Are you sure I got time to wash up?" he asked.

"I'm positive," she smiled, then grunted as a slightly stronger contraction made itself known. "There's no need to rush, honey. Even at

404

the best, this is going to take hours still. But hopefully, not twenty-six of them."

Tom slowly released a long breath and she watched forced calm spread over him as if he pulled his anxiety off with his shirt. "I got the feelin' that two's gonna pass like twenty till this is done."

"You and me both, honey." Dee rubbed her knotting abdomen. "You and me both."

⚃

As if she were made of spun glass, Tom held onto her supportively as they made their way inside, Chris pacing alongside like a nervous sheepdog. Then it was a flurry of questions and paperwork and a brief separation while she was gowned and prepped and Tom was given the standard labor-room etiquette rundown.

By the time Tom rejoined her, she was pronounced well dilated and almost through her first stage of labor. The time for waiting and waddling was over. Within hours, she would be holding her baby in her arms at last.

Jon's baby.

Dee clenched her teeth against a moan. No, this wasn't Jon's baby, not once from the instant he knew she was pregnant.

"Are you hurtin' bad?" Tom cradled her cheek, his eyes dark with worry.

She shook her head. "No, only a little overwhelmed. I'll be all right."

"You're gonna make it through just fine, darlin' and I ain't leavin' your side." His words came out with the tone of a vow, and he bent to press a kiss against her forehead.

Dee looked up at him as all thoughts of Jon faded like mist in the noonday sun. Her baby's true father stood faithfully beside her, his hand in hers, his solemn blue gaze steady on her face.

⚃

"Here's your healthy baby girl!" The doctor laid a noisy, besmirched, squirming mite of humanity onto Dee's belly.

Dee reached down to stroke her daughter's soft, blood-smeared skin while the physical cord that joined them was severed forever. Her baby was the sole focus of her awareness for that precious moment.

"She's so beautiful, Dee...."

Tom's choked voice brought her back. She looked up to see tears standing in his eyes. His hand shook a little as he cupped his palm over the baby's head.

"Of course she is." She smiled up at him. "She's your daughter."

"And yours," he answered, his husky whisper as intimate as any kiss.

"Do you have a name chosen for her?" one of the nurses asked as she scooped the baby up to clean her, warm her and make sure she was healthy.

"Madison Elizabeth Dorin," Dee answered.

"Maddie-Beth," Tom murmured, and Dee knew he would call their daughter nothing else for all his days.

It seemed like forever, but it was less than ten minutes later when the neonatal nurse returned with Madison cleaned up and swaddled in a striped flannel blanket, a perky little pink knit cap pulled low over her ears.

"Let Tom hold her first," Dee told the nurse. "I've had nine months to cuddle her, after all."

Tom was already reaching out. He cradled Madison against his chest with a sure hold, his focus intent on her little face.

The overflow of the tears standing in his eyes didn't surprise her, nor did his tender crooned words to his tiny daughter.

"Hey there, Maddie-Beth. I'm your Papa, sweet baby."

It was the broad, handsome smile lighting up his whole face that startled a tiny gasp out of Dee.

The joy glowing in that smile transformed him instantly into who he truly was: A good man in the first decade of his adult life, rejoicing in his love for his wife and his newborn child.

"Happy birthday, sweetheart," Dee whispered to both new lives in the room.

CHAPTER THIRTY-NINE

~ Later that day ~

"She's so adorable." Chris couldn't seem to take his eyes off the baby nestled in his arms. Tom was certain his whisper was as much from awe as from consideration for Dee, asleep nearby.

"She is," Tom agreed, his own voice low as he stood by the chair. "Your brother done real good with her."

"He sure did." Chris traced a fingertip over the little fist Maddie-Beth held against her cheek. He looked up. "And I'm sure my other brother will do even better, raising her."

Tom laid his hand on Chris' shoulder, and smiled down at him. Chris reached up and covered Tom's hand with his own. He smiled back at Tom. There was the slightest shadow of sadness in it, but no scorn at all.

~ Fourteen months later ~
June 6
Polk County, Tennessee

Even for Tom, the drive seemed long as their directions wound them away from an almost unrecognizable Benton, deeper and deeper into the rural countryside.

Paved road turned to gravel, then into a set of ruts. The tall weeds hissed against the undercarriage of the car while woody brush scraped up the sides of their rental car something fierce, until finally Chris braked in front of a wide metal gate.

He got out with the caretaker's key and swung the gate open, jamming it into the blackberry briars to one side.

"If that thing bounces back, our deposit is screwed," he commented as he got back behind the wheel.

"If all those bushes scratched up the paint as badly as it sounded, then the deposit's already toast and we'll have to duke it out with the insurance company," Dee commented from the back seat.

"I'll make it up to you," Tom promised him.

"Nah, don't worry about it. This isn't the first time I've trashed a rental." Chris pulled forward to another chorus of twigs on sheet metal.

Past the gate, the road faded into a pressed down pair of tracks in the weeds, so rough it had Chris cussing under his breath and Tom wishing for a good horse.

The baby was the only one in the car who thought the jouncing was fun, squealing and clapping her hands from her car seat beside Dee.

"Stop," Tom said as they topped the ridge.

Chris braked before the trace curved down across the face of the rise. "What is it?"

"Nothin'." Tom already had his door open. "I want to have a first look."

Chris and Dee stayed in the car, but Tom probably wouldn't have noticed if they'd been at his heels.

The first sight of Cooper's Creek in desolate ruins had stunned him to his core. The sight of the uninhabited farmland below only set a surge of old, worn-smooth regret rising up in his chest. Even in his own time, he hadn't expected it to stay the same.

A big, two-story house with no windows and very little surviving roof rotted away several yards west of where his house had been. An unfamiliar barn was in slightly better repair, but it listed to the east, propped up by cedar poles.

Of the home he'd left behind in 1861, nothing remained but a vaguely rectangular patch of briars and vines.

It wasn't the old house and outbuildings he'd flown across the country to see, anyway. He'd said his goodbyes to the land almost two hundred years before.

One spot of the grown-over pastures stood out. A path had been mowed to it from the road, and barbed wire protected the original iron fencing from the itchy sides of grazing cattle.

Tom turned away and got back into the car.

"Are you okay, honey?" Dee asked very softly. She reached up to stroke her fingers through the back of his hair.

Tom nodded, his eyes still on that deserted valley. "There's a path mowed from the road out to the graveyard. The rest of it's not too bad but the grass is likely over knee-high. Looks like the place is bein' used for growin' hay now."

"At least it's not covered up in trees," Dee said.

"Or been turned into a subdivision," Chris added.

Nothing more was said until Chris stopped near the derelict house. "I'll take a hike while you two look around here," he said.

"We'll call when we're ready to go," Dee said.

"Or I'll call you when I get lost." Chris grinned.

Tom shook his head at that and got out of the car. "Thanks, Chris."

"De nada," Chris shrugged.

"Be careful around that patch of saw-briars down there," Tom said, pointing. "Our well was about seventy-five feet uphill of the far left corner. It may not be covered good if that other house still used it."

"Ugh, thanks for the warning!" Chris shuddered. "That's a trip down memory lane I can do without!"

ଔ

Whoever kept the old family plot and the path to it mowed didn't do it often. Tom waded through the daisy-studded grass, a bouquet of roses in his hand.

Dee walked beside him, murmuring to Maddie-Beth as the little girl squirmed on her hip. On the uneven ground he didn't quite trust his altered sense of balance with the baby in his arms, despite no longer having the unwieldy lengthening frame around his right leg.

"Dow'! Dow'!" Maddie-Beth insisted and Dee set the little girl on her feet. Quick as a shot, Maddie-Beth headed for him but Dee was quicker.

"Nooo! Papa! Up!" Maddie-Beth strained for him to the limit of her chubby captured arm.

"Stay with Mama for a few minutes, sweet baby," Tom urged.

The little girl's lips crimped up as prelude to a wail, but Dee was as quick on distraction as she was on her feet. "Oh look, sweetie! Pretty daisies! Let's go pick some for Papa and Uncle Chris."

Tom watched with a fond smile as his daughter happily toddled away beside her mother, squatting every other step to snatch the head off a daisy or a clover.

The old gate squealed on failing hinges as Tom went inside the ornate, rusting wrought-iron fence. Gravestones had sunken into the fertile soil over the decades, leaning at every angle. Three small marble ones were worn smooth, the lambs atop them rendered featureless by wind and rain, mute reminders of the younger sisters he'd lost long before the War.

The two largest markers were granite, and the lettering on them was softened by time and lichens but legible still.

Tom laid his hand on one, the rough stone as warm as living flesh beneath his palm. "I'm sorry, Pa," he whispered.

After a moment, he moved to kneel in front of the stone beside it. Tom brushed away matted grass and dead leaves from the base of it, then settled the roses against the old stone.

"Ma," he murmured, fingertips brushing across her name. "I've finally come back to you."

ॐ

"That's odd," Chris muttered under his breath as worked his way through the underbrush towards a glimpse of dressed stone.

"I'll be damned, I've found the black sheep of the Dorin clan." Chris squatted in front of the lonely marker.

"I'd like to know what you did to get the ultimate cold shoulder. How did you screw up so bad that you were even kicked out of the family plot?"

He peeled a thick coating of plush green moss away from the face of the headstone.

Chris yelled, dropping backward onto the leaf litter, but distance did nothing to lessen the shock of the inscription.

Jonathan Madison Hansen
Died March 13, 1874
Genesis 23:4

ABOUT THE AUTHOR

Theresa Crawford writes professionally
and for pure entertainment.
My Name Is Tom Dorin is her first novel.
She lives with her family on the beautiful southwest coast of Florida.

Theresaccrawford.wordpress.com

How I Met Tom Dorin

It all started with a dream, and not the 'I want to want to write a novel' daydream. In fact, despite being a voracious reader, I never considered writing a book. I also had no particular interest in the Civil War, past the vague information remembered from history classes, and absorbed by osmosis as a Southerner.

All that changed when I had a dream. A horribly vivid, strange dream, like none I've had before or since. In this dream I wasn't a participant, or even an observer. I wasn't even *me*.

I was a young, nameless Confederate soldier. I looked out through his eyes, thought his thoughts, felt the pouring rain through his skin. I knew I was in Georgia, but I (he) wasn't quite sure where. The once plowed ground I crossed was a wasteland of sucking red mud. I was fiercely hungry, exhausted almost past going on, wet to the skin and cold to the marrow. I was a sniper, and it was my duty to find a high vantage point. When I approached the farm's burnt-out house, I discovered I wasn't the first to take possession of its attic....

When I woke, I was gripped by an unshakable resolve to write this man's story. I feel I've fulfilled my obligation to that cold, muddy, disheartened young man from so very long ago. I hope he feels I've done him justice, whoever he was, wherever he may be....

As for me, I'm working on my second novel, a tale I dreamed up all on my own this time. I live in southwest Florida with my family. While I love the climate and the friends I've made here, I will always, like Tom, carry a longing for the Tennessee mountains deep in my soul.

If you've enjoyed this book, I hope you'll take the time to leave a review online. Every positive review helps another reader decide to take a chance on a new author's title. Thank you for taking that chance on mine!

COMING SOON

SETH CONWAY

and

Falken's Fantastical

FLYING CIRCUS

*Being a
Steampunk Fantasy
set in an England
that might have been,
in the year of Our Lord
1887*

Chapter One

It is said that he stood with his spine
as straight as a Lord Noble...
and his eyes downcast like a slave.
≈ARCHER TALENTS, ROYAL HISTORIAN≈

Seth accidentally caught the gaze of a small boy looking out of the window of a butcher shop. He ducked his head and hurried his pace down the street. It was late afternoon but already dim, for the sky drizzled misty rain and cold fog thickened with every passing minute. He huddled within his ragged frock coat, hat pulled low to meet his turned up collar. He kept his hands tucked within his coat's overlong sleeves. Cold fingers were clumsy.

"The Lasrach are just a myth, boy." The butcher ended his assurance with grunt as he hung half a pig from one of the heavy iron hooks in the shop's window.

"But Papa, I do see one! He's walking down the street."

"Don't be daft." He frowned at his son, old superstition prickling across the back of his neck. "No man sees a Lasrach and lives to speak of it."

"So they are real!" The boy hurried to the shop's open door and stared up the street, a plucked chicken dangling forgotten from his hand.

"No, Archer. They're naught but tales told to frighten wayward women and children. Hush your foolishness and get back to your chores or it won't be the Lasrach you have to fret over."

"Yes, Papa." The boy turned away from the door and handed him the chicken to join the other meats on display.

Meeting no one's eyes, careful to be nothing more than a tattered shadow in their peripheral vision, Seth sized up every passerby. A bit of fine lace and silk peeking out of a passing reticule somehow made its way out of the lady's possession and up into his left sleeve.

Handkerchiefs didn't bring much at hock, but a few coins were far better than no coin at all. Just as food in the belly and a roof overhead were more comforting on a raw wet night than the ease of a conscience untroubled by petty thievery.

Fortune hadn't smiled on him today by granting honest work, but he still walked free, so he counted himself among the lucky. As he turned into the street that was the day's meeting place, he caught a furtive bit of conversation, the voices dulled and hollowed by the thickening fog.

"Coo— look at that bit o' fluff, will ya? What I wouldn't do t' that...."

A low, vulgar laugh. "What would you know of it, y' little poof?"

"I ain't no poof! I was with one of Madam Tremaine's, just last night. She said I'd break me share of hearts, she did."

Seth heard the rising click of a woman's heels against the cobbles. He crept closer, flattening himself into the shadow of a back stoop staircase. A scavenging roach scuttled out from underneath to nibble at the mud on his boots. Seth shoved it aside and it fled, dragging two of its six metallic legs against the pavement. Those devices never functioned properly for long, especially in this part of the city.

The furtive conversation just beyond his hiding place took an uglier turn.

"Ye're a flamin' liar. If ye're so fine as y' say, show that one there what that heartbreaker of yers is for."

There was a scuffling sound, a woman's gasp of surprise.

Seth eased close enough to make out the shadowy figure of a young woman, bracketed by a pair of strapping men.

"Evenin' darlin'," one of the men crooned. "Whatever are ye out here by yerself for?"

The woman walked faster.

"Maybe we should keep her company…" the second man offered as he moved in front of the woman, turning around to look at his companion, who dropped back behind their prey.

"Go away!" the woman snapped, and tried to sidestep the man in front, but he moved with her like a dance partner.

"Maybe we should teach her why pretty lasses shouldn't walk alone," the man following close behind her countered, with a throaty laugh.

The woman dodged and ran, but she was grabbed up into a punishing embrace by the man behind, his dirty hand clamping across her mouth before she could scream aloud.

Seth slid a hand into his pocket, slipped his fingers through the rings of heavy brass knuckles. The man behind was the one to take out first. Seth moved as quickly but quietly as he could. The pair was too focused on ripping the struggling woman's bodice to notice any slight scrape of boot-soles against stone.

His fist lashed out with all the power he could put behind it. Just as the blow connected with a stubbled jaw, Seth recognized her attackers. It didn't matter, at least not now.

Fergal went down in a dead sprawl and didn't make a sound.

Charlie bellowed and shoved the half-naked woman to the road. She crawled towards the curb. Charlie trampled over her skirts to get to Seth, a knife appearing in his hand as if it was conjured there.

Seth feinted, then snatched Charlie's knife hand. He backhanded Charlie in the nose as he gave that captured wrist a vicious twist in a direction Dame Nature never intended it to go.

The sound Charlie made usually only came out of rutting cats. He went to his knees, snuffling blood and cradling his arm. "Y'broke it! Y'broke it, y' bloody sheep-bugger!"

"Shut your gob and go before the coppers get ya!" Seth hissed.

"Y'll pay for this, Conway!" Charlie swiped his sleeve across his face, smearing blood from his nose across his upper lip and cheek. "Me and Ferg will fix you proper, y' boot-lickin' judas."

"Lookin' forward to it," Seth told him with a smile that was more a baring of teeth. "How 'bout now?"

He took a stride towards Charlie. Charlie backed off fast, scrabbling like a roach.

"Get him out o' the road and yourselves far from here," Seth gave his former compatriot a swift parting kick in the arse.

Charlie lurched to his feet, then grabbed Fergal by the coat collar. He staggered away up the street towing Fergal behind, a human donkey harnessed to a heavy load. Seth watched until the two disappeared around the corner. He remembered the woman then, and turned, expecting to see nothing but deserted street. She stood at the curb, staring at him, her arms wrapped around her bosom.

"He knew you," she said, her tone accusatory.

"Yes." Seth picked up his hat and knocked a clot of mud from it. Nothing would help the shape of the thing, for that had vanished years before. "They were right about one thing, Miss," he went on. "You shouldn't be walkin' here alone."

She gave an unladylike snort. "Thank you for stating the obvious. I'm not stupid, you know. I was abandoned by my cad of an escort, and lost my way."

"I beg your pardon, for no offense was intended." Seth shrugged off his coat and held it out to her. "Here, Miss. It's not clean, but you needn't fear to wear it, for I'm not lousy."

She glanced down at his offered coat, one eyebrow arched, before she nodded and turned her back so he could assist her into it. "I'm Delia Falken. You may have heard the name. My father owns Falken's Flying Circus." Her voice rang with pride.

"Well then, aren't you one of the lucky ones," Seth murmured as she slipped her arms into the sleeves and settled the tattered wool close around her, as if it was a queen's cape. She was a very pretty, and very brassy, little piece of baggage. He favored women who had more sass than polite society veneer, but his preference didn't matter, now or ever. Miss Falken was a helpless young woman of far higher class than his own, unavailable as the stars for the likes of him. "If you'll allow it, I'll see you back home safe, Miss Falken."

Her eyes traced over his form, from battered hat to cracked, filthy boots. Her shaken demeanor changed with a flutter of her eyelashes, as if she tucked her fright away like a discarded garment. Delia looked up into his eyes, chin tilted at an aristocratic angle, though her cheeks were still pale. "I'd be honored, Mr. Conway.

That is what your filthy-mouthed friend called you, isn't it?"

So, brassy and changeable as the wind, then. He answered her first with a little huff of scorn. "I wouldn't go so far as to call him friend," Seth answered. "But aye, my name's Seth Conway." He gave her a slight bow. "At your service, Miss."

She stepped to his side and tucked her fingers into the crook of his elbow with a proprietary grasp. "Now, when escorting a lady, a gentleman holds his hand in front of his chest, like so." She settled his hand into a loose fist, just above his stomach.

Seth allowed himself to be posed like a doll, compliant in amusement. "I do know some small scraps of refined manners, Miss Falken, for all my reek and rags."

Her pale cheeks flushed. "I'm sorry, I should have known better when you rescued me instead of joining in."

They strolled a bit closer to the yellow pools of light and safety cast by the gas lamps on the main street. "If it was me you met in the fog, you'd have had no reason to scream," Seth assured her.

"Why? Would you have ignored me?"

"Most probably," he shrugged. The truth was, he may have accosted her himself, though for nothing more nefarious than a glancing, 'drunken' stumble to allow his hand access to her skirt pocket.

"I don't like the sound of that," she huffed.

Seth shot her a shocked glance, for one wild second afraid he'd spoken his thought aloud. "What do you mean?"

"Being ignored." Delia bowed her head, looking up through long lashes at him with a pout pursing her plump lips. "I don't like it."

Was she being coy with him? Seth felt shoved off his balance by her sudden swings of demeanor. Miss Falken was an intriguing puzzle in a very appealing package, but she was also a dangerous complication in his already tangled life. He would be happy to see her off.

"My advice is to develop a tolerance for it, Miss," he said. "If you were ignored by all tonight, you wouldn't be relying on the likes of me to escort you safe to a 'pod."

She stopped short, halting them both within the weak circle of light cast by the cracked globe of a street lamp. "The likes of you? Do I need fear you'll force yourself upon me as well, Mr. Conway?"

He withdrew his crooked arm from her grasp and told her a sliver of the truth. "I don't force women into letting me have my way, I charm them into thinking it's all of their own free will."

His reply brought a splotchy flush to her cheeks and wiped away her coy pout. "You haven't deigned to practice any of that charm upon me, so why should I believe that you're experienced in beguiling hapless women?"

"Why does it matter?" he asked.

"I told you, I don't like being ignored." A sly little smile flashed across her lips. "I strive quite diligently to be admired by all."

"If Fergus and Charlie hadn't expressed their vile admiration of your person, my own may have cost you the gold chain on your wrist at the least."

She sucked in a startled breath. "You would have robbed me?"

He shrugged. "I would have picked your pockets. That's naught but petty thievery. I would never harm your person."

Miss Falken took his arm again and set them walking. "I appreciate your moral restraint, Mr. Conway, but you've hardly convinced me of your irresistible powers of charm and seduction. Though the fact that you're escorting me rather than stealing me blind is somewhat a balm to my vanity."

Seth looked down into this brazen little chit's eyes and gave in to the urge to rock her inner equilibrium as she did his. After all, he wouldn't be seeing her ever again, once the 'pod carried her back to her privileged life.

"I was born and reared in a brothel catering to the quality," he began. "The Madam took a liking to me as a babe, and schooled me in literature and pretty manners from the day I could stand up on my own. She molded me into a dainty little prodigy before I was out of skirts and ringlets, well-practiced in charming all manner of men and women, no matter how jaded. I was scarcely five when my mother died. The evening after her burial, Madam cashed in her investment by replacing my mother's lost earnings with the first of my own. I made my escape when I was seven."

Her lips sucked into a horrified 'o' around a gasp. "That's… unspeakably ghastly! It breaks my heart to even imagine such heartless depravity being inflicted on a little child!"

"I'm hardly the first, or the last, and I survived." He shrugged, banishing ugly memories back into their mental pit, and gave Delia his most delectable smile. "Since then, I'm free to be charming only when I choose to be so. And I could still steal you blind before we reach the 'pod."

She blinked and turned away to face forward again. They took a few paces in silence.

"You'd make a good roustabout, you know," she said as if they'd been discussing the possibility for half an hour. "You have a mean right hook, so you must be strong."

"Is that an offer of employment or simply an observation?" Seth asked as they neared the platform for the flying peapods. At this hour, and in this part of the city, the shadowy elevated platform was deserted.

"Both!" she said gaily, leaning her head against his arm as they ascended the ornate, soot-caked ironwork of the staircase. "Well, as much as I can offer. I'll give you a shining commendation to my father for saving my life. I'm certain he'll offer you a job on the spot."

"We'll see, I suppose." Seth stepped in front of her as the cylindrical peapod rattled and swayed up to the platform before them, its iron pulley wheels screeching at a painful pitch against the single rail that suspended the peapod over the street.

He clapped a hand to his hat to keep it from being swept away by the downdraft from the rotors that shoved the coach along. The 'pods were notorious for lifting unwary ladies' skirts, so it was more engrained courtesy than concern for her questionable modesty that prompted him to block the wind from her.

The 'pod braked to a stop with a hiss of steam and a down-pitched roar from the slowing rotors, tattering the gritty fog around the platform. Yellow lantern light spilled out of the 'pod as the door opened with a pneumatic wheeze. The conductor waited to one side, his palm out at the ready.

It was Seth's turn to flush in shame then. "If you'd be so kind as to tell me where I may find your father, I'll come in the morning to speak with him. I don't have the brass to take the 'pod."

"I think, Mr. Conway, that recompense for saving my life would at least begin with fare to see my father. I'm sure by this hour, he's becoming worried about me." She smiled as Seth handed her up into the 'pod. "Please?"

"As you wish, Miss Falken," he nodded with an answering smile and stepped up after her. Once the conductor punched their tickets, Seth settled onto the leather seat opposite Miss Falken and tucked his chilled fingers under his arms. If nothing else, at least this 'pod would carry him out of Fergal and Charlie's easy reach.

She was quiet a moment as the 'pod roared away, her expression indiscernible in the shadowy interior. "Will anyone worry for you tonight, Mr. Conway?" she asked, her voice softened slightly, though whether from remorse or pity or simple weariness, Seth couldn't determine.

"No, there's none to worry over me," he answered, just as softly. His lips tilted into wry disgust. He had no doubt he was the center of many a heartfelt thought just now, but it wasn't worry they were wasting on his memory. He'd seen Charlie gut a man like a trout once, for far less offense than he'd served up in the middle of that street.

"Ah," she answered, as if she had been enlightened by some profound reply. She leaned back against the seat and closed her eyes with a weary little sigh, her skirted knees somehow insinuating themselves into the space between his.

Seth shook his head and looked out the window, making careful note of the passing stations to keep his bearings about him. Wherever this peapod left him, if it was within the bounds of Manchester, Seth knew he would be wise to walk on further.

Chapter Two

Ambrose Bierce defined it best:
'Circus: n. A place where horses, ponies and elephants
are permitted to see men, women and children acting the fool.'
Archer Talents, Royal Historian

When he stepped down from the 'pod at the Old Trafford's Botanical Gardens platform, Seth stopped, so stunned by the sight spread before him that he forgot the woman waiting, trapped inside the compartment, behind him. He forgot even to breathe.

The main tent rose at least three stories into the sunset-streaked, smoky sky. The ruddy light drew out the brilliance of the blues and greens, yellows and reds that spiraled up its sides. It looked like an enormous candle, topped by a huge Union Jack fluttering proud in lieu of a flame. But even more awesome than the massive, cylindrical tent were the airships behind it.

The largest hung so high, it almost seemed another moon, but one flattened like an onion. It glowed from within, and twinkled in the beams of light playing over it from below, almost as if it was studded with stars.

A round gondola hung halfway down the stalk that tethered it to the earth. Seth could make out tiny figures, small as ants, moving about past the windows. Men, he realized, the crew of the magnificent ship.

Smaller dirigibles of the usual oblong shape encircled the large ship. They spelled out the name of the circus on their sides, as colorful as the tents and booths on the ground below. Their gondolas gleamed with polished brasswork and glossy paints.

The whole fleet floated within a pearly haze, the city's filthy fog mingling with the white plumes of steam released from the boilers below. The low-pitched, thrumming rumbling piston-beats of the engines they drove blended together into an uneven rhythm, the thudding heartbeat of some great sleeping beast.

"It's grand, isn't it?" Delia said, voice light and airy with pride as she, too, took in the sight of her home. "I still get all weak in the knees when I see it from a distance, and I grew up with the Circus."

Seth twitched, startled by her voice at his shoulder. He quickly turned to smile up at her. "Grand is hardly the word for it all," he answered, and didn't care that he sounded awed even to his own ears. "Beautiful, surely. Even magical...." He shook his head with a little laugh. "I've never seen so much light and color all at once in my life."

The 'pod conductor tugged the cord that blew the tardy whistle.

Delia gave a little shriek and jumped down from the car, shoving Seth forward. Seth probably jumped half a foot, himself, then staggered a little as she landed against him.

"I beg your pardon, Miss," he blurted and swung her away from the danger of the departing 'pod.

"Oh hush," she giggled. "It was fun to see you almost jump out of your boots."

She tucked her fingers into Seth's elbow again as they descended the fog-slick platform stairs. "On show-days, there are omnibuses pulled by zebras to bring people to the ticket-gates, but tonight we'll have to walk."

To Be Continued Soon

23918989R00239

Made in the USA
Columbia, SC
16 August 2018